GUILDS & GLAIVES

Other Anthologies Edited by:

Patricia Bray & Joshua Palmatier

After Hours: Tales from the Ur-Bar
The Modern Fae's Guide to Surviving Humanity
Clockwork Universe: Steampunk vs Aliens
Temporally Out of Order
Alien Artifacts
Were-
All Hail Our Robot Conquerors!
Second Round: A Return to the Ur-Bar

S.C. Butler & Joshua Palmatier

Submerged
Guilds & Glaives

Laura Anne Gilman & Kat Richardson

The Death of All Things

Troy Carrol Bucher & Joshua Palmatier

The Razor's Edge

GUILDS & GLAIVES

Edited by

S.C. Butler
&
Joshua Palmatier

Zombies Need Brains LLC
www.zombiesneedbrains.com

Interior Design (ebook): April Steenburgh
Interior Design (print): ZNB Design
Cover Design by ZNB Design
Cover Art "Guilds & Glaives" by Justin Adams of Varia Studios

Kickstarter Edition Printing, August 2018
First Printing, September 2018

Print ISBN-10: 1940709202
Print ISBN-13: 978-1940709208

Ebook ISBN-10: 1940709210
Ebook ISBN-13: 978-1940709215

Printed in the U.S.A.

COPYRIGHTS

Table of Contents

SIGNATURE PAGE

S.C. Butler, editor:

_____

Joshua Palmatier, editor:

_____

Lawrence Harding:

_____

Howard Andrew Jones:

_____

Esther Friesner:

_____

Jenna Rhodes:

_____

Anita Ensal:

_____

Violette Malan:

_____

Leah Webber:

_____

David Farland:

_____

R.K. Nickel:

_____

Ashley McConnell:

_____

D.B. Jackson:

_____

James Enge:

_____

Jason Palmatier:

_____

Amelia Sirina:

_____

Justin Adams, artist:

_____

Introduction

S.C. Butler

Stop right there! If you like your fantasy filled with fellowships and noble quests, this anthology is not for you. And if you love lengthy tales of politics and power, then it won't be to your taste either. But if you like a little intimacy with your evil, and your vengeance short and sweet, with perhaps a pinch of silliness in the witchcraft, then these fourteen delicious sweetmeats of sword and sorcery will prove right up your alley. And it will be a dank, twisting, fetid alley, too.

Jump from body to body with a soul runner, hungry for true freedom. Swap masks with a maskmaker as he desperately tries to hide from his fate. Laugh with an unmage while she unsuccessfully tries to persuade first her Inquisitor—and then her Insurance Adjustor—that she isn't what they think she is at all. Duel with the Gray Maid, creep out with the Tirribin and the Belvora, dive headfirst into the Asps' Nest, even pull King Finehair's immaculate man-mane. In this book you will find no high elves (only low), no politics (unless assassination is involved), and certainly no nobility. What you will discover will be all the finest points of … GUILDS AND GLAIVES.

In the Asps' Nest

Lawrence Harding

One might have expected the guards to be especially alert tonight, but Katja Shade-Eyes knew how guild hierarchies inevitably resolved themselves. Tonight was a night to be seen—to boast, to impress and, if necessary, to brown-nose one's way into the good books of the Grand Master and her lieutenants. To be left guarding the doors on a night like this was a disappointment, if not an insult. The best and brightest would be inside. And besides, what was the worry? No one would be insane enough to break into a guild-hall on a Pledging Night.

No one except Katja.

Still, alert or not, there were three guards at the door. That in itself was no bother—and the knives that had once been her namesake thirsted for their throats—but tonight's contract did not call for bloodshed. At least, not yet.

That left stealth. So that is what she had planned for.

Nor were the guards the only protection the entrance had. There were also the alarum wards across the doorway that would alert the guards—inside and out—if anything unauthorized should pass through. Besides that, lesser wards had been laid around the surrounding streets like tripwires, so that nothing could approach undetected. Unfortunately for them, Katja had a way with wards.

She had watched them setting the lesser alarums earlier from a convenient rooftop. She knew where they were and once she had seen the way the runes were carved it was quick work to creep down and alter them for her own purposes before they were activated.

A ward a street away was about to go off for no reason whatsoever, other than that she had told it to. Her timing had to be precise. The whole hit depended on it. Any second now ...

One of the guards cocked his head at the sudden sound. "Something's tripped a ward."

His fellow shuffled, looking out into the chill night air. "Probably just a cat." This earned him a meaningful nudge and a sneer from the third.

"Grayfang told us to be on extra high alert tonight, and that's what we're going to be. You stay here. We'll go check it out since you're so lazy."

Two of the guards drew their knives and disappeared round the corner, leaving the remaining guard at the entrance, staring nervously out into the gloom. That meant he was facing away from Katja when she dropped from the gutters behind him and shoved half an ounce of ha'lik against his unprotected face. He struggled for a moment, his cries muffled against the hand clamped over his mouth, then relaxed and allowed Katja to lean him gently against the wall.

Ha'lik was useful stuff. A mild opiate and hallucinogenic, it induced the notion that one had just had a pleasant daydream. Of course, any rogue with any experience knew the signs of it—probably even the grunts guarding the outer doors tonight—but by the time they worked it out it would be too late.

The guard's eyes drooped as he stared off into space with a lazy grin while Katja stuffed her soiled glove safely into her pouch. He began to hum while she carefully unclipped the sigil from his tunic and pinned it to her own breast. She allowed herself a small, satisfied smile as she slipped through the outer wards into the Asps' Nest.

It was time to go to work.

* * *

"So," Katja asked the hooded figure sitting opposite her. "What's the job?"

They were in a private room of The Golden Sheaf. This, contrary to the belief of most lowly rogues, was where the real business happened. If you wanted to impress an underling or intimidate them into doing something, you took them to the Ritual Chamber of a guild-hall and filled it with smoke and candles. If you wanted to get serious business done, this was the place to do it.

Outside in the taproom rogues, pickpockets, and knifemen of all gangs and guilds rubbed shoulders. The Golden Sheaf was the only truce-house in the city. No one drew steel on another here—not twice, anyway. Even cut-throats needed time off.

The voice from within the hood was deep and velvety. "The Black Asps."

"You have business with them?"

The hood chuckled. "Everyone does, sooner or later."

Katja drummed her fingers against the table. "True enough. I'm not un-familiar with them myself."

"So I have heard."

"Oh?" Katja leaned back in her seat and stared hard at her potential em-ployer. "And what have you heard?"

* * *

A scream echoed down the corridor behind Katja and the lanterns set into the wall began to pulse with an unnatural red light. The screaming was almost drowned out by the dull bass of the alarum charms throbbing from the wall—but not quite. In the meantime, everyone in the area would be very much aware that some sneak had fallen foul of the Black Asps' wards and was suffering a world of pain. Discretion had its merits, but sometimes it paid to advertise.

The guard would recover, eventually. And he'd been taught a salutary lesson—never lose hold of your guild-sigil. And if you do lose it, don't trip your own guild's defenses before you notice. As an added bonus, any min-ute now there should be …

She ducked around a corner and lost herself in the shadows as best she could. This time she didn't need to make much of an effort—the guards from the second ring of defenses were rushing to deal with the apparent intruder caught in the wards. They weren't expecting anyone to be inside already. She let them blunder past, each eager to be the one to apprehend the victim and claim the credit and a better posting next Pledging Night. She counted them as they went past—all three, a full complement. Some god or another must be smiling on her for them to leave their post unguarded. When their footsteps were lost in the distance beneath the alarum wards, she snuck round the corner to the now-deserted guard-post.

She'd underestimated the Asps. Clearly someone wanted this particular Pledging Night to be secure—there was still one guard manning the post. She stopped abruptly and launched herself backwards round the corner. She could only count herself lucky that the guard had been facing the wrong way. Katja swallowed a hissed curse. Gods above, how could she have been so sloppy? She flattened herself back against the wall, deep in shadow, and held her breath.

He didn't raise the alarm. It didn't sound like he had moved, much less noticed anything amiss. He was probably fresh meat, too, dumb and unobservant, obediently staying put while his more experienced handlers checked out the racket at the entrance. So much the better. She crouched and produced a tiny mirror from a hidden pocket in her sleeve. She screwed it onto a piece of wire, which she bent into a suitable angle. Carefully, she edged it round the corner, low to the ground, where it was less likely to attract unwanted attention.

He was definitely alone. That was a blessing. He was huge and resolutely filled the doorway, which was not. He was also built like an ox; luckily, she still had enough ha'lik soaked into her glove to stun one. She judged that she was maybe six paces away from the guard. An ideal distance. His stance caught her eye, too—the stance of a young street-brawler before he'd been bloodied enough times to stop fearing pain. There was a nervous aggression to it, better for warning off the weak than warding off an attack.

She slipped the mirror away and, pulling her scarf firmly over her nose and mouth, she re-donned her soiled glove. She took a deep breath, then sprang around the corner.

Her estimations had been correct. Not only was the guard green, but he was nervous and, frankly, didn't seem the quickest on the uptake. By the time he had opened his mouth to raise the alarm, her fist had connected with his jaw hard enough to stun him for a few seconds. It would suffice. She rammed her other hand against his nose and mouth, pressing hard to force him to inhale as much of the remaining ha'lik as possible. The huge man's eyes widened, then his lids drooped dreamily. He stood as if resuming his guard as Katja slipped behind him and away, further into the den of the Asps.

If she got this right, she would have a clan again. It would be a challenge, but she was a woman of her word. She could do this. And she would.

If she didn't, she had no future.

* * *

"I heard that your last encounter with the Black Asps got you expelled from the Spiderkin."

Katja kept her face blank. Her interlocutor continued.

"I heard that it was a simple mission. A hostage-exchange after some of the more overconfident low-rankers started an unsanctioned turf war. I heard that people died …"

Katja didn't need to listen. She was too busy fighting off the memories that came flooding back, as if summoned by those words.

She knew that she wasn't at fault, but that didn't stop her blaming herself. The violence had erupted almost as soon as negotiations began. The Asps shot first, of course, but the only survivors had been herself and the Asp ambassador. It was her word against his and his word had actual weight. The Spiderkin had had no choice. Katja had to go.

Work enough was forthcoming—even with a black mark against her, her reputation was sufficient to find jobs from clients who preferred to operate beneath the notice of the guilds. It was murky business but, in a way, she'd never been freer to pursue contracts—even if they were less savory than the guild-work she had been used to. She'd kept herself alive and in coin, and she could take a certain amount of pride in that. And yet …

She may have swum where others would have sunk without a trace, but compared to her old life she was barely treading water. The clanless life was lonely—no allies to call on, no safehouses to rely on, no one to watch your back … and no future to speak of.

She had been given a year's grace ten months ago. Time was running out. And yet the memories of the night of her banishment stalked her as if they had only happened yesterday.

* * *

Katja couldn't see the face of the Mistress of the Spiderkin, hidden as it was behind wisping webs of smoke and incense and the silken gauze of her mask, but she could feel its expression. Regret, apology, and, worst of all, sympathy. That was the knife that cut the deepest.

"Katja Blade-Weaver, I hereby cast you from the Spiderkin."

Katja simply bowed. There was no point resisting. Any objection would only lengthen this humiliation.

"You have failed our order. You have cost us wealth and lives. But, in light of your previous service, you will be allowed to live."

Katja bowed again. "Thank you, Mistress."

The Mistress stared down impassively at her from her dais. "Before you leave this place, never to return, you must shed the signs that joined you to us." She gestured curtly to two guards who emerged from the shadows to stand beside Katja.

"First, your weapons."

Katja unclipped the belts that criss-crossed her torso and handed them to her guard. Then she bent and removed the two knives from her boots, another from each sleeve. As she handed the last blade to the other guard, the Mistress held up her hand.

"Now your mark."

This was difficult. Her eight fighting-knives and other blades were costly but could be replaced. But giving up her insignia meant giving up her identity. There would be no going back. She kept her face impassive as she scraped the blade across the skin of her bare arm, cutting away the spider emblem tattooed there. Gritting her teeth, she handed knife and the bloody flap of skin to the guard. Another rushed over and pressed a poultice to the wound, binding it tight with gauze. Katja looked into the eyes of the Mistress, who nodded approvingly.

"I admire your spirit, Katja. I always have. I advise you to fix your other tattoos as soon as possible." Katja's hands strayed to the spiderwebs etched around her eyes. Of course. Another trap she had laid for herself. She nodded.

The Mistress waved her away. "Now go. You have a year of grace. No Spiderkin will harm you. Good luck, Katja. I hope I never have cause to see you again."

Katja was led from the torchlit chamber in silence, wondering just who she was now.

* * *

Katja took a deep breath, mentally shaking herself to banish the memories, then opened her eyes and stared hard across the table. "So you know I've had dealings with the Black Asps in the past, and that they went catastrophically. Why, then, are you asking me to do anything?"

She thought that her would-be client would chuckle, but he did not. Instead, the cowled head nodded magnanimously, like a teacher whose pupil had asked the right question.

"Call it a second chance. A chance to hit back. Think of it, Shade-Eyes. Your greatest triumph, the kill of your career, against the very people who wrought your downfall. Blade-Weaver would be born again. And if you fail, what have you lost? At the very least, you win an honorable death."

It all sounded so tempting. Of course it did. It was meant to. Katja leaned back in her seat and folded her arms, burying her wounded pride and her thirst for redemption beneath her long-hardened armor of professionalism.

"So. You want to take out a contract against the Black Asps. That's a lot of people, and they're all a mean bunch of bastards. And I'm just me. Who's your specific target?"

Her visitor spread his arms. "Why, Grand Master Zavine."

Katja's eyes narrowed. "Big hit." But she didn't ask why. You never asked why. Her knives never questioned their wielder, so why should she? "You're asking more of me than you know."

"I assure you, my dear, I know exactly how much I am asking of you."

Katja began to stand. "I'm not sure you do. I'm good. But to take out Zavine—"

"Calm yourself, my dear," came the placid reply. "I have every confidence in your ability. And as for your willingness—your little … incident with the Black Asps …"

Katja's frown darkened. "What about it?"

The figure chuckled and motioned for her to sit.

"What if I told you I knew who was responsible?"

* * *

A shadow loomed around a corner. Katja ducked back behind the crates and held her breath. The shadow was followed by a familiar figure. He was small, unassuming, dressed in simple black robes. Only the iron snake-pin—the single adornment on his austere outfit—gave any sense of how important, and dangerous, he was. That, and the shark-like smile that hung about his lips.

Bazan Grayfang.

As he passed Katja's hiding place, her hand slipped to one of her concealed blades. They called to her, pleaded to be wielded, yearned to sink into the flesh of his back. It would be so easy. He was alone, undefended. He was hers for the taking. It took every ounce of her willpower to resist the siren song of their steel.

She dearly wanted Bazan's death. But that wasn't part of the plan. As he disappeared around another corner, she slid the half-drawn blades back into their sheaths. She had a sweeter revenge planned for him. She just had to be patient.

It would be worth it. It had to be.

* * *

Slowly, carefully, Katja sat back down. Her client inclined his head. "I thought that might get your attention," he mused, too smug for Katja's liking. But he had the information she craved.

"You have it. What's the deal? You keep this hanging over me until I do everything you want?"

"Oh, lords above, no!" The client sounded almost affronted. "Not at all. Rather, my dear, I will give the information to you now. Call it a … show of good faith."

Katja mulled this over. Good faith it may be, but it would also mean she owed him an honor-debt. It would mean there was little chance of escaping this contract. Still … her hand traced the dark skull-like pits tattooed around her eyes that hid her once-intricate Spiderkin guild-tattoos. Nothing could replace that loss. But revenge might soothe it a little. And here was her chance. Could she turn it down? No.

She folded her arms. "Right. Tell me what you know and I'll consider your contract."

"His name is Bazan."

Katja's eyes narrowed. "The Grand Master's right-hand man."

The cowled figure shrugged. "One of them, yes. No Grand Master worth their arsenic would trust in only one right hand."

Katja scowled. "That's a name. But how do I know you're telling the truth? Tell me how, and why, and if I believe you then you have my blades."

The cowl seemed to smile. "Distrustful, but honorable, with a healthy dash of cynicism. Yes, Katja Shade-Eyes, I think you will do nicely."

"How. And why."

* * *

Katja wished that the damned Black Asp representative would stop smirking. They were on neutral ground. It wasn't even a high-level exchange—just a bunch of hotheads from both Spiderkin and Asps who'd tested the turf boundaries and been clumsy enough to get caught. How dare he act superior to her? She could tell he was trying to intimidate her, but she had heard much of this Bazan Grayfang. Practically second-in-command of the Asps—and didn't he know that he was honoring her by lowering himself to so routine a meeting with her, a mere rank-and-file assassin? But she had been entrusted with this hostage exchange and would show him what Spiderkin were made of, so she met his knowing gaze defiantly. The air was taut with tension.

The atmosphere was shattered as one of the Spiderkin acolytes scuttled up to Katja. "What is it?" she snapped, and then she saw his expression.

"Mistress, it's the prisoners. They're …"

But Katja didn't let him finish. She thrust him out of her way, back to the huddled figures bound behind her. As soon as she saw the first bloated, blue-tinged face, she knew that something had gone disastrously wrong.

"What's wrong?" called Bazan. "Are the prisoners safe?"

Katja turned back to him. Bazan Grayfang, ambassador of the Black Asps, raised a perfect eyebrow. She found herself unable to speak, but he spoke for her.

"If our men have been harmed ... then you leave me no choice."

He jerked his head in a curt signal and the crossbow bolts began to fly.

* * *

Though Katja couldn't see the smile, she knew it was there. She could hear it behind her client's suppressed chuckle.

"They were poisoned, weren't they?"

Katja said nothing in reply. She just glared, daring him to avoid the point any longer.

"But you never left their side. Not until the exchange, and then there would have been no time."

Katja nodded curtly.

"How, then, could that have happened?"

"You tell me," snorted Katja. "You have the answers. If I knew them I wouldn't be sitting here now. I'd be out on a ... personal mission."

Another chuckle. "No doubt you would, Shade-Eyes. I would expect nothing less of you."

Katja idly traced a finger around the cuff of her jacket. She knew that her client would know what was concealed there, ready to be wielded at a moment's notice. He seemed to take the hint.

"They were poisoned before you took them prisoner," he declared, smugly folding his arms. Katja pulled a face.

"Impossible. There's no poison that could pull that off."

"The Asps know their poisons," chided her client. "And they are known to experiment."

Katja studied the hooded figure. He clearly knew what he was talking about. There was no point speculating who he was. If he didn't want to be identified, then he couldn't be, that much was obvious. Instead, she listened to her instincts, and they told her to trust him. She hoped that this time they were right.

"And why? Why me?"

The figure shrugged. "No reason. You just happened to be the unfortunate in charge." He cocked his head to one side, as if appraising her pityingly. "I'm sorry, Katja Shade-Eyes. You were the least important part of his plan."

Katja tensed. If her client had meant to rile her, then he had succeeded. But then, it made sense. She'd been respected among the Spiderkin, but hadn't broken into the inner circle that would bring true esteem and power. And now she never would. She tried to control her temper and leaned nonchalantly in her seat, aware of the blades at her side. They urged her to take the contract. Any chance at Bazan was a chance for revenge and regained honor. They thirsted for it. But, Katja knew, this situation was not so simple. "I admit," she allowed, "that the prospect of revenge is tempting. Now I have the information, of course, there's nothing stopping me acting on it anyway."

"Apart from the debt of honor you owe me. There is still honor in you, is there not?"

Katja's eyes narrowed. "I like to think so. Very well. But that honor compels me to ask you something before I agree to this contract."

"By all means, ask away."

Katja leaned forwards, hands firmly splayed on the tabletop.

"Why do you want Grand Master Zavine dead?"

The figure seemed to grin beneath its hood and spread its hands in a small, quiet shrug. "I have my reasons."

Katja narrowed her eyes. "I am sure you do. And I would be interested to hear them."

The figure waved a gloved hand dismissively. "I am sure that you would. But you have no more need to know them than a knife needs to know the motives of its wielder. You are my means to the end."

"You are aware that she is my aunt?"

The hooded figure sat back with an air of satisfaction. "I am indeed. I was wondering when that matter would be raised. Yes, Grand Master Zavine is your aunt. But, as far as my sources tell me, you have not had contact with her since you joined the Spiderkin over a decade ago. I would hazard that you are hardly close."

"Nevertheless, you are asking me to ignore the obligations of blood. To place a contract over my own kin."

The man cocked his head. "All assassins are expected to place their clankin over their blood-kin. That is the way of things."

"But," Katja replied archly, "I do not have a clan. So why entrust me with this? Surely there are many who would be happy to bring about the fall of the Black Asps."

The man leaned back over the table. "Exactly. The Black Asps have many enemies. As unaligned kin, the Grand Master will trust you. And if I can trust you to do this, I can trust you to do anything." There was a long silence as Katja and her would-be employer stared across the room at one another.

"Despite your … status, you have a reputation for loyalty, Katja Shade-Eyes. I trust that it is not unfounded."

* * *

Once she was past the guards, the Asps' Nest was easy enough to navigate. She'd found what she was looking for in the tunnels between the storage rooms. She scurried up the stacked barrels and stole along the long ventilation shaft bored into the rock, making sure to wrap her gauze scarf around her face. Even at this distance from the Ritual Chamber, the scent of incense was becoming overpowering.

It didn't take her long to reach her destination. No sooner was she in the shaft than the pounding of drums echoed towards her, leading her on through the perfumed murk. She found the loosened tiles—just as promised—and slid them carefully aside. That done, she readied her weapons and looked down into the Chamber below.

The Ritual Chamber was low, wide, circular, and lit at regular intervals by incense-spewing braziers. The flames illuminated the shadowy figures of the Asp guilders filing across the tiles, jostling for places near the ambitious and the influential. Streams of scented smoke wound to the top of the roof, partly obscuring Katja's view from her position in the chimney that bore most of it away, but it also concealed her and right now that was crucial.

Directly below her was the object of the Asps' attention. A wide, marble platform, circular like the chamber, with a large pillar at its center. Three figures had arranged themselves around the platform, standing with the cool air of born killers who were willing to die for their leader. Bodyguards, lieutenants—at their level it amounted to the same thing. Katja scanned them quickly, judging distances and stances. Once satisfied that she had their measure—as far as such professionals ever allowed anyone their measure—she transferred her attention to the fourth figure.

Grand Master Zavine. Her target. The biggest hit of her life. The legend among assassins stood at the front of the pedestal, surveying her massed followers. Below her was a low bench—the Pledging Stone, upon which each guild member would prostrate themselves and avow their allegiance. There was a steady flow of figures taking their turn to affirm themselves. And at the head of the queue, just discernible through the smoke, was a familiar figure. Grayfang.

Katja took a deep breath. It was time to make her entrance. Open, in full view of everyone. It went against every instinct, everything that years of training and experience had taught her, but those were her instructions: to be as dramatic as possible. As she tensed to spring, the words of the note her client had left whispered from her memories.

Make an entrance. Make them remember you, at that moment. If you are successful, you need not fear the guards. They will pledge themselves to you.

She stretched out her arms and leapt down into the smoke-filled chamber below. She landed a few feet behind her target, rolling into action even as she hit the platform. Zavine could be given no chance to move, no chance to react. Luckily, Katja had been a killer since childhood. Her limbs knew better than her mind what had to be done.

First, the guards. Even in the depths of her lair, Zavine needed those of assured loyalty at her side. Assured loyalty and skill.

They were quick—almost inhumanly so. The first was on her in seconds, but she was still moving from her landing. She rolled under his swing and swept her leg into his, sending him stumbling. Leaping up, she stamped hard on the back of his head. There was a crunch, and he went still. The second came at her, knives in hand, but even as she sprang to her feet she began drawing hers. She parried once, twice, then backhanded the burly woman in the center of the forehead with her knife-pommel. She followed up with a headbutt for good measure, sending her tumbling off the pedestal.

The third bodyguard never reached her. As her second assailant fell, Katja sensed him moving towards her. She spun on the spot and hurled her knife, taking him in the chest. She leapt forward to barge him against the central pillar. His head cracked and he went still.

Her entrance had taken maybe thirty seconds. Now she was behind Zavine. The Grand Master was at her mercy.

After that, everything became mechanical, like the sparring fights from her training years ago, in the backyard with her parents—and her aunt. Her aunt whose life she held in her hands. As her mind dwelled on this, her body fulfilled the contract.

Her knee to the back of the elder woman's leg, forcing her to the ground. Left hand around the top of the head, holding her steady and exposed. Right hand gripping the blade, slashing with practiced accuracy across the neck. The blade entered her aunt's throat, sliding easily through skin and cartilage. Grand Master Zavine of the Black Asps smiled up at Katja as the blood spilled from her throat.

* * *

Katja folded her arms. To an outside observer, she was simply considering the offer. Anyone who knew her reputation, however, knew that her fingers now brushed the handles of the two knives sheathed beneath her arms. "I have only one question before I give you my answer. Who wants my aunt dead? And why?"

There was silence as her companion regarded her from beneath the hood for what seemed an age. Then the figure shrugged. "Very well."

The hood was swept back, revealing a hard-faced woman with strands of gray streaking her braided black hair. She spat out a wad of the zathani gum used by guilders to deepen their voices. Then she smiled at Katja, though it was twisted into a grimace by the scars of a long and colorful career. Grand Master Zavine of the Black Asps. Her aunt.

"Hello, Katja."

Katja tried to cover her surprise. "You want me to kill *you*?"

* * *

The hall was silent. Katja could almost hear the blood dripping from the corpse at her feet, trickling and slicking into pools at the base of the dais, the acrid tang of gore mixed with the sweet incense wisping through the air. All eyes were on her. Her next movements would make or break her. She was a scorpion in an asps' nest and she had to prove that her sting was worthy of their respect.

She recognized someone skulking at the back of the crowd.

"You." She pointed a long knife, still dripping with Zavine's blood, at the black-robed figure. "What is your name?"

The thin-lipped man bowed his head slowly. "Bazan."

She could have him killed now, right then and there. Her blades could drink his heart-blood at long last … but no. They had drunk well enough tonight, on worthier blood than his. Better to make the bastard squirm a while.

"Bazan …?"

The question hung in the air. Everything hung on his answer. If he answered as the age-old laws of usurpation dictated, then she would rule them. If he showed his true colors and refused, there would be anarchy. Some would side with him. Others with tradition. There would be blood and the Asps would be as good as destroyed from within.

Just how brave was he?

"Bazan ... Grand Master."

Not so brave that he was a fool. Katja flashed him a viper's smile.

"Very good. If that is my rank now, Bazan ... why are you not kneeling?"

Bazan stared at her for what seemed like an age. His gaze met hers, held it for a long moment, then flinched away and quivered over the sight of her bloodied knives and the opulently-robed corpse at her feet. Slowly, he knelt.

The rest of the chamber followed his example. Grand Master Katja Blade-Weaver of the Black Asps knew then that they were hers.

* * *

"It has to be you, Katja," said Zavine.

Katja raised an impassive eyebrow. "Why?"

Zavine grinned ruefully. "Because every Grand Master falls eventually. I want to choose the time and place."

Katja shook her head. "But why die? You're a master of disguise—why not just ... slip away?"

Zavine's eyes flashed. "Do you take me for a coward, Kat? What would your mother say? We raised you better than that."

Katja looked away. They had, it was true. That was why she was still here, in this city, when she could have gone anywhere to ply her skills. To run was cowardice and a denial of herself. This city was home. Where else would she go?

Zavine sighed. "More to the point, slipping away isn't an option." She tugged the neck of her cloak down, revealing a bluish tint around her throat that made Katja's blood run cold. It was barely discernible against her dark skin, but once one knew what to look for it was unmistakable. "There's no point running from a knife that's already in you."

They sat in silence for a few moments and Zavine re-covered her throat. It was Katja who broke the silence.

"When?"

Zavine shrugged. "When did I notice? Well, Bazan doesn't think I know about his little invention, but I have my ways. I did a little digging myself after my favorite niece was disgraced."

"Only niece."

"Nevertheless. But if you mean 'when' as in my meeting with Mother Dark, then I'm almost certain I have a little under a day. Bazan, bless him, has a flair for the dramatic. How better to usurp me than to step in when I'm taken ill at our own Pledging Night? No mess, no fuss, no risk of a knife in him."

"A coward's way."

Zavine smirked. "Quite. It goes against all our codes of succession, but who would know but him? If, however, a certain renegade assassin was to make an unscheduled appearance, then …"

"… then his plan is ruined."

"And he has to concede to the challenger or risk exposure as a poisoner." Zavine leaned back contentedly and observed Katja through half-closed lids. "Will you take the contract? On me? For me?"

Katja nodded. "Yes. I will."

Zavine practically cackled. "That's my girl! I knew I could count on you. I just wish I could see his face. Make sure you make the bastard squirm for me."

Katja smiled thinly. "At the very least."

"I'm glad to hear it." Zavine rose from her seat. "Revenge aside, Katja, I have to face facts. I'm not getting any younger. It's time to bow out gracefully. At least this way I get to set my own terms." She tossed a coin-purse on the table. Its weight echoed against the wooden surface in a way only gold did. Katja shook her head.

"No charge. Not for a … personal job like this."

Grand Master Zavine shrugged. "It's not as if I'll need it where I'm going." She walked to the door, redonning her hood. She looked back over her shoulder as she left the room and nodded.

"See you tonight. Don't be late."

The Sword and the Djinn

Howard Andrew Jones

In the days of the first Uthman caliphs there lived a brave youth named Bakri, talented in all ways with horses. Not only was he an exceptional rider, he was a gifted trainer, one of those to whom horses instinctively respond. Those who saw him working the animals swore that he understood their language. Even graybeards deferred to him in matters of horseflesh, and so it was that he was master of the stables.

Bakri was nephew to a fierce warrior named Ghaffar, who called himself general and was honored by the caliphs because he so zealously protected the border. In truth Ghaffar was little more than a bandit whose conversion to Islam was borne out of convenience. He had been raised a pagan, and it was said he pledged the copious blood he spilled to demons worshiped by his family in former times. These rumors were widely spread, but the caliphs looked the other way, for it was better so deadly a warrior fought for them than against them.

Ghaffar never took a wife, nor lay with women, and he suffered no women to serve him, even to the preparing of his food. Only grudgingly did he allow his lieutenants and servants to keep wives or women in their rooms, and none were allowed within fifty paces of Ghaffar himself, on pain of death.

All of Ghaffar's male blood relatives had perished in battle save Bakri. Ghaffar looked with some favor upon the young man, both for his skill with

horses and because he closely resembled his uncle. Both were tall and fair
to look upon, though where Ghaffar's mouth bent sourly, Bakri could sometimes be seen to smile in true joy, especially when he was in the saddle.
Ghaffar made noises about the youth becoming his successor, but Bakri had
no love for the man, though he honored him and held his skill with weapons
in great esteem. He had less regard for Ghaffar's treatment of women, and
animals, and even the men who served under him, for Ghaffar was harsh
and ill-tempered, and when he drank of evenings he grew very cruel. Yet
Bakri served him, for he knew no other way of life.

    And then, quite suddenly one day, Bakri fell in love.

    It happened in this way. Ghaffar's chief lieutenant was a scarred and
pockmarked Syrian named Habab and he returned from a raid one night
with a herd of horses and a beautiful girl. Bakri was roused to look over
the animals. He came from his cot in time to see the woman being bundled
away under guard, not toward Habab's rooms, as was usual, but toward the
central keep. The moon was bright and swollen and the stars hung like frost,
and so when the girl twisted against her captors there was light for Bakri
to see her slim figure. Her veil had been torn from her and so he briefly
glimpsed a clear-featured face of astonishing beauty.

    When she was cuffed across the cheek so that her struggling would cease,
Bakri himself winced and started forward.

    Scarred Habab laughed. "Best keep your hands off, boy. She's a beauty,
but your uncle wants her unharmed."

    "Why?" Bakri asked. His uncle had never before barred the same from
any of his men.

    "He's holding her for ransom and means to return her in the condition
he found her."

    "Who is she?"

    "Adilah, of the clan Njed."

    Ghaffar had been warring with the clan for almost half a year, and while
he had captured women before, he had never before tried to ransom them.

    "What is so important about her?" Bakri asked.

    "She's the sheikh's favorite daughter. Some say he loves her more even
than his sons. She's not," Habab said again, "for you."

    Bakri then pretended interest in the captured horses. Even though three
of them were very fine animals indeed, long-limbed and sleek, he was thinking of entirely different features, and after he led them to the stables and
returned to bed he was tormented by memory of that beautiful face. He lay

awake for a long while, thinking of her, wondering if she could possibly be as lovely as that glimpse had shown him. He deceived himself into thinking that she could not possibly have been, that a simple look would cure him of his infatuation. Surely there would be blemishes or flaws that the darkness had obscured. Excusing his fascination thus, he rose, dressed, and crept down the worn stone stairs to the fortress dungeons, convincing himself he went only to confirm his conclusions.

Below the storeroom were four dank stone cells, closed with thick bars. Bakri advanced into that darkness with a lantern. There was naught in the first two cells but empty pallets, but in the third the light caught the wide eyes of Adilah, huddled modestly under a coarse wool blanket. She was even more lovely than he had imagined, with light brown eyes almost the color of amber, smooth clear skin, and a wide rose-lipped mouth. Her hair was long, dark, and straight. Clearly, he had startled her, but as he stood there, dumbstruck, she drew herself together and stared boldly at him.

"Who are you?" she asked. Her voice was high and clear.

Bakri advanced to the bars. He had to clear his throat before he could properly answer her. "Bakri," he said. And he decided that he would not mention his lineage, adding only, "The stablemaster."

"Don't you mean the stable boy?"

"No," he said, but was still struck too dumb to take offense.

"And what does the stablemaster want with me?"

He set down the lantern and stared at her. He had no proper answer. "Are you being well cared for?"

"Oh, yes," she said sharply. "I have this fine bed, and this luxurious blanket, which hardly smells at all. I am quite well."

The youth felt foolish then, though the young woman's wit and mettle impressed him. "Have they given you food, water?"

Adilah peered at him, uncertain what to think. "I have had none," she admitted.

"I will find some for you," Bakri promised.

"That would be very kind."

She rose from the pallet and stepped nearer the bars, though she stayed out of his reach.She moved with such grace, and her form was so lovely beneath her soiled and rumpled garments that Bakri imagined a woman decked in the costliest jewels would seem a crone by comparison.

"Why does my ..." Bakri hesitated, for he had almost asked her what his uncle wanted with her. He fumbled for the waterskin he kept at his belt and passed it over to her.

She accepted it cautiously, peering at the stopper, then back at him.

"There is nothing wrong with it," he said, "though I would that it were cool and fresh. I have not filled it since this afternoon."

She drank and he spoke on. "Indeed, had I the means, I would give you far more than this water. I would give to you precious jewels, and splendid horses, and all fine things a woman might desire."

Adilah was no stranger to the flattery of men, though she was not one of those shallow maids who encouraged and thrived upon it, for her elders had taught her better, and she had natural sense besides. Still, she had been lying awake without hope wondering how she might find the courage to hang herself in the cell. Standing on her cot in that dark place, feeling the cold wall, she had discovered a hook, probably used for hanging lanterns. And then the boy had come and hope had crept slowly out from the darkness of her heart. It was not that she felt the stirrings of love—how could she, in such a place, in such a state?—but she understood something of it in his eyes, and for the first time in hours she thought that she might yet live to ride her gray mare in the lands of her father and feel the hand of her baby brothers in her own as she led them, singing, outside to chores. She stepped closer to the bars, and her voice was a whisper. "Why have you come?"

He wondered at his words as he answered, for never before had he thought to say such things. "Once I had seen your beauty," he confessed, "I could do naught but follow so that I might witness it again. I am like a man lost in the desert who has witnessed a flowing pool of water."

She handed the waterskin back. He took it, fearful that she had misunderstood him. He was not, after all, thirsty for water.

"Do you mean to let me go?" she asked.

He had not thought that far. Indeed, he had hardly thought at all, but now his mind raced onwards. He knew that the girl might come to a bad end in his uncle's dungeon. If her family could not pay the ransom, she would as like be killed. If she was to be safe, she needed to be removed, but if he took her from here, he would be abandoning clan, home, and everything he knew.

He spoke gently. "I know Ghaffar is ransoming you. How much does he want for your life?" He had a mad thought that he might trade for her, for he had some coins of his own, then felt foolish, for the girl was worth more than his small trove.

"You *do* want to help me, don't you?" she asked.

"I do. What does Ghaffar want for you?"

She hesitated only a moment before answering him. "It is not money. It is a sword. And Ghaffar will never have it, for my family will not give it to him, lest it be blade first."

"Ghaffar fears no weapon," Bakri said. "He cannot be killed. Don't you know? I have seen him ride unscathed through a storm of arrows that slew or skewered every man to his left or right."

"He wants this sword," Adilah insisted. "One of the finest ever made, said to have been forged in the dim past for the hand of a dead and mighty king. No man who wields it will face death by the sword, and it is keenly sharp and perfectly balanced."

Bakri felt the stirrings of interest then, for something other than the young woman.

"Ghaffar is a scourge already," Adilah went on. "If he were to obtain the Gray Maid he would be truly unstoppable."

"The Gray Maid?" Bakri repeated. He pressed himself to the bars. "The sword is named The Gray Maid?"

"Yes, it …" Adilah fell silent, for the boy's nostrils flared and his eyes brightened. She perceived something now in his features that she had not noticed in the past, a decisive, regal air.

"Where is the sword?" he asked.

She shied away, but he pressed closer to the bars. "Can you lead me to it?"

"But you will give it to him!"

Bakri laughed. "Aye, point first, as you said!"

"But you just said no weapon can harm him!"

"I think that this one can." Bakri's teeth gleamed in the dim light as he grinned. "He does not covet the weapon to wield, but because he fears it."

Adilah took a hesitant step closer.

"Will you show it to me?" Bakri pressed.

She was not sure what to think, but then he stepped around the corner, returned with a rusting ring of keys, and tried them on her lock. It seemed to her that they jangled very loudly in that small space, and that it took over long, but in a moment the door was open and she stepped forward into uncertain freedom. The youth was there, holding the door and the lantern. Might this be some kind of clever trick? A ruse to get her to reveal her family's secret?

But the boy did not seem to be acting; he appeared caught up in the moment. Quickly he closed the cell door behind her and started up the stairs. "Come," he whispered, beckoning her on.

Bakri's heart raced as he reached the height of the stairs, but there was no one in the dark storeroom, nor in the central hall. He paused at the door to the courtyard, then slipped out of his cloak and set it over the girl's shoulders.

"Pull up the hood. Can you swagger, like a man?"

"I shall try."

"No one will mistake you for one at close range," he said, "but we will be in the shadows. Can you ride?"

"As well as you," she promised.

"That shall be seen," he said with a brash smile, then blew out the lantern.

Bakri was sure that Allah watched over him, for clouds now obscured the moon. It was a chill night, and the wind fingered his hair as he and Adilah crept through the shadows toward the stables. Adilah burned with questions, but she knew better than to ask. She could see the outline of two sentries on the wall above the fortress gate and knew that at least two others walked the walls on the other sides, for she had seen them when she'd been led inside.

Bakri threw on another cloak and worked swiftly and quietly, saddling his favorite horse, Kutb, a black stallion with a white blaze, and a swift, sure-footed white for the girl. He prayed that she was as fine a horsewoman as she claimed. He pointed the girl to meager supplies, a bow, some arrows, and these she gathered. There was no time for anything else; they would have to obtain more water at the village fountain below the hill.

He was relieved to see that the girl climbed nimbly to her saddle and sat it like a queen. In a moment he was beside her with Kutb, trotting for the gate.

The two guards frowned down on the youth and his companion as they rode up to the gate. They did not much care for the night watch and, like many in Ghaffar's employ, were surly to begin with.

Bakri pushed back his hood. "Open the gate," he said. "The general demands more wine."

"So he sends you?" the guard called down.

"What is it to you?" Bakri asked haughtily. "He will be ill-pleased with any who cause delay."

Grumbling, the guards raised the portcullis and Bakri and Adilah rode free, down the hill toward the darkened little village. Adilah could not help pushing to a gallop, and Bakri followed, catching her. After a moment she heard that he laughed, and when he grinned she could not help but grin back. Almost she kicked into a full gallop across the plain toward home, but something stayed her. She thought at first it was because she realized the need for water.

They stopped at the stone pool in the village square and filled up their waterskins. Around them were only shuttered windows—it might have been the deep desert, so quiet were their surroundings.

"What makes you think," she whispered, "this sword will kill him?"

He shook his head. "Not here."

Thus she rode with him quietly until they were beyond the village and out into the scrub lands that were not quite desert.

"How will you explain to your family that you mean to give me the sword?" he asked. "It must be me. I can re-enter the fortress; I can challenge him."

"But you said no blade could harm him."

Bakri glanced over at her and was distracted for a moment, for her hood had come down once more and her long straight hair bannered in the wind.

"My uncle has kept from all women for fifteen years because a sooth-sayer once told him he would never be killed, or even injured, until he met a deadly maiden, in gray."

"Your uncle?"

He had not meant to tell her that, but he pressed on. "Don't you see? The soothsayer must have meant the sword, not any woman. Ghaffar's learned of it—he knows. He means to hide it or melt it away. But I can slay him."

"He is your uncle?"

"That is not my fault," Bakri insisted. "His heart is black. He would rather ride a hundred leagues to raid the smallest village than pass food across the table."

He could see that she did not yet believe him, so he spoke on. He feared that she might bolt, now, and he had foolishly given her the faster horse. "He did not mean to tell me his secret," he confessed. "He was drunk when he confided it to me. Once he sobered, he beat me nearly to death as a demonstration of would happen should I whisper a word to anyone of what I knew. It was three months before I could properly walk again."

She did not doubt that Bakri spoke the truth, for his uncle's cruelties were legendary. "What will you do once you slay him?" she asked.

Bakri had not thought that far. "I suppose … I shall rule in his place, but not in his way. I think men would serve better out of loyalty than fear. You would have better men, too," he added. "I have seen it with horses. Aye, you must be stern, but if you treat them well, they will risk their lives for you. If you give them only kicks, they will serve only so long as you control them. And," he added, "I would study the Holy Koran, and see that my men did also, for my mother used to tell me wise sayings she had learned within its pages, and my uncle will not suffer the book to be anywhere near him."

With these words she grew more intrigued, for she loved well the Koran. With her father's guidance she had memorized nearly half the surahs herself and was teaching them already to her youngest brother. She saw the potential in Bakri, you see, and it was that which kindled her love, for women love nothing so much as a man who needs a few improvements.

"The sword," she told him, "is not with my family. It is hidden in the wilderness."

He could scarce believe her. "If it is so marvelous, why aren't they using it?"

"My grandmother did not like the thing," she said. "It had brought my family victory for generations, but my grandmother said the price was too high, and on my grandfather's death she made my father swear that he would hide the thing away. This he did."

"Can you take me there?"

Still she hesitated, and bit her lip as she considered him. She knew she might be making a mistake, but she was young, remember, and was growing taken with young Bakri. "If you can keep up," she said, and set her mount curvetting, spun it, and dashed away over the flatlands to the north.

Bakri let out a glad cry and set Kutb galloping in pursuit. They rode out into the scrubland this way, under the stars, the moon unveiling itself or hiding behind clouds from moment to moment like a flirtatious maiden. Sometimes Bakri chased and sometimes Adilah, so caught up in the joy of the moment and the thrill of being young and beautiful that they almost forgot the grim purpose of their journey until they arrived at a low line of rocky hills standing starkly up from the plain.

Adilah paused to refresh her thirst, then arrowed east. Twice her father had led her past the cave, telling her that, as the oldest, she must know the location of the sword, should her family need it one day. "For if I fall in battle," he had said, "the sword's resting place would be forgotten."

Still, she had seen its location in daytime, and things look different by night, so that she did not find the proper place until the early hours of the morning.

The two dismounted and stood looking up at a blocky cliffside. It was as if Allah had set aside an unfinished block of stone after smoothing out one side, for neither could see clear handholds in the thing, just the near vertical surface stretching some forty feet. "The cave is there," she said, although neither could see it. The stone was but a black wall of darkness topped with a sky strewn with stars.

"Well then," Bakri said, hoping he did not sound too discouraged, "I shall climb there."

He divested himself of his cloak and took everything from his belt but his sword. He wound a coil of rope around his shoulder, for Adilah had insisted she would join him.

There, apart from the girl, with only the unyielding stone and tiny wedges and projections to focus upon, he found himself doubting reality. The rock was not quite as smooth as it had seemed, but he had no easy time finding handholds. He pressed up and ever upwards, slowly, upon uncertain footing. Was this but a dream? Had he really ridden into the hills in search of a sword he meant to use to cut down his uncle? Could he dare? Even with a mighty blade, could he really slay such a man, a lion among warriors? Briefly—only briefly—he even wondered if he should lower himself back down, take the girl prisoner, and return her to the cell.

But he would not do that.

At last he saw a narrow opening in the rock a man's height higher, and a sword length to his right. Grunting, he shifted his position and pushed on. This was the hardest stretch yet, and twice he nearly fell, but finally he was gripping the mouth of the cave and pulling himself within. Out of breath, shaking with muscle fatigue, he crawled into the wide, dark chamber beyond and sat for a moment before returning to the cliff and lowering a rope. Adilah attached a bundle with a small lantern and a flask of oil and he hauled these up and lit them. He saw that he rested within a large natural cave. The light barely stretched to either side—a little over six good paces—and could not reach the depths. The floor was fairly smooth, sloping only a little downward, and the ceiling arched above him. A thick spider's web lay over the upper half of the cave opening, but apart from the insects woven into their shrouds he saw no other sign of life within the place.

He secured one end of the rope about the bottom of a stalagmite, then lowered it once more. Adilah tied it about her waist and, using a combination of his pulling and her climbing, she joined him, flush and bright from her exertions. His flesh stirred as she took his hand for help through the opening.

She smiled at Bakri, taken now with the adventure, but the youth was troubled. "It is too quiet here," he said. "Too empty."

"We must go to the back wall," she told him. And so they did, she carrying the lantern, he with hand to the hilt of his sword.

Yet there was nothing to the rear of the cave but a field of rocks and boulders and a narrow rift too small for even a child to slip through. He wondered if the sword would be hidden within and stopped in surprise when Adilah bent down beside the field and pushed over a mottled brown rock. A cavity lay beneath it, and within that cavity was a black lantern, which she brought forth. She smiled nervously at the boy, then rubbed the lantern's side. Immediately there poured forth a stream of white smoke, and both she and Bakri sat back.

"What is this?" the youth demanded. "Where is the sword?"

"The sword is guarded by a djinn," Adilah told him. "You must let me do the speaking."

Bakri had never expected this, nor did he expect the beautiful woman formed all of vapor who appeared within the smoke. Her hair was white, blending now and then with the discharge from the lantern so it was challenging to know where smoke left off and hair began. Her dress was all of shifting shades of blue, as though it had been woven from the sky when it was in different moods. She barely took note of Bakri, looking instead directly at Adilah with eyes formed all of the shifting blue of her dress, for they had no pupil, or whites.

"You have called," she said, "and I have come." The djinn's voice was musical and bright, but different from the speech of men, almost like the ringing of bells.

"I am of the clan Njed," Adilah said, bowing her head with great respect. "I have come for my father's sword."

"I see." The djinn stared down at her, face placid, expressionless. "I have need for the sword and would trade you for it."

Adilah looked up. "I am interested in no trade: it is the sword I need."

"You have not heard my offer," the djinn told her.

"Speak, then," Bakri suggested.

The djinn glanced at him, then back to Adilah.

"I shall offer you a palace, and a handsome prince, and you shall want for nothing, living a life where all comes to you with ease."

"That I do not want," Adilah said.

"Then I shall offer you the very prince of horses," the djinn said. "He will sire a breed of champions, swift as the wind, surefooted as the antelope, hardy as the lion. They shall make you a wealthy woman."

This sounded of great interest to Bakri, but Adilah answered without even glancing over to him.

"I do not wish a horse," she said.

"Then I can only offer you the sword. But it shall bring enemies and heartache."

"I shall take the sword, then, and all that comes with it."

The djinn did not move, but suddenly in her hand was a long, straight sword, pointing downward. She extended her hand and Adilah rose, putting hand to the pommel. Bakri stepped forward and put his hand upon the hilt as the djinn passed it over. Her hands felt like nothing—he might as well have been waving his fingers through mist—and he did not understand how she had clasped the weapon.

Adilah relinquished the blade to him after no more than brushing the pommel with her fingers. He took it gingerly, then turned its blade toward the light, studying its surface. He saw that symbols had been etched into the blade. Many were characters he did not know, for one set named a pharaoh in a dead tongue, and others were letters of Greek and Latin. Some few were in Arabic, but while Bakri recognized them, he did not understand them, for he had never been taught to read.

Taking the sword in two hands he lifted it toward the cave ceiling. He found it superbly balanced, and knew the sort of joy a man knows when riding the finest horse, or when winning the smile of the fairest maid. This was a blade of kings. He grinned over at Adilah, then remembered the djinn and looked over to her.

"The first of your enemies are here," she said. And as she vanished, who should appear in her place but Habab and two guardsmen. They looked astonished, at first, to find themselves in the cavern, but at sight of Bakri their hands fell quickly to their blades.

Bakri threw a shielding arm in front of Adilah and urged her back.

"How did you bring me here?" Habab demanded.

"We need not be enemies," Bakri told him. He had wielded a sword, it was true, but never against three men at once.

Habab's wide smile showed blackened teeth. "Oh, I think we do," he said, unlimbering his blade. "I've followed you since you left the fortress.

I think your uncle will reward me well for bringing him that sword. Maybe he'll even give over the girl."

The two warriors with him were muttering about the witchcraft that had brought them from the bottom of the cliff, where they'd waited, but Habab barked them silent.

"Lower the sword, boy, and I'll make this swift. You're no match for me."

"Don't!" Adilah shouted. But she need not have worried, for Bakri did not mean to give up so easily. His uncle had once told him that he who strikes first wins, and he'd seen it was often true.

Thus he stepped forward with a mighty blow.

Habab sidestepped and brought up his sword to parry, then felt the weapon ring in his hands as the Gray Maiden struck with such force it notched into his blade. Habab staggered back to gain time, flexing his numbed fingers. One of his men ran forward with a shout, only to meet the boy and the sword. Bakri's blow sheared off the top of his opponent's head and he collapsed in a spray of blood.

Bakri laughed now, sounding a little mad, and urged the others to come at him. Adilah had backed toward the exit, warning him to be cautious even as she bent to the ground to look for rocks.

"You come from the left," Habab said to his remaining soldier, and they advanced on Bakri. Habab knew he had simply been too cocky. Certainly, the sword was sharp, but it was said to be a great blade, which was why he supposed that the master desired it. He had not been cautious enough. The boy was young and apt to be rash and nervous, for he was no veteran. "Are you worried, boy?" he asked. "I'm going to get close and cut you from ear to ear."

At that moment Adilah hurled a rock. It soared through the empty space a foot to the right of Habab's companion, but it distracted the fellow long enough for Bakri to drive forward with a brave shout and deliver a blow that tore the man open from shoulder to navel, straight through cloak and leather armor. The fellow sank, keening in agony.

Habab snarled and ran in. Two wild blows set Bakri on the retreat, and a third might have taken him in the neck, but that Bakri parried, not with the flat of his weapon but the edge. And so mighty was that sword that Habab's already weakened blade broke upon it like a wave upon a rock. The point twirled away from him and rang against the cave wall. Habab stumbled, and the last sound he ever heard was of that point tinkling as it hit the floor, for at that moment Bakri clipped the older man's head from his shoulders.

Bakri then stood panting, looking at the carnage he had wrought. He lifted up the blade and saw the blood streaming down it in rivulets. "Gray Maiden," he said, "I know now why men praise you." He turned to Adilah, still a little stunned.

"Will the djinn return?" he asked.

"I do not think so. She was tasked only with guarding the sword until we asked for it once more, but …"

"Well, she tested us," Bakri said. He considered the blade a moment more, then bent down and wiped it clear of blood with one of the soldier's cloaks. "And we have passed. Allah willing, we have seen the last of her."

They found the horses of their attackers picketed very near their own and supposed Habab had planned to ambush them when they came down from the cave. It was then but a few hours before dawn, and though Bakri and Adilah were both spent, they rode out, knowing that their best chance lay with striking tonight. Never again would Bakri have free rein to ride into the fortress. If he did not return now, he would be viewed with great suspicion, and getting close enough to his uncle to strike would become nigh impossible.

They were an hour still away from the fortress when the pre-dawn light showed upon the horizon, and Bakri knew that they would have to press hard. Their horses were as tired as they, but they forced them into a gallop. Thus it was that they reached the village outskirts just as the sun's light first touched the earth, but poor Kutb's heart burst and the horse dropped like a stone, sending the boy tumbling from the saddle. He rose and staggered to the side of his mount, too stunned yet to mourn the faithful beast.

"Ride with me," Adilah said, but her horse was shaking and flecked with foam, and Bakri thought it likely that it too was ruined. Instead, he offered up his hand to her and helped her down.

"Stay here," he told her. "I will find my uncle."

"I am going with you," she insisted.

There was no time to argue. He found the strength to stride forward and before very long he came to the village fountain. Not until they were nearly abreast of it did a set of long shadows detach themselves from the nearby building. There were nine men there, awaiting them, two closing on every side, and Bakri knew from the profile that the one behind the two directly ahead was his uncle.

Ghaffar's presence was no accident. Habab had seen the boy heading toward the dungeons and had reported his exodus to his master before following. Another man might have supposed that the boy had left with the beautiful young woman, never to return, which would surely have been the smarter course. But Ghaffar had been roused to action, certain that the boy meant to return and kill him. Thus he had wakened all his men and set most upon the battlements, watching the distance. He himself had led another four all around the walls, testing stones to make sure that all were secure, for it was one of Ghaffar's fears that there might be a secret way in or out. Of course, nothing was found, which had made Ghaffar that much more agitated, and he had lost his temper and sliced open a man he had caught rolling his eyes at him. He had sworn that all men who did not obey would meet a similar fate, then strode back into the fortress.

All this had taken place in the hours before dawn. At the same moment that Habab was breathing his last, Ghaffar had been tossing and turning on his bunk. When the woman all in blue appeared before him he'd sat up, shivering, certain that his reckoning was come. He begged her not to kill him, but she merely regarded him with lambent blue eyes.

"The boy has the sword and rides for you," the djinn said.

"He shall never breach my fortress," Ghaffar answered, hesitant, for he was not sure what this spirit wanted.

"If you sit in your shell like a turtle, he shall rouse your enemies and force you out, and you shall die. You must be ready to meet him."

A crafty look came into Ghaffar's eyes as he considered the glowing woman floating beside his bed. "Who are you, and why do you offer counsel?"

"I was tasked with warding the sword. It is useful to me. I shall deliver the boy to you, and you shall deliver the sword to me."

"So that you, then, can kill me with it?"

The djinn stared at him a long while. "You have no interest for me. I want only the sword."

Ghaffar frowned. Here, obviously, was a creature of great power. "Why don't you simply take it yourself?"

"I cannot intercede directly," the djinn told him, "owing to the oath I swore to the sword's original holder."

To Ghaffar's thinking, this seemed direct enough intercession, but he was not familiar with the obsession with rules and rituals held by djinn and demons. There are those who say the difference between man and such creatures is souls, which is partly true, even if djinn have them, but anoth-

er key difference is adaptability. The djinn was fundamentally unable to conceive of breaking an oath Ghaffar would have tossed aside like a bone sucked of marrow.

Though Ghaffar could not understand the why of the djinn's oath, he realized he could work it in his favor, so he bargained that she would swear never to bring the sword into his presence so long as he lived, and since Ghaffar had become certain he would never be killed except by this sword, the deadly maiden the soothsayer had foretold, he had been entertaining the thought of immortality the whole time he and his small force had waited near the village fountain. There was no sign of the djinn, but he was certain that she would return the moment the boy was dead.

At the same time Bakri saw his uncle he understood the man's error. Ghaffar, given his own invulnerability, was inclined to ride straight ahead and slash until everything was dead.

Bakri and Adilah had advanced on the east side of the fountain. The two men approaching from the southwest and the two approaching from the northwest could not immediately close upon him, owing to the square bulk of the fountain itself. If he moved fast, he could engage Ghaffar's guards before the others neared. A slim chance, indeed, but then he had seen what Gray Maiden could do. He snarled and charged.

This Ghaffar had not expected. "Stop him!" he shouted.

Even a trained warrior can hesitate when facing a running man with a weapon. Their swords were out, but the first went immediately on the defensive, swinging up to parry. He lost his arm at the elbow for his efforts and fell screaming. His companion thought to slice Bakri while he was distracted, but the scream was unsettling, the slice astonishing, and his blow uncertain. Bakri half turned, sucking in his chest, and only the sword's tip struck, slicing through his clothes. Behind him he heard Adilah shout that the men were dogs, and to his left he heard men splashing through the fountain, but he had eyes only on the warrior before him, who was partly off balance. If that warrior's blade had been as supremely balanced as the Gray Maiden, it might be that he could have recovered his footing, but it was a simple sword, and when Bakri struck him through shoulder and neck he fell stone dead and motionless.

To Bakri, Ghaffar's eyes seemed wide almost as saucers. The sun was rising now, with enough light for the boy to recognize actual fear in his uncle's face. The older man held his sword out before him protectively as he backed away, and the gems in its hilt caught a little of the daylight. Bakri advanced after him, almost negligently slicing to his left at the sound of rushing feet and dropping a man with a solid blow to the chest. His uncle's thugs muttered amongst themselves in amazement, for in the space of a few heartbeats the boy had stilled three hearts forever.

Three of them had wrestled Adilah into submission and two held her now, one with a knife to her chest. The other lingered, not wanting to advance, and the remaining two followed Bakri but did not rush his back. Not after what they had witnessed. Too, they recognized Ghaffar's fear. Service with Ghaffar had brought them riches and women, but he was an uncertain master, and they had little wish to die because of a problem of Ghaffar's own making. Thus they hesitated as Ghaffar commanded them to strike.

The boy turned sideways as he walked, so that he could see both Ghaffar before him, and the men behind.

"My men have the girl," Ghaffar told him, slowly retreating.

"You will not distract me."

"They hold a knife to her, now. If you do not surrender, they will kill her."

The djinn had suggested this plan, though Ghaffar had thought the matter an unneeded precaution at the time. He would never have supposed Bakri would prove so dangerous. It was the sword, he knew, from which he could not take his eyes. So it is when men first spy the maid they are destined for.

"Look," Ghaffar said, his voice quavering a little. He forced steel back into it as he went on. "I will order the others back, so you can see. And I will step back, out of range." So saying, he retreated almost to the mud wall of the tanner's house behind him, and Bakri remained two sword lengths out. Ghaffar barked at his men, so that when Bakri looked south, to his right, they were eight paces behind, and stepping back, their swords down, so that the two holding Adilah might push her forward. He saw her beautiful eyes, glinting fiercely.

"Surrender the sword," his uncle said, "and I will let you both ride free."

"Lies," Bakri said. He'd meant to say more, but somehow that seemed enough.

"You are wiser than I realized. You know that you will die, when you turn it over. But this I promise you. I will have them let the girl go, and you will set the weapon down."

"No!" Adilah shouted to him. "Do not listen to him!"

Bakri doubted this as well. Like as not his uncle would order the girl killed as Bakri lay dying, so that he would hear or see her fall. He was not sure what, now, he could do to save her, and the surge of anger and energy that had fueled his advance was now faded. He was bone-tired after his long journey, and the choices which had only moments ago seemed so effortless now were wearying.

Even from twelve paces off Adilah saw his hesitation, and it came to her that he meant to sacrifice himself for her, because she had seen the love in his eyes from the first. That she could not allow, partly because she did not think herself worth the life of one so brave, but mostly because she did not want such a sword to fall into the hands of so evil a man as Ghaffar. She acted then with more bravery than many seasoned warriors. She resumed her struggling, swaying away from the knife, and as the soldier tightened his grip on her hair and brought the blade closer, she thrust herself upon it.

Her own soft gasp as the weapon pierced her flesh was drowned out by the cry of dismay from the soldier with the knife. It was a deep chest wound, and the blood flowed swiftly out.

"I didn't mean to, general!" he cried, stepping back. "She just … threw herself at it."

The gathered soldiers looked back and forth among themselves, and the slumping girl, and Ghaffar.

Bakri let out a wordless cry of rage and swung forward.

Ghaffar could scarce believe it. Everything had come crashing down so swiftly. A moment ago he had been the most feared man in a week's ride. Yesterday it seemed he would soon have the only weapon that could kill him, and he would melt it down. Moments ago he'd sprung an ambush that surrounded Bakri nine to one, and after that the girl's fate had frozen the boy with indecision.

He felt the hand of fate upon his shoulder. That is not to say that he did not fight, for he raised his weapon and struck at his nephew with a curse.

Bakri felt that slash to his shoulder only dimly. The whole of his attention was focused upon the neck where his sword struck, and the long clean line he drew through his uncle's flesh, and the blood that sparkled in the wake of the head that went flying from the body. He was a little mad, then, and slashed the body twice more as it fell. He spun and charged toward Adilah.

The warrior who'd been holding her had set her down, almost tenderly, and the others withdrew, for they wanted no part of what they sensed would follow. Too late, the man with the knife threw it aside and fumbled at his blade. In moments he too lay dead, and Bakri snarled at the others to get back. This they did. He was aware, too, that shuttered windows had been thrown open and that closed doorways around the square now framed bleary-eyed villagers. This was not a fully Muslim place, remember, so there had been no call to prayer.

He knelt down beside the girl, setting Gray Maiden at his side, and cradled her head. She was breathing fast, and there seemed a great deal of blood already on her clothes. Her blouse was soaked. She looked up into his eyes and raised a hand toward his face.

The warriors watched. They began to think of the youth's exposed back, and the sword that lay apart from him, and how it might feel to wield such a weapon themselves, and they licked their lips and glanced at one another, trying to summon the courage to act.

The djinn appeared in a shimmer of blue in front of the fountain. The villagers gasped and the warriors drew back, but Bakri looked up slowly, with little fear.

"Give me the sword," she said, "and I will heal the girl."

He looked down at Adilah, who blinked blearily at him but did not speak. Color had drained from her face. And Bakri looked up at the djinn, and he thought of how the creature had summoned Habab and the others against him, and how it had said it desired the sword. "You brought my uncle here," he said, knowing as he said it that he spoke the truth.

"We made a bargain," the djinn acknowledged. "Now I shall make one with you. Give me the sword and I shall heal her. But you must act fast. Her life ebbs and I cannot raise the dead."

Bakri reached out, put his hand to the sword, rose slowly, and sliced at the djinn.

It was like striking the finest silk, for there was the barest resistance as the Gray Maiden passed through the creature's waist. Finally there was a changed expression, one of shocked surprise, as the djinn fell into bright fragments that then faded to nothingness as they settled toward the earth. With a cry of rage he thrust the point of Gray Maiden into the soil and called for the villagers to bring a healer.

But there was nothing that could be done for Adilah. She died in his arms while he wept and told her he would do everything he promised.

He kept his word. He brought Islam to the warriors who thronged to serve Bakri, djinn slayer, and to the village, and to the regions he conquered. He was just, and honorable, though he had changed overnight into a grim and humorless man. He took wives, but had no sons, and when in the fullness of time he died, it was said the last words upon his lips were not from the Koran, which he had long since memorized, but the name of the girl, Adilah.

As for the sword, it passed into the hands of the caliph as a gift, and from there to the treasure rooms, where it lay, undisturbed for decades, waiting until a righteous hand might come to wield it once more.

Honors Among Thieves

Esther Friesner

Ladies and gentlemen of the Pitchbrook Chapter of—

All right, all right, settle down. Yeah, I know what I called you. My old Da always told me to start off a speech with a joke and that was it. So—!

Miserable, poxy, lowlife ragamuffins, cutpurses, second-story men—sorry, Snaggletooth Lil, I meant to say second-story *persons*—thugs and thugettes, light-fingered rapscallions and assorted embarrassments to the Pitchbrook Chapter of the Greater Salamanzor City Thieves' Guild, as your duly elected Chief Filch and Pilferer, it is my inescapable obligation to introduce tonight's guest of honor. Unaccustomed as I am to public speaking that is not before a magistrate, I am nonetheless eager to fulfill my duties. I've got a tale to tell and I guarantee it'll warm the heart of your cockles.

Or if it don't, there's plenty of brandy on the tables. Some of it's still in the bottles. Enjoy.

It's a wise thief who knows better'n to rush things. We don't dawdle in our profession, but we do take what time's needful for the job. You know what happens if you just jam your hand into a gent's coin pouch without first making a careful study of your best getaway route and if he looks fit to chase after you, should your fingers fumble. And what do we call the hasty burglar who fails to give sufficient study to the house he's got in mind to loot?

I don't know either, but it always begins with "The late, lamented." So drink up and bide patient. You won't regret it.

This story begins some years ago, during the reign of Duke Salamanzor the Fourteenth, better known to us and all his woebegone subjects as Duke Sal the Enthusiastically Vicious. It was winter, though to be honest—Shut up, Lil, that wasn't a joke—while old Sal was infesting the throne, every day seemed like winter. Those were lean times for us hard-working guild-folk. The penalty for stealing was a slap on the wrist. Trouble was, they used an ax to do the slapping.

But this was winter for real, the sort of winter where rats breathed icicles, dogs were scared to lift their legs against iron gates, and my old lady actually *welcomed* me into her bed. It was a foul, cold night, and I was hanging around—Oops, pardon my non-sensitive language there, all you members of the Gallows 'n' Gibbets Surviving Spouses Book Club—I was *waiting* around the Guild headquarters in case any of our members needed to avail themselves of our All Night Loot-Fencing service. There came a knock at the door, and when I went to answer it, there they were.

I recognized *her* right off: Mimosa Claycraw, thief among thieves, troll among trolls, and five-time winner of the Duchess Amabel Memorial Flower-Arranging Competition.

I didn't see *him*, at first. How could I? He was in her shadow. You young sprats in the audience were born too late to see Mimosa alive and kicking—and many's the man still walking funny who found out just how hard she could kick—but let me tell you, that troll was *big*. Massive. Epic. Not so much big on the toes-to-topknot line but definitely on the crossways stretch. There weren't many doorways in this town she could walk through straight on, and some were a challenge to her even when she tried sidling over the threshold. When that happened, she just plowed herself a new doorway, and that's why Salamanzor City's known for its two-oxen-abreast tavern entrances.

"Evenin', Mimosa," I said, pleasant as you please. "What've you got for us tonight?"

"This," she said, and she reached her right hand back a ways and gave *something* a gentle shove forward.

I got my first good look at him as he crouched there in the light spilling into the street. He had a badly patched cloak covering him, the hood so deep that you'd think the troll was dropping off a bundle of laundry. Then she said, "What'd I tell you, Ash? Stand up straight! Be proud of what you are!"

He obeyed her right away, which was all the proof I needed that he was a smart'un. He uncurled his spine, pulled back his shoulders, and let his hood fall away from a filthy shock of short, tangled hair likely to harbor its fair share of head lice. I couldn't gauge the poor mite's age by looking at him, but a rough guess placed him somewhere between Nothing But Porridge on the one end and Starving to Death on the other, with cheeks gaunt enough to declare he was leaning *much* closer to the second one. He was snub-nosed, mud-and-worse-stained, and ugly as a dungeon piss-hole, but there was one thing he was not:

He was no troll.

I was baffled. I guess it showed, because Mimosa snorted hard enough to cover me with snot-gobbets and said, "No, he ain't no troll, but he's still my boy, and I want you to take him on as a Guild Trainee, and 'Prentice rank to follow that."

"How—?" I began, glancing back and forth between the two of them so fast I swear I heard my eyes rattle like dried peas being shook up in an empty box. I just couldn't believe it, y'know? Our Mimosa, she wasn't exactly famed for looking after anyone but herself, and the notion that she was seeing to the welfare of that little mite left me drop-jawed and right boggled. "Maybe we'd best take this inside," I said, expecting a long explanation and not willing to freeze my dumplings off while Mimosa gave it.

The troll just shook her head. "No thanks. I got … reasons. Him an' me, we can stand the cold. And you best be able to do the same or I've still got the means to make you regret it."

When Mimosa Claycraw made a threat, there was teeth behind it: dragon's teeth. I leaned against the doorframe, tried hugging myself warm, and told her to carry on.

She took a deep, shuddery breath. "I found 'im," she said. "Some years back, when Duke Sal first come to rule here, back when that toad-ticklin' slop-slurper was doin' the city-wide sweeps to bring in folk like me. You remember."

I did. We all do. Most of us lost friends and family to those bad old days, and the so-called honest citizens of Salamanzor City who'd been happily jabbering about how much safer they'd feel o' nights now that a strong hand was comin' down hard on the riffraff, well, they soon found that strong hand clutched tight around their own fat throats before it dug deep into their pockets. It was the first time them 'n' us found common ground, tryin' to survive Duke Sal.

"Where'd you come across the lad?" I asked.

"Outside of Lulu's place."

Friends, a moment of silence to honor the memory of Miss Lulu, one of the finest practitioners of the more complex, warm-an'-sticky amorous arts that our fine city ever knew. Things just haven't been the same around here since she shut up shop, pensioned off her girls, and changed her name when she married into the royal family. A fine citizen and a social climber to be reckoned with, that 'un!

Anyway …

"He wasn't more'n four years old then, near as I can tell," Mimosa went on. "Bold-faced little thing, half-starved but never a whimper out of him when I grabbed his arm and nigh broke it."

"Break a little kid's arm? Gods above, below, and sideways, Mimosa, that's harsh, even for you!" I said.

She snorted again. "I said *almost* broke it. And you'd done the same to anyone you caught with his grubby fist buried in your coin purse. Thanks be, I had good reflexes back then and I stopped myself the moment I saw how puny and young he was. Ain't that right, Ash?"

The kid nodded vigorously and his thin lips lifted in the ghost of a mischievous grin. I sized him up some more and for no sane reason found myself liking him.

A lot.

Maybe too much. It was a weird feeling that I couldn't lay a name to or find a reason to back it up.

"He still looks kind of young and puny," I said, trying to reclaim my professional attitude. No one comes to the Guild house except as they've got business to transact and a con or two to try putting over on the hard-working fence on duty. It wouldn't do for me to go soft.

Shut up, ladies.

"He is." Mimosa shrugged and might've been about to say something more, but instead she began to cough. It was a chilling sound, like a landslide coming at you fast. Clouds of white dust spewed from her mouth. I can see by the looks on your faces that some of you know what a cough like that means to a troll: nothing good.

She fought back those racking sounds and continued: "Yeah, he's young and he's puny but he's *mine*. I hauled the brat into Miss Lulu's, to see if he belonged to any of the girls an' they told me he was street sweepings. Showed up on the doorstep one night and acted worse'n a cat. Wouldn't let 'em take him in, wouldn't move on, though he was willin' enough to eat whatever they gave him. They gave him plenty, too, to hear them tell it. Far as we could learn, he was orphaned with nothing to his name *but* his name. Only keepsake he had from his kindred was a ring of braided goldy hair. Said it was his ma's. Said yes when I asked if he'd like to range with me. It just seemed … *right* to take him on." An odd look crossed her face when she said that. "We've been together ever since. Taught him all I know, I did, and damned thankful I trained him proper."

"Nice story, Mimosa," I said. "Very touching. But what's it got to do with—?"

She didn't give me time to finish the question, just undid her belt and dropped her breeches.

I'll tell you, friends, *there* was a sight I'll not soon forget. Her flesh— well, it wasn't flesh any more, not so's you could call it by the name. Trolls are thick-skinned creatures, but this was leagues past that. Ankles, calves, knees, thighs, everything'd had gone hard and gray and crazed with count- less cracks, every one of 'em leakin' grit. I cast a look around back of her and saw a trail of it in the street marking her passage up to the Guild house door. No denying the worst: Mimosa'd caught that scourge of all scourges, Rocky Pneumonia. It can sweep away a troll's life *that* quick and complete- ly unpredictable, leaving their ruined bodies as no more'n a heap of stone.

I confess, I teared up something shameful when I saw what was afflicting her. Then she coughed and I just missed getting à blast of sand in the face. The disease had progressed even farther than I first thought. No wonder she wouldn't come inside! A loyal Guild member to the last, she wouldn't burden us with the effort and expense of hauling away several tons of her remains.

"I'm sorry, Mimosa," I said, and I meant every word. "It's going to be hard on the Guild, losing you. You're one of our oldest, most respected members. If there's anything we can do—"

"Take him," she said, and shoved the young'n into my arms so sudden, so forceful, that the pair of us went tumbling backwards in a tangle. By the time we managed to get back on our feet again, she was gone.

I suppose I could've trailed her by the grit, but what would be the use of that, except to rob her of the dignity of dying the way she wanted? I took the kid inside, gave him a place by the fire, a plate of bread and cheese, and a mug of cider. He dropped all of it, flung himself into my arms, and bawled. To tell you the truth—Lil, if I've got to tell you to shut up *one more time*, I'll stuff a hamster in your gob, see if I don't!

Ahem. As I was saying, to speak truly, I joined my tears to his and we both mourned Mimosa together. He clung to his grief longer'n me, as you'd expect, yet even so, he came to accept his new circumstances eventually. You all remember how he was raised, eh? No single one of us guildfolk wanted the responsibility of replacing his foster ma. I would've done it— Mimosa did say she wanted me to have him—but with seven of my own kids at home, an eighth on the way, and a wife who pitched the sharp and heavy cookware at me for no reason whenever I came home, it wouldn't'a been safe for him. Our brood knew how to duck. Ash might've been less adept.

No one else volunteered to step in and help the boy. Our poorer brethren couldn't hardly feed themselves, nor their own brats. Our more successful members picked up gentry ways and found excuses more readily than pity for the poor mite. Fact is, 'twas Bela Goldtouch first suggested we make Ash's upbringing a community project, so we found the lad some space in one of the Guild house storage closets, a bed that once belonged to old Goldtouch's favorite hound, and added his feeding and training and such to the To Do list of anyone on duty. It worked.

Except for the training. Even though Mimosa claimed she'd trained him proper, let's just say that the hard evidence of it was sore lacking. I never met a being less cut out for the thief's life. Ash was eager to please and he tried his best, such as it was, but he couldn't even get the hang of a simple maneuver like Pennikin's Grabchat or master the art of the Tilt-Topple-Toddle. When it was my lookout to give him lessons, I started him out with easy targets to build his confidence. I took him into dark alleys hard by the worst taverns in our fair city, a resting place for sodden drunkards sleeping it off so soundly that the rats managed to marry, start families, and raise their pups atop the poor guzzlers' bellies. Some of 'em—the sots, not the rats—wore their coinpurses so plain to see that a rank amateur could cut 'em without laying so much as a fingertip on the client.

Not our Ash. Whenever I'd sic him on a mark, the boy always managed to touch 'em. *Always.* And not by accident, neither. I caught him doing it deliberate, putting a hand on the tosspot's brow before going for the man's purse. It roused the prey every time! What's more, it brought 'em back to their unaddled senses same as if they'd never had a drop of ale. Good thing we were both fast runners, in those days, else we'd've seen the whipping post or worse more times than I find healthy.

It was no good remonsterating with him after. "Damn it all, Ash," I'd say once I got my breath back. "Why'd you have to go and do that for?" He'd say sorry, and say he didn't know why, just that it seemed like something he was *supposed* to do, and swear he wouldn't do it again.

But he did. Every time.

"Now look here, boy," I'd say. "You're growing up. There's likely lads younger'n you who've already passed from Trainee to 'Prentice, and even some ready to take their Housebreaking exams. If the rest of us in the Guild didn't hold your foster ma's memory in such high regard, you'd've been out on your own hook long since. Is that how you want to live your life? As a debt and a burden on them as cares for you?"

Because that was the truth: we all *did* care for Ash, even them of our proud membership who didn't fancy kids at all, except as a side dish.

Huh. I guess that joke worked better back when we still had a couple of ogres on the membership roll.

Anyway, there was just *something* about the lad. We didn't know what it was, back then in the lean times, and we didn't have the leisure to think about it much. Too busy trying to earn our livelihoods while staying three steps ahead of Duke Sal's patrols.

For a while, we thought we'd found the answer: magic lessons. We had more'n one failed wizard in the ranks, men who'd done well enough learning the basics of the craft but washed out when it came to casting the serious spells. It never hurts to have a little of the old hey-presto-look-at-that-phantom-giant-marmot-I-just-whipped-up on your side when the lawmen got you cornered and you need a distraction. If the boy couldn't filch, he could still learn a trick or two and be a valuable getaway asset for his cronies.

Except no, he couldn't. Grendel "Stumpwrist" Borgumvetter tried teaching Ash the simple tricks even *he'd* mastered before the incident that led him to earn his nickname. No joy, my friends, no joy. The lad could not deliver the goods on something as simple as a fake fireball spell. It was the fake part that tripped him up, and that's why we had to rebuild the north tower. Twice.

So we got on with our lives and we kept trying to turn Ash into a halfway decent thief and *he* kept bollixing up his every lesson until we simply couldn't handle it no more and a Guildwide meeting was called.

It was held here in the Guild house, as is only proper, and Ash was told to shut himself up in his storage closet and cover his ears until someone came to fetch him. It was a grim get-together, I'll tell you that. We all knew what was coming: Mimosa or no Mimosa, we couldn't afford to carry deadweight any longer. Jennie One-Eye-Seven-Fingers-Extra-Toe was weeping when she said what no one else had the heart for:

"He won't make 'Prentice an' he don't make profit. He's gotta go."

I volunteered to give Ash the verdict, though I could feel my poor heart breaking with every step that took me closer to his hidey-hole. I could picture his face, especially those big, sad eyes of his. That boy could teach cats how to improve their gods-given talent for making a man feel guilty. By the time I rapped on the supply closet door, I'd resolved that I was going to adopt the lad right off and have it out with the wife later. She might get angry, but I trusted that one look at Ash's gaze would bring her around.

It wasn't needful. I knocked at the door once, twice, three times, and … nothing. I opened the door slowly and found he was gone. All that remained was a message on the floor and the ring of braided golden hair he'd always carried with him. I guess he'd dropped that and never noticed.

The message said: *I know it's wrong to eavesdrop but I couldn't help it. I overheard what you all decided. I'm sorry I'm no good as a thief. I'm leaving and I'm not coming back until you can be proud of me. Thanks for everything. Love, Ash.*

Now here's the funny thing—no, *two* of 'em—about this:

First off, he'd managed to sneak out of the Guild house without any of us being the wiser, which was really strange when you recall what a blunderfoot he was and how the only escape route passed *through* our meeting space.

Second, he hadn't left his farewell note on a scrap of paper or cloth or chalked up inside the closet, no. The letters were etched *right into the stone wall*, wide and deep enough for me to fit the first joint of my smallest finger. When I fetched the rest of meeting to witness this, more'n one of us swore they could smell the tang of something burnt. Someone suggested maybe it was done with sorcery, but ol' Stumpwrist said Ash didn't have the spell, the talent, nor the concentration needed to pull off a feat like that.

We were still puzzling over this weeks later when word came about the public execution. You all remember who the main attraction of that little bit of street theater was gonna be, right?

No, Lil, not *me*. Do I look executed to you?

Don't answer that.

I broke with Guild policy and went to see it happen. We guildfolk know better'n to show our faces at executions. No sense giving the authorities any ideas. I didn't care. I wasn't about to let that boy go to his death without him seeing at least one friendly face in the crowd. I made sure to take that ring of braided hair with me. He was going to have his one treasure back in his hands when he died, I was set on that.

The scaffold was set up in the plaza in front of the duke's palace. The space was big enough to accommodate a healthy crowd and convenient enough for His Loathsome Lordship to have a good view of the proceedings while he had brunch and wenches on the second-floor terrace.

I used all my skills to slip through the mob until I was close enough to the execution platform for my purposes. I was right by the path from the ducal dungeon to the three steps Ash would have to climb to meet his doom, close enough to reach out and tap the lad right quick when the guards brought him past. Good thing my hand could move like lightning in those days, else one of the duke's hired swords would've lopped it off at the elbow for my daring.

Ash turned his head at my touch and gave me a look so full of love and regret that I felt my lips begin to form the words, *Don't kill him, my lord! Take me instead.* No idea where that came from. Not then.

They marched him onto the platform kind of slow. That was odd, seeing as how the usual way was a brisk pace up the steps and over to the noose or the block or the cauldron or one of Duke Sal's more inventive devices for parting souls from bodies. The guardsmen acted like they was … *reluctant,* you know? That, in spite of how some said they'd had their hearts replaced with lumps of sun-dried beef to keep 'em from feeling anything human. Our Ash was young, but some of Duke Sal's victims was younger yet. The guards could either lose their hearts or lose their minds.

Did I hear one of you lot say, "Or lose their jobs"? Ha. And their heads along with that! Our duke always did have a different notion of employee severance.

All of which made the guards' actions even more bizarre. I caught a glimpse of Duke Sal's face while his men dawdled Ash up the scaffold steps. He wasn't happy. I swear, I could hear his teeth grinding, he was *that* furious at the delay. His fist closed over the jeweled medallion he always wore, the lawful mark of office passed down from one city ruler to the next. Fencing *that* gewgaw could provide funds to feed the poor hereabouts for half a year; more, if you threw in the thick gold chain it hung by. The commander of the guard was on duty up on the terrace and recognized the danger signs as the duke's complexion went from its usual sallow shade to bright red, to deep crimson, to—what's the name of that color? Puke?

Oh, right, *puce*. Thanks, Lil.

Like I was saying, when the commander saw Duke Sal's face go through that rainbow-from-the-Demon-Teeming-Pits-of-Garnoth display, he acted fast, shouting at his men to move things along. Before you could say boo, Ash was on his knees at the block and the executioner was testing the ax, making sure the edge was nice and dull, just the way his nasty master liked it. A dull ax means it takes more than one chop to get the job done. That's Duke Sal for you: rush the condemned to where they'll die but make sure they take their painful time doing it.

I shoved my way to a spot in front of the block and hissed Ash's name real low. He looked right at me. The boy always did have the most uncanny keen hearing, like we all learned when he overheard that meeting. I held up the braided ring of hair and it would've broke a heart of iron to see the gratitude in his eyes.

"I thought it was lost," he murmured. His hands weren't tied—Duke Sal got his jollies watching the futile way some poor souls tried fending off the ax—and he stretched them out to take the keepsake. The boy pressed that circlet of golden hair to his lips and wet it with his tears, then tucked it safe into the bosom of his tunic. He turned his gaze to the executioner and nodded. There was a grand dignity in that simple gesture, a calm acceptance of fate you don't usually see in someone that young. The headsman jerked back, like a thunderbolt'd gone through him. He wore a half-mask for the job and everyone up close could see how he licked his lips nervously as Ash laid his head on the block.

The ax rose, shaking. I gritted my teeth, saying a prayer that against all odds the blade fall straight and true and do the job in one blow. There wasn't a single sound in the plaza. Even the dogs and the birds fell still.

A roar from the duke's terrace broke the spell. Old Sal was on his feet, bellowing with rage. "Do I have to do everything myself?" he shouted as he leaped over the stone railing. You wouldn't think he was such a nimble bastard, to look at him, but he had no trouble landing on his feet from that height. The crowd fell back as he plowed his way to the scaffold. He grabbed Ash by the hair and yanked his head off the block.

"What have you got there, damn you?" he demanded. Ash just crossed his hands on his chest. I began edging away, but I reckoned without the duke's sharp eye. "Guards! There's the man who gave it to him," he said, jabbing a twiggy finger right at me. "Seize him!"

That's how I found myself sharing the scaffold—and likely the upcoming execution—with our Ash. Unlike the way they'd dealt with him, the guards didn't show a crumb of reluctance when it came to pinning *my* arms behind me and awaiting the duke's twisted pleasure.

Duke Sal wasted no more time questioning his prisoner. He slapped Ash's shielding hands aside and grabbed the boy's tunic, tearing it wide. The glimmering ring of hair fell to the planks. The duke scooped it up and glared at it with all the lip-curling disgust you'd use while dangling a dead rat by the tail. "What is this filth?" he sneered.

"Please, your grace, it was my mother's," Ash said. "I scarcely knew her before we were parted." A few scattered sobs rose from the crowd to hear all the sorrow and yearning in the lad's voice.

"Indeed?" The duke grinned. He turned his head toward the terrace where his commander of the guards still dithered and said a single word: "Torch."

The flame was brought fast. Duke Sal motioned for Ash to be hauled upright, then pressed the tiny golden wreath back into his grasp. "Burn it," he snarled.

Ash gaped at the heartless order, then shook his head. "I can't, my lord. It's all I ever had of her. You may do what you want with it—I'm powerless to prevent you—but I—I can't do it," he said.

"You can and you will," the duke replied. "For if you won't, your friend here will have a death in my dungeon that will make him envy yours." He grinned at me like a death's head. It was all I could do to hold my water, I'll swear to that. I closed my eyes and prayed that the Guild wouldn't let my poor wife and kids starve once I was worm food.

I heard Ash take a deep breath. "All right. I'll do it," he said.

I opened my eyes and saw him holding the circlet of golden hair above the torch. "No, lad!" I shouted. "Don't let this filthy bastard make you sacrifice what's dear to you! He'll kill me anyway, and slow, and make you watch while he gloats for having tricked you. Don't—"

One of the guards backhanded me hard, so hard my eyes were blinded with dancing lights and my mouth filled with blood. The duke laughed.

"Come on, boy, do it! It's rude to keep your betters waiting," he called, in the best of humor. "Ha! But where are *my* manners? Calling you 'boy' when you're facing a man's doom. They told me your name is Ash. Is that so?"

Our Ash bowed his head and answered, "Yes, m'lord."

"How fitting," said Duke Sal. He grabbed Ash by the elbow and forced the lad's hand into the flames.

His hand and more. The duke made sure that Ash's sleeve caught fire, too. My nostrils reeked and my belly churned at the smell of burning hair and flesh. The blaze raced up Ash's arm and engulfed him so quickly that it was all the duke could do to leap back and save himself. The crowd shrieked and groaned and wailed, their hearts torn to witness such a barbaric death.

And the duke? He laughed again and preened over the wonderful joke he'd made from his victim's name and fate. He laughed and commanded his shuddering guards to make sure nothing valuable caught fire from Ash's blazing body and started for the scaffold steps with his chest puffed out pridefully, pleased with himself.

Something froze him before he could take the first step down. I saw him pause and turn at the edge of the platform. His ugly face was creased with a puzzled frown. He stared into the flames wrapping Ash from top to toe. The sickening stench of scorching hair and skin was gone. There were no screams of pain, no need for the guards to use their weapons to keep the boy from jumping off the scaffold in a useless bid to outrun fiery death. Friends, it was the *calmest* human bonfire you could ever hope to see.

He stood still, our Ash, a cool shadow inside a husk of fire, and didn't make a sound. Not one.

The duke's face contorted with rage. "How *dare* you defy—!" he began. He never finished, which is pretty sad, actually, because yelling at someone for the treachery of *not* dying would've made that the single stupidest thing Duke Sal ever said.

But what can you do? The dazzling, white-hot flame that shot from Ash's radiant shell and pierced Duke Sal's chest robbed history of a great quote and a rotten man. He died surprised.

He wasn't the only one; to be surprised, I mean. The guards stood flummoxed. Should they brave the fire and seize the lad who'd just roasted their piggish patron? Should they rally a bucket brigade? Should they just shout thanks and scamper off until someone else took charge and told them what to do?

The crowd was too stunned to react, likely weighing up their choices. Was it safe to cheer? Was it wise to flee? Before they could decide, their choice was made for them. Hoofbeats rumbled loud and louder as every exit from the plaza was blocked by a shining company of mounted warriors. The late duke's guards did a quick us-versus-them headcount and took early retirement on the spot. The newcomers rode magnificent mounts, yet these were also steeds that looked too fine-boned to carry a man. Good thing none of their riders *were* men.

I won't ask you lot if you've ever seen elves in full war gear. Who hasn't, by now? Golden lances, silky hair streaming behind their glittering helmets, rich and regal garb under silver-chased armor, perfect faces and bodies, weird ears, all the stuff of which epics, sagas, ballads, and more'n a few dirty jokes are made. What you *don't* know is how their leader came riding straight to the scaffold and in one graceful sweep leaped from his saddle to the platform.

"My lord," he said, dropping to one knee before the firestorm enveloping our Ash. "Praise all, we have found you at last. Come forth, that we might pay you the tribute of our fealty!"

No, I don't know what *fealty* means. Whatever it is—maybe some kind of sausage?—that elf went on about it for a while until the flames on the platform died, probably blown out by the gust of all that speechifying.

Ash stepped away from the last tumbling sparks, except he wasn't *our* Ash any more. He'd grown taller and twinkly in the fire, with flossy, glossy hair down to his mother-may-I and a face that sent every female in the crowd—and a few men—into sighing, swooning, squealing bidders for his favor. It wasn't just his looks did that, either. Elves have the gift for making folks fawn over 'em for no reason. It's whatcha call it, *carissima*? The stuff that made us want to save him when he still looked like a grubby little human kid, and kept the guards from hustling him onto the scaffold, and gave the executioner cold feet. He had that, plus sharp hearing, with or without pointy ears on display. And a way of leaving notes in stone walls that he melted with a touch. And a healing hand that purged drunkards from the fumes of ale and wine. I guess all that should've tipped us off that he wasn't what he appeared to be. See, this is what happens when you don't pay attention.

As for *who* he was, though—

There'd been a big dust-up among the elvish royal houses, a round of Assassination Tag that led some of them to take refuge with us mortals, slumming to survive. A few refused to run away from the fight, but not before slapping a human disguise spell on their kids and putting them somewhere safe. And just in case the ugliness went on for centuries and yesterday's haven turned into a hell-hole over time, they gave the brats a way to send a *Help!* message home.

I see you nodding. Yeah, you get it: that ring of his mother's braided hair? It was set to summon their family's household troops if it got damaged or destroyed. Ash was so young when he came here that they sent a guardian along with him. Too bad Salamanzor City's so … *lively*. Something *real* lively must've happened to Ash's guardian before he could tell the kid what his keepsake was really for.

Thanks be for Duke Sal, eh? And that's the last time anyone'll ever say that. Though frankly, back on that fateful day, our Ash did seem to realize he owed that swine a debt. He stood there, hearing his kinsman tell him it was not only safe to go home again, but that their clan had won the throne and he was all sorts of royalty, and a funny look came over that pretty face.

With a massive sob, he flung himself on the duke's corpse, hugged that heap of scorched meat to his bosom, and began yowling about how sorry he was, how he'd never meant to kill anyone, how he had no idea he had the power to turn a churl into charcoal. His kinsman begged him to stop, but he groaned, "How can I, when I've robbed these good folk of their leader?" He dropped the body and clapped his hands to his bosom. "He left no heir. Alas, now wicked men will battle to take his place. Their vile ambition will destroy this city and its people! What can I do to save the innocent? What, oh *what*?" He paused for breath and softly added: "Unless …"

And then he told everyone his idea. His loyal legion of heavily armed fighters agreed that it wasn't half bad, as such things go, and might be worth a fair try. The late duke's guards agreed readily. The crowd followed suit. It was better than taking an arrow to the throat, that being the elvish way of gently reproving nay-sayers. The final verdict was sealed when we all saw the flash of gold from the jeweled pendant suddenly hanging around Ash's neck, like magic was at work. Someone shouted, "The old duke's medallion! It's a sign! The gods have spoken!"

Not that such a declaration made any sense at all, if you thought about it, but it made the elves happy, and they had the swords and the lances and at least one of them had the gift of setting cheeky folks afire, so we started cheering and that night the whole city got drunk.

Which brings us to the purpose of tonight's banquet.

Miserable, poxy, lowlife ragamuffins, cutpurses, and yada-yada-yada, it is my honor to give you our glorious, benevolent, and all-powerful ruler, Prince Ashkelion Elvenborn, monarch of the Seven Lordships of Radiance, Commander of the Realm, Vessel of the Fires of Shavann'ahyrkut, Wielder of the Sword of Especially Messy Death, Guardian of the Elixir of Relatively Eternal Life—

—and our Guild's newest accredited 'Prentice. If filching the life out of a tyrant, having the brass ones to rob his corpse, and then pocketing his whole dukedom doesn't count enough to qualify him for that, damned if I know what does. Steal big, my friends; always steal big.

Mimosa would be proud.

Rainbow Dark
Jenna Rhodes

His uncle dragged him howling down the alleyway, calling for his sister Maude until a fist came across his mouth in lightning fury and white pain. Crimson spurted from split lips. Cristane put the back of his hand to his mouth and realized that he could not hear Maude crying after him. And why should she? The house had been golden with warmth, its lights spilling across the sleeted and muddied street. A woman with nails painted the blue of a spring sky had drawn Maude towards her with a coo, and his little sister had gone eagerly. His uncle then pocketed a gold coin and grabbed Cristane up.

He tried to mark the street, but this was no part of town he'd ever seen before. Twisting about, Cristane caught sight of the House's corner lantern, a crescent moon illuminated by a fat yellow candle. He hoped he had marked the house, noting the chestnut hue to the muddy streets, different from the toasted nut color of the dirt in their quarter.

They crisscrossed town, passing quarters both low and high, but his uncle's hard grip did not lessen. He suspected that their tangled path was meant to lose the way. It would not. He would find Maude no matter what.

Then, on the outskirt, not far from the smelly environs of the tanners' sheds and drying racks, his uncle let go of his wrists and dug his fingers into Cristane's shoulder.

"Stand up, lad, and look alive."

He did not recognize the guildhall until they entered, then he stood as if struck dumb.

"You wanted shoes," his uncle husked. "You will find them here."

Shoes were nothing compared to losing Maude. Cristane shrugged his shoulder as if he might dart away and his uncle's hand tightened.

A handful of men stood at the far end of the building, arguing among themselves, voices raised and arms gesturing, taking little notice of their entrance. Massive rafters held up a ceiling that existed not only to hold back inclement weather, but to cradle the collected rainbows.

He tilted his head back to catch sight of all the banners and swags of cloth hanging from every eave and rafter, each its own brilliant color. All the hues that dye could render to dazzle the senses waved faintly in display, stirred by a nearly undetectable breeze. The solemnity of the place struck him like a temple, allowing only a quiet sigh of awe. Maude would have spun on her heels, hands out-flung in joy.

Then his own thoughts and wants rushed back to Cristane. The day had started with two promises: an apple for Maude and footwear for him, tempting offers for the wary two of them.

He had to ask, because she would have, and he wanted to know so he could tell her when he saw her again.

"Is this where they keep the rainbows safe against the storms?"

"Shut your mouth, lad. I will not have you thought a simpleton!"

Cristane's jaw tightened. Winter had already fallen on them all, the streets churning with mud, rocks, and sleet.

A man approached them, scrubbing his huge hands together briskly, his cheeks ruddy from a fire's warmth, his clothes tailored for his prosperous build, his coal-dark half boots shining to be admired, and so Cristane did.

"What have we here?"

"I want to apprentice the lad."

The guildsman frowned and bent slightly to take a look at Cristane. The starched white collar of his shirt rustled as its wearer shook his head. "We do our pickings in the spring. He stinks, as do you, of desperation. We have no vacancies. Move along with you."

"You will get him cheaply and be better for the bargain."

Cristane twisted about, to stare at his uncle's face. The man had not talked that way about Maude earlier that day. She'd been praised as a gem, and a virgin besides, young and cheerful with a singing voice that would be an asset to the house of ladies. A gold piece passed between them as they haggled and then Maude was gone.

But he had little value? He'd protected his little sister with all the strength of his wiry arms and the fleetness of his bare feet and the pounding of his knuckled fists. He had worth. His chin jutted forward. "Test me."

That drew both their attentions, crossing over their mutterings, which had begun to sound like two alley cats yowling lowly at one another just before springing. His uncle smiled, a thin drawing of his lips. "Aye. Try him."

The guildsman tucked his thumbs into his waistband, a cross-silk piece of darkest mulberry, which set off the redder tones hidden in his purple night-black trousers. "Is that what you want, lad?"

"I want a pair of shoes. And a dry spot by the hearth."

The guildsman brushed a hand over his face as if hiding a smile. "A trial it shall be, then." And he looked down and asked his question, a glint deep in his sorrel brown eyes. "Do you believe in miracles?"

His uncle thought himself the object of the question. "I do, by the Sunlit Lady and the Cold Man who pursues her. Or any other god you care to name, I kneel to them all. What other way can I hope to improve my lot? Test the lad and let's be done with this."

The guildsman waved aside his uncle's words. "I address the boy. I know by what way you intend to benefit yourself." Cristane felt his icy regard sweep over him.

What did he know of miracles? Cristane stood still. He'd thought the guildsman would ask him of the colors he saw, the verdants, the damsons, the crimson and ceruleans taught him by a near forgotten mother, along with the dozen different whites, the pinks, the grays, and the browns that echoed in his own eyes, but this took him aback.

"I ... I do."

"And what would qualify, lad?"

He could feel the tension in his uncle's hand and knew that he ought to say something smart, something important, if only he could think of it. What temple should he mention? What special rites that some of the fringe followed outside the sanctified churches? Or perhaps, as many of the lower folk muttered about Tradesmen, his only god came minted in gold coins? His thoughts chased one another futilely. The guildsman's gaze bore down on him.

"I see a miracle every day from my hut's window," he finally offered.

"You have a window?"

"My father took it from a fine mansion that burned down, when the rioters went to loot it. He brought back a pane of glass that you can look through and put it in our hut. My mother looked out it until she died."

"Did he now."

Cristane did not hear approval. Not yet. He swallowed and nodded. "My home is buried." And the listener inclined his head in understanding. Many hovels were half-buried along the back streets of the city, to retain what heat they could in the winter, and coolness in the summer. They climbed up to leave and down to enter. The huts could, and often did, flood in heavy rains and that's when they lived on the rooftop. Cristane held a finger up. "A plant grows against our window on the outside. I can see its roots reach out of its seed, down in the dirt, and its stem climb upward every day, reaching toward the sky."

"What do you see here?" Thick fingers beckoned about the hall's rafters and eaves.

"Flowers. Roots. Colors from boiled shell and bone and mines. The sky and earth harvested and melted into cloth."

The guildsman pursed his lips a moment, before waving over his shoulder. "There is a courtyard. Go wander while I talk with your guardian."

Cristane took a deep breath and shook loose from his uncle. The wooden floor met his feet without splinters, but a chill crept up through its boards, except where colorful woven rugs crossed it. He pushed on the swinging door and found himself in a small square between buildings. He could smell the heat of many vats, perhaps in one of the outbuildings, some of the aromas noxious and others perfumed. Like his neighborhood, he thought, the bitter with the sweet.

He nearly tripped over the silver-haired and wizened woman sitting just inside the edge of the threshold. She caught at his shirt, as much to steady herself as him, and made a cluck of disapproval.

"What are you doing here?"

"Staring. And smelling. And tripping." He did not mind that she kept a grip on his clothing, although she might yank him down so she could slap his ear or pinch his cheek harshly. He deserved it; he'd nearly run her over.

"Who sent you into my courtyard?"

Cristane hadn't caught a name, so he described the man by his bulk and the colors he wore. Her eyes, narrowed at first as she listened shrewdly, opened a bit wider as he finished.

"That would be Skagan. Master Skagan."

"He gave me a trial."

She blinked. Her hair, he noted, was not simply silver, but a bouquet of faded gold among the tarnish, with a note here and there of pure, absolute, snow white. Someone had scissored it haphazardly, or perhaps it had grown out raggedly from its last cutting. She did not look elegant, but the cloth draping her form did. It flowed in liquid colors of the sea, the water in rain, the tide in full sunlight, the deep waves where they lay, and the shallow pools over pebbled sand—all the blues he could imagine from the brief time he'd gone to see the ocean. It roared nearby but he had no business there.

His father and his uncle had woven cord that made the fishing nets, but they sold their skeins of it, tainted from the blood of their fingertips and calluses, and rarely, if ever, saw the end product. His job had been to gather the wool leavings from the shearing sheds, to be carded and combed. To steal what fleece he could, ill-tended, to increase their output beyond what they could buy fairly. He could weasel in and out of sheds and corrals like the varmint the herders called him and run like the wind if he had to.

"Did you hear me, lad?"

"I was thinking."

"Should I ask about what?"

"The colors of your gown."

She looked down and brushed her hand over it. The blues rippled in answer and he realized her eyes echoed the shades of her dress. "How many colors do you see?"

"At least four, lady, but I haven't names for all of them."

"Well, you wouldn't, would you? You're not a part of the Dyers Guild. But do you intend to be?"

"Will I be given shoes?"

"Shoes? No need for long trousers or a full-sleeved shirt or even, by the gods, a jacket?"

"Shoes," he said firmly. She must be daft if she thought he could ask for more. She waited, so he added, "Maybe someday I could earn the others." Not likely, not for the likes of Cristane, but he might be able to beg for more if he wore an apprentice's sash.

She used her hold on him to claw her way to standing and pushed her foot out from under her hem. She wore slippers of fine, soft leather that came to her ankles, their laces colored to match.

He shook his head. "Not like those, lady, too soft. I need tough leather shoes, hard as boiled armor and without leaks."

"A practical lad." She released her hand from his shirt and patted his arm. "Can you bear one last question?"

"If we can walk, lady. I would like to see …" he stared at the outbuild-ings, imagining the beauty that might come out of odors that could make him spew. Master Skagan and his uncle would come to throw him out at any moment. "I would like to see the vats." The drying racks, too, but he knew he could not push his luck.

"If you can tell me what you see there." Her blue-veined hand pointed to a corner across the way, where a flag stood in shadow, a banner he'd not spotted before and now drew him like a moth to flame. He walked, taking her with him, as close as he dared get.

The banner teased him. As he approached it, the sun found it, and he stopped in awe with a gasp he couldn't smother. He'd never seen anything like it, now light where he'd spotted dark. It shone strongly enough to make him throw up a hand to protect his eyes and squint. As he did, the stronger colors returned. Red as fresh blood. Blues that echoed the lady's gown. Glints of gold and green. Muddied browns that looked as if they came from river stone, wetter and all the more glorious for it. It embodied hues that rippled down the fabric before disappearing. His jaw dropped.

"Well, what do you see?" Her voice hammered sharply against his ear.

"Many colors." Before he turned back to her, the banner subsided into a warm ivory like the pages of a book scribed for a temple. He knew, because he'd seen one, once. He stammered as he told her what he thought he'd seen and watched her lips grow thinner and thinner in her age-etched face. He halted. "I saw it. I don't lie."

"Never said you did."

His gaze searched out the flag again, which hung still and shadowy in the corner.

Both turned on heel as the two men came seeking them. Cristane shiv-ered. The banner behind him unfurled a little in the winter breeze and some-thing touched him, a peculiar warmth stealing over him. He wanted to look back, to see what might touch him besides the flag, but did not dare. His uncle's face pinched with annoyance.

"Come away with you. This Goodman here, Master Skagan, will put you where you belong."

No sash dangled from Skagan's thick hands. No look of welcome on the master's face. Cristane drew back in spite of their words. It seemed he had not passed the trial.

Skagan bowed in the direction of Cristane's escort. "Lady Sea. Good day. Are you doing well?"

"Well enough for an old lady. My tides are ebbing and the sun is lowering, as it does for us all." She lifted a finger to Skagan. "Did you make a deal?"

He inclined his head. "We did. He'll be brought to rendering."

His uncle came forward, slapped a hand up the back of Cristane's head, saying, "Good luck, lad. Do the job." He scurried out of the courtyard doors, back into the hall and, Cristane felt certain, hit the street at an even faster pace.

As his relative disappeared, Lady Sea took a step forward, putting herself between the master and Cristane.

"Not rendering."

"It's what we do with … the leavings."

"This one is more than blood, skin, and bones."

A cold chill ran from the bottom of his soles to the top of his head. The noxious smell. He knew it now, from the tallow pots at the candlemakers. From the stew pots behind dubious tavern kitchens. Flowers and roots made dyes. Sometimes animals and minerals. He knew of beetles, dried, that made the most brilliant of reds. Bone and blood? He backed up another step and that peculiar flag covered his shoulders.

"Lady Sea, you have standing here, but I remind you that you have retired from your duties and that standing, how shall I say it, is precarious."

She tilted her head enough that her hair, silver and gold and snow white, tumbled down over one shoulder towards the curve of her torso. "This boy sees the pennant."

"Which one?"

"This one."

The ruddy coloration of Master Skagan's face fled, going chalk pale. "He—"

"Indeed. You are finished with him. I have enough sand left in me that I can train an apprentice." She ripped the sleeve off her gown and handed it to Cristane. "You have your sash. The shoes, we shall see about later."

* * *

They hauled him to the fields. Others were already there, working; backs bent as they harvested dried bud and seeds from the frost-browned ground. Skagan tossed an empty bag at him. "This here's the new lad. Show him the ropes."

Seven faces upturned to him. Hands waved, fingers tinged with earth and the dust of their gatherings. One boy put a knee to the ground and pointed to Cristane. "Here. Like this. We want these and these, but not these. Keep your hands from your eyes, nose, and mouth, cause this here is night marrow and it can make you sick if you take it in."

Cristane squatted by his teacher. He reached out to strip the plant indicated, filling his bag with its delicate remainders. He'd seen these bloom in the spring and summer and never thought much about them once their violet petals were gone. "What does this do?"

"Combined with copper, the powder can make the truest of teals, popular with the ladies, aye? Better to be here in the fields than down in the trenches. Soon, a good wind will sweep through here and then our chance to harvest will be gone. Call me Salvado, if you must."

"Cristane."

His tutor nodded. "All right then, get to work." And he took his knee from the ground, curled into a squat himself, moving quickly through the dried wildflowers. It seemed easy enough for Salvado, but Cristane found himself left with hands of powder more oft than not, and the others laughing at him.

From the field, the gang of laborers went to a small, cheerful brooklet where they washed quickly and splashed each other mercilessly, laughing at those who could not dodge the waves in time. Cristane got the worst of it and stood shivering in thin sunlight as they marched off toward the edge of the forest.

"Now what?"

"Roots, and then we're done for the day because the light is going." Gertha, a freckled and fire-haired girl, smiled at him. "Dinner then, and bed. Early roll out tomorrow."

"Same thing tomorrow?"

"Until this field is stripped, yes. Harvesting is near done for the season. We'll have classes then and you'll wish you were out here, fresh air and no madman Hopper droning his bookwork over you."

"Madman?"

"Shush it, Gertha." Salvado brushed past them. He threw a look at Cristane. "They'll cane you for calling them names."

Gertha shrugged and ran by, tagging Salvado as she did, laughing and disappearing into the forest dimness.

"What is in here?"

"Woad shrubs. We need the leaves."

Woad he knew, for its blue, although he couldn't be certain he'd ever seen the bush itself. By the time the light fell and they trudged back to the guildhall, his hands were raw from shredding leaves from stubborn branches and stems. He had blisters on the bottoms of his feet and his palms and Salvado told him of a salve they could get when they returned to the dorms.

They ate. Big, steaming bowls of porridge studded with bits of jerky and dried berries and flavored with cream and a sprinkle of salted butter. He ate until he thought he would burst, let the others point him to a heap of blankets on the floor next to their cots with a promise he'd have his own cot on the morrow, collapsed, and fell into sleep.

He dreamed of the world through its colors. Then, the universe turned as it was wont to do, and he loved it again as it revealed itself through dark hues as well as light. It would, this work, make him taller and tougher. Cristane had some doubts that height would help him—it did not seem to disqualify Lady Sea as she barely came up to his shoulder.

He did not stir until Lady Sea woke him with a boot toe to his ribs. She put her spindly hand over his mouth and waited until she could see him aware. Her voice, hushed and yet crystal clear, reached his ears.

"On your feet. The tides will not hold for me any more than they will stir for you." She dropped a set of waders on him, worn but still splendid looking, and he slipped them on. Snug they were, but the footwear part hugged the curve of his feet admirably. He knotted the ties into place and then rubbed his eyes open as he hurried after her. She carried an empty but large net bag over one shoulder and tossed a second to him.

"We hunt tonight." She picked up a short lance, weighed it in her hand before passing it to Cristane, taking a second one for herself. "Mind you, you aren't to use this." She shook the spear.

"Then why carry it?"

"Because you might need it."

"What do we hunt tonight?"

"The scale we use to make dragon blood cloth. The flag you pointed out to me."

A pit opened in his stomach and his mouth fell open, without words to utter. He knew—it had been *rumored*—that the dye came from such a creature, that once they held a nest on the shore, but everyone knew they no longer lived, if they had ever really existed. Kings and princes and warriors came for shirts of dragon blood cloth, more valuable than gold, to wear under their armor. Wizards came for its scraps, to write upon for their tomes of magic, or so the streets whispered. "Dragon blood?"

Lady Sea cuffed him under the chin, shutting his mouth with a snap. "Don't gape at me like a fool. I won't take a fool hunting with me."

"Yes, lady." He wrapped his fingers tightly about the spear and managed a short bow. She went to the door and waited for him to open it.

She led and he followed. Through the town gates, over hill and dale and down rocky coast, until they finally stood on a cliff above the shore. As he watched the phosphorescence boil off the receding waves, he calculated what might be used to duplicate the color and the desirability of the hues, for that faint and eerie green might not flatter many complexions. She paused as though knowing his thoughts.

"We have a sight, you and I."

He gave her a sideways glance. Of course they did … or else they'd be blind.

"Someday you may understand." She pointed off the sea cliff. "There was a time," she added finally, and quietly, "that one did not dare stand here. A drake would have plucked you from the rock and swallowed you down. In halves if not whole."

"Truly?"

"Sincerely." She held an arm up, letting her sleeve fall open, to reveal a long and jagged white scar that ran from the ball of her palm to the pit of her arm. "How do you think I got this?"

Did she think he had grown as old as he had swaddled like a baby or coddled like an heir to an estate? He saw accidents like that every day of his life, or nearly. "I hadn't thought about it, one way or the other."

"A drake caught me. Its teeth are like daggers but even its flippers and wings are sharp as razors."

"It attacked you?"

"Would not you, if something invaded your nest?"

"Surely, but—did you not have guards?"

Lady Sea brought her sleeve back into place. "The drakes, few enough of them left now, have secreted their nests and caves. I don't come to kill them, but to gather what they shed."

He caught at her words. "Like a snake. And if you did not come?"

"The guild would turn loose its greed, its hunters, its soldiers, and not a drake would survive. Although, goddess knows, there are few enough as it is." She nudged him. "Learn my trade and you will have all the shoes you can ever think of wearing, and fine clothes and cloaks, too. Perhaps even a horse."

"Could I buy my sister back?"

She regarded him. "If she wished. She might reach for a destiny of her own. I cannot say what your sister wants."

Cristane thought on that. She had not wailed, but her laughter had followed him down the alley as the house had glowed from within, spilling outward. He had no idea if she would welcome his rescue or not.

Lady Sea put a bony elbow into his side. "Finish your reverie. We have work to do this night." She pointed her spear at the moon. "We've just enough light." With that, she stepped down onto a path he could barely see, daring him to follow.

Old or not, the lady climbed like a goat. He slipped after her more than once, and even did an ungainly somersault head over heels to land on a wind-carved boulder in front of her. She leaned down to squint at him. "Done?"

"I hope so." He groaned as he stood up and checked his limbs. All in one piece, near as he could tell. The boulder peeked up from a blanket of sand; Cristane had managed to hit the only rocky spot on the beach.

Lady Sea rearranged his net over one shoulder and picked up his spear, returning it to him. "We don't use these unless rushed."

"Rushed?"

"Charged. Which it won't do unless we threaten it." She paused and then pointed at the surf line. "Wade in and catch me a fish."

"What?"

She turned full on him. "What did you not understand?"

"I've never caught a fish before."

She waved her hand negligently. "The surf is full of them. Watch the curl. Throw the net. Catch one."

Cristane sputtered. "I thought we were Dyers."

"We are survivors. If you wish to get through this night, catch me a fish." And Lady Sea's mouth closed to a thin line.

Cristane turned to do as bid, thankful he at least had the waders and hoping they might be warm as well as watertight. As the sea closed about his ankles, and then his knees, the shivers crept up as well. How could a fish live in water this cold? He watched the curl of the water and, as she had said, dark forms darted through the moonlit foam.

He threw his net out and watched it sink, empty, almost beyond his reach. Using the spear, he pulled it back. Again. And again. And then he caught the sense of it, the rhythm, the music of the tide washing up against the shore, hearing his sister Maude's teasing voice in it as she chided him for being tone deaf. But he wasn't, not this moment, not under this moon, its color like that of ice crystals, near transparent yet touched with silver.

He threw the net and dragged it back, filled with not one but two squirming fish, their scales dark green and charcoal, their gills fluttering. Water surging about his thighs, he returned to Lady Sea, who nodded before walking off, leaving him no choice but to follow.

They worked their way off the beach sands and back onto rock, stone pounded sharp and threatening against intrusion. Lady Sea motioned for silence as she moved along the cliff's foot, avoiding tide pools which lay glistening under the moon's eye like tiny mirrors. She headed straight for great black, knife-like cuts, where even the moonlight could not pierce, and his stomach knotted again in fear. If he followed her in, he would drown when the tide came roaring back, unless he could climb higher, sight unseen, out of reach. If a drake did not swallow him first.

She ducked under an overhang and fumbled at the pouch at her belt, withdrawing a tiny globe that sputtered and gained illumination, a fuzzy mimic of sunlight. "We haven't long before this will fade."

"It—"

"Not magic. It absorbs sunlight and emits it later, in darkness." She held it with her left hand, right fingers still curled tightly about the spear.

His net slapped against him, fish fighting now and then for their freedom. Cristane felt a little as they did: out of water, afraid, struggling, wary of what might wait ahead.

He heard a rumble, a low vibration of noise against his eardrum, and halted. Lady Sea stopped and turned a puzzled look his way. "I heard something."

"What?"

"A … a rumble. Maybe a growl."

"Low in tone?"

He nodded.

Lady Sea made a face. "These old ears!" She pinched an ear lobe. "We are near then. Search the nooks and crannies as we move. That's where our treasure will be found." She bent and began to creep along slowly.

Cristane blinked and followed suit, feeling foolish. Perhaps this was no lesson, but another trial to see how he followed instructions, no matter how foolish they seemed. His waders, no protection against the cold of the ocean, actually seemed to carry a little warmth in the cave. He could hear the drizzle of a long-ago tide draining through the cracks of the rock. That low vibration of something … breathing? Humming? Growling? The harsh noises of Lady Sea as she struggled with her own inhalations. It was then he realized that her heart fluttered a bit now and then, that her steps faltered, and that he could lose her even as she struggled.

He caught her arm. "Rest."

"What!"

Firmly, as he remembered his father saying to his mother years ago, "Rest. I will do the searching."

"You don't even know what you look for, boy!"

"I think I must." He wedged the edge of his spear into the pebbled bottom of the cave, swept his hand aside and found a thing of marvelous color wedged in the barnacled rocks next to them. "It has to be this." He held it up to her orb.

"Ah." She breathed softly. "It is indeed." Lady Sea smiled then. "You do have the sight for my work. All right then. I will take a short recess, but do not roam beyond the circle of the light. You may see its scales but you have no idea how to deal with what may wait beyond."

Cristane stowed his find in his net, next to the still yawning fish. "You want me to feed it."

"Only if we meet it head on. A distraction while you retreat. Otherwise, we will simply put these at the entrance when we leave and hope it has caught our scent and know we are no enemy."

"It's a beast."

She lifted her eyes to his. "Oh, aye. But a very smart and shrewd beast."

He stepped away then to continue his search and barely heard words he felt certain she did not intend him to hear. "And there may be more than one."

The orb she carried shed very little light, almost as sparing as the sea drake was in shedding its scales. He found two more that had been rubbed off on the cave walls, both of them slick and glistening with colors that chased themselves around the surface before disappearing, a wondrous sight.

At the edge of the illumination, he saw an arch of sea dragon color, an entire skin of scales, shed and lying limply upon the cave's bottom, where light could barely reach it.

It could be worth a guildhall's season. Perhaps even a king's ransom. Enough that, if he were careful, he might pinch a scale or two to buy Maude's freedom. He did not think of his own. The colors of this world spoke to him and, if he learned all that Lady Sea could teach him, he would have all the freedom he needed.

Cristane leaned into the crevice and reached for the skin.

A hiss cut across the cave. The arch heaved and slid about to meet him. Two golden eyes, pupils slit from bottom to top in onyx, opened upon him. He froze.

Far behind him, he could hear Lady Sea.

"Don't move."

That she'd heard, the sharp and whistling warning. "What do I do?"

"Nothing. Be still. Quiet. If it comes closer, put the fish out and try to back away and go still again."

He thought it might attack anyway. The hissing went higher in pitch. The golden eyes fastened on him, then gave a long and slow blink. He could see two of the drakes. No. One. Its scales hung about it oddly. Cristane stared at it before realizing it had begun to move forward, slowly, pulling its new body out of its old. They had caught it in the midst of a shedding. Cristane had been raised in the slums, but he knew about the skins. He had seen them hanging from merchant stalls in the great market, trophies from immense serpents in faraway lands, though not dragons. They might adorn ladies' hats or the belts of fine gentlemen or any other uses. But these … these he knew held a magic he could not imagine or calculate.

Hand shaking, he reached back and liberated a fish from his net, shaking it loose from the four scales he'd already found. He hesitated, wanting to throw it, but thinking that unwise. Instead, he took two steps forward, a long pause between them, and put his fish down, stepping back just as cautiously.

The beast whistled at him. He tilted his head, wishing he had a talent, like Maude, to whistle back, because it sounded like a question, one he wanted to answer. The drake shuffled after him, with grunts and low mutters, attempting to pull the old skin off itself, a birth as difficult as any he'd ever heard. He retreated again, to give it ground.

"Careful, lad."

"It's shedding, Lady Sea."

"Poor timing on our part then. It will do whatever it must to protect itself. It is more vulnerable now than at any time in its long span. Come away, for your life's sake."

"I gave it a fish."

"Which will do little good if it decides it is in peril. Return to me, slowly, and we'll leave."

"No." Cristane swallowed tightly. "There's a whole skin here. Or will be."

"No good to us if we're dead, as useless as it will be to the drake. Do what you are told if you wish to keep that new sash of yours."

Cristane looked at the fortune upon the sea cave floor. Would it be there if he came back or would the tide suck it out and swallow it down forever? He could have all he wanted or could ever think he wanted. Everything in one night's work. His fingers twitched, reminding him that they were empty. He'd left his spear embedded in the sand and pebbles, with Lady Sea.

The sea drake nodded its head downward and he could see the glint of many pointed teeth as it opened its jaws to take up the fish. He could also see that his lady had been lucky to receive only a jagged scar, instead of losing an arm to another such beast. He wondered what such a wise woman had done to gain such an injury. It surely had been nothing as foolish as what he was about to do.

Like a cat with great glistening scales and long dark whiskers, the drake settled down and bent its head over the fish, picking its flesh off bones delicately and swallowing it down, golden eyes intent upon the prize. Even as Cristane watched, the light thrown by Lady Sea's orb faded considerably and the beast blended into the night dark of its cave. With that, he could feel his hope being torn away.

Cristane pulled the last fish from his net and plunged forward, startling the drake. Its hiss boiled like a kettle in his ears. He could hear the smack of its jaws opening and smell its breath as it jerked toward him. He reached for where he thought its lose flap of skin hung and stabbed the fish forward into the teeth raking the air in front of him.

His hands burned like fire, ragged edges of the scales catching him. Cristane clamped his mouth shut on the pain, reeling up the object and tugging it free, hearing the drake roar in pain and loss, choke a little on the fish in its maw, and then give a bellow as he tore the skin from its body.

It gave way and he fell backward, tumbling over rock and shell as the drake struck, but Lady Sea stood there, spear in hand. She bellowed back at the beast as teeth clashed against the spearhead.

The sea drake reared back, readying to strike, fresh, raw scales glittering in the faint light of her orb.

"You know me," she said lowly.

The sea drake gave a faint whine.

Cristane started to crawl away, hauling the skin with him, as his hands blazed with agony and his face grew wet with tears. His prize made a slithery noise and the drake's head whipped around to track him.

He got to his feet between Lady Sea and the beast. She lunged with her spear to repel it, and advanced, pushing it back and back, her breath wheezing as loudly as its hissing. She would fall there, he thought, covering for him.

His mistake, his price to pay. He gathered the old scales to his chest, the skin covering him from chin to toe. Harsh, razor-edged … and tough.

The drake bit at him. He lashed back with an arm covered in scale, and it slashed an edge across the creature's new covering. It thrashed away from him and towards Lady Sea. Cristane leapt, wrapping an arm about its sinuous neck, his weight bearing it away from her.

"Run."

"Let it go."

He tightened his arm about it, feeling the squish of the newly revealed skin against the hardness of its old armor, his face pressed against the sea dragon, and thought it would burn through his skull. It snaked its head about and their gazes met.

The ability to move fled him. Locked into place, he fell into the sea dragon's regard. He could see … he could see a man sit at a table, pick up pen, and a book, and prepare to write. The paper held the likeness of the dragon blood pennant in the Guild hall … ivory fabric with hues running across it that were anything but light … colors that fled as soon as the writer put nib to the surface. The man began to scribe words that turned Cristane's blood cold, and as he watched, the writer turned his head enough that Cristane could see who it might be, what the dragon blood pages could hold to the world's joy and sorrow. Although the man's cheek had been heavily scarred once, it had paled and could not disguise the identity. Cristane looked at himself. Beyond it, as if mirrored, another book being written, and then a third. None of them held a bright aspect. All of them sent a chill through him.

How could a thing that held the rainbow in its essence become so dark?

He saw the sea drake emerging from its cave, hesitant, perched on ocean rocks, flinging its wings out. It must fly, he realized, to live. It must go skyward, to free the rainbows of its existence.

Deeds, he thought, intent. The only thing that could free and lighten his own colors. He loosened his hold on the sea drake, its breath piping heavily through its throat, and yet bore it away from Lady Sea. He shook his dragon skin. "Your life," he whispered to it, "for mine."

The dragon closed his eyes, shutting away the vision of future Cristanes writing away. It lowered its head and he realized he had been dangling above the sea floor. His soles touched.

Lady Sea whispered, "Come away."

"When it knows me." Cristane rubbed the back of the beast's head gently, as he would soothe Maude whenever she cried. "Eat your fish," he coaxed, "and let what you shed go, for you have no need of it, and I do."

The beast groaned faintly and put its head down to the fishes, one spat out and one half-devoured, and snuffled at them. As it lipped at the carcasses, Cristane let go entirely and left it, trailing the skin behind him. His face felt as if a hot iron from the blacksmith's forge had been laid upon him, and his hands wept blood sluggishly.

Numbly, his mind filled with what he had seen in the dragon's eye, he followed after Lady Sea.

On the cliff's edge, high above the tide once more, she took his skin and net from him and used her spear to dig a hole. Most of the skin went down in it, after she took another few scales.

"What …"

"A bounty, for later. Sowing a harvest we will reap more than once, while you learn." She touched gentle fingers to his face. "And heal."

* * *

He took a length of dragon blood cloth to the ladies' House and asked for Maude. She refused to come. The scullery maid looked at him in sympathy.

"She has a patron," the skinny young woman told him. "Already. He treats her as a cherished daughter. Would that I had that luck." Her gaze flicked over his wound, raw as it still could be, but out from under bandages to let the air heal it. His look frightened a few people. Surely it had not frightened Maude.

A shutter clattered overhead and Cristane shot a look upward. He caught a glimpse of bright tresses withdrawing, but before the shutter locked tight, he heard her soft laugh. "Love and life to you, brother."

He tucked his cloth under his elbow. As Lady Sea had warned him, she seemed to be seeking her own destiny. Cristane left her be. He had a trade to learn.

The Three Assassins
of Lord Slaughter
Anita Ensal

"I wonder what it would be like to run the city," Lord Slaughter said thoughtfully during a House dinner. He wasn't speaking to the entire room, just those sitting closest to him, so Lady Slaughter, who was at the other end of the long table, didn't hear him.

His eldest son, Marco, shrugged. "Probably difficult, time-consuming, and boring, father."

Marco's best friend and Lord Slaughter's First Lieutenant, Dean Hodos, nodded. "Marco's surely right, my lord. But if anyone could run the city well, it would be you."

Lord Slaughter smiled fondly. "You are too kind."

The House of Slaughter's newest assassin, Melissa Katano, shook her head. "No disrespect meant, my lord, but, despite assumptions, assassins tend to make terrible leaders. We don't like compromise and we really don't care for the idea of dealing with issues in daylight, particularly before mid-day. It's why I left my home city and came here, after all."

Lord Slaughter sighed. "You are most likely right, my dear. And I would not contradict your experience or impressions."

Melissa looked thoughtful. "Yet … you, my lord, not only rose to the top of our Guild, but you did it at a remarkably young age. You have ruled us for many years successfully with no successors even wishing to attempt to usurp your seat. That was not true of any Guild in my home city and is not true of any Guilds other than ours here in Jannpar."

Lord Slaughter chuckled. "That is more likely due to my good lady wife, Marco, Dean, and, these last ten years, yourself, Melissa." He sighed. "The city is in disarray and our politicians do nothing. Guild houses are far better run, regardless of changing leadership. I wish …"

They waited, but Lord Slaughter didn't continue. "You wish for what, father?" Marco asked gently.

Lord Slaughter shook himself. "Melissa is no doubt correct, as she so often is."

Marco noted a tinge of regret and longing in his father's voice. He looked down the table at his mother, who was laughing at something said to her. However, Marco felt the laughter was forced. His mother looked and sounded bored, though it was well hidden—just not from her eldest son, even at a distance. He turned back to Lord Slaughter. "Mother might enjoy the prestige, though."

"And she might laugh at the mere idea," Lord Slaughter countered. "No, it's a passing fancy, nothing more. Nothing to even think about as you go out on your assignments tonight."

They returned to casual conversation and their meals, but Marco didn't listen to his father's suggestion and instead pondered the idea of his father becoming the City Leader. He was sure that Dean and Melissa were pondering as well, and not just because the three of them outranked all others in the House other than Lord and Lady Slaughter.

That Marco was one of the top three assassins in the House wasn't a surprise—his father and mother were both Master Assassins and they'd trained their children in the family business from birth. Marco's younger brothers and sisters were all accomplished and, currently, all on assignment in other cities in the land. Marco, as eldest, remained in Jannpar in order to ensure that their parents were protected.

Protection of Lord and Lady Slaughter also fell to Dean, who was as enthusiastic about the charge as Marco. The House of Slaughter had taken Dean in when he was just a small, orphaned child living on the streets of Jannpar. They met when he tried to pick Lady Slaughter's pocket. He didn't succeed, but she was impressed with his attempt, seeing as the only reason she knew he'd gotten her purse was that Marco had spotted the lift and had, therefore, tackled Dean in the middle of the Night Market.

Normally, someone picking an assassin's pocket would end up dead—either from touching an object prepared with poison or because assassins had rules, and one of them was to kill anyone trying to rob them. But, at age five, Dean had charmed Lady Slaughter—after she had separated the two boys, retrieved her purse, and determined Dean's history—and he was brought into the House, where he and Marco quickly bonded and then went about beating up anyone older than them who was doing things they disapproved of.

Melissa's rise in the house had been unprecedented. No one other than Lord Slaughter himself had risen in rank so quickly. The House was extremely picky about who was allowed to join, and most new recruits failed the tests of entry—most by dying, some by running away—even those who had been raised in the House as children. Melissa, however, had passed with highest honors. She'd even outdone Marco and Dean and, considering those two held the highest entry scores for House Acceptance, Melissa was impressive indeed. Lady Slaughter always said it was because Melissa was a woman and so was naturally more dangerous than any man could ever hope to be. Considering Lady Slaughter's vast and successful record, no one argued this point.

After the meal was over, Dean parceled out the night's assignments. Some of these would be long-term—where the assassin would have to stalk his or her prey to determine the best method of achieving the death requested—and were paid for fifty percent in advance. Some were faster jobs, where death was required but subtlety was not. Naturally, some assassinations were required to take place in the daylight hours, but most were done in the dark of night. Marco, Dean, and Melissa worked daylight as well as night, though not all in the House of Slaughter were allowed that rank.

But there were no daylight assignments, and Dean had determined that the few long-term assignments were dull, the quicker ones even duller, so had spared himself and his two closest friends the boredom. Meaning, ultimately, the three top assassins had nothing to do.

"Shall we wander the Night Market?" Marco asked once all the others had left for their night's work.

"I can always get more jewelry," Melissa said. She didn't actually wear a great deal of ornamentation, unless a job called for it, but she liked the getting and having more than the wearing.

"One can never have enough knives," Dean agreed. So, they headed out.

Assassins have excellent night vision, are trained in how to improve it, and there were spells that cost a great deal of money that enhanced it as well. The House of Slaughter was well-funded—every working assassin had the enhancement spell cast on them every fortnight. So the three assassins took no torches with them, meaning they could travel along as if they weren't there, since assassins trained to walk in shadow as hard, if not harder, than they trained to see perfectly at night.

They walked along unseen for about a block before Marco spoke again. "Do you think Father meant it?"

"About ruling?" Melissa asked. Marco nodded. "Maybe," she said slowly. "But he might just have been wondering aloud."

"Couldn't have a better ruler," Dean said loyally.

"Can't with the way things are," Marco pointed out. "Father would have to offer himself up for the candidacy and you know he never will."

"We could do it. Nominate him," Melissa suggested. "It's allowed."

Marco grabbed their arms and pulled them into an alleyway. They did a quick perusal to ensure they were alone, then he spoke. "We could, but Father won't do what's needed. He's afraid that Mother wouldn't like the limelight."

Dean snorted. "And I thought your parents knew each other well."

Melissa looked thoughtful. "Lady Slaughter would never admit to wanting that much attention, but, after the career she's had, she might enjoy it. She and Lord Slaughter never go out on assignment anymore."

Dean nodded. "They tell me to ensure that the younger assassins get the experience. Though they both do keep their hands in."

Marco shrugged. "They'll never be better than the best, but even so, the best sometimes like a rest. And Father's run the Guild well. I've looked into the records."

"Not as closely as I have," Melissa said. "I wasn't saying it to gain favor—Lord Slaughter has run this Guild better than any other Guild in the land. And I don't mean just assassins. I mean any Guild. He's a natural leader and a wise one, too, and that combination is very rare."

"He hasn't been killed by his rivals because he's the best assassin still," Dean added.

"And his main rivals in the House are the three of us," Marco pointed out. The others nodded. "So, do we do it?" he asked. "Do we help Jannpar by putting the best leader in as Chairman?"

Dean cleared his throat. "This must be said. Without a fee or an assignment, we're breaking House rules. The punishment for that is death or ban-

ishment, depending. Are we willing to risk losing our home and our liveli-
hood over this?"

The three of them looked at each other. They put their fists over their
hearts as one. "Yes," Melissa said. "Let's do what should be done."

* * *

The planning for Lord Slaughter's unknowing rise to power took a few
weeks. The list of those who needed to be removed was long and all the
deaths had to look accidental. They agreed on death for all opponents, because dead men and women could share no tales of threats and persuasion.

However, they'd been taught to always have at least one backup plan.
Said plan was to ensure that, should those in authority start investigations,
they would find a secret conspiracy to overthrow Jannpar's stability. The
conspiracy would, of course, implicate the dead or those who might need to
be dead who hadn't been removed yet.

The existing Chairman had to go, of course, or there would be no new
election by the Houses. But they determined that removing the potential
candidates prior would be wisest and ensure that Jannpar retained stable
leadership.

While the Heads of all Houses could run for Chairman, as could any
landed noble or citizen with enough money to ensure they could afford to
leave their current occupation and still keep their property and such, most
would never have an interest. Other than those from the Merchant's Guild.

The Merchant's Guild was the largest Guild in Jannpar, and the land
of Tavaria as well, and had provided the majority of Jannpar's Chairmen
over the years. Though the Guilds of Educators, Military, Religion, Financiers, and even Thieves had all had representatives running the show at one
time or another, seven out of every ten Chairmen came from the Merchant's
Guild.

The Guilds of Healers, Whores, Entertainers, Builders, Artisans, and
Farmers had never successfully put forth a candidate, and the Guild of Magicians was never allowed to offer one. The Assassins had never put forth a
candidate, either. And, technically, they weren't doing so now. At least not
yet.

Marco, Dean, and Melissa planned and, while they went about their normal routines and assignments, they studied their future targets and set up
their backup plan.

While Melissa poisoned the man who had gotten her wealthy client preg-
nant, then run off to seduce a slew of other woman—using the age-old tech-

nique of feigning sexual interest and then giving him a tincture of aconite in his 'before the sex' drink—she rifled through his things, finding several convenient weapons, disguises for both Marco and Dean, as well as a listing of most of the influential families in the city. This list had the names of all the females of birthing age, listed in order of years of expected child bearing and attractiveness—with the least attractive first.

"We're well done of you," she murmured as her target expired. "Though I credit you with an interesting and, no doubt, enjoyable plan to control and influence the wealth of our land."

She also left a set of clues—well-hidden yet findable should someone keen on the job be searching—that would implicate him in the conspiracy.

Marco and Dean created a bar fight that gave them an almost laughably easy way to knife a tradesman who'd kept more than his share of Marco's client's profits and an ambitious young financier whom Dean's client wanted dead versus challenging for said client's position. They also lifted papers from several merchants who had access to those they'd deemed likely candidates and planted evidence of the conspiracy on these merchants and some lower level financiers, because efficiency was a House watchword.

And so it went, assignments assisting in the setup of the overall plan, spare time spent shadowing targets, planting fake evidence, and casing various buildings—they had the layouts of every building in Jannpar memorized, but people tended to be less predictable than clay and wood—all while biding their time until they felt everything was in place with nothing left to chance.

* * *

Plan finally in motion, Melissa headed out at dusk. Early for a normal job, but she wasn't officially working. She was taking a few personal hours; at least, that's what she told anyone in the House who asked.

She walked with purpose to the Artists Quarter. While the Guild of Artisans had never forwarded a successful candidate, one of their members was quite popular and looked to be a real challenger for the Chairmanship.

Iria was an exceptional artist, skilled in paintings, tapestries, and pottery. Melissa, Dean, and Marco had spent quite a lot of their earnings on her works in recent days. Not so much as to draw attention, but enough, once Iria was dead, to ensure a good return on their investment.

Therefore, Iria greeted Melissa with happy expectation, particularly since the Quarter was shutting down and almost devoid of customers. Melissa returned the greeting, ignoring the pang having to assassinate Iria gave her. "Shall we go for tea once you close?"

"I'll close right now," Iria said.

"Excellent, I'll meet you there and secure our table."

Melissa went into the alleyway they used to get to the tea stall and waited. Iria came into the alley a few minutes later. "I have the table and realized I hadn't given you a greeting hug." She included a special extra.

"What was that?" Iria asked as their hug ended. "I felt something prick my back."

Melissa looked around and squinted. "There's a bee nearby."

Iria went pale. "I … I am allergic …"

Melissa slammed her hand against the wall. "I've killed it. Let me see." She turned Iria around and pulled her blouse up. "I don't see anything much," she said doubtfully.

Iria grabbed her neck. "My throat … closing …"

"I'm sure I have an antidote with me." Iria gasped as Melissa fumbled around in her pocket. Melissa pulled a needle out and shot it into Iria's arm.

"Thank you," Iria gasped, right before she stopped breathing.

Melissa heaved a sigh. She wanted to close Iria's eyes, but that would indicate someone had been with her. Instead she let the body fall as it would in a case of anaphylactic shock and hurried off to her appointment at the massage tent at the other end of the Quarter. She was almost asleep when news of Iria's untimely death reached them.

Dean had arranged for the Merchant's Guild dinner to be imported quail. That the quail had all been fed hemlock-laced feed—which the birds were immune to—and that, therefore, their flesh was deadly if ingested, was seen as terribly bad luck. It was considered a tragic choice by the Guild's chef for buying food from outside of Tavaria and the Chef was only fined, not imprisoned or executed.

Marco, meanwhile, had weakened a footbridge several of the potential candidates from the Guild of Religion used when attending monthly meetings at their favorite bar. A collapsing bridge wasn't exactly news, nor was it a surefire way to kill anyone—unless those falling hit onto rocks sharpened to a knife's point and tainted with arsenic. The river's water washed away the arsenic traces, and the water would dissipate the poison enough that others wouldn't be harmed and some might even gain a slight immunity. It was a public service, really.

And so it went—a choking death here, an allergic reaction there, a mugging gone badly, even a suicide. All normal deaths for Tavaria's largest city.

They'd decided on a slow death for the current Chairman, in no small part because he was a terrible leader and the very reason Lord Slaughter had been musing about leadership in the first place. Melissa had ensured that pills the Chairman, and the Chairman alone, ingested daily were treated with a slight dusting of arsenic. Since the pills were those the Chairman took to give himself more sexual virility in order to indulge his sexual appetites, this method allowed him to, essentially, kill himself, which the assassins found rather poetic.

As they moved to more obvious targets, less obvious methods were required. Tragic accidents required many moving parts, but they were one of Dean's best skills.

Horses being spooked were commonplace, and something a top assassin shouldn't need to bother with, but they tended to do the trick. How the horse or horses were panicked was where the skill came in—on any given day, there was something happening in Jannpar to upset the most nervous of the Gods' creatures.

Dean was quite good with all animals and he enjoyed using their natural natures to assist him in his work. Nothing spooked a horse faster than a deadly snake, and then the snake was there to ensure the target died if the horse didn't do the job. Sadly, despite their effectiveness, asps and other deadly serpents were rare in Jannpar these days, so his preferred choice was out.

Flying insects were plentiful, however, and a good sting on the rump could cause many a horse to throw its rider. A swarm of stinging beetles was effective to the point of certainty—even the best trained warhorse didn't want stinging beetles in its face and would react from nature and by instinct versus training. And, if the right circumstances were in place, the situation and resulting death were unsuspicious.

So, just before dawn, Dean broke a jar of honey over a pile of dung outside the entrance to the brothel the Chairman and several of their top targets preferred. This location was perfect, since three potential candidates—and therefore, three targets—worked at the bank across the street.

He joined the others on the roof of the bank and waited to watch the show. "Those in the brothel should be leaving just as those going to the bank arrive," Marco said softly. "Wait to trigger the beetles until we see the Chairman leaving, though."

"I wasn't trained yesterday," Melissa replied, with more humor than rebuke in her tone.

They waited. And waited. People came and went, but none went into the bank or came out of the brothel. "Why aren't the financiers arriving?" Dean asked. "They should have been here an hour ago."

"Why aren't those in the brothel leaving to get to their homes or businesses?" Melissa added.

"Something's wrong," Marco replied. "Get ready to run for the House. Alibi Number Twelve."

"Spent all night playing cards because we had no assignments," Dean said. "Check."

Melissa jerked and put her hands on their arms. "Wait."

They froze and then the men heard what Melissa already had—women screaming.

Whores ran out of the brothel, screaming their heads off. The three assassins listened intently. "Customers died in their beds," Melissa said. "Several of them."

"I heard at least one name, and it was a name on our list," Dean added, as town guards began to arrive.

"Time to *go*." Marco grabbed the others' hands and pulled them away.

They headed back to the House quickly but carefully, put the beetles back in the storeroom, and were all in Melissa's room playing cards and looking tired when the door opened to reveal Lady Slaughter.

"I apologize for not knocking," she said. "But I've been looking for you three and I already checked Marco and Dean's rooms."

"Mother, what can we do for you?" Marco asked casually.

She shook her head. "Nothing. I wanted to let you three know—several murders happened last night. None of them ordered by the House."

"Do we need to investigate?" Melissa asked.

"No, not yet. But please be aware that someone seems to be working outside of our laws or has taken assignments without advising the House, meaning stealing from us." She smiled fondly at them. "Though, not you three, of course."

She closed the door and the three looked at each other. "What now?" Dean asked softly.

"Now," Marco replied, "we find out who was killed and how many of them were on our list."

* * *

"All of them," Melissa said hours later, as she returned from the Day Market and joined Marco and Dean in Marco's room. "Every person who died last night was on our list. And they all died in their beds. Some from 'explainable' reasons, some from their throats being slit."

"Father is at a Guild meeting," Marco told her. "Explaining that our House is not responsible for any of these deaths."

"We aren't," Dean pointed out. "We didn't kill them. We planned to, but someone beat us to it."

"Far less elegantly," Melissa added with a sniff. "Even if they were effective."

"The problem isn't elegance or effectiveness," Marco said. "The problem is that it was done all at once and in an obvious manner, meaning that someone else is likely after the Chairman's position."

"Which is now open," Dean said. "Since the Chairman got his throat slit at the brothel."

Before they could fret about this, or formulate a counter plan, there was a knock on the door and Lady Slaughter put her head in. "I just wanted to let you all know—a conspiracy has been discovered. I need you to come to an All House Meeting right now."

They pointedly didn't look at each other as they followed Lady Slaughter to the meeting room. All the House, other than Lord Slaughter, were in attendance.

"There appears to be a conspiracy to undermine the stability of Jannpar," Lady Slaughter said without preamble, "which would then undermine all of Tavaria. All assassinations are, therefore, in abeyance until the city has stable leadership."

"What do we do, then?" Dean asked.

"We wait. Our Guilds are choosing a new Chairman as we speak."

The three assassins still didn't look at each other, but they all felt discouraged. All their planning was now useless, because someone from the Merchants Guild would likely step in and it would be dangerous for the House if that person was killed.

"Where does the conspiracy originate?" Melissa asked. "Do we know?"

Lady Slaughter nodded. "The Magicians Guild has contacted their Houses in Tavaria's other cities—none of those other Guilds will admit to being involved and we have confirmed that by contacting my other children, who know of no Houses working against us. This, in fact, tracks with what's been discovered here in Jannpar. The threat seems to be from outside Tavaria's borders. As near as we have determined based on the clues found so far, assassins not associated with any known House have taken the assignment to disable our government. Signs point to either Cadnis or Veed, or both."

So, their backup plan was working. One small victory. "Is retaliation planned?" Marco asked.

"Not as yet," his mother replied. "Our tensions are always high with those lands, but since Jannpar is nowhere near either lands' border, we are waiting to see what those who run Tavaria feel is best."

"Politics as usual," Melissa said quietly.

"Perhaps," Lady Slaughter replied. "Perhaps not."

* * *

The Guilds' selection of a new Chairman took a week. The Magicians Guild hadn't had this much work to do for a long time—every member was using all their powers to speak with Guilds across the land. Marco hadn't talked to his siblings this much in ages, either, so there was an upside.

But finally the decision was made. Everyone who could squeeze in was at the town square in front of the Chairman's Office. The Assassins were all on the roofs, however, so they had a good view without being crowded—the rest of the city felt safer this way, as well.

The Head of the Merchants Guild was speaking, his voice projected by a spell. Aldroth droned on for a bit, talking about the conspiracy and how Jannpar and Tavaria's enemies would not be allowed to triumph, but he finally got to the relevant part of his speech: who was to be the new Chairman.

"Think he's going to introduce himself?" Dean asked.

"Unlikely," Lady Slaughter replied. "It's bad form."

"Didn't stop them from nominating the last Chairman," Marco muttered.

"Hush," Lady Slaughter said gently.

"After much careful deliberation, we have chosen a new Chairman who we feel will send a strong message to our enemies," Aldroth said.

"Going to be from the Military Guild," Dean said. "Mark my words."

"The Gods help us," Marco replied. "We'll be at war forever if that happens."

"Hush now," Lady Slaughter said.

"Our new Chairman did not seek this position," Aldroth continued. "He, in fact, tried to refuse it. But his sense of loyalty to Jannpar and Tavaria overruled his desire to remain a simple Head of his Guild."

"By the Gods, he *is* going to announce himself, isn't he?" Melissa gasped.

"Hush, children," Lady Slaughter said a bit more strongly.

"I am therefore pleased and gratified to present our new Chairman," Aldroth went on. "One who has proven time and again that he is a man of honor and of his word. And a man who these rogues who want to destroy us will fear more than any other. I give you … Chairman Slaughter!"

Lord Slaughter walked out to the cheering of the crowd. The Assassins were, of course, the loudest of those cheering, but no one seemed upset with the outcome, other than Lord Slaughter, who looked a little embarrassed.

"Our new Chairman is the greatest Assassin in the land, nay the world!" Aldroth exclaimed. "These rogue assassins fear him, as well they should! Our Assassins Guild is the strongest in all of Tavaria, and, as his last act as Head of the Assassins Guild, Lord Slaughter has pledged them to find and destroy those who have done this treachery, sparing our brave soldiers any unneeded bloodshed. Therefore, in his first act as Chairman, Chairman Slaughter has proven he's the leader Jannpar needs!"

The cheering got louder. Lord Slaughter waved. "I appreciate your support and pledge to run Jannpar as I have run my House—with fairness and compassion for all but those who wish to destroy us."

The cheering and celebrations went on all day and into the night. Many hours later they were all back in their House and Lord Slaughter was in bed, sleeping the sleep of the exhausted but victorious.

Marco, Dean, and Melissa were in Marco's room, waiting until they were sure the rest of the House was sleeping to discuss the day's events, when Lady Slaughter came in without knocking.

"Mother, is everything well?" Marco asked as she shut the door tightly behind her.

She nodded and flicked her thumb—a silence web encircled the four of them. This was an expensive spell and Lady Slaughter had never used it with them before.

She smiled at their shocked and nervous expressions. "I just wanted to compliment the three of you on your backup plan. It was truly well-executed and made things so much easier. Only a few things had to be altered."

"Excuse me?" Melissa asked, as Marco and Dean stared.

Lady Slaughter chuckled. "You were so meticulous, but you were just taking far too long. I couldn't keep feeding Lord Slaughter the right things to think and say forever, children. I allowed you to set the stage, but I believe I understand the political landscape a bit better than you three do. Mass hysteria is a very useful thing if you've planned properly."

The three assassins all gaped. "It was you?" Marco asked finally. "All of them, in one night?"

"There were over two dozen, in all parts of the city," Dean added.

Lady Slaughter smiled modestly but didn't reply.

"It would be close to impossible," Melissa said. "But not for the best assassin in the land."

"Thank you, dear," Lady Slaughter said. "We'll keep this between us, of course. Due to your father's move to Chairman, I have taken the post of Head of the Guild. I'll be assigning our top assassins, ergo, the three of you, to the hunt for these 'rogue assassins' and other conspirators. Enjoy your 'banishment' during your grand tour of Tavaria and be careful when you go into Cadnis and Veed—we don't want to start a real war, after all."

"You can count on us, Mother," Marco said.

Lady Slaughter hugged each one of them. "I know. But, this time … you'll be following *my* plan. Agreed?"

The three assassins looked at each other, then back to Lady Slaughter.

"You mean, we'll be following your plan *again*, don't you?" Melissa asked.

Lady Slaughter smiled. "I have no idea what you mean, dear." And with that, she flicked her finger and the silence web disappeared. She nodded to them and left the room.

They were quiet for a few long seconds. "How long do you think she had this planned?" Dean asked.

"Months?" Marco suggested.

Melissa shook her head and grinned. "Knowing your mother? I'd say she had this planned, potentially, before she met your father."

Marco grinned back. "Well, she is the best."

Dean laughed. "And long may she reign."

Footprints of the Hound
Violette Malan

"Which of them, do you think, is trying to kill the other?"

Dhulyn Wolfshead shrugged but didn't look up from the tracks she was examining. "Naru's the one who hired us, so let's try keeping *him* alive."

Parno Lionsmane nodded, returning his sword to its sheath. "So what made these prints?" He had done a fair amount of hunting when he was still part of a House, but everyone knew that Outlanders made the best trackers—he'd wager Dhulyn could track a fish in water. So he was more than a little surprised when she didn't answer right away.

"What?" he said. "Shamans of your tribe didn't draw these in the snow for you to study when you were a baby?"

His Partner snorted. "Unlikely. This isn't a what, it's a who. Rather too exactly what we would have expected to see, given the tales we've been spun."

"The footprints of a gigantic hound?"

"Too gigantic, and not very hound like."

"The daemon, do you think?"

Dhulyn straightened and shot him a look that made him laugh as she dusted her hands off on her leather trousers. "What makes you think there *is* one?"

Parno nodded in the direction of the elaborate tent in which their client was taking his rest after spending most of the evening making offerings to his family gods. "He thinks so."

"*He* thinks losing the Sakarai market for coriander is worth risking his life."

"If people *didn't* think that way, we'd have far less work."

"Granted." She frowned at the marks, drawing down her blood-red brows. "In any event, these prints are false."

He glared at her. "When were you going to tell me?"

She gave him the smile she saved only for him. "Apparently, now."

Parno shook his head. Outlanders and their sense of humor. "False, hence who and not what. I'd wager the younger of the cousins." He looked at her sideways. "We *are* sure one of them is trying to kill the other."

"No way to be sure unless we see more of the game played out."

"So what about these marks?"

"Remove them." She smiled her wolf's smile, the tiny scar pulling her upper lip back in a snarl. "Then watch to see which of them goes looking in the morning."

* * *

Three days earlier, Parno had looked up from examining the edges of his daggers when a hush fell over the patrons of the Werquon Inn. The same thing had happened when he and his Partner, Dhulyn, had arrived the day before. Since Dhulyn went bareheaded by habit, everyone saw her Mercenary Badge right away, whereupon the talk, gambling, and grumbling had resumed. A few of the patrons had nodded at them, and one or two even offered them drinks. Since Dhulyn was Senior Brother, Parno left it up to her to refuse the offers. Somehow people, even here in the most southerly mountain crossroads of Berdana, were more likely to take the Wolfshead seriously and not persist in forcing their hospitality on her.

Strictly speaking, the Werquon Inn wasn't an inn at all. Strictly speaking, it wasn't even a building. True, it was anchored at one end by the remains of a stone wall and a vast fireplace—apparently used for both cooking and heat—but the walls and ceiling were a combination of thin leathers, heavy canvas, and swathes of woolen fabric. Its "rooms" were made up of similar materials, either attached to the main structure or detached, depending on how much the traveller wanted to pay. It had taken Parno the better part of the previous afternoon to feel warm enough to shed his fur-lined cloak. Meanwhile Dhulyn had sat reading her book of poetry, bare-headed and bare-armed, with no sign of discomfort. An Outlander from the frozen plains well to the south, she was apt to find the chill of spring in the foothills of the Syrena Niweff Mountains refreshing.

"Your pardon, you are Mercenaries, of the Brotherhood?" The speaker was the older of two well-dressed men, obviously both Berdanans from their dark coloring and formal headscarves.

Parno gestured at the red and dark yellow tattoo reaching from his temples to above his ears. "As you can see from our badges." Dhulyn did not look up from her book. "I am Parno Lionsmane, called the Chanter, I fight with my Partner, Dhulyn Wolfshead."

"Called the Scholar," she said, sitting up as she closed her book on a finger.

"It seems such a stroke of luck," the younger of the two men said. "To find Mercenaries, just now, when we are in need of guides to take us through the Guadil Pass." A frown ghosted its way across the older man's face, and Parno thought he knew why. Letting people know how badly you wanted their service wasn't the best way to get it at a good price.

"I am Naru al Difor, a spice merchant of Suwala, and this is the son of my mother's brother, Simka al Difor," the older man said, indicating in the Berdanan way both the family and business relationship. "I must be at the trade fair in Kadib by the fourth day after the full moon."

"Eleven days from now, in other words," the cousin chimed in. Dhulyn smiled her wolf's smile and the young man took a step back, his enthusiasm suddenly dimmed. "The Guadil Pass is the only route that will get us there in time. When we saw you …"

"It's not our usual practice to turn down work." Dhulyn produced a slim-bladed knife out of nowhere and used it to mark her place in her book. "But do you really need Mercenary Brothers to guide you? There's the road, right there, you can't get lost, and you have armed people with you." She gestured with her book at two men standing not far off.

The merchants exchanged glances before the older one leaned in. "We can afford the Brotherhood," he said. "And it's not to guide, but to guard." He gestured at the bench on the room-side of the table and, when neither Mercenary objected, sat down.

Dhulyn waited in silence. She could outwait any townman, that went without saying. The two cousins looked at Parno, instinct telling them he was the more civilized of the two Brothers, but Parno merely smiled and recited the steps of the Turtle *Shora* to himself.

"It's because of the curse," the younger one, Simka, finally blurted.

Dhulyn lifted one blood-red eyebrow and looked at her Partner. Parno looked back, careful to let his face show only the mildest of polite interest.

"If we have to deal with Mages, I'm not sure you *could* afford to pay us," Dhulyn said.

This time it was Naru al Difor who answered, shaking his head. "It's a family curse," he said. "Generations old. No one knows how it started—"

"Or if it's even real," said Simka. His eyes flicked for the merest of moments to his older cousin.

"In any case," Naru reasserted himself with a pointed look at Simka, "I have no choice. I must be in Kadib in eleven days and only the pass will get me there in time."

"What form does the curse take?" Parno asked. "We're Mercenary Brothers, not Healers, or even Menders."

"No, no, it's bodyguards I need," the merchant said. "Stories of the curse have been handed down in our family for generations ..." he hesitated, clearly unsure how to go on.

"We're from this area originally," Simka said. "Hill people, but traders even then. The pass is vital to trade in these parts, as you might well imagine—we *had* to use it. But then the daemon came, in the form of a huge sand-wolf, attacking always the most senior family member present in the caravan." He exchanged a look with his cousin. "It's said they tried sending only employees, but business suffered. Finally, our great great-grandmother moved the whole family to the river valley, and then the sea coast, to escape the curse. It's said she had only the one child, and the family would have died out if she hadn't moved."

"Can it be killed, this daemon? Always supposing it still lives." Trust Dhulyn to ask the practical questions.

"The stories say it can," Naru said. "But that eventually another comes— or the same one returns from the dead. I cannot risk it. Since our grandmother's day, we travel always around, by land or sea. But this time I cannot. Not and meet my commitments honorably."

"And *you* are not concerned about the daemon?" Parno asked Simka.

It was as clear as though he'd written it down that the younger man didn't believe in it. "I'm not the heir," is what he said aloud.

But you'd like to be, Parno thought. Daemon curse or no daemon curse.

* * *

It had taken the better part of three days, the road climbing steadily, for the caravan to reach the Guadil Pass. Parno could see that most of the other travellers, and even some of the ponies, found the air at these heights thinner than was comfortable. As the Brotherhood had a *Shora* for this—not that they shared all their Schooling with others—he and Dhulyn had no trouble.

"We'll have to move more slowly," he told her, "if we don't want people becoming ill. We can make up time on the downslope."

But though she nodded her agreement, from the look on Dhulyn's face, their clients' shortness of breath was not what occupied her attention. She tilted her chin at the two merchants standing almost a full span beyond their packed and folded tents. "Tell me, what do you see?"

"Considering that's just about where we saw the tracks last night, I see one man trying to frighten the other. And unless you noticed whose idea it was to walk that way, we still don't know which is which."

"The younger cousin went into the elder's tent, but they came out together." Dhulyn frowned, drawing air in through her nose. "But there is more. The old servant, Bertol, has been with the family the longest, and his father before him. He says the Scholars have records of the family's original holdings, just on the other side of the Pass, which was, in fact, under their control. So we know it must have been something drastic, to make them give up such a trade advantage. The family was indeed moved after several killings by large, wolf-like animals, possibly a daemon. So at the least we know the tale is no recent invention."

"I'll wager you my second-best dagger young Simka sneaks out of his tent to make more footprints tonight," Parno said.

"Following the failure of last night's display, the guilty party may rethink his strategy. We may see prints, or something different, or nothing at all."

"So is it a wager then?"

As the night passed with no incidents, Parno could consider himself lucky she hadn't taken him up on his wager. The merchants' people were breakfasted, packed, and ready to be on the road when the sun had risen only a fingers-width. After silent consultation with her Partner, Dhulyn nudged her horse into step with Simka's. She was now close enough to hear the laboring of his breath as his lungs tried to deal with the thin air of the Pass.

"Long, slow breaths," she told him. "Take in as much air as you can with each one."

"You've encountered these conditions before?" The man took a deep breath and let it out slowly.

"We're Schooled in every type of condition." Would he notice she hadn't answered the question? "I would ask a favor of you."

"Anything."

Dhulyn was familiar with the gleam in Simka's eye. Many men—and women—were attracted to Mercenary Brothers, of both sexes. It was partly the thrill of being with someone who had killed, and partly the knowledge that this bedmate would not be staying to complicate their lives. There were others who found Dhulyn's Outlander coloring exotic, since her pale skin, hair the color of old blood, and gray eyes were rare among civilized people.

She was experienced enough in flirting, however, to know that Simka merely attempted to distract her. She held his eye, her face impassive, until he looked away.

"Refrain from making any more tracks to unnerve your cousin."

"You saw them? It was you who removed them?"

Really, townmen were too easy to trap. His blink and startled look alone were all the proof of guilt she needed. "It's our business to see them," she said. "Just as it's our business to keep your cousin safe and healthy. This altitude is hard enough on him, without his being frightened."

"I hadn't thought of that." The young man frowned, a furrow appearing between his brows. "It was meant as a joke. Naru's so *serious* all the time."

"Remember, if some joke of yours kills him, it will be part of my job to ensure you will never find anything funny again." Without giving him a chance to respond, Dhulyn nodded and let her horse fall back until she was riding next to Parno. "He's the one planting the tracks all right."

"Demons and perverts," Parno swore under his breath. "How did you find out?"

Dhulyn related the conversation. "He'll have to be a better actor if he plans to make a living as a trader," she concluded.

"It's clear he plans to make a living by taking his cousin's."

* * *

Dhulyn rolled to her feet, sword in hand, before the whistle faded away. She waited, and sure enough another whistle signaled which direction she should go. That it hadn't come immediately told her there was no urgency. As she went, she noted that both Naru and Simka's tents were open, and she moved faster. Sun and Moon strike them blind, she and her Partner were fools. They should have stood guard inside the man's tent, instead of limiting themselves to a perimeter watch.

She found Parno several spans up the hillside, where the waxing moon gave light to a small clearing among the pines. He stood over a body. It was hard to see color in the moonlight, but Dhulyn thought from the clothing that this was the old servant Bertol, who had spoken with her about the al

Difor family, not their client. Her breath came more easily, but she was still angry.

"Have you moved the body?"

"Am I an idiot?" Parno looked around. "Step around that way, there's a lot of blood here."

"That is not what killed him, however. Look here, the man fell backward onto this rock." She reached her fingers carefully around the slack head. "Feel his skull, here."

Parno did as she asked and then sat back on his heels. "He was fighting something off. There's his staff over there, where it fell from his hand."

Dhulyn picked it up, shaking her head. "Look there, on his forearm, the blood and the bite marks. Evidently an animal. What's not evident is who attacked whom. The end of the staff has a small amount of hair on it, as if he managed to strike his opponent. It could be a case of defense on both sides. Anything running off as you came?"

"Not a thing." Parno stepped back, frowning. "From the other side of the camp I thought I saw movement. By the time I reached here—" He gestured at the ground, his voice tight. "This is more than footprints. Do we conclude the cousin also did this? Killed an old family retainer and made it look like an animal attack?"

Dhulyn stood motionless, her head to one side. "Stand further back," she asked. "Out of the light."

"What light?" But he moved.

Dhulyn crouched down on her heels and examined the ground from one side, at a shallow angle. She measured something with her spread fingers, and finally laid her dagger next to it. She shook her head, moved slightly, and examined another spot of ground, to Parno's eyes identical with the first. Placing her feet carefully, she paced to the far side of the clearing. Again she spread out her hand and measured something. She stood and let out the breath she'd been holding.

"There are two sets of tracks. The ones we've seen before, here and here; and a second set, there and here. This," she pointed at the first spot she'd measured, "is one of the false prints we've already seen. These," she indicated the line she'd followed across the clearing, "these were made by a real animal."

"You can tell this by moonlight? Sorry," Parno held up his hands, palms toward her. "Of course you can. Which are the prints of the killer? Could this be the curse?"

"To answer your first question I need the light of day to examine the wounds. As for the second, a wild animal, in and of itself, does not constitute a curse," Dhulyn pointed out. "And besides, if it was the daemon of the legend, why attack this poor fellow? No, these tracks belong to some native creature, something like the snow leopards in the southern mountains, only larger."

"I always thought *they* were legendary."

"I assure you, they are not."

Parno grinned, sure that his Partner could see him. "You've got that look again."

"What look would that be?"

"The I'd-like-to-kill-someone look."

"Don't I look that way all the time?"

Next morning the camp was like an anthill doused with water. Much exclaiming, much scurrying, much backing and forthing, much calling upon the gods, and precious little in the way of practical activity. Both al Difor cousins looked shocked by the news of the old servant's death, and both showed signs of stiffness, as if this was the first day of travel and not the seventh. Or as if they'd fought with someone in the night. Dhulyn tapped out a rapid rhythm on her sword hilt. Impossible to know which had been out of camp killing servants.

When they were once more on the road, Dhulyn and Parno separated the two cousins; Dhulyn rode at Naru al Difor's side.

"You were out of your tent again last night. You are not the first to think that hiring Mercenary Brothers frees you from acting in a reasonable manner. If you do not stay in your tent, one of us will stay in it with you. Is this clear?"

Naru shook his head slightly from side to side, as if he wanted to argue with her, but when he spoke, it was to change the subject. "I wish I had not lost Bertol. He has been with me since childhood. If his death was meant for me, I sorrow that it found him instead."

"If it consoles you at all, his death wasn't brought about by your family's curse. His killer was no great wolf."

"Was it not?"

Dhulyn didn't know what to make of the look on the man's face. By daylight she had seen the unnatural look of the bite marks, but that still did not explain which cousin ... She sighed. "Tomorrow will see us out of the pass."

"I am relieved to hear it."

* * *

The mood in the camp was subdued after the activity of the evening meal had ended. The al Difor cousins were sitting a little apart from the others, Naru stabbing at the air with his finger, Simka frowning and shaking his head. Their quarrel made the servants nervous and no one asked Parno to bring out his pipes, as they had done every other night on the road.

Finally, Naru leaped to his feet. "What are you saying?"

Simka was up as well. "I only said you should have left Bertol at home. He was too old for this kind of journey."

Dhulyn circled around the still seated servants to approach the cousins from the far side.

"So his death is my fault, is that it?" Naru swung his fist at his cousin, but the inexperienced blow barely grazed the younger man's face. Simka defended himself with an equal level of clumsiness. By this time the two had abandoned the common tongue entirely and were shouting in Berdanan so fast that Dhulyn could only pick out the odd insult here and there. Approaching from another angle, Parno moved a dumbstruck servant to one side and reached out to yank Naru out of what danger there was.

"Wait," Dhulyn called out. Parno stopped instantly and trotted round to her side. "Let them fight," she added in the night watch voice. "We'll step in before the point of apoplexy."

Parno shrugged in agreement. "They're too clumsy to do each other much damage."

Even as they spoke, increased anger turned Naru al Difor's face a dark red, his breath grew shorter and shorter, until it seemed he could not draw another. This time, when Parno stepped forward to put a stop to things, Dhulyn did not hold him back. Before Parno could reach them, however, Naru al Difor fell to his hands and knees, and Simka stood looking from his fists to his cousin and back again.

"I never touched him!" He even approached closer, hands outstretched to help Naru to his feet, but stopped, frozen in his tracks. There came a heavy ripping sound, like canvas sails tearing in a high wind, and a most unusual smell.

Dhulyn, her lips pursed in a silent whistle, grabbed Parno by the wrist. Naru al Difor didn't appear to need anyone's help. In fact, Naru didn't appear to be Naru any longer. Where the merchant had been on hands and knees, struggling for breath, stood the largest wolf Dhulyn had ever seen.

His fur was thick and dark, except for some light dustings of gray.

Naru must dye his hair. The totally irrelevant thought passed through Dhulyn's mind as she grabbed a quarterstaff from one of the guards fleeing into the darkness under the trees.

Meanwhile, the wolf had leaped, pushing Simka to the ground and snarling into his face. Dhulyn ran forward, calling out and swinging the staff around in a blow that landed square on the beast's sensitive nose. It backed away, howling, far enough that Dhulyn could put herself between him and Simka.

"Kill it! What are you waiting for? This is the beast that killed the servant."

"Professional courtesy?" Parno hauled the man away with a grip on his upper arm. "After all, she *is* Dhulyn Wolfshead."

"How long can she keep the beast at bay?"

Parno glanced upward. "We'll have to hope long enough. When the moon sets we'll have less light to fight him by, and she will tire eventually."

All the time Dhulyn faced the wolf—fencing him in with quick strokes of the staff—she spoke to him in the soft voice she used to calm frightened horses. He'd begun to settle, his pace slowing, when an arrow came whizzing out from the trees. One of the guards had chosen that moment to remember he'd retained his bow. Dhulyn knocked the arrow aside without taking her eyes from the wolf. But in doing so, she stepped backward onto a metal cup, dropped by one of the servants as he ran away. She regained her balance in an instant, but in that instant the sand-wolf leapt, knocking her to the ground.

Like the old servant, Parno thought.

But unlike the old man, Dhulyn landed cleanly, managing to keep hold of her staff. As the muzzle came down, she thrust the staff into the sand-wolf's jaws, as one puts the bit in the horse's mouth. Parno stepped forward, sword raised, but stopped after only one pace. She would not thank him for killing their client.

She still spoke softly, calling Naru by name, switching to the Berdanan tongue. Finally, the beast calmed enough to stop snarling and simply stand still, its eyes flicking from one human to another, before fixing them on Simka. Dhulyn rolled out from under its paws.

"What is she doing? Why doesn't she kill it?"

"I'd say she's earning our pay, wouldn't you?" Parno's statement was met with a look of utter disbelief.

"Look," Dhulyn said. "He likes you. Shall I let him come nearer?"

"Keep it off me. Keep *him* off!" Simka huddled behind Parno, holding to the back of his sword harness. Parno pulled the man forward by the scruff of his neck.

"Now you know why your granny *really* moved the family."

* * *

Whether the moon had anything to do with it or not, it wasn't until it had set that Naru al Difor returned to his usual shape.

"I always knew he was greedy," Naru said as he watched them truss and gag his younger cousin. "I never thought he'd try to kill me."

When the sun rose, there was some talk of resting another day where they were, considering the very little sleep anyone had had during the long night before, but no one really wanted to stay where Naru might become an enormous sand-wolf at a moment's notice. Consequently, it was later that same morning that they began their descent from the Guadil Pass.

"You say you didn't believe?" Naru twisted round in his saddle to check on his cousin, slung face down over the back of his own horse.

"Not at all," Dhulyn admitted. "I thought it was your cousin trying to kill you, using the family legend as a way not to be blamed."

"Well." He glanced back again. "It appears you weren't wrong."

"And neither were you," Parno said. "There *is* a curse, just not the one you expected. Not that anyone could have expected it."

"I've read about such things," Dhulyn admitted. "But I always assumed they were tales alone."

"Did any of these tales explain why I've never changed before? Why I don't change all the time?" He shivered. It would be a long time, if ever, before he stopped waking up shaking.

Dhulyn shook her head. "They often link the change to the moon, but obviously there is more to it, otherwise you would change everywhere. Putting together what I've read, and the histories of your family, there must be something about the Guadil Pass itself. One account does suggest that great pain or stress can bring on the transformation."

"Between worry, fear, anger, and the physical stress of the altitude, I'd say that's the explanation." Parno, at least, was satisfied.

"But Simka didn't believe in the curse, did he?"

Dhulyn shrugged.

"And he did not change his plan when I hired Mercenary Brothers. How could he be so stupid?"

"Greedy, ambitious people often are."

Naru nodded in a way that told Dhulyn he'd encountered such things before. "Why did the change not come to my cousin as well?"

Dhulyn exchanged a look with her Partner. "In truth? I'd wager my second-best sword he isn't the son of your mother's brother."

Eyebrows rose and mouth fell open as Naru realized what she was saying.

Parno patted their client on his shoulder. "Would you like us to tell your uncle?"

The Witch That Wasn't
Leah Webber

A man walked through the door to Esther's cell covered head to toe in oiled leathers and clutching a black-bound book in front of him like a shield. One frantic step in and the door slammed behind him, making him jump. The various charms hanging all over him jingled in the musty dark. They obviously didn't like him enough to give him the benefit of a lamp.

Esther sighed.

"Look, are you going to tell me why I'm—"

"You are not permitted to speak!" the man shrieked. His voice bounced dramatically off the bare stone walls.

"Because why?" Sitting on the hard stone was making Esther's rump ache and she was cold and tired.

The man commenced frantic waving with one hand. "Your tongue will be still! You cannot cast your vile death magics upon me! I am of the White Watch! Dark magic will never cast out the light!"

"As stimulating as I find your company, I'm pretty sure if I could do vile death magics I wouldn't be trapped in here right now." She propped her chin on one hand, thoughtful. "As a matter of fact, I'm pretty sure this whole dungeon would be deathified by now."

A faint glow started somewhere in the cover of the book. It floated freely up from the man's hands, which started making complex gestures at her. "By my sacred bond with Ores, who rules the day and sees into every shadow, I take your powers of speech. I seal you under sun and sky and bloody stone. I BIND YOU!"

Esther blinked. "Yeah, no. Not happening."

The man blinked back. The book thudded to the ground, its light fading.

"I mean, solid effort, but that was never going to work on me."

"Hideous witch!" he screamed, pointing a finger at her.

"Now, that is just uncalled for. I mean, my nose is sort of crooked, but—"

"You will pay for what you've done!"

"Which is WHAT, exactly? You people grabbed me out of the bar with no warning—I didn't even get to drink my beer, by the way, and I'd been saving up for that for a solid week. I paid in advance! Then you drag me down here and dump me in a moldy dark cell, and every time I try to talk, someone threatens me with glowy magic fingers. What exactly have I done?"

The jingling began again. The man was shaking, sending all his little charms tinkling. "E-ESTHER WARKLIN—"

"Worklin."

The man froze. "What?"

"It's Worklin, not Warklin."

The man's eyes widened. The book shot up, brighter than before and humming loudly. His finger arrowed straight for her eyes, his shoulders thrown back, chin tilted up. "ESTHER WORKLIN, THE BLACK BLADE OF SINDARIA, I BIND YOU BY YOUR NAME! I HOLD YOUR SOUL ENSLAVED! DARK TO LIGHT, MOON TO SUN, TREE TO EARTH, YOU ARE IN THRALL TO ME!"

The echoes rattled the cell's stones a bit, shaking free some dust to cloud the already close air. Esther coughed, rubbing the grit out of her eyes with her sleeve. "Gods, could you not? My allergies are already hating me in here."

He snatched the book out of the air, genuinely puzzled. He looked at her, then at the glowing book. He gave the book a shake, thumping the cover as if he could knock the magic back into alignment. Its glow intensified. He looked at her hopefully.

She shook her head. "Sorry, no."

The light went out with a pop, but not before she saw the blooming horror in his face. "The bindings don't work on you."

"Solid analysis."

"You're too powerful."

"Seriously? No. Come on, now. Would I even be here if I was the all-powerful Blade of Sindartha?"

"Sindaria."

"Right, that. This is obviously just a terrible mistake."

A stone dropped out of the ceiling and bopped the man neatly on the head. He crumpled to the ground.

Esther gaped in surprise. "What the actual fucking hell? Just, how?"

She reached out to poke him to see if he was still alive and he recoiled. He started screaming, a long, incoherent wail of terror. The door flew open. Large meaty arms reached in, glommed onto him, and yanked him back into the hallway. The door slammed, leaving Esther in darkness once again. The wails quickly receded down the hallway and silence descended.

Esther stood, dusting off her pants and smacking a spider from its hopeful perch on her knee. She walked to the tiny barred window in the door.

"You know that wasn't me, right?"

Silence. Either the guards were too afraid to talk or they'd all made a run for it.

"I'm pretty sure he knocked that stone loose himself, with his boomy lighty enthrally spell. That didn't work, because nothing magic works on me! I am the opposite of a witch here! … Hello? I'd really like to know why I'm in here! Hello?"

Silence.

"For gods' sake, can't ANYONE answer a simple question around here?"

"Well, that depends on what you want to know."

Esther spun, knocking an elbow on the door in her haste. Then she had to divide her attention between hissing and holding her throbbing elbow and staring at the nondescript man who had somehow appeared in this place where that was supposed to be impossible.

He looked around the drab little cell with obvious distaste, arms wrapped around his torso as if to keep its ickiness from getting on him.

"They certainly do know how to cater to stereotype, don't they? If this was any more gloomy and damp and covered in spells against black magic… wait, you've broken the wards … well done, you!"

Esther blinked at him. "Do I know you?"

The man perked up. "Now THAT is an interesting and worthy question. Not even in the philosophical blowhard 'Can any of us really know anyone?' sense, but in truth. Because the answer is yes, but no."

Some of the sting was leaving her elbow, so she stopped rubbing it and braced her back against the door. "I'm fairly certain it can't be both."

His smile broadened. "Oh, but it is, and only because you are who you are. The great Esther Warklin, Black Blade of Sindaria—"

"I keep telling people, I'm really not."

"Yes, I know. I heard you say that, too. I assure you that you both are and are not, currently, the Great Black Witch of the West."

Esther sat, back against the door. "Okay, I'm very confused now."

"To be expected! All will be explained in due course, but we need to get out of here first."

"I'm not against the idea … but, how, exactly?"

"Your policy covers post-incarceration extraction if you notify us of the possibility in advance of the felonious spellcasting and reserve a ward breaker. It's quite expensive, but you always did have foresight."

This was becoming surreal. "My policy."

"Anyway, let's go. I like to leave them guessing how you got out. You let them see the trick behind the magic and then the next time they'll build to type and we have a devil of a time getting the next mage out."

"And we wouldn't want that."

"No, then we'd have to raise our rates and that just makes everyone unhappy. The lesser mages start dropping their catastrophic disaster coverage, we end up with not enough working capital, and we have to up our rates AGAIN. The whole cycle gets vicious."

"Nothing you're saying makes the slightest bit of sense."

He crooked out an elbow in invitation.

Esther bit her lip. "If you're planning to magic us out of here, it won't work. Magic doesn't work on me."

The man smiled wider. "Under other circumstances that might present a problem, but as I've moved the space itself and not you, you merely need step through. I'm not casting ON you, as such."

She stared at his proffered arm. "Well, as the alternative is staying in here and most likely being tortured and executed, I suppose I must."

"That's the spirit!" He smiled again.

She levered off the door, dusted her hands, and grabbed his proffered arm.

And then they were someplace else.

* * *

Esther liked to think she'd lived and experienced a great deal as a migrant who traveled in search of work requiring her particular brand of magic immunity. She'd once been stuck overnight in a collapsed barn with a prince (who she'd had to wallop for getting too handsy). She'd once had to take tea with a magician so old and demented that he kept exchanging the teapot for a badger, the sugar cubes for potted ham, and the cream for orange juice. They'd made the best of it by toasting cubes of ham dipped in orange juice over the fire, sharing with the badger so it wouldn't maul them … overall not a half bad afternoon. But Esther had to say that being popped out of a deep dungeon like a cork from a bottle, marched through an office buried in filing cabinets that casually stepped out of one's way when told to budge off, and plopped on a sofa with a blanket and a cup of strong coffee, well sweetened, with a file folder of paper as thick as her arm labeled 'Warklin, Esther P, MIGS' took the prize trophy for odd days.

The office was bright, open, and airy, with windows facing into the cheerful morning light. It smelled of books, leather, and ink. She looked at the man, seated comfortably behind his desk in a big squashy chair. The nameplate on the massive mahogany desk read 'Carlin Murgen, First Adjuster.'

"So what's a MIGS, then?" she asked.

Carlin propped his elbows on the desk, tenting his hands. "Mage In Good Standing. It means you're paid up through the end of the fiscal year and not currently in trouble with the guild for other reasons."

So many questions to that. She opened the file. On the top of the gathered sheaf of parchment lay a sheet titled, 'Request for Ward Breaker to Remain on Retention in Case of Unexpected Incarceration.' It was stamped 'APPROVED' in bright red.

"Hand me that, would you?" Carlin reached out an impatient hand for the form, opening a drawer in the desk with his other hand.

She passed it over.

He pulled a stamp and a pad of ink from the drawer, rolled the stamp several times over the pad, and thwacked it heavily onto the paper. He passed the paper back. The new stamp read, 'Cashed Out, No Return on Client Deposit.'

Esther stared at the bold red blot, then at Carlin as he leaned back in his chair with a small smile of satisfaction. "So, I'm a witch?"

"Mage."

"Sorry?"

"Only the non-magical refer to us as witches and warlocks. We're mages."

"We? Are you a mage?"

"Oh, yes. You have to be to work for the guild."

Esther blinked. "What kind of magic do you specialize in?"

"Oh, standard Adjuster magics. Wards, reassembly and disassembly, animation and disanimation, tracing and hiding, etcetera."

"Animation?"

"Bringing things to life." He wiggled his fingers at his own cup of coffee, where his spoon began to enthusiastically stir in his cream and sugar.

"So with your god-like powers of life-bringing, you chose to become some sort of magic … clerk?"

He winced a bit. "Insurance adjuster. I manage policies for guild members, execute claims, and manage recovery up to reanimation, as necessary."

His tone struck her. "Is it prestigious?"

"Oh, yes. Had to relocate three other applicants for the position to parts unknown. Job security. Low chance of sudden dismemberment or enkindling. Reasonable pay after materials. My own office, now I've been promoted to first rank."

Esther nodded. She well understood the value of a stable job. "So I'm a mage, then. A black mage?"

"Smudgy dark gray, really. It's a whole spectrum of light to dark, not so you'd hear it from the white mage's guild. They whinge on about natural law and sins against gods and no death, blah, blah, blah. We're not bad, just not entirely legal under some interpretations of the law."

"If you're legal, it's squinting at the law sideways through a glass of dark beer, by what I've heard."

Carlin waved a dismissing hand. "Unfounded rumors, mostly."

"Why don't I remember I'm a smudgy dark mage?"

"Spell gone dodgy. I analyzed the remains of the orphanage after the explosion—"

"I blew up an ORPHANAGE?"

"Well, not on purpose, but backfirings do happen. Near as I can tell, it was simply a case of wrong place, wrong time. Channeling near all that unbound mental chaos is bound to misfire now and again. There was an interesting study done by Mertigan the Third on how an overabundance of children in the vicinity of a spell can crimp the flow of dark magic until it backs up and rebounds on the caster. I hear mages usually just blow themselves up. You seem to have more rebounded your rebounding and splattered everything around you—clever way to survive a bad casting, really."

Esther gaped at him, cold sweat breaking out all over her. "Are they all… dead then?"

"Who?"

"The orphans!"

Carlin blinked at her. The thought had apparently not occurred to him. "Oh, yes, I suppose. Probably why they imprisoned you."

She fought tears. "So I'm an orphan murderer?"

"Murder implies deliberation and planning. I would categorize it more as accidental child slaughter."

"I don't care what you call it! Those children are all fucking exploded because of me!"

"I believe I listed among my skills the reanimation of the dead. The snotty little monsters are very much alive again, with only minimal brain damage. Not a dire outcome, considering how little they need their minds. However, it makes long-term cleanup much easier if there aren't large groups of outraged citizenry out for your blood. I have to say that is an interesting side effect of a backfiring spell-induced mind wipe, though."

"What is?"

"You seem to have developed a warping in your morality, divorced from logic. We'll have to note that in the post-incident study report."

"Inconvenient, is it, the crippling grief of destroying innocent lives?" Esther gripped her coffee mug harder, considering whether he'd blow her up if she threw it in his face.

"More annoying, really."

She chucked the cup at him. He held a hand up and the mug arrested itself mid-air, its lukewarm contents slopping a bit over the side and onto the paperwork on the desk. Carlin hissed, quickly hovering a hand over the puddle and muttering under his breath. The liquid pooled up from the paper, floated back up, and plopped back into the cup. The paper was unstained, as if it had never been touched. Esther blinked.

"As I WAS saying, the spell backfired at you. You did seem to channel most of it away from you, but it's not unheard of for there to be residual effects. Missing memory is high on the list of expected additional bother. You blew all your protection magics and tracking spells right off, as well. You can't imagine what I had to do to track you down after you'd blundered away from the crater."

"But I don't have any gaps in my memory. I can tell you everything I've done for the last week, right up until I was having a beer at the inn where they arrested me, and none of it involves exploding orphanages."

Carlin shrugged, plucking the mug out of the air and setting it out of her reach on his side of the desk. "Minds and memories are funny things. They don't like holes. They fill them with stuff."

"What about the fact that magic doesn't work on me?"

"That is a first, but if one extrapolates the idea that your last act was to furiously channel harmful magics away from you, you may have done so by making yourself magically impervious."

"But I've been this way my entire life!"

"Holes, remember. Filled with stuff. It was a brilliant save, but I have no idea how it will affect your recovery."

"My recovery?"

"Your policy covers the revocation of harmful magic, curses, or otherwise resetting from ill-effects of magic gone wrong. Third page of your policy file." A page shifted out of the stack and floated up to her hand. "We will attempt to reverse what you've done. Not my area, but there are specialists on call."

Esther looked at the word-packed page and thought about this. "What if you can't reverse it?"

"Well, there is a rider on your policy in case of irreversible debilitation. You'll have a monthly stipend, and you'll be resettled in secret and hidden by wards for your defense against those who would take advantage of your weakened state. Addendum three, page seven." Another page extracted from the folder and handed itself to her.

"So I'll be paid to go away and live peacefully in the country somewhere?"

"Yours is an excellent policy, but then you've always had good reason for paranoia, a mage of your skill. Still, it's a pitiable state, stripped of your power and even your memory. But hopefully it won't come to that! With any luck, we'll have you right as rain and back to your research."

Esther felt like she was drowning. Nothing in this made any sense at all. "… Do I want to know what subject I'm researching? It isn't using orphans as bits for spells, is it?"

Carlin considered her across the desk, glanced briefly at her coffee cup still perched on his side of the desk, opened his mouth, reconsidered, closed it, then smiled brightly. "Let's introduce you to the memory specialists!"

* * *

Esther gave it considerable thought and concluded that the only difference between a dungeon and a medical examination room was the fact that the latter was cleaned far more often. However, the smells, sights and sounds were remarkably similar.

She'd been shuttled from this room to a tiny suite upstairs in the tower every other day for a month, to be stared at and poked by a group of people in leather aprons. They talked over her head and used alarming terms like 'exsanguination and replacement of her bodily fluids' as possible treatment options. (She tried very hard to ignore the occasional far-away scream coming from down the hall somewhere.)

Today, like every day, they ended their session with disgust and splatters of rebounded magic smoking lightly on their apron fronts.

Being in her room was almost worse. She had nothing to do, save reading some of the many books on her table, full of impossible titles like 'A Measured Sky: Interpreting Moon Phases for Reliable Spellwork.' Not one adventure or fairy tale book in the whole lot. No wonder these people were all mad, if this was all they were subjected to. She read them anyway, while eating the bland food and drink they brought her. The alternative was contemplating that everything that existed in her mind, her full sense of self, was a lie.

There was never any beer, which was her starkest indication that she was still in a special kind of incarcerated hell.

Carlin visited her once a week to update her on things like 'billable hours against remaining retainage' and 'inconclusive investigation findings.' His pronouncements were heavier each time he saw her, though nothing seemed to have really changed for the worse in her opinion.

Unexpectedly, only three days from his last visit, he showed up in her tiny tower again with a ladies' jacket draped over his arm and an enormous smile. She'd come to realize that the larger his smile, the more dire the situation.

Esther didn't smile back. "Have we reached the 'ship batty old Esther off to the country' phase already?"

Carlin tossed her the jacket. "Not quite yet. We've exhausted all magical options, which means we have to switch to more … mundane methods."

"Does it involve them sucking out my blood? Because I think I'd rather be stuck in the countryside forever."

"No, no exsanguination. They disproved that theory. The barrier isn't in your blood."

She shrugged into the jacket. It was a perfect fit, because of course it was. "That's good to hear."

Carlin examined his nails. "They think it's in your skin, actually. Luckily, they decided flaying you wouldn't remove the barrier, so you get to keep your hide today!"

Esther blinked at him. She could never quite tell if Carlin was joking with her or not.

"No, when I say mundane, I mean truly non-magical methods. We're going to try some bland old exposure therapy. See if we can jog your memory."

"What happens if I do remember?"

"You fix yourself, hopefully. Then I can close out this case file and go back to boring desk work, you can go back to warping reality, and we'll all be the happier for it." He clapped his hands together.

"So what am I being exposed to?"

"The black manse ... dark corner of the bladed hills where no good soul dares to tread." He wiggled his fingers at her dramatically. Definitely joking, then.

She finished buttoning the jacket, found gloves in the pockets, also a perfect fit. "Sounds ... fun?"

He dropped his hands. "Oh, decidedly not. I don't know your security spell codes, so we might very well get incinerated or eaten."

Or maybe not joking. "Are you sure I can't just go get flayed?"

"No good. Wouldn't work. Come along, Esther. Let's take you home!"

*　*　*

The house sat tucked in a secluded dead-end street on the outskirts of the city. It had a solid looking wrought iron fence with 'EW' scrawled into the gate, a pleasantly shady wooded yard, and a bright red front door. There were purple tulips and herbs in the window boxes, buzzing with bees against the cheerful yellow siding.

Esther squinted through the gate. "Are you sure we have the right address?"

Carlin pulled a card from his pocket, then checked the number on the gate. "Yes, it's definitely your house. First time I've been here. Very nice, east-facing windows. Must be lovely in the mornings."

She cocked her head. "Is it an illusion, then? Hiding the wicked black house?"

He looked puzzled. "Why would it be an illusion?"

"You said it was black. 'Where good men fear to tread' and all that."

"Look, when you're not popular with the local constabulary, you need a certain off-putting reputation to keep most people away. The addition of misdirection keeps the brave ones from finding you as well, so you can get on with your spellwork in relative peace."

"Were you lying about the incineration and getting eaten part, then, too?"

"Sadly, no. Now be quiet a minute. I need to see if I can get us in the gate without setting anything off." He placed a hand on the gate, muttering to himself. His eyebrows drew together and the muttering intensified. He jerked his hand away from the gate and stepped back, a small crackle of lightning zapping the spot where he'd been standing. "Damn."

Esther tried not to smile. "No good?"

"To be fair, you ARE the best mage in the region. I'd have been surprised if it had been easy. I may have to go get some components, maybe a few friends here to get this open. It's a very sensitive trigger."

"What happens if a common thief gets in?"

"Nobody misses them."

"Or a child?"

The fat false smile bloomed. "Then I get overtime pay."

On impulse, Esther reached out and grabbed the latch. There was a popping noise and the gate swung open. She wiggled her fingers at Carlin's open-hanging mouth, smile completely gone. "Impervious to magic, remember?"

"You might have died!"

"Considering all the magic I've had bounced off me recently, I thought it unlikely."

He looked alarmed. "Can I ask you most sincerely to not do that next to me again? You might be immune, but *I* most certainly am not. I'd rather not be in the way of a rebound."

"You might want to go for a quick walk, then, as I intend to walk up the path and trip everything."

Carlin blinked. "I can't decide whether that's brilliant or mad."

"That seems fitting for the Black Blade of Sindaria, I suppose. Decide while walking away, please!" Esther stepped through the gate.

Carlin jogged quickly around the corner.

When he returned five minutes later, she stood calmly on the porch. Her hat was missing. A pot of hydrangeas was tipped over, and a smoking crater marred the front lawn, but otherwise all was as it should be. He stopped at the gate, checking the area.

"Did I get everything?" Esther called from under the eaves.

"Not hardly, but the walkway is clear. Just don't step off the path while

I'm nearby, all right?" He joined her on the porch, where the door hung open in an inviting manner.

As they stepped inside, Esther looked around. Warm wooden floors strewn with brightly colored carpets led to a very ordinary-looking sitting room, a dining room, and what looked to be a library. She was amazed to note that she owned more books than she'd ever seen in one place. A quick scan of the shelves revealed that none were adventure stories. The library did have the benefit of a large fireplace, a full bar of liquors, and both lay-ing settees and squashy chairs. She approved of her mage self's furniture choices.

At the back of the house was a set of locked doors. While Carlin popped back out to the porch, she despelled them, but they remained locked.

"That's likely your work room. We might have to get a locksmith in, unless you have a key on you?" She turned out her dress pockets, dropping a few pieces of lint on the floor, but no key.

Carlin mused. "Do you feel anything here, Esther? A tickle at the back or your mind? Déjà vu?"

Esther tilted her head in thought. "Nothing rattling free at the moment, but it does suit me, this house. It's comfortable."

"Well, I suppose that's something."

"I like the carpets."

Carlin sighed noisily and sat in one of the squashy chairs.

"The books need a bit of work, but that's not the worst thing."

His eyebrows drew together. "It's one of the most extensive libraries in the nation. What could it possibly be missing?"

"Well, there is an abysmal lack of pirate stories."

Carlin blinked at her. "Pirate stories."

"Maybe a book about genies."

He laughed. "Well, there is a treatise on magic-based familiars some-where in here, but I'm guessing that's not what you meant." He cast about for a few minutes, not really looking at the books. "Look, perhaps we're rushing it a bit. Let's have you stay here for a few days and see if anything in the house jogs your memories, eh?"

"What, alone?" Esther exclaimed, mildly alarmed. "In a strange fancy house? With no food or beer?"

Carlin laughed. "All right, I'll go get lunch, and we'll see about arrang-ing for someone to stay here with you." He settled her on the sofa in the sitting room and left, leaving the door open behind him.

She poked the sofa. Should a sofa be familiar? What about the arched shape of the windows, or the view of the garden, or the painting above the fireplace (a landscape she didn't recognize)? Was that painting of a place she had been? What do you do when your memories might not be your memories, just place-fillers for the things you had accidently knocked loose, soon to fade?

The panic that tickled under the surface of her mind threatened and she agitatedly walked out onto the porch.

A woman stood in the walkway, barefoot, with a torn, dirty, and burnt dress, hair unpinned and wild around her shoulders. Her eyes were wide and angry. "How did you get in?" The woman whispered.

"Oh." Esther gasped. "Well, I walked in."

"I couldn't get in. The gate hurt me before and now it doesn't. How did YOU get in?" The woman said, walking up to the porch. "Who are you?"

"I'm not really sure at the moment." Esther sat on the step. "I used to think I knew. I don't like not knowing."

The woman seemed at a loss for a moment, then sunk down to sit beside her. She whispered, "Do you know me?"

Esther took her in afresh. She'd known a lot of characters in her day, but very few wild-eyed savage women. "No, should I?"

"I think I know this place. I don't know how I got here, and I don't know who I am, but this place feels safe. Do you live here?"

"I think I do." Esther looked at the porch lamp. It was shaped like a dragon. She loved it, but she loved it as a new discovery, not an old friend. "I don't know."

"Damn, I was hoping for answers. Why can't I remember anything?"

"I know exactly how you feel." Esther smiled a bit and extended a hand. "I'm Esther. Esther Worklin."

The woman stared hard at her hand, eyebrows drawing tightly together. "Esther. Esther? Why do I know that name?" She stood, walking agitatedly down the walk toward the gate, muttering.

A man walked through the gate. He was dressed in oiled leather, covered in jingling charms, holding a large leather-bound book. Different face, but the clothes were the same as from the prison. Esther jumped to her feet. The woman in the walkway froze, planting her feet.

"I've finally found you, you parasite!" The man cackled. He raised the book above his head. It began to glow. "By Ores' Holy Flame, I will cleanse you from this world!" A tower of flame shot from his hands.

Esther backed away, ankle hitting the steps. She fell backward on the stairs, knocking the wind out of her.

The tower of flame hit the woman. She screamed and fell backward, crawling back up the walkway. The fire grew larger and hotter, swirling into a funnel. The woman stopped crawling and her screams cut off. With a roar, the flame burned out and a dusting of ash blew across the lawn. The woman was gone.

The man ran towards Esther. She screamed, throwing up her arms in defense.

He skidded to a halt, hovering over her. "Are you all right, ma'am? Did that monster hurt you?"

Esther froze, peering at the man between her arms. "Sorry?"

"You're so lucky I got here in time. That woman was the worst kind of witch. She'd have killed you for certain." He grabbed her arms, levering her to her feet.

"You … you just incinerated a woman in front of me and SHE was the dangerous one?" Pins and needles were in her hands and feet. Spots were in her vision. She thought she might faint.

The man bowed low. "Madam, I'm so sorry for that violent display, but I assure you, what I did was highly necessary. That woman was a demon."

"She didn't even know who she was! She was asking me for help!"

"I know it. I've been tracking her for weeks since she escaped me by blowing up an entire city block and lost her mind in the process. Even without her memories, the Great Witch of the West was a formidable foe."

Esther stopped breathing. "Great Witch of the West?" She whispered.

The man struck a proud pose, his charms jingling. "Yes. You've just seen the demise of Esther Warklin, the Black Blade of Sindara."

"Sindaria." Esther said absently. She sat heavily on the step.

"Pardon?"

"Oh gods, this has been the worst month of my life." Esther lay back onto the porch and threw an arm over her eyes.

The man crouched down and patted her knee awkwardly. "I advise you to go drink a tonic and forget this ever happened. You've had luck today, thanks to the White Watch."

"Thank you?"

He looked at the overturned hydrangea pot, the smoking lawn crater, the still smoldering pile of ash, and coughed uncomfortably. "What is your name, madam, so we can reimburse you for the damage?"

Esther broke into a cold sweat, sitting up abruptly. "Oh, no. No. I'm sure we can manage it. I couldn't possibly burden the … White Watch."

"The Protectors of the City." The man beamed.

"Yes. Your help here was quite enough for me."

He looked around uncertainly. "Well, I'll have to note the owner of the house in my follow-up report. What was your name?"

Esther blinked at him, looked past him, and zeroed in on the initials on the gate. "Elizabeth. Elizabeth Woods." She stated firmly.

* * *

An hour later, Carlin strolled up the path with a basket over his arm. He paused several steps past the smear of ash when he saw her sitting like a sack of potatoes on the step, exhausted. "Esther, what is the matter? Did something jog your memory?"

"You could say that." She sighed.

He set the basket down and sat beside her on the porch.

"Carlin," she began hesitantly, "you know me, right? From before I lost my memory?"

Carlin propped his chin on his hand. "Only by reputation. I'm newly promoted to the office. I worked case files on the other side of the city as a Second Adjuster. The previous First Adjuster retired after his eyebrows stopped growing back."

"Those mages who worked on getting my memory back, they knew me? From before?"

"I'd imagine not. You move in very elite circles within the guild." He looked puzzled.

The dread settled home in her stomach, yet she started to feel better. "How did you know who I was, then?"

"Well, they arrested you. It was pretty simple to confirm it. And after all, you still remembered your name."

"Esther Worklin."

"Yes, Esther Warklin."

"Carlin, what is my middle name?"

"Philomena, I believe."

"It's Lavinia."

Carlin's eyebrows drew together. "No, that's not right. Esther P. Warklin."

"Esther L. W-O-rklin, Carlin." Finally, finally, she knew who she was.

His mouth opened, worked silently for a few moments, then closed.

"That's … not possible."

She nodded, feeling better and better. "But close enough for the White Watch to mistake it and arrest me. Similar age and a funny way with magic."

Carlin slumped down in shock. "Oh, my god. Then where's the real one?"

Esther looked at the pile of ash. "About that. You can resurrect people, right?"

His eyes slowly followed hers and he swallowed hard. "Well, depending. How intact are they?"

Esther coughed delicately. "Let us suppose not very."

Carlin looked at the pile, then at her. "How not very?"

"Particles?" She pointed.

He leapt off the porch, ran over to the pile, and crouched over it. Several minutes passed as he waved hands over it, circled it, poked at it, then finally dropped his hands and walked very slowly back to her. He dropped dejectedly onto the step next to her.

"Are you going to lose your job?"

"In a manner of speaking, I'm going to lose a lot of things. Possibly my limbs. Maybe my mind. If I'm lucky, my life. And my gods, the paperwork. So many mismanaged accounts! She had no next of kin, so at least we won't have to pay out the death benefit." He put his head in his hands.

"I don't suppose what they'll do to me will be any great shakes, either."

"Your death will likely be swift and painless, as you're not responsible for the losses and not a beneficiary."

Esther felt surprisingly calm about that idea. "It's a shame we can't just pretend that I was Esther all along and send me out to the countryside."

Carlin snorted out a little laugh. "No, of course not. That would be … entirely plausible."

She smiled a bit, folding her arms. "Better fun would be to retire a fictional Esther out to the countryside, pocket the stipend, and give me a job as a magic breaker in the guild."

"You're not a mage, Esther."

"No, I'm like an unmage. Which is rarer than a mage and worth more. Think of the things I could do for you that no one else could!" She nodded.

"Esther, I am somewhat alarmed at your willingness to bend the spirit of good fellowship in our guild to your benefit."

"So you'd rather die horribly?"

"I didn't say THAT." He snorted.

"Carlin, I never claimed to be an angel, just not an orphan-exterminator.

A good con for money is right up my alley."

"You'd fit right in." He looked at the sky. "I suppose I could modify the medical staff's memories to Esther's actual appearance. This could actually work! You'd have to study on all the policies and addendums so you could work by guild law, but it's not as if you're an imbecile. You can read."

"Thanks ever so. I want a desk. And maybe to keep this house."

"Don't push it, Worklin."

She winced. "I think I'll need a new name."

He gave it some thought. "Lavinia?"

"Lavinia Woods, Ward Breaker, Spell Sunderer, and Black Hammer of the Hills?"

He laughed. "No. For gods' sake, you don't give yourself titles, woman, the peons do." He held out a hand for her to shake. When she reached for it, he dropped a massive black key into hers. "Work room key. Found it in the ashes."

Esther—Lavinia—mused at the key, dusted the ash off it, and burst out in a pained laugh. "Oh, this is just awful. That poor woman." She pocketed the key and opened the basket, fishing out a sandwich, and was quietly delighted to see two bottles of beer. She handed another sandwich to Carlin, keeping the beer for herself. "I'm putting pirate stories in the library," she decided, taking a bite.

Carlin looked at his sandwich and chuckled, resigned. "Lavinia Woods, welcome to the Black Mages Guild. Try not to burn it down on your first day."

Oathbreaker

David Farland

The King's Despatcher was a man of few words. He spoke more in soundless gestures and said all that was needed in a sigh or a look. He was old, Dval knew, but he didn't know how old. He'd had a name once, but seemed to have forgotten it. Yet his mind always seemed to be going, and the Despatcher often lay awake at nights, just pondering.

There was something otherworldly about the man—the way he seemed to smell an ambush on the road ahead, or the time three months back when he was twenty leagues from town and suddenly stopped, mid-stride, and said, "The king needs us."

Tonight, as they climbed a peak high above the Courts of Tide, the Despatcher seemed to be responding to some sort of alarm. Their route lay straight up the face of the mountain, not by an oft-trod footpath that doubled or tripled its distance with switchbacks, nor even a scant trail made by the horned goats that sprang from crag to pinnacle to browse on spiny grasses. The moon had yet to rise and so they felt their way in darkness, probing outcrops and stone pockets for handholds and toeholds. This was no handicap for Dval, who was born with the night vision of his people, the Woguld.

In his year or so as an apprentice, Dval had learned never to question the King's Despatcher. Finally, he could not hold his curiosity any longer. Dval touched the Despatcher's nearest boot, soft-soled for walking silently and climbing. "Master," he asked, "where are we going?"

For a moment the only sound was wind sighing over rocky ledges. The Despatcher said nothing, then whispered, "Patience," and crept higher.

Dval wondered. Were they storming some marauder's hideout, or did the Despatcher just want to get high enough to view a layout of the land? The lights of the Courts of Tide were a muted orange glow, like stars on a dim night.

Perhaps it is only a test of my climbing ability, Dval considered. But he had been born in the mountains and lived in the underworld. He did not fear climbing at night. He inched higher.

At the crest minutes later, a hand reached over a wall of scree to grasp Dval's, a younger hand than his master's scarred one. Its grip guided him through the rubble into a hollow a dozen yards across, shallow as a wooden trencher, but rougher. Curved fragments of stone, some as long as his body, lay crumbling against the encircling talus as if swept there. They smelled of ancient decay and Dval wrinkled his nose. Bones. Old bones and egg shells.

Dval froze. *This is the nest of wild sea graaks. They will be enraged if they return while we are here.* The leather-winged creatures were large enough to grab a man in their jaws and send him over the precipice.

Before he could question his helper, he spotted other dark shapes standing about. All of the men were hooded and robed in black: Despatchers.

His helper flung back his hood and grinned. Surprise surged through Dval once more. This Despatcher couldn't have been more than five or six years older than his own fifteen years.

"Brooding season is long past," the young Despatcher said. "The chicks that came from these shells are ancient themselves, if they still live. No graak nests in this aerie now." Still eyeing Dval, he added, "I call myself Three. I am third in line among all of the king's Despatchers. Your master is First." Among Despatchers, this young man seemed gregarious and long-winded.

Dval nodded.

At that moment the moon burst clear of the clouds crowded on the distant horizon, separating the sea from the sky. Its silver face sparkled among the crystal-faceted towers and spires of the Courts of Tide, the castle and city built on the shore of the Carrol Sea. There reigned King Harrill of Mystarria, known as "the Mad" since the death of his queen in a carriage crash two years before.

And there lives his daughter, the Princess Avahn, Dval thought, but quickly banished the longing that welled in his heart. He had saved her from dire wolves once, at the cost of injuries to himself.

The moon's brilliance outlined the distant peaks of three black Toth ships as well, shaped from stone and teeming with monsters. Dval shuddered at the memories of darkness and stench and snatching hooks inside one obsidian hull. All three ships had been conquered weeks ago.

"Son!" His master's voice snapped Dval from his waking nightmare. "Come."

His master joined with two cloaked figures at the aerie's center, around a simple altar, a low table made of a single carved stone.

In the moon's glow Dval recognized the others as more of the king's Despatchers, these middle-aged, and with a hardness in their eyes that spoke of warriors accustomed to killing without a second thought. Dval recognized their faces, but he didn't know their names any more than he knew his master's. They were all just Despatchers.

A meeting? he wondered. *But who called for it, and when?* Dval had not seen another Despatcher since midwinter. *Do they always meet here on the midsummer's full moon?*

Dval followed the youth who called himself Three to stand with the other men.

His master stepped back and tipped his head up to search Dval's face, because Dval stood at least a head taller than all of them. With his white Woguld skin and silvery hair like a smooth waterfall down his back, Dval knew he appeared as pale as a specter in the full moon. He bore the gaze, waiting wordlessly. *He is judging me, assessing me for some purpose.*

Dval surveyed his master in return. Far older than these others, he knew, by his leathery visage and wrinkle-shrouded eyes. The old Despatcher remained as broad of shoulder as a bull, with thighs as thick as the forest elms, and his hair still gleamed black as a raven's wing, untouched by the hoarfrost of his years.

At last his master said, "You have proven yourself in the king's service time and again. I consider you my son, though you are not of my loins. I judge you as ready. But if you are to join the Despatchers in full you must take our oath. That's why we have revealed to you the ancient circle." He thrust out his jaw as if pointing and turned his head slowly to trace its boundary.

The rising moon, well above the water now, revealed to Dval what he hadn't seen before. The broken shells of graaks hatched centuries before camouflaged carved stones set in a perfect ring. The largest, its top shaped to a point, stood in exact alignment with the place from which the moon had risen.

One of his master's companions stepped forward, a bear of a man. "Do you fully understand the gravity of our duties, boy?"

Dval thought he knew, but the man's stare filled him with uncertainty. "We are the king's elite guard," he said with a shrug.

"In part," the man said, "but there is more."

Dval paused to remember what his first teacher, Sergeant Goreich, who trained the king's guard, had once told him.

"A Despatcher is part scout, part spy, part saboteur, and in need, he may be an assassin," Dval said. "It is his duty to discover the movements of enemy forces and halt them. He may do this by poisoning their draft horses and the livestock they keep for provisions. He may burn bridges or cause avalanches to block mountain passes to stop their advance. He may be sent to slay enemy kings or to hunt outlaws."

"Very good." His questioner gave a scant nod. "But there are deeper things still."

The fourth man strode forward, strong and wiry. "Our duty is to protect *both* the king *and* his people," he said in a growling voice, like tumbling gravel. "We accept the tasks that no one else dares or can accomplish. You have killed Toth, and that is a deed that few can boast. Yet you must learn to take more difficult actions still, ones that may challenge you in ways beyond your physical strength."

Dval puckered his brow, questioning what that might mean. *What more can I give?* he wondered. He had sacrificed pleasure and suffered pains, risked his life a dozen times over now. But these men wanted more from him.

His master must have seen his expression because he said, "More often than not, my son, the greatest dangers to our kingdom arise from within. Sometimes we are called upon to do what men of good conscience cannot."

Dval thought he understood at last. *They want me to give up my conscience?* He considered the outlaws he'd met last month in the Kingswood. They were robbers, in tents with their wives. He'd refused to kill the men's wives, but the Despatcher had shown them no mercy. "I see," he said uneasily, wondering just how cold he could become.

"When you take this oath," Three said, "it is not without consequence. It will *change* you."

Dval bit his lip, considered. He had lost so much already. Was he willing to give up more? He wondered in his heart if he could keep an oath when he did not know how terribly it might affect him. "I am ready. I will not fail you again."

"Then place one hand upon your heart, to signify your loyalty to our king and to his people, and the other upon the hilt of your sword, to represent the strength of your arm in their service, and listen with care to each word, for you must repeat them after me. This oath must define you."

He and the other four men positioned themselves about the stone altar. With them and the moon's solemn face as his witnesses, Dval vowed to "protect the king and people of Mystarria, whether great or lowly, from all enemies, within and without our land, in whatever form they may take, and to defy the darkness."

Dval felt somber afterward and wished for time alone to ponder the weight of the words and their deep meanings. But the gravelly-voiced Despatcher said, "Now comes the binding of the oath upon you by the greater powers. Kneel upon the altar."

Dval dropped to his knees on the aerie's ragged floor. "Receive the swiftness and the binding of Air," he said, and blew a deep-chested breath about Dval's head and shoulders. The breath surrounded him in a whirlwind strong enough to lift and tug his pale hair before it dispersed on the night breeze with a shriek like a falcon's.

The second drew a flask from beneath his dusky cloak and splashed water upon Dval's face. "Receive the power and the binding of Water." Dval knew it was seawater by its scents of salt and kelp and creatures swimming in the deep, scents stronger and sharper than those borne on a summer pond.

Next, his master drew a flaxen cord from the leather pouch at his belt, a cord bearing four runestones the size of Dval's knuckles, but each a different color and carved with a different shape. He hung the cord about Dval's neck and said, "Receive the strength and binding of Earth."

Dval's knees had begun to ache from kneeling on the rough surface, so he shifted from one to the other to ease their discomfort and noticed something strange. His knees suddenly felt at one with the stone.

"Hold," ordered Three, and he planted a short-handled torch between the altar's stones that Dval hadn't seen him light.

Dval narrowed his sensitive eyes and recoiled from the scorching heat on his face.

"Hold," Three said again, more firmly this time. He dropped to his own knees across the altar from Dval, and through the fluttering fire Dval saw that the open friendliness in the young man's face had sunk into a deep sorrow. He said no more but began to stare into Dval's eyes.

Dval held, despite the torch's blistering heat and painful brightness. He had felt such heat in the flying sand and dust of the training arena, under the summer sun and stern but fair tutelage of Sergeant Goreich. *It is another test*, Dval thought. *Perhaps their final test. I endured the burning then; I will endure it now for as long as I must.*

But the brightness! After a long space Dval realized that the blinding light did not come from the dancing torch, but from the eyes of the young Despatcher. More and more brilliant they burned, as if they held the sun itself within them, the full sun of high summer. Then something twinkled, like a prominent star in a cloudless sky, and released itself in a towering flare.

In that ethereal burst Dval glimpsed a white creature, a man-figure made all of light, brighter than the summer sun, a man of brilliance, of ... glory. Dval could find no other word. *Yes, he is a Glory!*

The Glory pressed forward to peer into Dval's soul, to search and study it, as if hefting its weight. Dval resisted recoiling once more, not from any heat this time, but from the Glory's fell scrutiny, its revelation of his every flaw. Dval became sensitive to his own weaknesses: his hatred toward the uncle who had slain his father and banished him from his own people; the anger and disgust he'd felt toward the Mystarrian youths who had tormented him during his training for the king's guard; and the forbidden warmth—no, heart-hunger—he felt for the Princess Avahn. How it tormented him, so much that even now he wondered how he had bonded to her in such a way. He was not a lover. He could never be that. But at some primal level he needed to protect her.

I see you, the Glory whispered. *Let me see all of you. Give yourself to me and I will make you a weapon to drive back the darkness.*

His face heated again, to his ears, but the heat came from inside him this time. It was all he could do not to lower his eyes in shame. *I'm not worthy. I'm not ready for this at all, and the Glory sees every smudge and smear of it.*

It seemed to take all of his courage and strength to remain upright, kneeling above the altar.

A voice filled his burning ears. Not the grave voice of Three but a thunderous voice as of great waters or wind. "I have seen you for what you truly are," the Glory said. "Receive the purification and binding of Fire and know that your offering of service is accepted."

There was a flash and light seemed to burn through him, burn all of his evil to ashes, and in an instant he felt an awareness of evil unlike anything he'd imagined. It was all around him. He could feel shadows, sense them miles away, down in the woods, in taverns, and in the Courts of Tide.

The Glory vanished, rising like a meteor that streamed up into the night, and Dval's last thread of strength left him. He crumpled to the ground beside the altar.

* * *

Dval woke to a familiar hand shaking his shoulder and a crinkled face leaning over him.

"Come now, Son," the Despatcher said, raising Dval with a hand. "You must eat, and then we will take the easier way down from this mountain and turn our faces toward Toom. There is a matter we must investigate."

Weakly, Dval rose and peered out across the shimmering seas, silver with morning light, and studied the crystalline bridges like strands of spider web strung between the islands at the Courts of Tide. The Toth's black ships had moved in the night, changing formation a bit, floating derelicts.

But everything seemed unreal. He could not sense the darkness he'd imagined in the world, and the other Despatchers were gone, had fled like dreams.

Strength returned to Dval after he'd eaten dried meat from his pouch. He still could not stomach many Mystarrian foods, but hunger as fierce as if he'd spent the night in battle drove him to finish a lump of hard cheese and empty his water-skin as well. Lingering shakiness, as he followed his master down a treacherous mountain trail, left him puzzled.

Yet amazement overshadowed his puzzlement. He stared, brow furrowed in contemplation, at the narrow path before him, at the tiny dust clouds raised by his master's soundless boot-falls. *Now I know that Despatchers are more than warriors. They are users of ancient magics, like runelords and wizards.*

He fingered the small stones on their cord, hidden beneath his tunic. He did not recognize the runes carved into them, but he could feel potency in them. *These are relics of great power. I have been granted great power.*

"Master," he asked, keeping his voice hushed in the early chorus of bird-song, "who is the—no, *what* is the being I saw last night?"

The Despatcher slid him a slight smile, bearing both deep wisdom and humility. "He is simply called The Master and he has sent you on your first quest."

Dval nodded toward the north. "To Toom? Are the hill giants crossing the borders again?"

"No," the Despatcher said. "In the past two months, two young women have been found dead and naked in the lands near Clifftor, where reigns our king's brother, the Duke Hamid. You must find their killer and avenge them."

He paused to fix Dval with a cynical gaze. "Here is the mystery: I did not learn of these murders nor receive a command from the king to search into them. Our Master told me of them."

* * *

As Dval climbed down into the wood, he had to wonder: when had the Master spoken to the Despatcher? Did the man hear words in his mind or just feel impressions?

Could Dval do the same?

They reached their mounts on a road in the morning and Dval made a discovery. As they passed a cottage, the beams of its roof so warped by time and water that it was no more than a hovel, Dval saw a hunchbacked old woman out at her gate, scattering seeds for a few red chickens that peeped in excitement.

There was something wrong with her—terribly wrong. He had to stop and try to figure it out. As he gazed at her, her body seemed to waver like the air above a desert trail and her face became shadowy and misshapen.

He peered at her in amazement and the Despatcher urged him along. "Don't stare. Our Master has given you new eyes, so that you see the stains on men's souls."

There was something disconcerting and hideous about her, and Dval hurried in the Despatcher's footsteps and wondered, "Is she evil?"

"No more than most," the Despatcher whispered. "In fact, she's one of the good ones. All men bear some stains on their souls."

Dval peered hard at his master, but could sense no darkness or stains there, nor in himself.

"Where are my stains?" Dval wondered.

"Our Master burned them away," the Despatcher said. "Last night. But take care, or they shall return."

And so they strode that day to an inn, where a kindly fat innkeeper offered a horse, and, as Dval neared the man, he not only saw the flickering shadows of corruption, but he could smell it upon the man—putrefaction, like rotting meat—and it was all that he could do to remain calm when the man shook his hand at the wrist.

Dval caught the Despatcher watching him with an amused gleam in his dark eyes, and, as they rode down the highways, Dval peered keenly at men, struggling not to see just their forms, but to really view them. He wanted to feel them, to know them.

"Study others carefully," the Despatcher warned that night. "Learn to truly see them. Listen for warnings. The harder you peer, the better you will learn to truly see. But if you grow careless, your vision will grow dimmer and dimmer and leave you altogether."

So they traveled by horseback, and when they reached villages Dval struggled to see men truly, to see through their stains and twisting shadows, and he began to realize why the Despatchers often sought solitude in the wastes, for just being near others drained him, left him feeling mentally and emotionally exhausted. For eleven days they rode.

On their last night, with the towers of the duke's castle distantly visible above the forest, they entered an inn whose sign bore a very fat hog wallowing among brightly painted squashes and melons. The sign swung on the evening breeze, creaking above their heads as the Despatcher pushed the timber door open.

While they devoured a savory pork stew, Dval listened to his master talk with the innkeeper, a woman as rotund as the pig on her sign. Like most people of Mystarria, she repeatedly darted wary glances at Dval and his white Woguld features. In the comfortable near-dark, where he didn't have to squint, he met her silent queries with his steady gaze. He could see almost no stain on this woman's soul.

His master finally seemed to become irritated by Dval's silence and turned to him. "It's *your* quest boy. Seek to know what you need to know."

So Dval looked hard at the woman, searching her face, and felt … light inside of her.

"Two young women have died this summer," Dval told her. "I must find their killer. Is there anything you can tell me about it?"

The matron's face clouded over and tears glistened in her eyes. "The first girl was from our village. Fair Meaghan, daughter of the beekeeper." She shook her head in genuine sorrow. "She'd taken pots of honey to the market at the castle, but she never returned. The other came from Cliff Haven, a fishers' village three miles up the coast. Both girls were found in the woods not far from here, naked and strangled, by the bruises on their necks, and probably ravished."

Dval shifted in the heavy chair. "Why were they naked?"

There was a clatter across the room as a patron spilled ale on the floor.

The innkeeper blinked and studied him. "When pirates take a man, young Despatcher, they strip him to his skin before they lock him in chains and sail away with him to Haversind. It keeps them from hiding weapons or breaking free. We lose a lot of poor folk to them every year—Pirates from Haversind."

Slavers! Dval thought. He searched his heart. Yes, he felt a brooding darkness to the north and east, out at sea. It was like a massive storm on the horizon, with gray swirling clouds. Pirate marauders were indeed involved somehow, he felt sure.

"Thank you, mistress," the Despatcher said, "for this good meal, this night's lodging, and for your help." He placed two steel coins on the trestle table.

The next morning, as they rode easily toward the castle, Dval spoke from under his deep, black hood. "Do we need to even go to the Duke's court? The pirates … I can sense darkness. I feel them, a cloud off to the north."

"Very good," the Despatcher said. "Our master is guiding you there. Learn to trust those feelings."

The castle was bustling when they reached it that morning, cocks crowing, bread baking, crowds gathering at the markets. Duke Hamid's man-at-arms stopped them at the castle gate, then admitted them into his great hall, announcing, "Two Despatchers from the courts of His Royal Highness King Harrill!"

From within the cowl of his robes, Dval peered about. The great hall was much smaller than the king's, but the stonework was exceedingly fine. High windows allowed the morning light to shine upon deep-blue tapestries that displayed saber-cats clawing the air.

The duke rose from his humble wooden throne, a broad smile lighting his face, though he didn't conceal his revulsion quickly enough when Dval dropped his cloak's hood. Dval could imagine him thinking, "The Gross Wurm," the epithet he'd heard so often from the king.

"Welcome to the Court of Clifftor," Duke Hamid said in a voice that was surprisingly jovial. "Twice welcome, indeed! May I ask what brought you? Was it my mad brother that sent you, or do you come on other business?"

The Despatcher peered curiously at the Duke, as if considering how to answer. Dval felt a deep reluctance to speak, and he peered hard into the

Duke, saw a curious darkness, but to Dval's surprise, the Despatcher said openly, "Other business. There have been murders in your land. Two young women ..."

The Duke's smile faltered and he whispered worriedly, "Yes, I have heard. Please, come feast with us tonight, and let us discuss ... in private, how to capture the men that did this."

Dval studied the man. Ten years younger than King Harrill, Dval guessed, with hair more blond than the king's sandy color. But Hamid shared his brother's hazel eyes, keen and searching, his facial structure, and brawny build. *He is a runelord, my master said, with a dozen endowments of brawn, sight, and agility, the gifts most sought by warriors.*

Dval tried again to reach out, to sense the shadow on the man's soul, and he felt stains there, but his heart urged him northward, toward the darkness.

"We understand that the killers might be pirates?" Dval offered.

"Perhaps," the Duke agreed, "but I'm hesitant to put the blame on the most obvious malefactors. Sometimes, there is more to a matter than it seems. Let us investigate this more deeply."

That evening the Lady Etelinda, Duchess of Clifftor, joined her husband at dinner. Dark as he was fair, with hair of rich mahogany, full lips, and brown eyes that sparkled with warmth and intelligence and humor, she alone of the court did not flinch at her first sighting of Dval. She extended a slender hand to him in welcome. *I like her better than her husband*, he thought, and touched her hand lightly with his lips in the manner his master had taught him.

He reached out with his mind again and sensed warmth from her, and light. Or was he just imagining it?

Seated several places along the head table from the duke, between his master and a knight presented to them as Sir Marin, Dval consumed the rare flank of beef with gratitude but could only pick at most of the feast. Many of the colorful vegetable dishes would have sickened him; even their aromas twisted his stomach.

The hearth behind them was banked low that night, and hunting hounds lay beside it, yawning and waiting for bones.

Sir Marin, a middle-aged knight, inquired in a tone more amiable than Dval had expected, "I hear that you've come to investigate the murders? The Duke has placed me in charge of the matter. How can I help?"

For the next few minutes he divulged a few details of the victims, telling how they had been found, and where. He peered at them and then quickly glanced down to his food. Slipping a sidelong glance at Dval, he murmured with sincerity, "I wish you *well* in searching out this horror."

Dval glanced to the Despatcher for his reaction, but his master remained silent.

Should I push for more? Dval wondered. But he felt sure that this was not the time or place.

Search for the darkness, Dval thought, and he tried to reach out with his mind. He felt it here, in the room, but it sought to conceal itself. He felt it to the north and east, in the isles of Haversind. And he sensed a great darkness still farther to the east—the monstrous Toth.

We live in a world filled with more dangers than we know.

He felt quite unsettled. He looked again to his master and the Despatcher nodded ever so slightly.

After dinner, the duke's chamberlain greeted the Despatcher and Dval graciously outside the high double doors when they left the feast hall. "Rooms have been prepared for you. If you will come with me."

Dval stepped to follow, imagining with relish a feather bed up off the stone floor, not a tick filled with scratchy straw and fleas and the stale sweat of previous sleepers.

His master stopped him with a firm grip on his shoulder. "We are truly thankful for your lord's kindness," he told the chamberlain, "but we must be on the hunt tonight."

"Oh?" The chamberlain arched dark eyebrows.

"We are investigating the deaths of the two young women," the Despatcher said.

"Oh," the chamberlain repeated, not as a question this time. To Dval's curiosity, he leaned nearer to them, peered gravely from one to the other, and whispered, "Blessings upon you in your search."

* * *

The Despatcher headed north into the wilderness, as if to challenge the darkness. In two more days' travel they pressed through some deep redwood forests and then climbed some rolling hills to reach a giants' village on the border of Toom. The village had no houses or inns, merely a cluster of thirty or forty brutish lean-tos made of gray stone slabs on the leeward side of a large hill. The stones were splotched with lichens in shades of metallic green, gold, and crimson. Sheep and donkeys grazed the rolling slopes beyond, on rich grassland spotted with stands of wild apple trees and natural hedges of blackberry.

"Hill giants live there," his master had told him the day before. "You have met one of them, Sir Bandolan."

"Yes." Dval had met one. On the hillside where the queen's carriage had crashed, when he had been accused of it, the giant had pinned him to the soil with a massive foot, nearly cracking his ribs. Hours later they had fought a Toth queen together and Sir Bandolan had pulled him out from under its massive carcass after he felled it.

"Our king," his master said, "employs dozens of them in his armies as mercenaries, mainly up here in the north. We are seeking Bandolan's brother, Dalmodir. He is a sage, of sort—a master at sensing the shadows that surround us and battling them."

They found him in late afternoon, apart from the village, seated in a shelter at the edge of the forest and carving intricate patterns into the six-inch wings of his massive bow. His blade seemed too small for such great hands, but he wielded it deftly. In the summer's heat he wore only a kilt of gray-brown donkey hide. Colorful stones tied into his full beard clicked softly together when he lifted his head.

Runestones like the ones my master gave me? Dval wondered. *Very different from the rat skulls woven into Sir Bandolan's beard.*

Dval felt no darkness in the giant, only a soft burning glow, as if he held a hidden fire.

Dalmodir assessed them through coal-black eyes from beneath his craggy brow. He was as silent as a Despatcher himself. He slapped the flattened turf before him in an invitation to sit, with a hand that could have spanned Dval's chest.

The giants of Toom could not speak like normal men. Some oddness forced them to speak in rhyme, aside from the odd exclamation. Once Dval explained what he sought, Dalmodir's eyes flashed in anger and his voice grumbled like a thunderhead approaching over the mountains:

"Welcome, welcome, have no fear,
Though one must beware
Of all out here.
Though pirates roam,
The woods are home
To things of darker nature still."

Dval wondered what would be darker than the pirates' hearts. *Magic,* he decided. He had heard stories of spirits in these woods, malevolent creatures summoned by sorcerers. He shivered where he squatted at the thought of pirates dealing in the ancient arts. *Maybe there are other creatures, too. Maybe even a Toth sorceress.*

At times, the past few days, Dval had thought that he could sense unseen… essences, spirits.

Dalmodir cast him a critical stare as if sifting his thoughts, but Dval held his tongue. The giant said, "Hmph," applied his knife to his bow once more, and rumbled what seemed to Dval to be a mournful song.

"Two maidens died not in one night
But each when the moon gave its fullest light,
After it grew wan and dim
And waxed to fullness once again."

The girls were killed a month apart, under the full moon, Dval realized. *The moon is waxing again. There could be a third murder in another two weeks.* He shot a glance at his master.

"Where do the pirates land?" Dval wondered.

Dalmodir did not glance at either of them, but rumbled:

"Search for tumbled rocks and trees
Where cliffs cast brooding shadows upon the seas."

The Despatcher bowed in gratitude and pushed himself to his feet. "We have a night's work to do," he told Dval, and started eastward.

Yes, Dval thought. *I can sense the darkness there.* He felt eager to greet it. He fell silent as they rode through fen and wood, where gray squirrels barked warnings from trees and jays ratcheted.

Four or so miles on, the crash of heavy surf reached Dval's ears. In another mile, brine and fish scented the air, stronger than in the graaks' abandoned aerie, and the pastureland dropped off the edge of a cliff more than one hundred feet high.

They skirted along the coastline for some distance, peering over often while the sun sank gradually behind them, until they came upon a cove where a section of cliff had fallen away. In the deepening blue at its foot, Dval distinguished tumbled boulders and windswept pines stretching for the sky. "There," he told his master.

There was a beach in the inlet, a tiny spit of sand where there had not been one for miles. Dval recognized that of course it could serve as a natural harbor, where none other existed around here.

His master nodded approvingly.

Even bearing all his weapons, including his sword and warhammer, Dval found this descent easier than his midnight climb weeks earlier. He led the way in the darkness and found cover behind mounded rocks at one side of the crescent-shaped beach.

He could sense a rising darkness out over the sea, even though he could not see it.

The moon rose, half full, and climbed. It passed beyond the cliff's top, darkening their ambush still more. Finally, through the shush of waves spilling up the sand, came a lap of oars and muffled voices. Two boats appeared from the gloom, visible at first only by a torch held aloft in each.

Voices fell silent before their owners slipped over the gunwales, scarcely disturbing the water, to haul the boats to shore. Dval heard the paff, paff of feet, the hiss of keels on wet sand, and counted the black-clad shapes. Eighteen, counting the torchbearers.

His master touched Dval's arm for his attention and shaped soundless directives with his hands: "Cut them off from their boats. Torchbearers first, then kill them all."

All? By myself? Dval considered how to do it. Sneak up and kill the torchbearers first, leaving the narrow inlet in darkness, and then take the men. If this was a test, it would not be a hard one, he decided. With his night vision, he did not need torches to defend himself, but his victims would.

Dval answered with a curt nod, nocked an arrow to his bow, held a second in his teeth, and rose like a shadow from his cover. The first torchbearer flew backward with an arrow through his throat, blocking any outcry. Wet sand doused his flame and his counterpart whirled. Dval glimpsed the whites of wide eyes a heartbeat before his second arrow pierced the man.

A shout rose as blackness swallowed the cove. Night-blind, the pirates drew swords, staggered into one another. Dval traded bow for longsword and danced in among them, slashing and lunging. Most felt the swift tip of his blade at their throats, but two he shoved hard, impaling them on their mates' swinging swords. The tide, already receding, couldn't reach all the splattered stains, like iron-scented ink, to sweep them from the pale sand.

Dval executed them in moments and stood with heart hammering, staring at their corpses. He'd had to kill men before, but never in such numbers.

He felt for the darkness and found that its source was gone.

As Dval retrieved his arrows, then cleaned his blade and the arrow points, the Despatcher leapt down from the rocks onto the beach and said, "A good night's work, that, but I fear our task is not yet finished."

Dval weighed his master's words and knew that he had done something wrong. He'd been sent here as a test and he had failed it somehow, or only partly succeeded.

* * *

For days Dval and the Despatcher stayed in a small village, both of them awaiting some unheard signal. Then one day, Dval woke and knew it was time to head south. Three days later, Dval and his master stood in Duke Hamid's audience chamber. The air was fresh with the scent of mock-orange blossoms strewn upon the floor and the Duke seemed to be in good cheer.

"We have slain the pirates who ravaged your northern coasts, my lord," the Despatcher announced. "There will be no more maidens stolen from your lands."

As proof, the Despatcher threw down a bag filled with the dead pirates' rotting ears.

Duke Hamid smiled, smugly Dval thought. He noted the gleam in the man's eyes when he said, "I am forever grateful for the assistance of my brother the king's Despatchers. Let me reward you. We shall feast!"

The Despatcher only bowed courteously. "Alas, we cannot. We have far to go this night. Our king still fears that more Toth might beach this summer and so we must refuse your graciousness. It is time for us to turn south to the Courts of Tide."

"At least let me reward you," the Duke suggested. "I'll give you some fine horses to help hurry you on your way, and silver so that you might dine at the finest inns. The Stag and Brew is sixteen miles down the highway, but with good horses you could easily make it by nightfall."

Dval hoped their job done and felt happy with his reward. But six miles down the road from the castle, the Despatcher cautiously guided his horse and palfrey into the trees, into the duke's private hunting reserve, and began to circle back toward the northeast. No village stood within the preserve's wooded boundaries, Dval knew. No place of refuge for fleeing prey, when the moon rose to its full. Only groves of scrub oak and pine, interspersed with barren fields of wheat burned white by the summer sun.

To Dval's surprise, as they reached a grove of pines, the giant Dalmodir met them in the bracken, beside a track made by the regular passage of many horses. At eight feet tall, he had to duck and stand between the lowest branches beneath the pines. He greeted them with an incline of his head, swung his warclub off his shoulder, peered about, grunted as if he had just made a discovery, and said:

"Behold the dark and awful place
Where the damsels' hunters love to race."

Dval wondered. There is no way that the giant could have communicated with the Despatcher. Not a word, not a note. Yet the Despatcher did not seem at all surprised.

They serve the same master, Dval realized, to his embarrassment, *and they have been summoned here. Yet I did not hear the call!*

Something inside him broke and he let out a whimper, resolving to listen harder, to learn to hear his true Master's voice.

Then he felt it—bloodstains on the ground all around him. The blood seemed to rise up like screams that chilled his spine and made him tremble. He felt the killing field.

Dval and his master dismounted and tied their horses in dense growths of oak a hundred yards away. Then they and the giant hunkered down on a hillock overlooking the forest to wait for nightfall.

Shortly after the setting of the sun, the moon rose bright and full, though it was bloody red from the cooking fires of a port city to the east.

They did not have to wait more than two hours past sunset.

Dval heard the girl's voice first, rising from the plains in the far distance, perhaps a mile away. Most likely, his master was not quite aware of it, for humans did not hear well.

Dval heard shrieks high with indignity and fear, but not panic. No gibbering or blubbering; she still had wit enough to protest her capture, to demand, "Let me go! What crime have I committed?"

The roar of a man's laughter gave answer, vicious and unmistakably drunken. "Your crime, my bird?" he slurred. "Is beauty now a crime? No, unless it be flaunting your beauty in the market. ... Yes." Another deep chuckle rolled forth. "That *is* your crime, and fanning to flames my hunger for it. ... Such piracy! For that you must pay me by satisfying my hunger when I catch you at the end of the chase."

Shock stiffened Dval where he stood. It was the duke's voice! *But he is a runelord. He has sworn fealty to his people, to use his endowments to pro-*

tect them, not destroy. By such deeds as this he breaks his oaths.

"My lord, do not this thing," the unseen girl cried. "I beg of you by all that's worthy!"

Once again raucous laughter echoed among the trees. He heard the muted plod of hooves on loam and the duke shouted, "Strip her and release her! Hold fast the dogs."

The girl screamed again, still unseen at this distance. But soon, orange torchlight appeared, dancing between trunks black as cinders. The torches halted and wavered on a gust. Dval heard cloth ripping and the girl's gasps and cries, outraged as much as frightened, and more chuckles at her distress.

Jaw and fists clenched, he questioned his master and the giant with a glance.

The Despatcher gestured toward the track below. "Wait for the maiden there," he murmured. "We will see to this duke."

When Dalmodir nodded agreement, Dval sprang away and raced down among the trees. He ran fleet-footed and silently for two minutes, scaring up a pair of stags that had been grazing in the grass.

He reached the trail. A limbless hulk of a long-dead oak leaned low over the track, forcing it to curve. His soft boots trod fallen leaves and twigs without a sound as he melded with the shadows of its hollow bole.

On a thought, he released his cloak's clasp at his throat, his long cloak with its deep hood, sewn by Sergeant Goreich's wife to protect his white skin from the sun. It was black as night and offered perfect concealment, turning its wearer into a shadow. *I have no need of it here,* he thought, *but this girl does.*

Her panting sobs reached his ears before he heard the hurried pats of her bare feet on the forest floor. The full moon's glow made a ghost of her in the blue-black night, running on long legs with her arms crossed over her breasts and her loosed hair rippling behind.

A shout sounded from the direction that she'd come and she cast a swift glance backward. Moonlight glistened silver from tears that streaked her face, but Dval saw determination in the set of her fine chin and the way her eyes searched the forest.

As she drew even with him, he sprang, cloak stretched out like the sail of a small ship in a fair wind, and wrapped it snugly about her. She cried out, a startled sound muffled by the cloak, and thrust an elbow into Dval's chest hard enough to take his breath. He gasped, but kept his hold. "Hush!" he hissed at her ear, and pulled her into the dead tree's shadow. "I came to help you. Watch."

A horse appeared up the track, mincing ahead of the men who bore the torches and restrained the wolfhounds on their taut leashes. Ears flicking every direction, it snorted through extended nostrils and advanced in small jumps. When it drew near enough that Dval could see the whites of its rolling eyes and the drunken leer of its rider, the girl shuddered against him.

Something man-sized hurtled from the undergrowth at the horse's feet, spinning a cloak in its face. The beast reared onto its hind legs with a squeal and thrashed the air with its forehooves. The duke somersaulted from his saddle, arms and legs flailing. He struck the turf hard on his back as his mount wheeled and lunged toward the castle, sending the men on foot sprawling. Dval heard the crash of underbrush and the yip of a kicked dog as the torch went out.

The bulky form in the dirt before him stirred and groaned. Dalmodir, club resting on his shoulder once more, stepped into the moonlight to join the Despatcher, who had approval emanating from his deep-set eyes.

The Despatcher motioned to Dval. "Remember the oath that you swore on the mountain."

And Dval suddenly understood his true test.

The words his master had spoken there rose clearly in his mind: "More often than not, my son, the greatest dangers to our kingdom arise from within. Sometimes we are called upon to do what men of good conscience cannot."

After them echoed his own words, spoken with his hands on his heart and his sword. "To protect the king and every person of Mystarria, whether great or lowly, from all enemies, within and without our land, in whatever form they may take, and to stand against the darkness."

Sometimes, Dval thought, *our duty is to protect the people from their lords.* He glanced at the girl, huddled in his cloak at his shoulder, and queried his master with his eyes.

"A petty, ignoble execution for an ignoble man," the Despatcher said.

Dval peered down at the Duke. There was a deep shadow in him, revolting and twisted. He had not seen it before and he realized something. The Duke was drunk, a cruel and dangerous drunk, and under its influence, it seemed that he had become a new creature, more foul and loathsome than a pirate.

Dval sank to his knees beside the duke. The man was so drunk that he now simply moaned in a fitful sleep, tossing his head from side to side.

My Master, the Glory, has been leading me here all along, knowing what we must do. Dval had worried that he himself might be an oathbreaker, but now he had an opportunity to prove himself.

A scuff and a rustle wrenched his attention upwards. The duke's men stood rigid mere yards away, Sir Marin's face as pale as the moon itself, as if he feared for his own life.

The Despatcher stood at Dval's back. "You will tell them," the Despatcher ordered, "that the duke died in a fall from his horse." Every word carried its own warning and Dval knew that his master's eyes, leveled on each of the men in turn, reinforced his threat.

None of them replied. The Despatcher nodded to Dval.

Dval studied Sir Marin and the men and thought he saw relief hidden beneath their fear. Like him, they were mere servants, following orders.

The duke stirred again and stared at Dval, eyes glazed with drink but wide with sudden fear.

"Oathbreaker," Dval whispered, and snapped his neck.

Blood and Onyx

R.K. Nickel

It was common knowledge that no one could steal from the queen.

That's why the guild sent Rivyn.

He crouched atop the roof of the blacksmith's shop, hidden behind the billowing smoke of the chimney. From here, he could study the movements of the palace guards as they circled round and round the high stone wall.

To the west, the sun licked the horizon. Almost time.

Rivyn hated the moments of waiting. Waiting meant time to think. Was he really going to break into the best-guarded building in the sovereignty? The last Soul Runner who'd gone after the queen's jewel had ended up extremely dead. Rivyn could attest to that. The royal alchemist had pickled the head and kept it in a glass display above the castle gates for a year and a day. The queen had never been kind, but it seemed as though, the last few years, she'd grown especially cruel.

But if he turned back, the guild would suspend its contracts and send every member after him. They couldn't take over his soul; no Runner could Bind another of their kind. But when they found him—for they would find him—the punishment would make the Ritual look like a night out with friends. Or so he assumed. Friends were a luxury Soul Runners were forced to eschew. No, if he wanted to keep his head, he'd simply have to play the role of fearless thief.

Action is identity.

Pretend to be brave, you are brave. Steal, and you're a thief.

There—on the wall—the guard Rivyn had seduced a few weeks prior. Rivyn cracked his knuckles, then scampered to the edge of the roof, drawing a shuriken from his belt. *You were a terrible lay*, he thought as he rolled the shuriken across his left arm, each of the four points drawing a pinprick of blood. He cocked his arm back. Waited. Waited. *Now.*

As the shuriken tumbled through the air, Rivyn thought he could just make out his glistening blood on the black blade. And then it struck home, right in the flesh of the guard's left shoulder.

Rivyn focused, channeling his will. Then Leapt.

The world constricted, light and dark merging into a single pinhole of lurching existence as an inexorable force tugged Rivyn forward. He burned with elation, with unfettered momentum. He was everywhere, and nowhere, and felt a whole lot like throwing up.

And then he was atop the wall, looking back at the chimney. The woman who had been Rivyn spun about, clearly confused, horrified. Rivyn had Bound her for nearly five weeks. It was a long time for a consciousness to be trapped, tamped down beneath a greater mind. She would remember none of it, of course—just a gap where her life should have been. Nothing of seducing the guard, nothing of the nights in the tavern, plying men for information. For five weeks, she had not existed. There had been no *she*. She was simply Rivyn.

Action is identity. And she had taken none.

Rivyn considered killing her—the guard had a dagger at his hip that would likely fly true, and it was certainly what the guild would have wanted, but whom would the woman tell?

Instead, he turned his attention toward the palace. This body was larger, heavier. But stronger, too. Rivyn felt the weight of the leather armor upon him, the remnants of a heavy meal sloshing in his stomach. His bladder was full to bursting. Why couldn't people take care of themselves?

There was nothing for it now. Ever since the previous Soul Runner's attempt, the Queensguard had been especially attentive to unusual behavior, like, say, pissing from atop the outer wall. So he'd simply have to hold it in. Rivyn pulled the shuriken from his flesh, grimacing. At least he wouldn't have to run it across his skin a second time. The blade already glistened with the guard's blood—his blood.

Bloodforged.

His thoughts flickered briefly to the ritual. Nearly a decade prior, but you never forgot your first time. Lying on the altar, a youth of sixteen, surrounded by the Unbodied—the guild's most elite assassins. And beside him, mouth gagged, limbs strapped down, the first person he would Bind. A stocky lad with short-cropped hair. An orphan, someone nobody would miss. Rivyn still remembered his eyes. Hazel. And filled with a fear Rivyn had never seen.

And then they'd plunged the onyx dagger into Rivyn's heart. The Blade of Making. There'd been a brief moment of darkness, followed by that now-familiar pull as he'd been drawn to the bloodforged wound. They'd driven an onyx spike through the orphan's left hand, and that's where Rivyn had entered.

The body he'd known his whole life was gone, a sack of flesh, and yet Rivyn lived—the true Rivyn, the idea of Rivyn, the mind. The *actions*. And once someone made his first Leap, became a being of consciousness, the path was ever open.

The bell rang in the royal tower. The changing of the guard. Hoping no one would notice the few drops of blood around his shoulder, Rivyn descended the stairs to the inner courtyard. Someone was coming his way.

"Samson," said a fellow guard.

"Alistair," Rivyn replied, then reached out his hand. They shook, interlocking their little fingers. It'd cost Rivyn a hundred claws worth of ale to get that out of one of the castle staff.

"The sun rises," said the guard.

"The panther stalks its prey."

The guard nodded, then released Rivyn's hand. The Queensguard changed the call and response weekly to ensure that everyone was who they appeared. Clearly that wasn't often enough.

Rivyn continued toward the barracks.

"Hey, Samson," called the guard before Rivyn had taken even three paces. "Aren't you forgetting something?"

Rivyn turned, slowly, mind racing.

"What do you mean?" he asked, fingers dropping to his belt, feeling the outline of the hidden shuriken.

"You still owe me for the girls last night, you dog."

Rivyn relaxed. "Yeah, yeah. Whaddaya say I meet you at Mistress Taneal's after your shift and we do it all over again. I'll cover."

"I like the way you think." Alistair flashed a devilish grin. *Men. Always making decisions with the smaller head.*

As soon as Alistair was out of sight, Rivyn turned away from the barracks and ducked into the kitchens. The smell of baking bread immediately assaulted his nostrils. This jerk may have been terrible in bed, but damn did he have a great sense of smell. No wonder there was so much food sloshing around in his stomach. If Rivyn's last body had been this adept at discerning the intricacies of the wafting oats and barley, he'd hardly have been able to resist.

The lone kitchen maid on duty looked up from her work and dropped a dish in surprise. It landed with a shattering crash. "Now look what you made me do," she said.

"Apologies," Rivyn mumbled, adding what he hoped was an appropriate level of shame to his gravelly voice. A constellation of freckles dotted the girl's face. This had to be the one.

"You were in here not but three hours ago, mister," she said, beginning to pick up the ceramic pieces from the floor. "Someone's going to get suspicious."

"I know, but I just can't help myself, m'lady."

"I'm no lady."

Rivyn bent down and helped stack the broken slivers. He looked at her. Their faces were close. She smiled.

Rivyn closed his hand around one of the sharper fragments, squeezing until a few drops of blood dripped between his fingers. Soul Runners quickly learned to tolerate a high threshold of pain.

"Heavens, Sam. Will you never learn to be more delicate with those ogre's hands? Come here." She took his arm.

"I don't want you to get in trouble for leaving the oven unattended."

"And what will cook say if she finds blood all over her kitchen? It won't take but a moment." She grabbed a cloth napkin and led him to the pantry, which she unlocked with nimble fingers.

"Now let me see," she said, closing the door behind them.

Rivyn thrust the sharp ceramic edge into her stomach, making sure not to cut too deep. "Apologies again, m'lady." Her eyes opened wide in surprise, and Rivyn Leapt.

The familiar pull took him, the darkness, the heavy, pounding pressure, weightlessness, the endless, throbbing tug, a tearing of the mind.

He pulled the makeshift weapon from his stomach and, just as Samson moved to cry out, rammed it into his neck. The kitchen maid's arms were surprisingly strong—kneading dough was its own sort of training—and despite her shorter stature, he had no trouble slicing straight into the jugular.

"She deserves better than you anyway. Fooling around at Mistress Ta-neal's."

Action is identity. Repeatedly cheat on the woman who loves you, you're a shitty person. And in this case, a dead one.

Rivyn looked over his clothes. Not too bad. He grabbed a fresh apron, then removed the shuriken from Samson's belt and tucked it into a sock.

He stepped back out into the kitchen, locking the pantry behind him, then took the fire poker from beneath the oven, thrust it into the flames, and cauterized the small wound in his stomach. *Gods be damned.* He clenched his teeth, trying to hold in as much of his scream as possible. Nothing hurt worse than burning flesh. But one couldn't wander around bleeding all over one's dress.

Now, to complete the disguise. Rivyn slipped the apron over his neck, concealing the blood on his dress, then looked around until he spotted what he needed: a tray loaded with fresh-made breads and marbled cheeses. He quickly picked up a cheese grater, then scraped it along the edge of the fire poker, which still had little bits of blood and flesh stuck to it. Thin metal shavings flaked off, and he forced them into the soft cheese.

"What are you doing?"

He hadn't heard anyone enter. Bad hearing? Great. It was always some-thing. What had the cook seen? Rivyn waited, tense.

"You were supposed to be upstairs five minutes ago."

"Of course. Going now." Rivyn tried to imitate the kitchen maid's in-flection. He should've gotten her to talk more. Rivyn took up the tray and hurried toward the exit, ferreting away a couple of napkins as he went.

"Fool girl," said the cook. "I ought to leave you to the jungle."

Just another girl without options. Like Rivyn had been. But if he com-pleted his task, the guild would have no choice but to make him one of the Unbodied. For the last decade, he'd been yoked, tugged wherever the guild desired. He'd joined because he wanted to be someone else. And now he'd give anything to be, well, someone.

No, he was someone. As long as he moved forward, made choices, took action, he was Rivyn. Still, a little freedom would be nice. A chance to sit beside a fire and read a book. To sleep with someone not because they had information, but because he was attracted to them.

What a thought.

And yet, even still, he could never feel at home, for always he'd be riding in an unnatural body, little more than a parasite. A powerful one, but a parasite nonetheless.

Maybe one day, once he'd proven himself a worthy Unbodied, he'd find someone in the guild to, well, not to settle down with, but to be a companion. Someone he could work beside, who understood his condition and his sacrifice, someone who loved him entirely for him, no matter which body he happened to reside in.

He reached the harem and, with a nod from the guards on duty, entered.

"Which one of you is serving the queen tonight?" he asked, puffing out his breasts a little.

"I am," said a gorgeous young man. Shirtless, he seemed mostly to be a solid block of abs. Exactly what the queen would want. Her lust was legendary. And legendarily shallow.

"The queen's meal," Rivyn said, trying to add a touch of flirtation to his tone.

If they'd simply wanted to poison the queen, how easy it would have been. But her treasure would be less valuable in an unstable market. And easy was a relative term, Rivyn supposed. This theft had been two years in the planning.

The queen's treasure, Rivyn thought as the slave took the tray. Though the Unbodied had tried to make the job sound routine, Rivyn wondered what jewel would truly be worth the risk. In Rivyn's experience, wealth was ephemeral. The sovereignty's true currency was information. With the right leverage, the guild would be able to elevate itself, cementing a place of power beyond the queen's scrutiny.

"She requested that you to bring it to her right away," Rivyn said to the slave and, with a slight bow, headed for the door. The man followed close behind.

After he'd gone a few steps back toward the kitchen, Rivyn stopped in his tracks. "Oh no," he said, then turned to the harem guards. "I forgot to set out the napkins. Please, the cook will have my head."

"Go on then," said the taller of the pair.

"Thank you. Oh, thank you. Stop by the kitchen in a couple of hours and I promise I'll make the two of you something special."

"Much appreciated," replied the guard. In Rivyn's experience, a man's stomach did nearly as much thinking as his groin.

It wasn't long until Rivyn caught up to tonight's meal. Both of tonight's meals. "Excuse me," he said meekly. "I'm terribly sorry, but I forgot the napkins. Here." He set them on the tray.

"Thank you." The pleasure slave turned to go.

"And, uh …"

The man gave Rivyn a withering glare. "Yes?"

"Tonight was my first time in charge of the cheeses. Could you, could you try some? I want to make sure I didn't make any mistakes."

His eyes narrowed. This was not going well. But Rivyn didn't dare use any of his usual methods. He needed the man's body to stay perfectly intact. After all, the queen would be seeing it completely naked. A single wound meant his task would be ruined and his life forfeit.

"You seem awfully nervous," said the slave.

"It's just, the cook beats me something fierce whenever I get anything wrong, but I've never been good with numbers, and just last week I added twice as much flour to the bread as I should have, and I think I might have put in entirely too little salt, and—"

Rivyn cut himself off mid-sentence. He could see he was making no headway. "Oh, forget it. I'll just take my chances with the cook. I hope you enjoy your meal. I slaved over it."

Rivyn turned and stomped off. But just before he rounded the corner—

"Wait." The man took a bite of cheese.

"It's good," he muttered.

"Thank you," said Rivyn, suddenly aware of the bloodforge created by dozens of immeasurably small cuts in the man's throat. Swallowed shavings were a Soul Runner's dirtiest trick—effective and nearly undetectable. "Sadly, I had nothing to do with it."

Rivyn Leapt, felt himself slip into the black, into the place that was no place—then dove forward and tackled the kitchen maid, wrestling her to the ground before she could gain her bearings. Rivyn almost laughed. The pleasure slave might look amazing, but the maid was the stronger of the pair. Beauty over utility. Or perhaps in the slave's case, beauty was utility. The maid tried to shout, but Rivyn slammed an elbow into her neck, bruising her windpipe. "Quiet."

He ripped off her dress, eliciting a fearful whimper. *Gods, what must she think of me?* "I'm not going to hurt you. I could, but I'm not." Rivyn tore the dress into strips. The material was tough. "Mostly because Samson was an asshole." Her face grew even more terrified. "Yes, I know Samson. He was bedding other women." Rivyn gagged the girl, tied her arms and legs, then dragged her into the first room he found—guest chambers, clearly unused at the moment. He dropped her into the bathtub, then grabbed his shuriken from her sock.

"If you tell anyone about this, if you whisper one single word, my guild *will* murder you. It could come from anyone. A friend. A mother. A lover. And we will dispose of that person when we're done with their body. You were attacked by a thief, just a thief. Do you understand?"

She nodded, eyes wide with fear.

"Someone will find you," he said, turning to go.

It was dangerous to let her live, and she'd always bear that unfortunate scar, but still, he did the right thing sometimes. When possible.

* * *

"Ah, excellent choice," said the queen as Rivyn stepped into her bed-chamber.

Rivyn took in his target. As a common woman, she would have looked, well, common, but dressed as she was in a formfitting slip of shimmering green, she did indeed look like someone who would indulge her lusts. Her hair fell draped around her smooth shoulders and a jet-black necklace plunged between her breasts, disappearing beneath the fabric of her dress. There was a hardness to her eyes he had not expected, a world-weary wisdom he was used to seeing in the faces of urchins struggling to survive on the humid streets.

"My queen," Rivyn said, carefully setting down the food on an oaken table.

Now came the hardest part. The guild didn't want the queen to fear Soul Runners any more than she already did. They certainly didn't want her to know that they could infiltrate her chambers. Which meant Rivyn couldn't simply Bind her and walk away with the jewel. Instead, he needed to play the game. He was a pleasure slave. He would provide pleasure. And when she fell asleep, he would find the jewel and escape. Betrayal by a kept man was hardly unreasonable. In fact, the papers falsifying the slave's disloyalty were already in the right hands.

His success all rested on whether he could be the person she wanted that night.

Action is identity. Provide pleasure under orders, you're a pleasure slave.

Rivyn sauntered toward her, preparing himself. The queen was not known for her gentle touch, but Rivyn had been through worse. "What would my queen desire this evening?"

The queen quirked her head, examining him. "Tell me about yourself, slave."

Odd. "What would you like to know?"

"Tell me what you most long for."

"I live only to pleasure you, your majesty."

The queen sat down on the edge of her bed and took up a pitcher of wine from a standing table. She poured a glass, then held it out toward Rivyn.

"Here. Drink."

"As you wish." Rivyn took the wine. This was not what he had expected. He couldn't tell yet if the difference meant danger.

She poured herself a glass, raised it, and drank. Rivyn joined her.

"There. Now we've broken bread. So tell me, what is it you most long for? And I do not want to hear a second lie."

"What lie?" Rivyn asked.

She narrowed her eyes at that. "A dishonest question is dangerously close to a lie, slave."

"I am uncertain that it would be wise to speak." Her face hardened and something in her look dragged the truth from him. "I would … like to be free."

"And why would you like to be free?" she asked. Rivyn sensed there was a deeper game at work, but he could not decide what it was.

"I …" Rivyn worked to think as a slave and quickly found it was not such a difficult part to play. Was he not a slave to the guild? They had rescued him from the streets, certainly, but they had ripped away his mortal body, leaving him as nothing more than an endlessly running consciousness, forever at their beck and call. To settle into a final body would be to consign the person he chose to Bind to a fate akin to death, and even then, he could never successfully evade capture by the guild, could he?

"I am not sure," Rivyn finished.

"That," said the queen, "I believe."

"Perhaps it was a foolish thought." Rivyn stood and began to slip off his shirt. "Now, let us put it aside."

"Hush. I am not finished with you."

Why did she refuse him? Had he picked the wrong body? Rivyn tensed, preparing for the worst.

"I know what it is to be trapped," she said, casting her gaze about the room. "The cells are lavish, but a queen is slave to duty, to her people, to her station. We are all trapped in one way or another."

"It is not the same, your majesty."

"No, I suppose it is not." She took a sip of wine. "Please, call me Anshalla. You expect to be my lover. Lovers should treat each other as people. Sex without intimacy is an empty thing."

Something was terribly wrong. The queen—Anshalla—seeking intimacy? Impossible. She knew. She had to know.

Rivyn worked to control his breathing. He would not tip his hand. Not yet. If he could just get closer, perhaps he could forge a connection by blood and Bind her. The guild would not be pleased. Not by half. But it was better than a catastrophic failure.

"We are on this turning world but a brief time," she said, eyes piercing, refusing to let him look away. "Would you truly spend it in fear? Each moment is one of choice. Each moment a chance to change our fate, to tell those who shackle us: 'No longer.'"

"Why are you telling me this?" Rivyn asked, thoughts spinning.

"Because I would rather this night end peaceably, Soul Runner."

Damn.

Rivyn shot into motion, hurling the wine into the queen's face. As she recoiled, he already had his shuriken in hand. It flew through the air, just behind the wine. She stood, turning to her side instinctively, but she wasn't fast enough and one of the blade's sharp corners nicked the flesh of her right arm. Little more than a scratch, but it was enough.

Rivyn Leapt.

He felt himself—

He felt himself rooted exactly where he'd begun. No darkness. No otherworldly pull. Nothing.

He Leapt again, shutting his eyes, focusing his will—and remained.

"What—"

"I said I would prefer to resolve this peaceably." She stood. "You Soul Runners are all the same. Guild puppets, to the core."

"It's not possible."

"Do not presume to tell me what is possible," she said, wiping the wine from her face with a sleeve.

There was only one way to gain immunity to the bloodforge.

"You're—"

"Yes. I'm one of you. A secret which, unfortunately, must remain close to the breast." She pulled a long knife from a hidden compartment beneath her bed.

"How did you know? I was careful."

"I knew because you are not my Damian. I keep up pretenses, but I must admit that I am a romantic. While I take many bodies to my bed, I always truly take only one lover. One man, one mind, but each day, different flesh. Endless variety, and the slaves themselves need never be involved. But Damian is delivering a missive to a subject at the Outskirts. His return is at least an hour off."

Rivyn could hardly process what he was hearing. Another Soul Runner? Who was he? Who was she?

She struck.

A blur of beauty and silver, stained red with wine. Rivyn barely had time to roll out of the way. He was a formidable fighter, but he'd never practiced fighting fair and he'd had no time to familiarize himself with this body.

She came at him, a blinding blade. Rivyn grabbed the tray and hefted it to block the blow. The steel clanged with a note he knew would ring through the palace.

"Shit," he said. *Think, Rivyn. Think.*

He needed to escape. To flee and take his chances in the wilds. Without the queen's treasure, whatever it might be, there would be no returning to the guild. And he knew their secret—they had failed to control one of their own. A secret they would surely kill to keep.

The doors burst open and guards poured in. A dozen of them, each armed and armored, men of training. Any of them alone might pose a threat. But twelve? Rivyn had died the moment the queen had seen through his flesh to the man beneath. It had simply taken this long for the blade to reach the soft of his neck.

"Assassin!" shouted one of the guards, and boots clamored. Swords rang from scabbards. Shouts filled the air and Rivyn felt it grow heavy with heat, as if the warmth of the jungle beyond had somehow been sucked into the room. He blocked another swing of the queen's blade—of course she could fight; she'd been trained just as he had—and the tray split in two.

His shield was gone, and with it, his time.

The guards were nearly on him. The guards … *the guards.*

With the split-second awareness of battle, Rivyn saw the tray in his hands. The queen's blade had left a sharp edge. Rivyn twisted, in a single motion dragging half the tray across his arm and hurling it at an oncoming guard. Two feet away, a foot, and the tray impacted, digging into the leather at the man's leg.

Please, Rivyn thought.

He focused his will. And Leapt.

Darkness. A gut-twisting forward drop. Light.

Rivyn's vision snapped into place just in time for him to see his own hand running the pleasure slave through with his sword.

Adrenaline coursed through this body, which pulsed with strength. He felt the armor where it touched him, felt the sting of the shallow cut on his leg, just above a strap that held a dagger. A thousand nerves giving him information at near-instant speed.

"Good work, Merrick," said another guard.

"He's a Soul Runner!" the queen shouted, coming at him. "Don't let him cut you."

Before they could react, Rivyn ran, bowling past them and to the door.

An alarum rang through the palace. Bells. So many bells. And a few fleet footsteps behind him, the queen, giving chase.

He turned a corner and smashed into a behemoth of a man. The two tumbled to the ground. Before the guard could recover, Rivyn pulled the dagger from his leg and stabbed the guard through the neck. But the queen was on him, blade swinging down.

Rivyn rolled, came to his feet, drew his own sword. Their weapons met, trading blows, dancing forward and back, gaining ground, losing ground, and beneath them, the guard's blood spread slick upon the hall's stone floor.

She's good, he thought, *but rusty. Too many years of comfort.* But how many years?

"The Soul Runner those years ago," he said, landing a kick that sent her tumbling back. She slipped on the red-stained rock and landed heavily. "It was you."

"No," she replied from the ground. "It was merely the body that carried me. A body I put on display to show my 'failure.'"

"And who would doubt that one of us had lost their life to the best-protected woman in the sovereignty?"

"Some have, but I've done well rooting out those who've suspected me. Though clearly someone in the guild still harbors suspicions." She clenched her jaw. "You know, Soul Runner, the guild is not an organization worth obeying. They are slavers, murderers."

"As are you."

Why do I not press my advantage? He willed himself to plunge his sword into her heart. But he knew the reason. She had escaped. She had escaped to live her own life. Though he had never allowed himself to truly consider the possibility before, Rivyn did want to be free. He'd hardly known it, but it was a yearning, deep down. Not in his gut, for he had none—at least, none that truly belonged to him—it was a yearning of mind, of spirit, a lust for life that went beyond thought. He'd seen it in stallions and in slaves.

And she had fulfilled that yearning.

But there'd been only one Soul Runner sent to infiltrate the palace that day ...

"Your lover ..."

She leapt to her feet, and their fight raged once more, flowing down the hall. Behind him, a guard came running. Rivyn cut himself, hurled his dagger, and Leapt, putting a hall's distance between him and the queen. But another guard appeared, and the queen threw a shuriken of her own—where had she been keeping that?—and then she was beside him. This time, in a stronger, deadlier body.

Back where they'd come from, the girl who years ago had been the queen began to scream. A soul-piercing scream. Rivyn and the false queen threw their hands to their ears. It was the scream of the mad.

Her mind had been trapped for years, tamped down. Hosts didn't remember what happened while they were Bound—that much they knew. Or at least thought they knew. Rarely had a Soul Runner lived in one body for so long. What might seep through? What horror might a trapped mind experience?

Rivyn recovered from the shock and once more ran. The false queen once more gave chase.

They sprinted down halls, traded blows, Leapt from guard to guard, gaining distance, causing wounds, stealing bodies.

Rivyn had danced once, long ago. Just the once, back before he'd become a being of mind. He'd scampered onto the grounds of one of the nobles, hoping to steal a bit of food from a feast spread upon a table. When he'd made it over the wall, he'd been struck by the beauty of the gardens, the grace of the people, the rhythm of the music.

There, he'd met a girl. Lashiva. Perhaps a year or two older than he and clearly there for the same reason. They'd stuffed their mouths, then their pockets, then scurried out of sight. But neither one of them could bring themselves to escape immediately. They hid behind a great hedge, laughing at their spoils, swaying to the music that drifted across the estate.

Once or twice before, the older boys Rivyn ran with had forced him to drink until he grew sick, but that night, that music, that girl—it was an intoxication of an entirely different nature. Somehow, the two had found each other's arms and they'd rocked back and forth together, the world beyond bleeding away into nothing.

And then the song had ended, and they'd been spotted, and Rivyn had fled. He never knew what happened to her.

He often thought it was the most beautiful moment of his life. Back when life had been his.

This, here in the castle, with the queen, was almost as beautiful. The music was that of swords, thunderous percussion that melted into high, ringing tones. The garden was one of stone and blood. The dance was a dance of death. And yet they did dance.

And the kinship was the same.

Here, Rivyn had found someone who truly understood him, and fate had placed them at opposite ends of a blade.

They twirled, thrusted, parried. Any guard they encountered had no time to react, stunned by the confusion of two of their brethren fighting so beautifully.

They did not tire, for when their muscles began to burn, they found themselves a fresh host, and their lungs filled with fresh air, and the dance began anew.

Until suddenly, the long-ago queen barreled into the hall from a side room.

They stopped. The false queen could not risk harming the girl, for once their fight was over, she would have to return to her guise. Rivyn, however…

Rivyn leapt forward and slid his arm around the queen's neck, holding his sword to her throat.

"If you kill her," said his fellow Soul Runner, "we both become outcasts, hunted by the guild."

"If I nick her throat," Rivyn said, "I become you."

The queen, the Soul Runner, the guard, grimaced.

"Maybe I should kill her," said Rivyn. "I can think of worse fates than running with you by my side."

"I'm sorry," spoke the false queen.

"Don't tell me you didn't sense it. We are cut from the same flesh. Think of what we could accomplish. Two Soul Runners together. We just might be able to escape."

"I think I could have killed you," she said, musing.

"I think I could have killed you."

She smiled, a sad smile. "I've already found my companion."

The young queen tried to speak, but Rivyn pressed his blade tighter, drawing blood. He felt the bloodforge then. After all, this sword had wounded his current body mere moments before. A focusing of will and he could become the queen.

"What do you want?" asked the other Soul Runner.

"You asked me that already."

"And?"

What did he want? Perhaps he should simply ask for the jewel and return to the guild. If he submitted to their mercy, they might allow him to live.

The jewel.

Rivyn felt something beneath his fingertips. A necklace. He curled his hand around it—there was a weight at the bottom, concealed beneath her dress. He lifted, slowly. The false queen's eyes watched him from across the hall, fierce.

And then he saw it. The object of his hunt.

An onyx dagger, dangling beside an onyx spike. The Blade and Nail of Making.

"Now you know why they pursue me."

"Damian," said Rivyn.

"I wanted a lover who would understand me. Not the flesh I wear, but *me*."

He had the jewel. He had the queen. His mission was complete. Bloodier than expected, and sure to unleash a hellstorm of retribution. But complete all the same.

He could Bind the queen, return the jewel. With such a powerful prize in hand, the guild would surely overlook his transgressions, especially if he killed this rogue Soul Runner. What a thorn she must have been, and still they'd kept her quiet.

How many others must there be out there, Soul Runners who'd escaped the guild's grasp? Each of them staying silent so that they would not be pursued, each of them playing right into the guild's lie that they had the power to punish any who sought freedom.

But Rivyn could change that. He could wander the sovereignty until he found someone he loved, and together, they could search for a pair of hosts who truly deserved death. He could forge himself a companion, and they could take the bodies without remorse. Together, they would live out their days somewhere and finally, when the time came, they would reveal themselves, a message of hope for all those who thought the guild was unassailable.

"You've made your companion," said Rivyn. "Let me have mine."

She looked at him then, considering. "You'd turn against the guild?"

"It seems to me," Rivyn said, "that perhaps we are not as easy to hunt as they say."

"We are not," she said, a smile gracing the great, bearded face she wore.

Rivyn snapped the blade and nail free from the girl's neck, then released her, tossing his sword to his once-opponent. She caught it, nodded, and drew the blade across her skin. The true queen's blood was upon it already. The forge would take but a moment.

Rivyn tilted his head, then turned and walked to the nearest window. He climbed onto the ledge and looked below. An easy jump, and from there only a few steps to escape the palace. He breathed in the cool night air with new lungs and cast his gaze once more toward the horizon. His sight was clear, his eyes sharp. Sharper than they'd been in any body since his first. As sharp, even, as the blade that rested in his palm. One day, he would put it to use. One day, he would draw blood and forge himself a new path.

But for now, he simply leapt.

The Charter

Ashley McConnell

"My lord, goodmen, and goodwife," the man at the podium said, leaning forward to glare at his audience. That audience, consisting of the two masters Vettazen and Firaloy, and the three apprentices sitting at the end of the bench against the wall, shifted uneasily.

My lord? Jazen thought, glancing over at Adri-nes. The man had definitely nodded in Adri's direction when he said it. Adri, for his part, leaned back, as if the bench actually had something to lean against, and returned only a polite, noncommittal smile. He, Meleas, and Jazen were not supposed to be important enough to acknowledge here.

"My lord the Chancellor has received your petition and has been pleased to send me today to review it. But I must tell you I am not inclined to recommend that he support it."

"And why might that be?" Vettazen, seated at the far end of the high table, asked mildly. "Ser Immatus, the petition is entirely in order. In form and content it is entirely unexceptional. It follows several such petitions point by point, each of which were approved without challenge or…" she paused delicately, "review." Next to her, Firaloy nodded in emphatic agreement. "We seek to study magic, to organize those with the gifts, to better understand them."

Immatus tore his attention away from Adri with difficulty. "Oh. Well, it is simplicity itself, Goodwife. In form I must agree, your petition for establishment of a Guild of your own is entirely unexceptional. But in content? No. I cannot agree. It is filled with nonsense, errors obvious to the merest child!

"My lord, Gentles, you are applying for a Guild Charter to study *magic*."

"Yes?" Vettazen encouraged. "As I said." *You idiot*, she did not add, though Jazen could hear the words in her tone.

Apparently Immatus could not. "But there is no need to study *magic*. We know the origins and source of all magic in the world. We have always known. Magic is demonic. It comes from the Yaan Maat. We do not need to study magic, we need to *destroy* it, whenever and wherever we find it, just as we destroyed the Yaan Maat. We do not need a Guild for that."

It sounded very firm and definitive, which made Immatus's yelp of surprise even funnier when one of the workmen at the other end of the room knocked over a scaffold holding up several buckets of plaster. Everyone jumped, in fact, and Vettazen closed her eyes and murmured something that goodwives probably shouldn't say in the hearing of imperial courtiers. Jazen smothered a laugh and got up to help the workmen try to limit the spread of the plaster on the stone floor.

No one else joined him. He didn't expect them to; it was the kind of work he was used to, and he doubted any of the rest of them had ever worked with their hands before. Well, Meleas, perhaps, but if it didn't involve animals, Meleas had no interest in it. Sweeping up dry plaster didn't involve animals.

On the other end of the room, Immatus was valiantly trying to regain both his composure and his control of the conversation, but Vettazen had taken advantage of the interruption. "Ser Immatus, is this recommendation the result of your own researches? Are you familiar with the studies of magic in foreign lands? Have you seen magic done?"

Immatus snorted. "I should hope I have not, Goodwife! Nor, may I say, have *you*, unless you are confessing to being possessed by a demon! As for magic in foreign lands, it is clear to the meanest intelligence that if the Yaan Maat could invade our own empire of Miralat, they could equally do so elsewhere. Any magic anywhere in the world is the work of those demons. And the Yaan Maat have been defeated." From around his neck, he pulled out a red velvet bag, opened it, and shook the contents out on the table. Pieces of what looked like ivory—shards and scraps, a couple almost the size of Jazen's palm—poured out on the table before him. Vettazen leaned forward and reached out for one of the larger pieces, but Immatus spread his hand over them protectively, preventing her. "Yes, Goodwife, these are mataals. Broken, all of them. This is all that remains of the Yaan Maat." He swept them back into the bag and tucked it under his tunic. "I carry these to honor my own family who fought and died in those wars. I know whereof I speak."

More than two hundred years before, the Yaan Maat had appeared in what was now the Empire of Miralat. They had possessed the Emperor, all his Court, wreaked devastation across the land. They had brought magic the likes of which no human had ever seen, power like that of the sun itself. Wide stretches of the Empire were still called the Burned Lands, the Waste. More than a million had died before humanity had discovered the link between the carved white plaques and the demons—and how to destroy them—before the current Emperor's great-grandsire had taken the throne away from the usurpers.

"This is *exactly* why we need to study magic. That is how your mataals were broken! By human magic!"

Immatus glared at her. "There *is no human magic,* Goodwife."

There was a little silence. Then Vettazen said, "Lord Lasvennat has been very interested in our work." Lasvennat was high in the councils of the Emperor, Jazen knew.

Immatus swallowed. "Lord Lasvennat is not the only voice on the Council, and the Chancellor agrees with me."

Adri-nes cleared his throat.

Jazen glanced back to see Vettazen's lips press together, hard, her head quivering in a "No."

Immatus didn't see it. "My lord?" he said. Jazen could almost hear the oil oozing from his lips. "Did you wish to add something?"

Adri coughed, glanced at Vettazen, and said, "Why, no. Just clearing my throat, Ser."

"I had the great pleasure of speaking to your lord father just the other day," Immatus went on. "He is looking forward to seeing you again soon."

"*Is* he," Adri said. He turned then and looked straight at Vettazen. "When my teachers give me leave, I will be very glad to visit him."

Oh ho, Jazen thought. But Adri *could* go home again; presumably so might Meleas, although he'd never heard the blond boy talk about his family. If Adri's father, someone who had influence at Court and in the Chamberlain's office, spoke against the petition for a charter, where would he, Jazen, go?

He couldn't go back to Smattac, the village he'd abandoned to follow

Vettazen and her little party to Mirlacca. Back in Smattac he was nothing more than a bastard forge boy, indentured for life to bellows and hammer, ever afraid someone might see something, accuse him of something. He wasn't even safe here, because truly, magic *was* demonic, and no one here really knew what kinds of things happened around him. He sneezed as the plaster puffed up in a cloud.

"Your *teachers*?" Immatus was saying incredulously. "My lord, you had the best tutors in the Empire! There is nothing these … gentles … can teach an heir to one of the Great Houses of Miralat!"

"Seventh heir," Adri said mildly. He would not call Firaloy and Vettazen his "masters," not before Immatus.

But that is what they were, Jazen thought. Just as he, Adri and Meleas were their apprentices. He had accepted that as soon as he had understood what these strange visitors to Belzec's forge in Smattac were all about.

Meleas was very good with animals of all kinds, true; Adri tried to write spells, but cheerfully claimed to have absolutely no magic of his own whatsoever; but as for Jazen—Jazen thought Immatus was right. Magic was demonic. He had seen the demons himself, in the forge of Smattac—the little red figures walking along the molten metal, dancing in the blazing coals. They even flared up in his own footsteps when he was tired and angry and discouraged. He knew demons were real. And all you could do with demons was destroy them.

"That will be enough," said Vettazen. Beside her, the other proto-Master of the Guild-to-be, her lifemate Firaloy, nodded. Adri slipped back into the role of an apprentice.

"I will return, if you please, in one week, to see if you have anything to add to your petition." It was clear Immatus, who was gathering together his scrolls and sheets of vellum, thought this unlikely. Firaloy and Vettazen were talking quietly to each other. The three young men glanced at each other and, coming to silent consensus that they were free to leave, got up.

As soon as they were outside the building and around the corner, headed toward the stables, Adri stopped and the veneer of a nobleman fell away as he sagged against the wall. He looked as if he wasn't sure he could stand on his own two feet. "I *hate* them," he said passionately.

"Who?" Meleas asked, as always the voice of reason itself.

"*Courtiers*. That evil little toe-sucker wants to gain credit with my father by telling him I spoke to him about returning home." Adri waved an impatient hand. "I'm a seventh son. I'm not needed for anything, my father didn't even have enough titles to give to all of us. I am *nobody*, but they refuse to see it."

Meleas snorted, but didn't pursue the argument.

"And I will *not* allow that little toady to quash that petition and prevent us from forming a Guild. Or make *me* a puppet in his Court games." For a moment Adri looked like a noble, again. Then he let loose a great sigh and was once again a man who had not reached his eighteenth year, one who felt helpless in the hands of other people and their machinations.

Jazen could sympathize. And yet—

"Why is it so important, this Charter?" he asked hesitantly. It was the kind of question that marked him as a country fool, he knew. So far the others had been patient with him, but there were times when he could *feel* them being patient with him, too.

This was one of those times.

"If we have a Charter for a Guild, of Exorcists or Sorcerers or whatever they plan to call it," Adri said, waving away the details, "then the Masters can assess fees from every member."

Jazen swallowed. "I cannot pay fees."

"None of us can, yet," Meleas assured him hastily. "But if we gain a reputation for knowing about magic, for being able to deal with demons for instance, we can charge for it, and some of that money will come back to the Guild. And in exchange, we get certain rights and are free of some taxes. We can set standards so people will know the value of what they pay for and discipline those who would cheat others, like false hedge witches and fortunetellers. It will make magic respectable."

Jazen blinked. Magic—respectable? "But how can demons be respectable?"

"That's the rub. If Immatus is right and all magic comes from the Yaan Maat, we might as well all just march into a bonfire and have done with it. But our masters say it isn't."

"And that's likely what Immatus hates most," Adri said dryly. "He probably gets some kickback from the taxes on kindling and stakes."

"Oh," Jazen said. The other two, heads together, headed back into the main building.

He wasn't sure yet that Adri-nes and Meleas were friends, exactly. He had never had friends in Smattac; people didn't make friends with clanless bastards.

But there were times, over the past month or so, that he'd begun to feel almost accepted. And now, in an odd way, perhaps he had something in common with them, if the masters thought he had a place here too. He was still nobody, but at least within these walls he was included in Adri's class of nobody. Although Adri's definition of "nobody" included more silk tunics than Jazen's did.

But if there was no Charter, and no Guild, then what?

Now that he knew where the metalworkers' quarter was, he had a chance to find work, if this Charter wasn't approved. He wasn't sure what Meleas would do—something with animals, doubtless—but clearly Adri-nes would simply go home again. It just didn't sound as if "home" was the bright comfortable place it ought to be, for a seventh son.

Ever since he had left Smattac, Jazen had carried in his pouch the iyiza he'd stolen from Belzec. It was a thick bundle of sheets of metal, tied together with wire. Each sheet was near half a finger-joint thick, half as long as his hand, and there were at least a dozen of them. It was heavy, even heavier than it looked. Belzec had never tried to make anything from the iyiza, but Jazen could. And today, perhaps—

He stopped by the kitchen house to beg bread and cheese and an apple from the cook. "Sit and eat here," she said briskly. "And before you go wherever you're going, get me some water." She glanced at the sky and sighed. "After it changes back."

Jazen nodded and sat down. It was nearly noon, and the fountains would change soon. Every day, as a reminder of the battles with the Yaan Maat, the fountains of Mirlacca ran with blood—human blood, they said, although he did not know how they could tell. He had been shocked, the first day he had seen it. Now he, like the rest of the city, had accepted the phenomena with resignation and eventually, indifference.

"Jazen! There you are. I have something for you." Adri, still looking upset, slid onto the kitchen bench beside him and filched a piece of bread.

Jazen, mouth full, lifted an eyebrow.

"It's a working," Adri said, with the slightly embarrassed look he always had when he talked about what he did. He had no magic of his own, he insisted, but he read everything the masters had and haunted shops looking for old books. Exploring Mirlacca with Adri was an exercise in strained eyes and sneezing. And Adri was always doing what he called "workings," attempts to create spells. The first time he had spoken of it before the masters Jazen had been shocked speechless. Such talk would have had him burned in Smattac as a demon, but instead it was the reason the ... *lord's* son ... was one of their community.

Was it only a month since they had told him, with straight faces, that Firaloy and Vettazen were only collecting stories and tales about magic and the Yaan Maat?

And Jazen had believed them?

"I know you work with metal," Adri was saying. "Try this, with the herbs, and, um, a drop of two of your blood. When you quench."

Jazen laughed. "Only a drop or two?"

Adri smiled and shrugged. "I don't know if it would work, but it might make something … useful."

Jazen nodded and thrust the paper into his pouch, where it crumpled against the iyiza. Did Adri know what he wanted to do with the bundle of metal?

"Well, perhaps I'll go see."

Adri smiled and shrugged again, staring at the fireplace on the opposite wall. "Will you let me know?" There was a trace of yearning in his voice.

"I will." Jazen got up and walked away, leaving the lord's son behind him.

* * *

He had marked this place on his first solo trip into the depths of the city. It was a small shop, with a forge in the courtyard in the back where customers were not welcome, but something about it drew him. The sign over the door showed an anvil and a hammer; the shop could have been for anything made of metal. This time he went inside. Bells rang as he stepped through the door, startling him. The interior was lit by half a dozen lamps backed with reflectors, making it brighter than the overcast sky outside.

An array of knives were displayed on the inner counter, under the watchful eye of an old man. A stack of cups was arranged beside them. A set of spoons of varying sizes occupied a shallow basin. A boar spear and a war axe were propped casually behind the counter. It was an interesting, varied array of goods. There were no horseshoes anywhere.

Jazen was pulled to the knives as if drawn by chains.

Two of the knives were long, double-edged, fullered, with jeweled hilts. He gave them no more than a cursory glance and studied the rest: a blocky, heavy chopping knife, almost but not quite a cleaver; a plain-looking single-edged blade with an interesting curve to the back and a pattern like water across the metal; some meat cutters the cook would no doubt like, next to a slender blade the like of which he had never seen before. "What is this?" he asked the old man.

"It's a filleting knife."

Jazen's hand hovered over the plain blade. "May I?" he asked.

The old man snorted. "Aye. It's for sale, if you've the coin."

Jazen picked it up, sighted along the blade, ran a thumbnail along the edge, and put it back. He picked up the chopper, swung it experimentally, looked at the edge and tested it against his arm. "If I had the coin," he said, "I'd buy this one."

The old man studied him. "Why?"

"It's the best one here."

"You're mad. Those are real jewels, and that layered blade is worth—"

Jazen shook his head. "I don't care about jewels. I care about metal. Those blades are warped. And your layered blade—" he pointed inquiringly at the watered-edge knife, and when the old man nodded, continued "—hasn't been tempered very well. The edge is soft. I don't know how you got that pattern—I like it—but as a knife, no. This one, it's heavy, but it's meant to cut. Branches, bone. You could trim a carcass with this, use it to clean the hide. It's a good working tool. It's sharp. It's not brittle. I like it best."

The old man laughed. "You've worked metal, boy. Who's your master?"

Jazen swallowed. "I have no—I mean, I am with Firaloy sr'Islit and his goodwife, but they aren't metalsmiths."

"Don't know them." And, since they weren't metalsmiths, the old man didn't care. "But you've been to the forge. I can see it in your hands. You have the scars from fire and blade and hammer. Where?"

Jazen swallowed. "I'm not from the city." If he told this man he was from Smattac, and word ever came about a runaway bondservant, Belzec might be able to claim him back. He wasn't sure. It would be safer not to say.

Again, the man studied him. "Runaway," he said at last, as if there was no question about it. "Not from the city, you say."

Jazen said nothing.

"Any good?"

Jazen lifted his head. He *was* good, even without the—extra help he sometimes had.

"My name is Gilé," the old man said. "I sent my last 'prentice on his journey two months ago. Not looking to bring along another, not at my age. But you sound like a likely lad. Know something about metal. Like to swing a hammer again?"

Jazen lifted the chopper. "Was this your prentice's work?"

Gilé smiled. "Mine, boy."

"I'd like to see your forge," Jazen said.

It was smaller than the forge in Smattac, but there were the bellows, the tongs, the chisels, the heap of charcoal as high as his shoulder against the wall of the little courtyard behind the shop. Underneath the shed-roof, the cubbyholes for tools, for bits and pieces of metal, for wood and leather and all manner of materials for hilts. And the forge: hooded by strong metal curved over the fire pit, smoldering, the smell of fire and hot metal so familiar he could not tell if the pricking in his eyes was from cinders or homesickness. The weight of the iyiza in the pouch at his waist was suddenly very heavy.

"There's an apron, boy," Gilé said. "Care to show me what you can do with this?" He tossed a round bar the length of his forearm to him.

Jazen took a long look at the bar, hefted it, and swallowed. Then he flexed his shoulders. "Yes," he said. "I would like that."

Gilé didn't tell him where anything was, but answered readily enough when Jazen asked, diffidently at first and then, when the old man sounded nothing at all like Belzec, with more assurance and finally with an abstracted concentration on what he was doing. As he stoked the forge-fire (*please, Gods of my unknown father, no demons now! Not now!*), Gilé asked *him* questions about what he was doing, what he planned to do. How hot did he want the metal to get? How could he tell? As Jazen tried the swing of several hammers before selecting one, why that one and not another? As the bar heated and Jazen turned it in the flames, pausing only to pump the bellows, what did he think the bar was good for? As he set the red-hot metal on the anvil *(thank you*—perhaps the demons couldn't find him in this huge city?) and got into the rhythm of his swing, what would he quench it in, and why? All manner of questions about methods of firing, and materials he had used, what he had made and by what techniques. At last, the third time the now-flattened bar was returned to the fire to re-heat, Jazen was able to spare enough of his attention to realize the man was probing him, seeing how much he knew, where the holes were in his ability and education. There was no accusation or condescension in the questioning. It was simply a matter of measurement. He also never asked what, exactly, Jazen was making. He was letting the younger man show him.

But it was the third time that disaster struck, as he was beginning to truly relax. The afternoon was wearing on, and Jazen was beginning to think he should ask if he could come back the next day. Gilé had stepped away to check the shop doors and get some more water for the two of them to drink. Sweat was pouring off Jazen's back and gathering in his eyebrows, itching at the nape of his neck where he had tied back his hair. The metal was beginning to redden again—

And there were demons dancing along the blade, celebrating the sparks that flew.

They were tiny things, a dozen of them at least, at first barely distinguishable from the sparks themselves, then the height of his thumbnail, but even so he could see the features on their faces, hear their laughter in the roar of the forge. As they twisted and turned and raised flickering arms, the metal beneath them turned redder, brighter, and Jazen cursed helplessly, pulling the metal out and slamming it onto the anvil, raising the hammer high to try to beat each one of them to death somehow. Instead of cooling in the open air, the bar stayed red-hot under their tiny, naked feet, and Jazen looked around frantically for the quench tub, desperate to try to drown them even at the cost of ruining all his work.

To see Gilé standing behind him, a skin of water in his hands, and an expression of utter delight on his face instead of the horror he should have felt.

"Oh!" Gilé said, just audible over all the noise. "The fire people! They come for you, too!"

It was late that night before the forgemaster and his new apprentice—he insisted on calling Jazen that, despite his half-hearted protests—stopped talking. By then they had eaten, and Gilé would not let Jazen try to find his way back to the Street of Scribes in the dark. He made a cot on the floor of the shop for him before stumping his way back into the two rooms overhead where he lived.

Jazen stared up at the ceiling, listening to the footsteps overhead, the creak of the boards. This was nothing like his little room in the house of Vettazen and Firaloy—it was cramped and really nothing more than a pair of blankets for him to lie between.

On the other hand, it was so much better than the dirt floor behind the forge in Smattac where he had slept for as long as he could remember.

Gilé had seen the demons—the "fire people," he called them—and had not reacted in horror or rage, had not called for Jazen's immediate death. He had agreed, chortling, that perhaps not mentioning them to anyone else would be a good thing. Even sophisticated Mirlacca would not accept little dancers of fire making their cutlery and door locks. But Gilé had not only seen them before, he had used them. They were a part of everything he made, although his previous apprentice had never once evoked them and Gilé had made quite sure the boy had never seen them in his own forging.

Did this mean he could desert the people who had taken him in, helped him escape his bond, given him a place among them, welcomed him? Could he walk away, take up the apron and hammer and learn—and he had so much to learn!—from Gilé instead?

And if Immatus refused to present the Charter to the Emperor, would it even matter?

He owed Vettazen and Firaloy so much, for not turning him away, for welcoming him, for not condemning him when they saw the demons in his fires. He wasn't sure what his role in their plans could be. Here, at least, he knew exactly what was expected of him, he knew what he could learn, and the old man wanted to teach him. And he, too, had seen the demons, and accepted them, welcomed them even.

It was a long time before Jazen got to sleep.

Over the next few days Jazen went back and forth between the metal-workers' quarter and the Street of Scribes. At night he puzzled over the spell Adri had given him, painfully sounding out the words, trying to identify the listed herbs. During the day he worked with Gilé, trying new techniques to forge metals he had never tried before, seeking to control the fire people so they wouldn't make the metal so hot it became brittle, learning what materials made the best hilts and how to fix them firmly to the tang.

Gilé was careful never to let anyone else enter the forge while they worked. It would not do, he said, to let others see the fire people. His own old master had been burned at the stake for letting his own wife see him talk to the fire people.

At the house on the Street of Scribes, the household met for the early meal, but no one was in the mood to talk much. Meleas stayed mostly in the stables. Adri seemed busy running errands. And the masters spoke mostly to each other and to friends they brought in. Jazen found he missed the comfortable exchange of small talk, even the reading lessons, but he was focused now on Gilé, and working metal, and more and more on the iyiza weighing down his belt pouch.

It was after Gilé showed him how to achieve the watered pattern in the steel by folding metal over and over on itself in layers that he realized what the bundle of metal was supposed to be for. He had made a half-dozen knives, sturdy working blades that had passed Gilé's critical eye, before he finally dared to bring out the iyiza and put it on the work table.

Gilé's brows raised. "Ah," he said, fanning out the metal strips with his fingers. "And this is yours? Do you know what this is, youngster?"

Jazen thought of the lifetime he had spent being beaten and cursed, working for no pay and bad food. He had learned more from Gilé in less than a month than he had in all his years with Belzec. "It's mine," he said defiantly. "I earned it."

His teacher gave him a long look. "Very well, then," he said at last. "What you have here is very high-quality metal, mostly high-carbon iron, but some other things as well that alloy well—*if* you can forge it properly. These bundles come from the north, mostly, and it's rare to find them bundled and ready for work like this. The superstitious say they're cursed, that things you make from iyiza are never what you intended. They're either very, very good, or they turn on you. Are you sure? Are you ready?"

"I think I am," Jazen said. "Do you?"

Gilé laughed. "Let us see what you can make with hammer and flame, youngster. Tomorrow, you can begin."

That night, Jazen reviewed the spell Adri had given him, assembled packets of the herbs the other apprentice had listed, sounded his way through the short verses over and over again until he knew them by heart. He wasn't sure why he was doing it; he was making a knife, after all, not casting a spell. But he recalled the look in Adri's eyes, and thought, *I am an apprentice here too. I may as well. What harm can it do?*

The next day, at Gilé's forge, he sprinkled the herbs in between the strips of metal, feeling a little silly as he did so. The next step was to weld them together. He bound them back together with wire and checked the color of the fire before using the tongs to place the bundle in the forge. Gilé watched approvingly, nodded, and then left him alone to take care of the shop. This was Jazen's work, and his alone.

Plus, he thought, a little magic. Maybe.

He pumped the bellows and set the bound iyiza into the flames. He thought he could almost see the shredded herbs catch fire, leap up and smolder into the block of metal as it heated, as he worked the bellows and turned it over, as it began to slowly turn red and begin to glow. And then the fire people, the demons, came.

They were bare sparks at first, along the edges where he could still see the different kinds of metal in distinct layers. They grew as the metal glowed brighter, and then they began to dive through the metal as if they were playing in water, and they twisted around and *looked* at him, laughing joyously as he sweated.

He pulled the glowing block out of the forge, set it on the anvil, and reached for his hammer.

You who come from fire and seed
Make this now to what I need

The hammer fell. The fire people laughed. He swung it harder, even blows, stretching the block into a longer strip, no more a stack of metal layers but one piece. As it began to cool, he hung the strip over the side of the anvil and began to fold it back upon itself until he could no longer feel it give to the hammer, and then he put the reformed block back into the flame and watched the fire people come again.

And again.

And again.

He lost count of the number of times he folded the iyiza, never letting it cool back to blackness, never letting the fire people die away.

This the tool that I do make
For all I need for my own sake

For a sorcerer, he thought, Adri made a poor poet.

And then, finally, it was the right length, the right thickness, and the demons were almost the size of his own hand, diving through coals and metal alike and reaching out to Jazen as he hammered, looking him in the eyes, and he felt a connection to the flames as he never had before, never at Belzec's forge, never, as if with each blow of the hammer he pounded a piece of his own soul into the metal fabric shaping itself at his hands.

You who come from fire and seed
Be this now as I shall need
You who come from seed and fire
Shape yourself to my desire
That this shall be my own blade
That fire and seed and magic made

It was almost enough. His hands were blistered and bleeding from holding the hammer, switching hands at every seventh blow. He lifted the shape with the tongs to plunge it into the quench and then remembered the last instruction.

He would not bleed on the red-hot blade and invite cracking. But he could wash the blood and sweat from his hands in the quench.

And as the knife went in, the fire people screamed and dived into the metal itself to hide from the cooling liquid. But there were no clicks and cracks in the metal, and as he drew it out it blossomed one last time in sparks and flame.

Gilé found him, then, slumped beside the anvil, staring at the metal lying there. Jazen felt he could not have lifted his arms for one more blow to save his life. What had been a pile of metal strips was now a recognizable knife blade with a sturdy tang, a shape with one long edge and a solid, curved spine.

"It needs honing," Gilé said. "Polishing. And a good hilt." He picked it up, inspecting the length of metal for warping, for cracks, and found none. He swung it experimentally. "This is good work, boy. Very good work."

Jazen nodded, rolled his shoulders, and winced. Gilé laughed. "Better than even you know, boy."

* * *

Immatus looked smug as he cut the flesh from his bird. "I understand what a disappointment this is for you, Ser sr'Islit, but the facts are the facts. There is no magic since the Yaan Maat was defeated."

"So the fountains do not stink of blood at noon?" Vettazen asked quietly.

Immatus took a deep drink of his ale. "There are some residual effects, of course, and that is the most notable. They were great and terrible sorcerers. But it does not last long, no one is harmed. We simply have no need for a Guild to study a magic which is fading away to nothingness. You are asking for privileges you cannot possibly earn."

At the other end of the table, Jazen spread butter across a roll.

"Ser Immatus, you are very certain of this." Firaloy sounded very sad.

"Of course I am. It is simple truth. If you really were able to produce magic, then of course it would be a different tale, but you cannot. No one can."

"Hedge witches …" Vettazen began.

"Ser, do not insult me. Do you suggest a Guild for the makers of herbal potions?"

Jazen was beginning to be very tired of the constant kicking his ankle was getting from Adri, beside him.

"I suggest there is more to all of this than you know."

Immatus snorted. "If you would give me some more of that excellent bread, Goodwife. Now that bread is something I might consider magical!" He roared with laughter.

Jazen got up and picked the basket of bread out of the air as it was being passed from Meleas to Firaloy, walked around Vettazen, and put it down in front of the Palace functionary. "May I offer you my spreading-knife?" he asked, offering it hilt-first, as was proper. The smear of butter on the wide, dull blade gleamed in the light from the torches. "Do be careful, Ser. It's sharper than it looks."

Immatus reached for another roll, good brown bread thick with seeds, then took up the offered implement. He sank the edge of the spreader into the roll, pushing it hard against the crust. The dull, rounded edge barely dented it. Immatus shoved it back impatiently to Jazen, who took it and pushed lightly against the bread in the man's hand.

Better than you know.

And Immatus yelped, as the knife transformed from a dull butter-spreader into a single-edged blade of water-patterned metal three times the size that went through the soft bread and into the meat of his palm. The roll was turning a mushy red as blood poured over the table. Immatus dropped it and stared at the sharp blade stuck in his hand and screamed.

Jazen reached over him and pried the knife out, panicking. He wasn't supposed to cut the man, just show him how the knife changed. He had no idea why it had turned lethal; he had barely used any pressure at all. He cast a terrified glance at the masters, hoping they understood the mistake. Meanwhile, Immatus's gaze followed the blade and watched it transform back into a small, meek, innocuous, and very dull butter-spreader.

"You cut me," he gasped. "You cut me!"

"Impossible," Vettazen said quietly. "There is no edge to that blade. No point. You said so yourself, Ser: There is no human magic. So how could a mere spreader cut you?"

"It was—" Immatus tried to clench his bleeding hand and cried out again as his hand refused to obey. "My hand!"

"I did mention, Ser—" But Vettazen caught Jazen's eye and shook her head sharply. She was watching Immatus and didn't seem angry at him at all. Jazen nodded with cautious relief, picked up another piece of bread and wiped the butter and blood away, then thrust the spreader—now a knife again—into the sheath at his side. Immatus's eyes grew wide, rolled back, and he slumped off the chair.

"Oh, dear," Firaloy muttered. "And us without a healing spell. Adri, I don't suppose—"

Adri shook his head, helplessly, just as Immatus's eyes opened again.

And opened wider.

And glowed.

He shook his head and snarled something in a language none of them had heard before, and licked at his hand. "Not enough," he said, and before their startled eyes the deep wound stopped bleeding and Immatus got to his feet. "Give me that knife, boy."

Jazen swallowed and stepped back, his hand on the hilt. "No, sir."

"*Give me the knife, boy.*" Immatus swung his once-injured hand in Jazen's direction and all the dishes and remains of the carefully prepared dinner went flying. Jazen, Vettazen, Meleas, and Adri staggered from a blow that never touched them. "Give it to me now and I might let you live!"

"Yaan Maat are notorious liars," Firaloy gasped, and from the floor threw one of their good goblets at Immatus's head.

Yaan Maat? Jazen thought, even as he leaped away. They had only thought to show Immatus he was wrong, show him the fruit of Adri's spell and Jazen's work. No one had said anything about Yaan Maat!

The demon snarled again and picked up the oak refectory table, swinging it up over his head. Jazen dodged, shoving Vettazen out of the way. Meleas ducked back. Firaloy, on the floor, was caught directly in the table's path and collapsed without a cry.

Without knowing exactly what he was doing, Jazen yanked the knife free from his belt.

You who come from fire and seed
Be this now as I shall need

He had no idea what he needed. He was no trained fighter, certainly not with the sword he found in his hand. He cast a despairing glance to Adri, who shook his head—Adri, who could use a sword, but if he took this one up, it wouldn't be a sword any more. The magic of the fire people had shaped it only to *his* hand.

So he slashed, and as the blade came down it changed again, from long narrow light blade to something else, wider at the point, chopping at the demon. Immatus glared and stepped back.

"The mataal, Jazen! Break the mataal!"

But the little velvet bag with the pieces of mataal, the inscribed ivory in which Yaan Maat lived when they weren't possessing humans, was safely tucked under Immatus's tunic. The demon laughed and raised his hands again. Smoke began to pour from them.

More than anything, he wanted to run away, but Jazen's knife—or sword—or whatever it was—appeared to have other ideas. Out of the corner of his eye he could see Adri and Vettazen scrambling through the debris for something, anything, to throw at Immatus. Meleas was muttering to Firaloy, who was on the floor, under the oak table.

Jazen lunged, since the knife seemed to think that was a good idea, and Immatus whipped his smoking hands out of the way. The smoke eddied over the prostrate Firaloy, who gagged and coughed, desperately waving it away. Vettazen threw a soup bowl, which smacked against Immatus's head and distracted him long enough to let Jazen get a stride closer. Obligingly, the knife lengthened and sliced.

But there were limits, it seemed. There had only been so much metal in the iyiza, and as sharp as his weapon was, at that length it had no heft and was impossible to control. The tip ripped at the demon's sleeve and drew blood, but it was only a scratch. Immatus cursed and reached for his own eating knife and threw it at Jazen. It buried itself in his upper arm and he almost dropped his weapon.

But he had hammered the iyiza knife with both hands, and he took it from the suddenly nerveless fingers of his right into his left and swung it again. Immatus swung his hands and a wind came up, creating a whirlwind of rushes and debris and broken crockery. Meleas shouted. Immatus laughed.

And then his laughter changed, suddenly, as a brown shadow appeared from the debris on the floor and launched itself at him. The demon screamed and beat at himself, but the rat ran up Immatus's leg and around his back. Jazen lunged from the floor and his knife, now back into its home shape, sank deep into Immatus's leg.

The demon screamed and Jazen felt a crushing blow out of nowhere, pinning him to the floor. Immatus had fallen, too, on his back, trying to crush the rat. Somehow Jazen found the strength to strike at the demon's chest, but it had no power behind it and the blade merely sliced through the Court finery, exposing a pudgy hairless chest—and a red velvet bag. Immatus staggered up, the wound in his leg healing itself as Jazen watched, but the rat—Meleas's rat—squealed and snapped, as Adri used Immatus's own eating knife and his own to deliver a double blow to the demon's back. The cord around the demon's neck parted. The bag fell to the floor. Before Immatus could raise his lethal hands, the iyiza blade transformed into a hammer and smashed into it.

With a shriek, Immatus swung his hands and more smoke poured out. But this time his wounds did not heal. The hammer in Jazen's hand descended again and again, in the rhythm he knew better than his own pulse, smashing the mataals, as Adri, Meleas, and Vettazen struck once more.

This time, the demon did not rise.

* * *

"Well," Lord Lasvennat said, surveying the hall. They had done the best they could to clean it up, but it would take days, and none of them were untouched. Firaloy had a broken leg and a concussion. Jazen's arm was bandaged. Meleas, Adri, and Vettazen all still had trouble breathing from the demon's smoke, and Meleas's eyes were red and swollen—although Jazen thought that might be because of the rat, which had also died.

"Well," the lord said again. He shook his head. "I didn't actually think there were any more Yaan Maat among us. It seems I was wrong." The red bag swung from its cord. He had taken possession of it, but was obviously not eager to touch it. In fact, he seemed relieved to hold it out to Vettazen. "I think this would be better in the hands of someone who studies such things professionally, Guildlady." He looked around. "And where is this famous knife of which I have heard so much?"

"It's Jazen's, my lord," Vettazen said.

"Ah, yes. The knifemaker. So, young man." Lasvennat raised an eyebrow. "Apprenticed in two Guilds? Unheard of."

Jazen swallowed, aware that all eyes were on him—this lord from the Emperor's own Court, Vettazen and Firaloy, who had brought him away from bondage, even Meleas and Adri-nes, who had befriended him. Fought with him. Lasvennat—summoned from the Court when someone, somehow, had to explain the death of Immatus—hefted the "famous knife" in his hand. It remained itself, one-edged, slightly curved. Nothing unusual about it at all.

It felt wrong, seeing someone else hold that knife. It called to him, as if it needed him. As if the fire people deep in the blade needed him.

"I … I have much to learn," he mumbled at last.

Lasvennat smiled and held the knife out to him, hilt first. "It is a terrible thing to kill a man," he said quietly. "But it is an honorable thing to protect your own. These folk, I think, claim you for their own."

Nodding, Jazen took the knife, stuffing it into his belt, and faded back into the little crowd and then out the door and away from all the stares. He could still hear them talking.

"I think he'll be coming back to us," Firaloy said, complacent.

Lasvennat smiled. "I'm certain the Exorcists and the Ironworkers can come to some accommodation."

"I hope so," Vettazen said. "We need his magic. As we need all the magic in this room."

"In this city," Lasvennat corrected. "Indeed, in the Empire. We had magic before the demons came. We never lost it. We need to bring it back. Smashing a mataal is not all it takes to kill a demon. It takes magic, too—*human* magic.

"Build us a Guild, Sers. Recall our magic. And—" he looked past them, out the door where Jazen had disappeared "—make sure that young man is one of you. I want one of those knives."

Vettazen laughed. "So do we, my lord. All of us."

Guild of the Ancients

D.B. Jackson

They gather on a promontory, in a glade of windswept cedars, far from the eyes and ears of humans. A sea breeze breathes in the branches above them. Surf pounds like a heartbeat below.

It is a moonless night, as always when they meet. Stars dot the sky, vanishing and reappearing as clouds scud past. They burn no torches among the trees. None of the Ancients require flame or moon glow to see in the dark.

The various septs cluster together, disinclined to mingle and thus suggest a lack of unity among their own kind. The Belvora have arrived first, as is their custom. Droë counts twelve of them, more than usual. That doesn't bode well.

The rest of the septs array themselves upwind of the winged ones, where they won't have to endure the stench of rot that clings to them. Perhaps a half dozen Shonla gather in the shadows of the wood, their mists coalescing into a single cloud of vapor. Droë discerns no bodies, but their eyes gleam dully from within the haze, echoes of the stars above. Hanev and Grajkim have come as well, though only a few of each. Nine Arrokad, the last to arrive, stand with their backs to the edge of the cliff. Brine still pools around their feet. Tall, sculpted, beautiful, despite their serpentine eyes. Their cold, bone-pale skin appears luminous even in the inky gloom.

Droë's own kind, the Tirribin, lounge on the forest floor, some picking at twigs and leaves, others speaking in low voices. Most cast occasional glances in her direction. Droë keeps herself apart. For this one night, she belongs to no sept. At least not until the others decide the question of guilt or innocence.

"Let us come to order, cousins," says one of the Arrokad, a black-haired male with golden eyes and a voice as deep and gentle as the ocean at dawn. "This gathering of the Guild of the Ancients, North Sea, is now convened. I am Lir of the Arrokad, and I shall preside over tonight's proceedings. Let all who have business before this body speak truth, hold peace, and keep faith with its collected judgment and wisdom."

Some of the Tirribin look Droë's way again. She knows all the Belvora do as well, but she does not allow her gaze to leave Lir.

"We will begin, as always, with matters of Commerce. All who would be heard, step forward and present yourselves."

One of the Shonla floats into the center of the space defined by the different septs. She remains shrouded in her mist, eyes aglow, her form barely visible. Droë's skin pebbles at the touch of the Shonla's cloud. She eases back, trying not to be too obvious. Others do the same.

"I am Flisze of the Shonla," the mist creature says, her words slow and thick. "I bring a question of Commerce before the Guild."

Lir opens a hand, motioning for her to continue.

"Long has there been … understanding, that human ships on the route between the Sisters and the isle they call Oaqamar are to be left unmolested, save at the discretion of the Arrokad. But with traffic along that route increasing, my kind petition the Most Ancient Ones to consider a new arrangement."

Lir's brow knits.

But it is another Arrokad, a female, also dark-haired, who says, "Terms?"

Flisze raises a blunt hand. "A moment, please."

She glides back to the edge of the wood and speaks in a low voice with the others of her sept. Among themselves, the Shonla do not speak the common tongue, but rather communicate with a series of clicks and guttural noises that Droë cannot understand.

Not that she cares. This promises to be a long night. Discussion of Commerce will consume much time, as will questions of Jurisdiction, Predation, and Legalities. The ancient septs do not convene often. The gentility of Lir's welcome notwithstanding, most of the septs dislike one another. Even within each of the bloodlines, suspicion, if not outright hostility, is the rule. Creatures of prey tend to see in every other predator a rival. It seems to Droë a small miracle that the Guild has survived for so many millennia.

Flisze drifts back to the center of the promontory and halts before the second Arrokad. "Six ships per fortnight," she says. "And in return we shall, each of us, for a year and a day, be subject to give one boon to the Most Ancient Ones."

"A boon of our choosing?"

"Of course. But only one from each Shonla."

The female Arrokad peers back at her sept for a tencount. "Four ships," she says. "And two boons, over two years and two days."

The Shonla shakes her head. "Four ships is acceptable, but one boon, over one year and one day."

"You ask much and offer little."

Flisze shrugs. "We take little from ships. Some screams, a song or two if the humans can be persuaded. Never lives. You know this. The ships will still be available to you for your … your pleasures."

The female Arrokad answers with a wicked grin, exposing needlelike teeth, similar to Droë's and those of the other Tirribin. An instant later she turns serious again.

"Five then. But two boons over two years and two days. That is as far as we will bend. Accept or refuse."

Flisze looks back at her kind. One of them nods.

"Accept."

"Then we have an agreement, your kind and mine, freely entered and fairly sworn before the Guild?"

"We have an agreement, freely entered and fairly sworn."

The female Arrokad dips her chin and turns to Lir.

"So be it," he says.

Flisze and the other Arrokad withdraw. Next a Grajkim approaches Lir to speak on behalf of his kind, who wish to enter into a new arrangement, also with the Arrokad.

And so it goes. One by one, Ancients take their turns petitioning the Guild, forging arrangements, or requesting accommodation, or disputing the rights of their rivals. Tirribin engage in their share of negotiations, but even then Droë pays little heed to what is said. She does watch Rissla, though. She wants to know where she is at all times. And she notices that Taibid bears a livid scar on his cheek. She can guess why.

At last, deep into the night, Lir says, in that same rich, ringing voice, "Finally, we come to Grievances."

A shiver charges through Droë, as if she has been enveloped in a Shonla mist.

One of the Belvora strides to the middle of their circle. She is taller than even the largest of the Arrokad; she towers over Droë and the other Tirribin. Her membranous wings remain folded against her back, but she holds her long, sinuous arms akimbo. Her skin is pale and leathery and her mane of golden hair dances in the wind. Amber eyes sweep over the glade, lingering on Droë for an instant. A snarl curls her lip.

"I am Jonji of the Belvora," she says, her voice harsh, like the cry of a hawk. "And I stand before you all to say that we have Grievance. All the Belvora, but I most of all."

Lir does not appear to be surprised by this. "What is your Grievance?" he asks, the words rote.

Jonji pivots with the grace of a creature born to hunt, and levels a taloned finger at Droë. "That Tirribin killed my brother."

* * *

Droë decided to leave Safsi soon after the Goddess's solstice. Life on the tiny isle had grown tiresome. She wanted change, an adventure. New years to taste. But how?

Tirribin traveled at speed over land, but unlike Shonla and Belvora, they could not fly, and unlike Arrokad, they disliked water. They were forced to depend on others for transport among the lands of Islevale. And since few humans trusted Tirribin, whom they called Time Demons, Droë had some trouble finding a way off Safsi.

In the end, she secured passage aboard a small boat whose captain welcomed her in exchange for a promise that she would forever spare him and his family. She had been happy to oblige. On the larger island she would find plenty of humans on whom to feed. The captain and his wife were old; sparing them would involve no sacrifice on her part. His children *were* full of sweet years, but she expected she would have no trouble preying on others.

Soon after arriving on the larger isle, she realized her mistake. She had thought she might find a circle of Tirribin she could join. Friends. Partners on the hunt.

Instead, on her first night, she found Rissla. Or rather, Rissla found her.

She had been alone, learning the pattern of the lanes.

"Look at how skinny she is."

Droë turned at the sound of the voice to find herself facing seven of her kind, all dressed in rags, as she was. They resembled human children, three male and four female. They were slight, waiflike, with large, pale eyes. Some were as dark-skinned as humans of the northern isles. Others were as pallid as those from the Inner Ring. Several leered at her, needle teeth gleaming with light from nearby oil lamps.

"She's not very pretty, either. Is she?"

The Tirribin who spoke had golden hair and skin the color of sail cloth. Nothing about her appearance established her as their leader, but Droë sensed her years. She was at least two centuries older than Droë herself, and a good deal older than her companions as well.

A few of the other Tirribin laughed, as if the old one had said something hilarious. One, a male, frowned.

"She's young, Rissla," this one said. "I can taste her years. You're being rude."

He had dark skin and bronze hair. His milky eyes showed a hint of green. Aside from the girl, he might have been the oldest.

"What's she doing here?" Rissla asked, watching Droë. "Maybe she's come to make trouble. Until we know …" She lifted a shoulder.

"Did you?" the boy asked Droë.

Droë shook her head.

Rissla's glare scraped over her, face to foot. "Then why did you come?"

Droë didn't know what she had done to offend the girl, but it was clear to her that the boy's interest in her, his defense of her, would only make matters worse.

"I was in Safsi," she said. "I was … bored there." She had meant to say "lonely," but she feared the ridicule this might provoke.

"So you've come to be entertained."

"I came hoping to find friends," she said. "A new leader to follow."

Perhaps if she made it clear that she didn't see herself as a rival …

"We're not interested in scrawny, ugly girls who are too young to know how to hunt."

"I know how to hunt!"

"Then why would you need a leader? Or was that just something you said to win my approval?"

Droë opened her mouth, then shut it again.

Rissla laughed and clapped her hands in delight. "I've silenced her. How splendid."

"Rissla—"

She rounded on the boy. "Tell me again that I'm being rude and I'll kill her now."

He didn't flinch, nor did he challenge her. He merely stared.

"She isn't worth this trouble," Rissla said, her gaze on Droë again. "I'm bored. Let's find some years to take." She started away. The others followed her, all except the boy. After a few paces, she halted and faced him.

"Are you coming?"

"I'll find you later."

Rissla's eyes narrowed. "You," she said, pointing at Droë. "You're not welcome here. Find another village. These grounds are ours. You're not to hunt in my demesne. Do you understand?"

Droë didn't answer straight away. Rissla bared her teeth again.

"Do you understand?" she repeated, biting off each syllable.

"I understand your words," Droë said, knowing she was being reckless. "I'm not simple."

Rissla stalked back in her direction. "But you will not obey? Do you challenge me?"

"I do not challenge you. But neither do I recognize your authority to keep me from hunting here."

The girl smiled again, a cruel, knowing smile. "You are a stupid child. You have made an enemy tonight, one for whom you are no match." She whirled away, her hair whipping around her face. "Come along."

The others fell in step behind her.

Droë watched her go, her hands trembling.

"That wasn't smart," the boy said.

"You think I should have given in to her?" she demanded, glaring at him sidelong. "You think I should allow myself to go hungry while I'm here?"

"I didn't say that. But you could have acquiesced and then hunted here anyway. Now it won't matter what you do. She hates you and she won't allow you a moment's rest."

He was right, and she was a dolt.

"Well, that's just fine with me," Droë said, rather than admit as much. She stomped off in the opposite direction from that taken by Rissla and the other Tirribin.

The boy walked with her.

"I'm Taibid," he said.

"I'm Droë." She had come searching for friends, but now that she seemed to have found one she wished he would leave her alone.

"Did you really come here from Safsi?"

She nodded, turning down a new lane that led away from the wharf, toward the hills that loomed over the town.

"Why?"

Her throat tightened and her eyes stung. *Because I was lonely. I'm always lonely.* "Does it matter?" she asked, blinking away the tears before they could fall.

"I didn't mean to—"

She halted, forcing Taibid to do the same. "You should probably leave me," she said. "I can tell that she cares for you and sees you as ... well, as someone who shouldn't be my friend."

He lifted an eyebrow. "So you'll hunt where she tells you not to, but you'll refuse an offer of friendship on the chance that she won't approve?"

Put that way, it did sound foolish. She eyed the lane they were on, followed it with her gaze into the uplands. "Am I likely to find anyone abroad in the streets this late?"

He considered the road as well. "Not this way. The wharf is the best place for hunting."

"That's where Rissla went."

Taibid shrugged.

"So where should I go? I don't know this town."

"Aside from the wharf, the market is best, but that's only during the day. At night you just have to roam the streets until you find someone."

"That's not very helpful."

"No," he said. "I don't suppose it is."

She turned again at the next corner, angling away from the hills, back toward the center of the town. Taibid remained with her, but said nothing. Droë didn't speak either and they walked together in uneasy silence. Yet she was thankful for his presence beside her. Awkward though it was, she preferred it to being on her own.

After perhaps a quarter bell, she caught the scent of human years nearby. Not as young as she would have liked, but certainly better than nothing. She and Taibid shared a glance and a smile. At Tirribin speed, with the care honed over countless years of predation, they approached the next cross street in tandem, eager to spot their prey.

As they stepped onto the next lane, they spotted the human—a burly man of perhaps thirty years. He stumbled through shadows in their direction, muttering to himself. Even at this distance, Droë smelled spirit on his breath.

Not her ideal prey, but she prepared to rush him and take his years. Before she could, he fell, as if knocked down from behind.

A form scrambled over him, latched on to the back of his neck. Another Tirribin. The man cried out, flailed. The Tirribin began to feed, a faint, pale green glow suffusing her body and covering the human as well.

As she ate, the Tirribin raised her eyes and peered at Droë, malice and pleasure in the gaze.

Rissla.

They watched her for a fivecount.

"We should leave," Taibid said.

They turned, but other Tirribin stood in their path.

"You're to remain here until she's finished," one of them said.

Droë and Taibid shared another look.

Rissla took her time with the man and then straightened, her feeding glow fading. The human lay at her feet, withered, his eyes and cheeks sunken as if he had been dead for days.

"That was lovely," she said, sighing the words. "He didn't look like much, but he had more years than one might have thought. You really ought to have had some."

"Why are you doing this?" Taibid asked her. "She hasn't done anything—"

"You will cease immediately to have anything to do with her," the Tirribin said, "or you will be outcast for ten centuries. I swear it."

"You can't cast me out." The words were confident, but though Droë had known Taibid for only this one night, she recognized doubt in his voice.

"No? How certain are you?"

He didn't answer, but sent a quick glance Droë's way. She knew he would choose Rissla and the others. Why wouldn't he? Who was she but a stranger who, in a matter of a bell or two, had thrown his life into turmoil?

Taibid lingered a moment longer, then crossed the distance between Rissla and Droë to stand with the older girl. Their friends still loomed at Droë's back.

"It seems to me that you were hunting where I told you not to," Rissla said, even more confident now that Taibid stood with her. "Isn't that so, little one?"

Droë looked at Taibid, but he avoided her gaze. She would have no help from him. "You were at the wharf," she said. "I kept my distance from you and your friends. This town has plenty of humans. You wouldn't have suffered for any years that I took."

Rissla prodded the dead man with her toe. "But I would have. Had you succeeded in disobeying me, I would have been denied this one's years."

Her gaze flicked past Droë to those behind her. All the warning Droë had. Hands grabbed for her.

Droë twisted away, dove to the cobblestone lane, rolled. They lunged for her, fingers like iron, teeth clacking. They were stronger than she, but she was fast. She always had been.

She squirmed away a second time, leaped to her feet. Her breath came in gasps. They closed in on her. At the last instant, she remembered Rissla, on whom she had turned her back. She heard a footfall just behind her, spun, dropped, rolled again. Rissla let out a snarl.

Droë darted at speed through a gap between Rissla and her companions. She swerved as the quickest among them darted after her and fled along the lane. At the first corner, she turned to head away from the shoreline. The other Tirribin followed, neither gaining on her nor losing ground. She knew Rissla would be with them, wondered if Taibid was as well.

She didn't have time to think on it. They pursued her and she ran. Rissla and her friends knew the town better than Droë did. Would they cut her off? Surround her? Did they intend to kill her or merely scare her off? She had gone much of the day without feeding and wasn't sure how long she could run at Tirribin speed before her body failed her.

She took one side lane after another until she couldn't say with certainty where she was or even which direction she would have to turn to find water. Fear drove her on.

Eventually, she realized they no longer followed. She slowed, breathless, sweating like an overworked human. She listened for the others, for any indication that they still hunted for her. Nothing. Probably they had returned to the wharf to hunt and to laugh at her. The child-Tirribin whom they had chased off.

This time, she couldn't stop her tears. She swiped at them, angry with herself for allowing them to hurt her feelings, and for caring that Taibin had chosen Rissla over her.

More than anything she wanted to feed. Then she would leave. There were other towns and villages, other places where a Tirribin might find prey. But it had grown late, and these streets had gone silent. She sensed no humans in the lanes. A dog or two. And cats. But she refused to lower herself to such a feeding. Their years were not as satisfying. No, she would find a human come the morning.

She entered a narrow dirt byway between two buildings, lay on the damp ground, and curled into a tight ball. In time, sleep took her.

Droë slumbered longer than she had intended, waking to bright daylight and bustling streets at either end of her alley. Like all of her kind, she preferred to hunt at night, but her stomach growled and, despite her rest, she felt weak, sluggish.

She stood, crept to the end of the lane, moving with care, keeping out of sight.

"Sleep well, little one?"

She stiffened, already too familiar with that voice.

"Don't bother running. You won't get far."

Droë turned. Rissla stood closer than she had expected. She couldn't stop herself from taking a step back. "So you're going to kill me now?" she asked. Somehow she kept her tone level.

"No."

Droë blinked. "You're not?"

The Tirribin shook her head. "There's no fun in that."

"I'll feed this morning and leave the village. You have my word. I have no intention …" She trailed off. Rissla was shaking her head.

"I don't think that sounds like fun either."

Cold dread crawled down Droë's spine like a drop of ice water. "Then what?"

"A game," Rissla said, a smile splitting her flawless face. "We won't allow you to leave, but neither will we allow you to feed. That, at least, is our intention. You can try to do either, or both. If you win, you'll have your meal and live to hunt another day. Or you'll leave this place and need never worry about us again. If we win, you'll die."

"Why are you doing this to me?" Droë asked, throwing her arms wide. "What did I do to offend you so?"

"You came here without seeking my permission. You chose to hunt without seeking my permission." Her voice rose. "You tried to steal Taibid from me without seeking my permission. So now, you will have nothing, not even your life, without my permission."

"I had only just arrived when you found me! If you had told me I needed your permission—"

"You should have known. Let that be a lesson to you, little one. A lesson you probably won't live long enough to put to use. When you come to a new port, a new village, your first task should be to seek out the dominant Tirribin and ask leave to hunt and live."

A number of replies leapt to Droë's mind, not least among them that she didn't appreciate being called "little one." She gave voice to none of them.

"The game begins now. I hope you'll be more clever than you've been thus far. If not, this promises to be rather boring."

Rissla turned her back on Droë, almost daring her to attack.

She didn't. She ran.

She thought her best hope would be escape. There had to be a dozen paths that led out of the town. Rissla and her friends couldn't possibly guard all of them, could they?

It didn't take her long to find that they could. The first lane she followed appeared to curve into the highlands, past copses and fields. She wasn't able to follow it far, however. One of Rissla's friends stood in her way. Two more stood in the grass on either side of the road. All three of them smirked at her.

Droë turned back, followed another lane in a different direction. Rissla's Tirribin guarded that one as well.

She struck out in a third direction, this time eschewing roads for brush and thickets. Before she could cover much distance, Tirribin closed on her from both sides, forcing her to turn back yet again. On her way back to the village, she encountered Rissla.

"You're following me," Droë said.

The Tirribin hiked her shoulder, her calm unnerving. "You don't make it difficult. So predictable. I hope you prove more of a challenge before this is over."

"Do you truly have nothing better to do than torment me?"

Rissla sauntered closer. Droë tried not to flinch away.

"You still don't understand, do you? This has nothing to do with torment-ing you, although that does make it more fun. It has everything to do with my authority in this town. You claim to know how to hunt, and I'll grant that you're quicker than some Tirribin I've known, but you have much to learn about what it means to be an Ancient."

"I'm sorry," Droë said. "I didn't mean—If you just allow me to leave, you'll never see me again. And no one will ever hear of any of this."

"I've already told you," Rissla said, turning and starting away. "It's too late for that."

Droë stared after her, despair flooding her heart. After a time, she could no longer see the other Tirribin, but she knew Rissla hadn't gone far. In all likelihood, she was near enough to mark Droë's every movement.

Yet, what could she do but try to survive?

Droë didn't fear individual humans, but in numbers they could be dangerous. She preferred to prey on single ones, and always by dark, when she was least likely to be seen. But as her hunger deepened, caution seemed a luxury she couldn't afford.

She skirted the town's marketplace, hoping to isolate a meal. In moments, however, she found herself in the company of Rissla and two of her friends. She retreated, cursing the other Tirribin, her hands shaking with rage.

So it went throughout that day and into the night. She couldn't leave. They wouldn't allow her to feed. At last, giving in to the hollow ache in her belly, she turned to hunting animals. But Rissla and the others wouldn't allow her even this consolation. They kept her from dogs and horses and cats. They did allow her to take a rat. Or perhaps they didn't see, or care. What she took from the creature couldn't be measured in years. A turn, perhaps two. Such a meager reward was hardly worth the effort. It did nothing to sate her need.

After repeated frustration in the lanes of the town, Droë managed to sleep, waking to a gray dawn and a chill fog. Usually the vagaries of climate did not touch her. A Shonla mist could make her shiver, but she thought nothing of wearing tatters through the worst of Trevynisle winters. This morning's cold, though, seeped into her bones. She felt like a husk. Tirribin were not meant to go so long without feeding. She could barely stand, much less move at Tirribin speed.

Still, she roused herself and crept through the streets, following a wide path around the marketplace, toward the wharf. They might not expect that. She would have preferred to run, to use all the powers she usually possessed, but she was so weakened she had to rely on guile rather than swiftness.

It wasn't enough. Rissla awaited her at the waterfront. Taibid stood with her.

They exchanged not a word. Droë spotted her and halted. Rissla flashed a savage grin. Taibid stared, his expression unreadable, his arms crossed over his chest. After a fivecount, Droë pivoted and set out in a new direction. She might as well have sat down and remained where she was. She had no more success, either hunting or exiting the town, than she had the day before. She grew more desperate with each passing bell. Thwarted for what felt like the hundredth time as she tried to leave the town along a footpath into the hills, she screamed her frustration, tears coursing over her cheeks, her throat growing raw. By nightfall, her thoughts were as muddied as a river in flood. Hunger gnawed at her.

The next day was worse still. She spent it in a daze, stumbling through the streets until she was too faint to hunt. She took refuge behind a bank of rundown wooden houses near the marketplace.

She no longer recalled when she had fed last. She, a creature of time, had lost track of the days and bells. She didn't even remember who her last meal had been. A sailor, she thought. Yes. It came back to her, as if through the same fog that still hazed the town. He had been young, ripe with years. The recollection brought with it another gut-wrenching pang.

"Droë."

She lifted her head. Even that took effort. Taibid stood over her. Panic gripped her. She quailed, pressing herself to the wood at her back, staring past him, looking for Rissla.

"She's not here. I came to help you."

Droë wasn't sure she believed him.

"Can you walk?"

"Do you know how long it's been since I ate?"

"A long time, I know."

He tried to pull her up. Droë's legs wobbled and she collapsed back to the ground.

"How long?"

"What?" he asked.

"How long? I'm asking. I can't remember anymore."

"It doesn't matter. We need to get you away from here."

"How? She'll find me. She always does."

"Not this time." He smiled. "I gave them a riddle—Rissla and the others. They'll be distracted for a bell or two at least."

Fresh tears leaked from her eyes. "You're sure?"

A riddle. If only she had thought of that. She even knew one. A good one. All Tirribin kept one in mind for occasions of this sort. No Tirribin could resist the lure of a fine riddle, and once presented with one, no Tirribin could leave it, even for a moment. She might have saved herself, if only she had thought to do so. Perhaps Rissla was right and she was still a child.

"It's the best one I know," Taibid said. "It once held me for an entire day. I wound up nearly as hungry as you are now."

"I doubt that."

He helped her up again and supported her as they made their way from the town into the farmland to the west. There, he left her for a time, returning to her near dusk, leading her to a prone form lying in a field. An old man, who bled from a messy wound to his head.

"For you," Taibid said. "He's alive still. Not many years, but enough to get you on your feet. After him you can hunt for yourself."

Before he had finished speaking, Droë was at the man's neck, draining him of his years. She barely heard the last of what Taibid said. Too soon, she finished. She straightened, breathing hard. The man had given her just enough to make her frantic for more. But she could stand. Her thoughts cleared. She thought she might even be able to move at speed again.

"I need more. Now."

"Then you should hunt. I have to go back."

"Yes, all right." She should have said more, thanked him for saving her life—he had risked a good deal on her behalf—but she could think only of finding more years, of finally satisfying the hunger that raged within her. "Goodbye. I'm in your debt."

She gave him no chance to reply, but dashed away along the farm road. After less than a league, she had nearly exhausted herself. To her great relief, however, she had come within sight of another village. This one was smaller than Rissla's town, but it was big enough. As dusk darkened the sky, she slipped into the village, following the road past fields and barns and homes, tasting the years within each structure.

Droë sensed the boy before she saw him. He walked toward her on the lane. Ten years old, no more. An entire life ahead of him. Years enough to begin to fill her once more.

She felt his fear, could imagine him in the gloaming, eager to be home, safe with his mother and father. Fear might make him careless, which would help her take him. Usually such prey would be almost too easy for her. But she was far from her best and she didn't know the land.

She tasted something else in him, something that might have held her back had she not been famished. As it was, she dismissed the danger. How could it matter? Out here in this tiny village, far from any towns or cities of consequence?

Easing off the lane, she retreated into shadows and watched for the lad. She didn't have to wait long.

He carried a stick, gripping it as a soldier might a war axe. His eyes scanned the road and the fields to his left and right. Surely he feared an encounter with highwaymen, or wolves, or some imagined terror of the night. It would never occur to him to be afraid of a girl, someone who, to all appearances, was no older than he.

She stepped out of her hiding spot. The boy halted, adjusted his grip on the stick. After looking her up and down, he lowered it slightly.

"Good evening," he said, his voice thin in the cooling air.

"Good evening." She kept herself coiled, ready to strike. Just a bit closer.

He took a tentative step toward her, glanced around again. It didn't seem to occur to him to check the sky. It didn't occur to Droë either.

The attack came without warning, abrupt and furious: the rush of wind in wings, a pale blur of motion, a truncated cry from the boy, a spray of blood that stained a broad arc of the dirt road and the pale grass beside it.

Even after Droë realized that the huge pale form crouched over the boy was a Belvora, it took her a fivecount to understand what had happened. Her prey was dead. This witless Ancient had taken it from her, spilling precious years the way one might slosh muddy water from a bucket.

"He was mine!" she said, rage turning her voice to a rasp.

The Belvora draped his wings over the body. Already blood stained the leathery skin around his mouth. He regarded her with placid surprise, as if he hadn't noticed her until that moment but cared not at all.

"Not so, Tirribin," he said. "Surely you scented the magick in him. He was mine to take, as are all creatures of power. Including Tirribin. You know Guild law. If you do not, you ought to."

"I was stalking him," she said, ignoring the implied threat. "I practically had his years already. They were mine!"

He flicked a hand, indicating the body. "It would seem otherwise." He turned his attention back to his meal.

Anger exploded within her. Rissla. The Belvora. The madness of near starvation. All of it had been building for too long. The death of the boy was as a flame to oil.

She charged at the Belvora and was on his back before he could react. She clamped her mouth to his neck, wrapped her arms around his throat. He bellowed, tried to break her grip, but she would not be denied this feeding. He buffeted her with his wings to no avail. She closed her eyes, locked her hands together, held on. And she devoured him.

His years went deep, deeper than any creature on which she had fed before. Belvora were shorter lived than most Ancients, but still he had more time in him than any human. The years were bitter, not as honeyed as the years of humans, but she was too famished to let that stop her. She ate, filling herself and more. Long after she was sated she continued to pull the years from him, spite blending with hunger into a ravenous frenzy.

When at last she had finished—when nothing remained within him—she released him and stepped back. He lay dead, prone across the body of the boy. His skin had shriveled, making him even more hideous than most Belvora.

Droë felt unsteady on her feet, drunk on years, but also more powerful than she could remember. She sighed her contentment and left him there, intending to find a new village, one in which she would be the lone Tirribin.

* * *

"Do you deny it?" the Belvora female demands, her taloned finger still aimed like a blade at Droë's heart. "Do you dare to claim innocence before this assembly?"

Droë raises her chin. "I am Droë of the Tirribin. I do not deny killing the Belvora. But I was on the hunt as well. I was desperate to feed. Near to starving. The human was mine. Your brother stole my prey."

"Then you concede that you were stalking a magickal creature. Not only are you guilty of murder, you also have violated ago-old agreements on prey and territory."

"I never admitted murder," she says, an idea coming to her with the power of epiphany.

She might yet find a way to avoid punishment. The Belvora himself—this creature's brother—has shown her the way.

Jonji scowls, the expression fearsome on such a huge creature. "You said you killed him. What more—"

"He was prey. I fed on him."

Whispers greet this, then silence. The Belvora spreads her wings. "Do you dare mock me?"

"I do not."

"Tirribin do not feed on Belvora!" The female turns to Lir. "I demand that she be punished!"

"Why can my kind not feed on Belvora?" Droë asks, facing the Arrokad as well. "Do Belvora not feed on us? Do they not claim the right to hunt all beings of magick?"

Lir raises both eyebrows at her question. "An intriguing point. Jonji, do you deny that your kind prey on others in this Guild?"

"We—we prey on humans who have magick. Primarily. It is rare for us to prey on other Ancients."

"But not unheard of."

As the Belvora falters, Lir turns his gaze on the other Tirribin. "Do you support the claim of Droë, that your kind should be given leave to prey upon the years of other Ancients?"

"Only those who prey on us," Droë says before the others can answer.

"Very well. Do you support the claim of Droë," Lir begins again, "that your kind should be given leave to prey upon the years of those Ancients who have leave to prey upon you?"

Rissla slants a glance Droë's way and for a moment Droë thinks she might refuse. But after a tencount, the older Tirribin nods. "I am Rissla of the Tirribin. We do support this claim. It seems only right and just." She sends a sweet smile Jonji's way. "I'm sure my Belvora cousins will agree."

At first, the Belvora can say nothing. Eventually, though, she gathers herself. "Even if we do agree, that does not excuse the killing of my brother. She cannot murder, and then, afterward, justify doing so."

"Even though he threatened me?" Droë says. "Even though he flaunted his right to hunt me down?"

"He did not!"

"He did. I swear it before this Guild and invite death should I be found to be lying."

"An empty vow, since none were there to hear!"

"It is fairly sworn, Jonji," Lir says. "You know this." He does not wait for her response. "I find that Droë's actions, while unfortunate, do not warrant punishment. Next Grievance."

No one speaks.

"Hearing none, I conclude our proceedings."

Droë exhales.

"But before we take leave of one another, I have a question. Why, Droë, were you so desperate for sustenance?"

"What?"

"You said so yourself. 'I was desperate to feed. Near to starving.' You, a Tirribin with the strength to take the years of a Belvora—how did this come to pass?"

She goes still, save for her eyes, which find Rissla's. The other Tirribin schools her features, but watches her, clearly interested to hear her answer.

"With all respect to you and the other Ancients here tonight," Droë says, "this is a matter for our sept. It does not fall under the purview of the Guild."

"I did not claim otherwise. This is why I concluded our gathering before asking. But I remain curious."

"A predicament of my own creation, I assure you. An error of youth, some might say."

She chances a second glance at Rissla. The Tirribin actually smiles back at her.

"Very well," Lir says. "Farewell all, until next time."

He moves off and, joined by the other Arrokad, begins the descent to the sea. The Belvora linger. Jonji glares at Droë, murder in her amber eyes. But she does not attack, at least not yet, and an instant later the other Tirribin gather around Droë. All except Taibid.

"That was well done, little one," Rissla says, her voice devoid of irony. "Very well done indeed."

"Thank you," Droë says, wary.

"You've found a new village?"

"Yes. I'm the only Tirribin there."

Rissla nods, eyes the Belvora. "That's just as well." She swings her gaze back to Droë. "But if ever you return to my town, you will be welcomed."

Droë does not hide her skepticism.

"'I swear it,'" Rissla says, "'and invite death should I be found to be lying.'" She grins again.

Droë does as well. She tips her head, a motion halfway between a nod and a bow, and moves off, keeping an eye on the Belvora as she retreats into the wood.

She has been fortunate this night, and even so she has managed only to exchange one deadly enemy for another. She decides, though, that she would rather be at odds with the Belvora than with her own sept. Her kind are cruel and canny. The Belvora are hunters, no less certainly, but no more either. Formidable as they might be, they are also predictable.

Still, from this day forward, Droë will have to make a habit of checking the sky.

The Cage at the End of the World

James Enge

"Things could be worse."

"How?" asked Morlock Ambrosius.

"You could be dead, too. Like me."

Morlock ignored his cellmate and continued to look somberly out the barred window. The eastern edge of the world curved away, only a few paces distant—dry and bare, like the rib of a monstrous beast, long dead and picked clean. A few vermilion sheep were snuffling through the dust near the world's edge, trying to pick the bone even cleaner. They ate bugs, and in some ways their faces looked more like pigs than sheep. But they had been bred from sheep by some of the members of the Collegium Necromanticum, the same order that now held him prisoner.

It had started, as many things did for Morlock nowadays, with a hangover. Morlock woke up in a ditch with his head throbbing like a Fenferlad's drums, his eyes crusted shut with a cement of tears and dust, dried vomit caked on his face and forearm, and a wound on his hand that he didn't remember and couldn't explain.

It was a better morning than many he'd had in the past few years. The ditch was relatively dry, at least.

Everything was dry. His eyes, when he managed to pry them open, still felt like they were coated with sand. His nose was plugged with black dusty dried snot. The wound on his hand was recent, red with unhealing heat, but the wrinkled brown lips of the wound were clamped shut. His mouth tasted like damnation salted with empty regret. Clearly, he needed a drink, and he crawled out of his ditch in search of one.

None of it puzzled him, except the wound. He didn't remember getting it and it seemed recent enough that it should still be oozing the occasional drop of blood. Maybe someone had sealed up the cut with a salve while he was unconscious or blacked out. Not out of charity, he was sure: few wasted their kindnesses on a drunk, as he knew from experience (and, as a matter of fact, he quite agreed). But his blood was a general hazard: it set any flammable and many apparently non-flammable things on fire. He wasted little thought on it, as it didn't seem important, which was probably the biggest single mistake he made on that ugly, evil morning.

When he made it all the way out of the ditch he realized that he had forgotten his sword, Tyrfing. It had somehow slid out of its sheath overnight and lay there, glittering like a strip of volcanic glass, at the bottom of the ditch.

Sliding down the ditch again would be easy, but he shuddered at the thought of repeating the laborious climb up the dusty slope. He held out his hand and croaked the sword's name: "Tyrfing." The talic impulse woven into its crystalline lattice lifted it up and it settled into his outstretched hand like a bird coming to roost.

He considered simply sheathing the blade without renewing the talic impulse. But what if he dropped the sword in another ditch or behind a piece of furniture or something and was too tired to pick it up? Morlock sluggishly reckoned future effort against current effort, the lazy man's calculus, and reluctantly took the steps to summon visionary rapture, allowing him to re-infect the accursed sword with a kind of life.

The mental discipline involved in summoning and dismissing rapture woke him more thoroughly than the sunlight, or hunger and thirst. He hid the blade in the sheath strapped to his crooked shoulders and stood in a single movement, defying the crescendo of pain-drums thundering behind his eyes.

"Very good!" remarked a fox who was lounging atop a nearby stump.

"Thank you," Morlock replied with reflexive courtesy. He looked more narrowly at the fox to be sure that (a) it was there, (b) it was actually speaking, and (c) it was speaking to him. All three things seemed to be true. It looked at him with a quizzical intelligence luminous on its narrow, pointed face.

"Not at all," the fox replied. "If I knew you could be so lively, I woody-bin more careful about clawing you last night."

"Oh?" Morlock looked at his hand. "Woody-bin?"

"Yes: woody-bin. My name is Gawr, by the way."

"Mine is Morlock. So you clawed me."

"Yes! Sorry! My friend wanted a sandal of your blood, so I clawed you a little tuney bit. Burned my paw, too! But my friend healed me up, and you, too. Sort of."

"So you're a familiar."

"That's rude. We prefer the term 'sorcerous adjunk.'"

"Oh?"

"No, I'm just messing with you. Yes, I'm a familiar: to Clivia the Life-maker."

"Eh." Morlock usually didn't get along with lifemakers, or necromancers as they were sometimes known.

"I guess I know what that means. Most lifemakers are pretty creepy. But Clivia's not like that. Usually. Sometimes. Maybe you'd like to talk to her? She can get you a drink, at least."

"All right. Sounds like she owes me one."

Gawr the fox lightly leapt down from the stump and trotted down the road towards the blue wall of the sky. The eastern edge of the world was very near here and the size of the sky was somewhat disconcerting.

They came over a ridge and went down into the last valley in the world. A city wall stood blocking the road; there was a soldier in tarnished armor standing with a spear in the open gate. He brought the spear up to guard, but the fox ran straight at him, screamed out high-pitched wheezing barks, dodged the slow swing of the spearblade, and arrowed in to nip at the soldier's bare ankles.

"Get the chaos away from me, you fornicating rat-dog!" the soldier screamed at last and the fox dashed onward into the world's last city.

As Morlock approached, the soldier swung his spear back threateningly and said, "You I can stop."

Morlock took the spear away from the soldier and handed it back to him without a word. The soldier looked at the spear, looked at the filth-caked figure confronting him, and snarled, "I'm quitting this stupid job!"

Morlock took this as permission to pass and followed the fox into the last city.

The street beyond the gate was full of peddlers. They stood silent by their carts, watching every passerby eagerly, but said nothing, and did not even gesture toward their wares. Morlock noted how odd these wares were. Who would need triply refined goat-piss, or dried baby-fingers ("harvested from freshly dead babies!" according to the ideoglyphs adorning the seller's cart), or jellied Hydra venom? No one … unless they were engaged in the more sinister forms of magic.

"Many magic-workers in town?" he asked the fox.

"Sure," Gawr said. "It's the magic guilds. For all intensive purposes, everyone in town is in one, or biting their time until they can get their mist in."

Morlock thought he understood most of this. "There are many magic guilds, then?"

"Oh, Lorbal Mighty, yes. My friend belongs to the Collegium Necromanticum, or she used to, and will again as soon as she passes mustard. But there is the Werewolf Conspiracy, Granny Stormfunk's Triple-Secret Coven, the Army of the Mystic Envelope—whores of others."

"Whores?"

"It means 'lots.' It's a hard word, but my friend taught it to me. I know lots of hard words," Gawr bragged, grinning a toothy, vulpine grin up at Morlock. "People can hardly understand me sometimes. Anyway, there are lots of magicians in town."

"That must be why the peddlers don't hawk their wares," Morlock reflected. The more magic workers there were nearby, working their various magics, the more likely a shouted word would send one of their spells awry, perhaps disastrously. This would be a quiet town. Also, a very unsafe one. Morlock was starting to wonder if this drink would be worth the trouble.

The fox was worried about something else. "Hawk? Are you sure that's the right word? I thought it was a kind of bird."

"It is, but sometimes it means to call out to people so they will buy your stuff."

"Oh, yes. No one does that. It is weird. I thought it was because of the fairs of wizards."

"What?"

"You know the old saying. Do not peddle in the fairs of wizards, for they are supple and quick tobbangers."

"What are tobbangers?"

"People ride them downhill for fun when there's snow or they've stolen a chicken or something."

"Never heard of them. Or your saying."

The fox peered up at him with a suspicious eye. "Are you sure you're Morlock Ambrosius? You don't seem to know much."

"I know your friend owes me a drink. Where is she?"

"Not far."

It was far. The fox led him on a circuitous path through the winding streets of the silent town drenched with magic and sunlight, past many a fortified tower emblazoned with mystic sigils. At last they came to a tall, many-towered, rambling house of many wings, standing in a field of tiger-lilies at the edge of the world. In the truncated fields nearby, vermilion sheep rooted in the dirt for bugs and other fodder. In the doorway of the house lounged a burly, greasy sort of doorkeeper with an unusual number of heads scattered around its body—several on necks protruding from the broad shoulders, a couple peeping out from the gaping armpits of the doorkeeper's tunic, one on each knee and so on. Morlock stopped counting at fifteen; there were almost certainly more, from the muttering sounds emitted by the doorkeeper's ragged clothing. He or it had seven arms; three of his hands held clay jars wearing thin gray lips. Periodically it held a jar up to one of its mouths and there was a high, keening sound, like the scream of a ghost.

Trolls protruded heads and limbs like that, before they split up into several smaller selves, but Morlock didn't think this was a troll. Seams of old scars crisscrossed the ancient body. It hadn't grown; it had been constructed in this guild of lifemakers. Morlock didn't need to ascend to rapture to see that the body was a harthrang, the corporeal anchor of a soul-eating demon or shathe.

"Making a delivery," the fox said to the many-headed doorkeeper.

The doorkeeper stepped aside and gestured with several of its hands. "Enter."

Morlock was ware of the spells woven into the threshold, the many-headed monster, even the orange flowers nodding on their long green stems.

"No," he said. "Not without some safeguards."

"You're shrew," Gawr the fox said approvingly.

"Am I?"

"Yes. That means," Gawr added helpfully, "that you chew right through something. These guys can't be trusted. Hey, Lesion!"

"Legion," the patchwork door-monster snapped irritably, from several mouths.

"Hey, Lesion," the fox repeated, "go call the High Sarkoptic or somebody who can take an oath."

"I'm here, Gawr," said a bald, bronze-colored, elderly man, coming out of the shadows of the entryway. He was not tall or imposing; his gray gown was plain and he wore no badge of office. But the doorkeeper stood respectfully out of his way, and even the brash little fox seemed abashed in his presence.

"Is this our distinguished guest?" the old man asked genially. "How shall I call you?"

"I'm Morlock Ambrosius," said Morlock Ambrosius. "And you?"

"People usually call me Xudnas," said the man who was not really named Xudnas. "We would be delighted if you could help us with our troubles."

"I'm not in the helping business."

"Of course not, of course not. I quite understand that you have … er … retired. From active practice. Nonetheless, you are a mage of some status and reputation."

"I don't bother with reputation. I make things. I used to. I still do, sometimes."

"Excellent. Excellent. The thing is, we have need of a visiting consultant, as it were, and we can't really trust—we would rather—"

The town was full of sorcerers and they needed one. But they would rather depend on a passing stranger than let a neighboring guild into their secrets. So Morlock guessed, anyway. It might have taken this stately gentleman many minutes to make this point, but Morlock's head was already throbbing like the soul-drum of an Anhikh komos.

"I get it," he said briskly. "What is it you need? The odds are I'm not selling it."

"We need your answer to a question—that's all it amounts to, really."

"What's in it for me?"

"Yes, that is the question, isn't it? We can certainly feed you, house you, get you that drink you're interested in. We can get you money, too, of course, but …"

"Eh." Like any competent magic-worker, Morlock could make gold by the cartload if he needed it, which was pretty rare.

"Well, we just slaughtered some vermilion sheep and the mutton in the refectory is especially good today."

Morlock's stomach turned at the thought of food, but he supposed he would have to eat at some point.

"Then. Your guild feeds me and gets me something to drink. I'll give you my opinion, for whatever it's worth. We'll both have to give self-binding oaths, of course." Morlock didn't like how the Sarkoptic had been waiting there, in the shadows of the entryway, for him to enter without safeguards. He glared this rather than saying it, and from the way that Xudnas dropped his sand-yellow eyes, Morlock gathered the message was received.

"Wait a second," said the fox. "You got your Ambrosius. What about my friend?"

"Fair enough." The High Sarkoptic made three gestures with each of his withered bronze hands and said, "Your friend is released and restored to her status as a provisional semi-permanent adjunct to the Collegium."

"Ha ha!" said the fox triumphantly. He dodged between their feet and was lost in the shadows of the guild-house.

Xudnas and Morlock each swore self-binding oaths that neither would harm the other nor let the other come to harm during Morlock's stay at the guildhouse. They each ascended into the visionary state to anchor the oaths in the talic roots that bound their lives to their bodies.

Once he was sure that the oaths were valid, Morlock descended from the visionary state and stepped into the guildhouse.

"I'd like to show you around, if I may," the High Sarkoptic said.

"Not unless it's necessary," Morlock said.

"I think it is," Xudnas responded. "You'll need to understand the issues before you can pass judgment on them."

Morlock grunted and opened his left hand in concession. Xudnas proceeded to talk a great deal. Morlock paid little attention to what he said, but waited for the flood of words to ebb away. When it showed no signs of doing so, Morlock started to count his breaths. After two thousand he would give up the prospect of a drink and a meal and walk away.

By the time Morlock's count had reached five hundred they had climbed a winding stair to the second floor of the guildhall's central tower. The floor was one large windowless room, in which a great many people were working at isolated work stations: some were reading, some writing, some fiddling with foul-smelling fluids or strips of dried meat. Near at hand, one played a slow silent tune on a flute carved from bone. Xudnas had a great deal to say about this, but his cheerful tone was beginning to sound strained; he may have begun to notice Morlock's inattention.

Then Xudnas touched his wrist, something Morlock noticed because he disliked being touched. While the Sarkoptic had at least part of his attention, he hurriedly said something like, "And here is someone you know, I think."

Morlock looked around and saw the talkative little fox, Gawr, sitting on the shoulder of a woman with reddish-yellow hair and a set, weary expression. A stream of noisome fluid was running out of a funnel, through a channel atop her work table, and disappearing down a funnel at the other side. She was painstakingly inscribing cursive letters on the surface of the dark fluid with a stylus made of a fingerbone.

"Don't let us interrupt you, Clivia," Xudnas said genially. Morlock guessed this was an instruction to keep working; Clivia certainly took it as such.

"You lied to me, little friend," Morlock said to Gawr.

The fox flinched and looked away. "I'm sorry—filled with rebets. But Clivia was in the meatlocker—was going to lose her rank. I had to bring the lifemakers something they wanted and they wanted you. Now you're here and Clivia is a temporary-permanent adjunk again, with a chance at permanent-permanent adjunk."

"Adjunct," Morlock corrected him.

"Gesundheit," the fox said politely.

Morlock turned to Clivia. "Did you teach him to speak?"

Clivia looked at Xudnas, who hesitated, then nodded benignly. "Yes," she answered. "But he teaches me things, too. There must be a balance."

"You should teach him to tell the truth," Morlock said. "There are other kinds of balance, and I also keep a reckoning."

"Hey!" squawked the fox, glaring down his orange snout at Morlock. "That sounds like a threat!"

"It is," said Morlock, and passed on.

The conversation had disrupted Morlock's count. He stoically resumed it at five hundred.

"So you see," Xudnas was saying, as they descended the stairway on the far side of the dim, ill-smelling room, "they do most of the mere work, while the full members of our collegium devote themselves to contemplation, design, and policy, as you will see when we reach the studium."

Morlock understood well enough. The temporary adjuncts did the work; the full members reaped most of the benefits. Morlock had walked from the western edge of the world to the end of the east and he had seen the pattern repeated more times than he could count.

"Now, let me show you," Xudnas said, waving his coppery hands like flags.

"Not needed," Morlock said.

"No, but look," Xudnas insisted, as if Morlock were arguing with him. When they came out on the ground floor, they were on the far side of the tower from the entrance, in a dark sweet-smelling room where elderly folk lounged on many a couch. Some were engaged in animated conversation; others were staring at nothing that Morlock could see—lost in abstraction, he supposed. Some appeared to be napping. One wrinkled hairless figure of indeterminate sex seemed to be choking on their own phlegm.

"You see how peaceful it is in the studium," Xudnas said urgently. "Each member has private chambers and laboratories staffed by adjuncts, of course. But most of us spend most of our time here in the central studium, engaged in reflection or conversation. Imagine how much thinking we can do, about things that really matter, when we are freed from the toil of working with base materials and our hands."

"I do my best thinking with my hands," Morlock replied, "and my feet."

"I sense your impatience," Xudnas replied soothingly, "but let me show you one more thing."

"One of your members is dying over there."

"Aha! So it seems, does it not? It's really opportune. Let's go down to the body farm."

Morlock made a face. Lifemakers were always messing about with bodies, living and dead. "Nine hundred," he muttered to himself.

"Excuse me?" Xudnas said.

Morlock didn't bother to answer. The aged Sarkoptic led him down another flight of stairs to a dank cellar lit with green lamps. From the moist dark earth of the cellar floor was growing many a green, golden-veined plant, radiant in the bilious light. The fruits of these plants were human bodies. Each plant bore bodies in at least three stages of life—a baby at the base of the plant, a youth midway of its length, and a young adult near its apex. The bodies stood next to the plant, but each one was connected by a green-gold tendril running from the plant's trunk to the crown of the body's skull.

"Beautiful, isn't it?" Xudnas said eagerly.

"Eh," Morlock replied. Living is not a nice business, as the philosopher says, but lifemakers always seemed to be intent on making it more horrible than ever.

One of the bodies was convulsing. It was the adult body of a strapping young woman, but its throat was gargling phlegm, much like the dying old body on the floor above. It spasmed, then leapt off the moist earth floor and opened its eyes to glare about like a woman waking from a nightmare. The body's breathing eased to something like normal. The eyes grew less wild. The head looked about. The house now had a new tenant.

"Long life to you, Colleague Suna!" Xudnas called out.

Suna smiled back at him. Her strong young hands reached up to snap the tendril connecting her to the plant. She turned her head to cough up a clot of dark phlegm. Then she turned back to Xudnas and said, "Long life to you, High Sarkoptic! And to you, guest Morlock. Your reputation precedes you."

Morlock's long life was a burden to him and his reputation an even greater one. He shrugged his crooked shoulders.

"You see how it is?" Xudnas said eagerly. "Full members of the collegium never need die. They are in constant empathic contact with a life tree that grows replacement bodies. The moment of our death is the moment of our rebirth." He went on like that for a while, and Morlock counted breaths.

"Let me show you my own life-tree," Xudnas said, taking Morlock by the arm and disrupting his count.

It was somewhat interesting to see four Xudnases at once: the baby resting on the ground, the pale youth standing asleep next to the green-gold tree, the bronzed adult standing on the far side, his eyelids flickering as if he were about to awake.

"Are they alive?" Morlock asked Xudnas.

"Technically. In a sense. Perhaps. But their identity will be erased when I take possession."

"So your rebirth will be their death?"

Xudnas seemed taken aback. "I suppose so. But they are not really people, you know—just extensions of myself."

The adult body on Xudnas' life tree opened its eyelids in a slitted glare at its progenitor. Morlock looked from one to the other and shrugged.

The High Sarkoptic didn't seem to notice the glare; his yellow eyes were intent on Morlock. "I can reassure you on this point, if you will give me a chance. Really, I can."

"It's nothing to me."

"But of course it's something. The life tree is one of the most important benefits of full membership in the collegium."

Morlock was startled, then dryly amused. Very dryly. "You're offering me membership?"

"Yes! If you'll take it."

"No."

Xudnas urged him to reconsider. He insisted that Morlock's personal qualities and skills would be a tremendous boon to the Collegium, and that the lifemakers could aid him in his work and in his life, that he owed it to the world to live as long as possible so that he could enrich it with his gifts, and many a similar argument. Morlock waited until he had run out of breath and then said, "No."

"You're inflexible?"

"I'm not a joiner."

Xudnas said some more words. Morlock considered that he had wasted enough time here and turned away to leave.

"Wait!" Xudnas said. "We have your answer, and we are sorry for it, but we still owe you a drink and a meal. I hope you won't mind my company during the meal; I still hope to change your mind."

Morlock walked away. The prospect of a drink was searingly bright in his hungover mind. But he was just sober enough to know there was something wrong here. All he wanted was out. He thought this, and he met the yellow eye of Suna, still standing and watching by her life tree. Her mouth opened in a strangely predatory grin and he heard something behind him.

That was the last thing he heard for a long time.

* * *

When Morlock woke, he was in the cage at the end of the world. He could see and hear and breathe, but could not move his arms or legs. His insight told him that Tyrfing was nowhere within calling distance, even if he could have wielded it.

Xudnas was standing over him, looking down with a sad, supercilious smile. "I'm sorry it had to happen this way," the High Sarkoptic said, "but I'm not surprised. We'd heard a great deal about you, much of it bad. You could have been an ornament to our collegium. But all we really need is your blood. It has the most amazing properties! It is a phlogiston-binder—I don't know if you knew that."

"I do," Morlock croaked.

Xudnas' pale eyebrows arched even further. "You can speak? Remarkable. We'll have to increase your dose next time. You've been slightly poisoned—nothing that will harm you permanently, but it will prevent you from making trouble when we come in to collect your blood. Over time, it will probably make you more docile, but that's to your benefit, too. You're far too willful."

"I activate your oath," Morlock gasped.

"Nonsense. You've no claim against us. We're not harming you. In fact, we're keeping you safe. You were drinking yourself to death out there, you know. We won't allow that. You're far too valuable a resource."

"I had two things," Morlock rasped. "My freedom and my sword. You took them both. There will be a reckoning."

Xudnas laughed politely, as if Morlock had made a joke that he'd heard too many times before, and turned away. He said to someone standing nearby, "You may begin. Remind Kamraph to increase the dose of narcopsallion in future collections: we don't want him causing any trouble." The High Sarkoptic departed. Morlock had a brief sense that Tyrfing was near, very near, but that quickly vanished.

Xudnas' place at Morlock's side was taken by the fox-haired necromancer, Clivia. Her familiar was still draped across her shoulders, and his narrow face gazed down at Morlock, squinting with concern.

"I don't know!" Gawr said to Morlock. "The guy says he wants to talk to you! I don't know he's doing this to you!"

"Shut up, Gawr," Clivia said. She pulled on a pair of fireproof glass gloves and stuck a needle in Morlock's bare arm, drawing a quantity of smoking dark blood into a glass jar.

"You shut up," Gawr said, after some thought. "*You* shut up. This is the same meatlocker you were in."

"It's not."

"It is."

"I was on a different floor."

"It's the same even if it's not the same!" the fox barked shrilly.

"We'll discuss this later."

"We'll discuss *you* later," the fox sobbed.

Clivia finished the job and wrapped Morlock's wounded arm with a fireproof bandage. "I am sorry, too," she whispered.

Morlock didn't answer and she left. His eyes could move enough to watch her go; he saw her use an intricate blackiron key to open the cell door. For a moment, just a heartbeat, as she passed through the door, Morlock could again feel the talic weight of Tyrfing somewhere on the other side. Then the cell door slammed shut and the connection was broken.

In time the poison left Morlock's veins and he could move again. The cell in which he found himself was much as Gawr described it: a meatlocker. There were human beings and other animals hung from the walls in various stages of disassembly: the upper torso of a sallow-skinned man, the ragged ends of his entrails neatly braided together; the left half of a goat, its internal organs glazed to prevent leaking; a gigantic newt with roughly a hundred eyes (and bleeding gaps for at least fifty more), floating in a globe of bluish fluid affixed to the wall, and so on. The warm-blooded animals seemed to be alive; their bodies were hot and stank like live things rather than dead ones. But none of them seemed to be conscious. If it weren't for the jars of dead necromancers, Morlock would have had no one to talk with at all, which would have suited him better.

There was a shelf of them: yellow unglazed jars about the size of a man's head, each adorned with a single waxen ear and a pair of grayish lips. Each one contained the soul of a necromancer who had been found guilty of some more or less serious infraction of the guild rules and sentenced to death. For those judged the most guilty, it was death without parole. When the time came, their jars would be taken out to be consumed by Legion. For the less guilty, this was a temporary death, and they would eventually be granted access to a new body (not necessarily their own).

They talked endlessly: to each other, to Morlock, to themselves; about their crimes, their appeals, the injustice or justice of their sentences, constant threats to inform the collegium about something some other jar had said. The chatter in the room was worse than the stench. He stood it as long as he could, and then he started turning the jars toward the wall so that their flapping lips were muffled by the stones. After he had turned three, the minds in the rest of the jars took the hint and ceased their endless babbling.

The walls, the cell, and the window of the cage carried some magical seal. They were opaque to visionary rapture, and sound did not seem to pass through them in either direction. The barred door of the cage was secured with a blackiron lock of no particular subtlety. But a blackiron lock can only be turned with a blackiron key.

Light and air passed between the bars of the doorway, however, and (even more importantly) the window looking out at the eastern edge of the world. He spent many hours pacing the narrow length of the cage, ignoring the muttered remarks of the jars, trying to think of a way out. When he tired of that, and of the dreckish, rotting reek of the cage, he stood at the barred window and breathed deep, watching the vermilion sheep and the endless blue beyond the end of the world.

At least once every day, he would fall into darkness. He awoke on his cot, with some of his blood gone and a tray of food and a goblet of water tinged with wine at his side. The food was plain bread and sheep's cheese—nothing extraordinary, but edible even in the slaughterhouse reek of the cage.

This went on for some time. He didn't count the days. But he was sensing the growth of something gentle and terrible in his mind and heart. It was not docility, exactly. It was despair. His recklessness and folly had put him here and he would stay here until he died—or until it was safe for the necromancers to let him out, because he had become so tame, so harmless. He doubted that day would ever come. But, increasingly, he feared that it might. Those were the darkest moments of all, darker than the sleep when they stole his blood.

One day he woke to find the wound in his arm deeper and wider than ever. His arm ached when he moved it. He wondered if this constant blood drain was beginning to kill him. It was the first hopeful thought he'd had in a long time.

It wasn't the last. He found that his arm hurt because something had been inserted in the wound. He drew it out carefully, spilling as little as he could of blood and fire. Eventually it lay gleaming in his bloodstained, smoking hand: a long, stiff wire of blackiron.

Morlock was not a thief, but he'd made many a lock and every locksmith must perforce have some skill at picking locks. But he had to work quickly: the next time they came in to take his blood, they might find the wire and take it as well. And he had to work out of the sight of anyone passing by in the corridor, and of the few remaining jars that he had not turned toward the wall.

Morlock palmed the wire and went to the window. He worked the wire by feel, seeing it in his mind's eye, gazing somberly with his body's eyes at the edge of the world, bone-bare and bone-brown like the rib of some monstrous beast.

"You're moping again," one of the jars said to him. "When will you stop?"

"At my convenience," Morlock said. "No one else's."

"Things could be worse."

Obviously, they could be. Morlock had discovered that, no matter how little you have, you could always have less. But he was more interested in deflecting the mind in the jar than engaging it.

"How?" he grunted.

"You could be dead. Like me."

The dead necromancers in the jars would betray him to their captors for anything, or for nothing. So Morlock believed. He kept on looking out at the edge of the world, at the vermilion sheep, and shaped the lockpick with his fingers and his mind.

The thing was done at last, or as close as it could be. He palmed the wire and turned toward the shelf of dead necromancers.

"Hey!" said one of the jars. "What's that—?"

He turned them all to the wall, muffling their empty, angry voices.

His heart was pounding in his chest, as if he were a child again, sneaking down to the workshop to implement his first fourth-dimensional seedstone. He'd blown up a big chunk of the mountain that night. Thank God Sustainer no one was killed. It was a huge disaster, a terrible thing. And it was the moment he had begun to know what he could do, who he was. Maybe it was time to remember that again.

The blackiron lock was as simple as it had seemed. On the fifth pass he had turned all three cylinders. The door drifted open.

The magic seal was broken. Sounds came to him: footfalls, voices. He felt a slight, unmistakable psychic pressure that had been missing: his sword Tyrfing. It was within calling distance.

He carefully moved the cage door aside and stepped into the corridor. No one was in sight. He turned to the left and walked quietly down the corridor of cells: meatlockers like the one where he had been caged, or worse.

Morlock followed the hallway around a corner where it crossed two others and ran into a necromancer in a stained smock with a sample dish and a clutch of dissection tools in his hands. His face was pale as marble; his blue eyes gaped wide as he saw Morlock; his mouth gaped wide, preparing to shout. Morlock caught his throat with his left hand and broke it. He caught the instruments as they fell, but the collecting dish slipped away and rang on the floor like a bronze bell.

Voices spoke in inquiring tones up the hallway to the left. Morlock ran straight up the hallway before him: it was dark and windowless. From the weight and feel of the air, he felt it was taking him underground. He leapt up the next stairway he found until he saw the light of a window.

He was standing at a side entrance into the vast workshop staffed by adjuncts. He recognized the finials on the arch of the main entrance. Opposite it, then, would be the stairway down to the body garden and its life trees. And the shape of his sword cast a shadow on his insight: it was near, very near.

Morlock entered the workshop. An adjunct stood in his way: gray of hair, of face, of eye. "Who the hell are you and where do you think you're going?" the adjunct snarled in a bitter, gray voice.

"Graverobber," he replied, "I am Morlock Ambrosius and I go where I will." He took the bitter gray adjunct by the scruff of his smock and tossed him into the nearest table.

"Ambrosius has escaped!" someone shouted and someone else cried, "Summon Legion!" and others began incantations of protection or attack.

Morlock threw back his head and called out, "Tyrfing!"

His sword flew across the room, smashing alembics and rune-hearths as it came. The grip landed in his hand like a bird coming to roost.

A shocked silence followed, and then Morlock heard the barking laugh of a talking fox.

"The wreckinging!" Gawr laughed. "The wreckinging!"

"Gawr!" hissed Clivia's voice. "What did you do!"

"I did it! You woody done it if you thought! These old farklebrugs say, 'Do this!' and you do it. But they'll never let you in! They'll never let you in! You'll always be an adjunk, you'll all always be adjunks!"

"The little fox is wiser than you, graverobbers," Morlock said. "I was a prisoner here, but you are prisoners in a worse cage than mine. Make them give you your due. They'll never give it else."

He dashed past them then and ran heedless down the stair. There was an ominous chanting in the shadowy studium on the ground floor: the full members of the collegium were aware of their danger and taking sorcerous steps to combat it.

But Morlock had a plan, long-simmered in his mind through the days of captivity. He leapt down the stairs a landing at a time until he came to the bilious garden of bodies under the earth.

Wielding his shining sword like a scythe, he began to harvest bodies from the life trees. As he cut the green-gold cords that bound them to the trees, the bodies fell gasping to the ground, their eyes snapping open as if they were awaking from nightmares.

"You know what I know, and more besides," he called out, as many had risen to their feet and were blinking at each other in wild surmise. "You know your danger and your opportunity. Your progenitors are coming to reclaim you. Fight them or die."

Some of the freed bodies began freeing their peers, gnawing through the green-gold branches of their life trees. Others began to climb the steps to the heart of the collegium. Morlock kept on slashing the branches until all were free. Then, although it took long moments he might have used escaping, he

rewove the talic impulse in Tyrfing's crystalline lattice. At last he followed
the riot of naked bodies climbing the stairs in quest of freedom or death

When Morlock reached the members' studium it was not the calm med-
itative place that he had once seen. The dim air was filled with cloudy, fire-
eyed spirits, summoned by the members to defend them. But each of the
members was struggling with one or more younger versions of themselves.
Morlock sauntered past Xudnas. He would have liked to say something
cutting to the High Sarkoptic—remind him of his broken oath. But it would
have been wasted air: Xudnas' infant self had climbed him like a tree and
was chewing with desperate intent on one of the High Sarkoptic's golden
eyes.

Morlock wove his way through the room, warding off stray spirits with
Tyrfing, and finally crossed the threshold to the entryway.

Legion was there waiting, an edged weapon in each one of its seven
hands.

"Get back to your pantry, meat," one of its heads said.

Morlock, in turn, said nothing at all. He knew better than to bandy words
with a demon. He raised Tyrfing to guard and barely fended off slashing
attacks by two swords and an axe.

That was not the real danger, though. He could hear voices whispering in
his head, offering assistance, offering power, offering escape.

He raised up his confidence like a burnished shield. He had learned the
way of the sword from Naevros syr Tol, greatest swordsman of the old time.
He did not fear death. He rejected the whispers.

Furiously, Legion spun around the entry, slashing deftly with all its
blades. Morlock guarded himself, shifted his footing as necessary, and
watched the thing move. It was ungainly to look at, as was Morlock himself,
but the body was built by people who knew how bodies worked. It could
threaten him, perhaps kill him.

But it was alive. It breathed. It sweated with exertion. It took moments
to rest. The soul-eating demon within was bound to this body. If it died, the
demon would need another host. Morlock juggled the risks, the possible and
impossible futures, in his mind.

In that moment, he felt an exaltation greater than any drunkenness. A
bright window opened to the past and future and he was again, for a moment, the man he once had been, the man he might yet be.

He rose to the challenge and ascended to the first level of visionary rapture. It was a fearful risk: the talic realm was the demon's native heath: it

could reach him there, perhaps infect him with itself, its despair, its insatiable satiation. But it was the risk on which all his futures hinged.

He saw the thing then in two realms: physical and non-physical, the sweating mask of matter and the dark knot of talic energy within. That was the place—there—where its heart would be, if it had a heart. That was the demon's anchor in this crooked house of flesh.

Morlock was ware of a talic incursion by the demon and dropped like a stone out of the visionary realm to the mundane one.

He threw Tyrfing like a spear. The black and white crystalline blade, glittering like volcanic glass, sank deep in the seamed chest of the shambling harthrang. The demon was bemused by the unexpected move and hesitated as Morlock dove past its weaving arms and plunged into the sunlight beyond the threshold.

"Tyrfing!" he called, and held out his hand.

The blade burst through the back of the harthrang, scattering gobbets of rotten flesh as it flew from the ruins of the monstrous chest cavity, spinning about to land in Morlock's hand like a bird coming to roost. The grip was a little slimy, though.

Legion's body staggered, dying, into the light. It let its weapons fall. It reached out with its many hands for supports that were not there. It fell to the ground among the tiger-lilies and was still. The body was dead.

But the demon lived. Morlock felt its approach like a cloud of dread through the sunny day. It needed a new host; it would have one; and Morlock's body was the nearest at hand.

Morlock leapt up into the talic realm, letting his body fall unregarded to the earth. His visionary avatar—a black-and-white tornado of talic flames, armed with Tyrfing, a weapon in both realms—struck out at the dark fiery cloud of the unrooted demon.

It expected no such resistance and quailed, fled toward the edge of the world. The only bodies nearby were in the flock of vermilion sheep and the demon settled amongst them, darkening the dim light of their souls with its hunger and its hate.

A streak of fiery tal approached, a wild fuzzy comet of a mind: Gawr. His necromantic insight perceived the demon in the sheep, knew what must be done.

Morlock fell from vision into flesh. His body lay aching on the ground and his sword lay, lifeless and bereft of tal, beside him. He seized it and forced his aching muscles to lift him to his feet.

The vermilion sheep were still convulsing from the onset of the demonic possession. Gawr was dashing at the edges of the flock, chivvying them towards the verge. Morlock rushed at them as well, shouting vile insults in Dwarvish. The sheep started to move, and then run away from these irritants, straight to the end of the world, bone-bare, bone-brown, with nothing to stop their plunge over the side.

Morlock and Gawr stood there in companionable silence, not speaking or needing to speak, as they watched the sheep fall into the endless blue beyond the end of the world. They watched for a long time, but the sheep kept on falling.

In fact, they are falling there yet. If you ever get to the eastern edge of that world (not impossible with all the advances being made in interplanar travel these days), you should definitely visit the Free Institute of Necromancy and Gawric Studies, on the site of the old Collegium Necromanticum. They have an array of far-seers and telescopes there, and in the more powerful ones you can still see the bright red sheep falling ever more slowly into the end of the world and time.

But don't expect to see Morlock there. He has long since moved on to the next town, the next drink, the next mistake.

Assassinsssss

Jason Palmatier

The hidden trebuchets groaned and whirled in the muggy darkness, flinging barrels from their slings in flat arcs that slid them just over the high walls of Castle Noway. The barrels smashed in a skittering mess on the innermost courtyard, releasing dark shapes that tumbled wildly before springing up in front of stunned guards.

Shing!

The first guard dropped, blood spurting from his slit throat. His killer spun around the body as it fell, slinging a second blade up the left nostril of a wall sentry twenty feet above who had leaned over to investigate the noise. As the sentry's body smacked onto the filthy cobblestones near the killer's feet, the victorious assassin threw back her jet-black hood and hissed to her BAFE (Best Assassin Friend Ever) Candace, "Baaaadddddd Asssssssss …"

Candace glanced over with a wicked gleam in her eye as she pulled a dagger from a third guard's chin and finished her friend Angela's catch phrase. "… Assassinsssss."

The two women high-fived, their matching auburn hair bouncing with a zest glam, before pulling their hoods back on. Then they ducked as a third barrel slammed into the central tower directly above them, leaving a prodigiously bloody splat and showering them with wooden splinters.

"Ooo. Jody didn't make it," Candace winced.

"Less talk, more killing," Angela said as she yanked her dagger from the fallen sentry's nose and stepped over Jody's bleeding-out body.

The door to the main tower opened silently. The two assassins swept in. Three more guards fell on the stairs, one to Candace's blade "Rat Bastard" and one each to Angela's main blade "Throat Slitter" and her Saturday Night Special blade "Ralph." The door at the top of the stairs glowed in the sooty torchlight. A quick game of parchment, rock, dagger gave Angela the main door and Candace the outside window.

Angela watched her friend find a grip on the stonework and slip out into the darkness, then counted out ten seconds. "One bloody dagger, two bloody daggers, three—"

She threw the door lever up on ten and rolled in, coming to her feet with Throat Slitter pointing just to the right of the king's Adam's apple. She shoved it home savagely, yearning for the pulsating arterial hit that would spurt blood all over her face and down her shirt.

Nothing happened. Her blade had sunk about a half inch into thick leather. She pulled back and found a regally-dressed sparring dummy staring back at her.

Someone cleared their throat behind her. She spun, throwing Ralph in a smooth motion that resulted in a high-pitched, metallic ring as her second-string-killing-thing bounced off a longsword. She drew back Throat Slitter for a second try, but a voice interrupted her.

"Ah, ah, ah …" King Reginald Noway the Fifth stood in his royal pajamas, wagging a finger from side to side. He pointed around the room. Six guards stood on the circular perimeter, all pointing cocked crossbows at her. Angela smirked, knowing exactly what she was going to do. She tensed.

"Nope. Feinting at me and dropping to the ground so they all shoot each other in a buffoonish crossfire isn't going to work," the king said. "We train for that."

Angela paused, taking in the king's total lack of armor and essentially useless-for-close-combat longsword. She could kill him even without taking out the guards.

"And, no, you can't kill me without taking out the guards because I have this," the king lifted the longsword from his shoulder where it rested casually. "Some people call it Assassin's Bane or King's Shield or whatever, but I call it Assassin's Ass In." The king gestured to the upper walls of the room where two dozen human butts hung like hunting trophies, all with longsword-blade holes conspicuously stabbed through them. The names below them read like a who's-who of assassin pedigree. There was Jenny

"Cut Up" Comeatian, Barbara "Slash and Bag" Barbary, Caroline "Shove a Knife Right Through Ya" Bunnylove, and, of course, Ted; all the greats that the bards still sang stories about. Angela paused a second time, then a smile split her face.

"You've thought of everything Reginald, except one … I'm not alone!" Angela dropped to the floor, listening for the whoosh of Candace's blade as it sailed from the window into the king's smug face.

Nothing happened. Angela jerked her eyes towards the window and found Candace staring back at her, the points of three pikes hovering just above her head from the parapet above. The two assassin's eyes locked.

Candace swallowed.

Sweat broke out on Angela's forehead.

Then Candace dropped from view in a perfectly timed get-your-assassin-out-of-here free fall.

"Candace!" Angela's mouth dropped open in disbelief. Her BAFE had just abandoned her.

"Well, well. Looks like you *are* alone now. How about we have a little chat, then," the king said.

Angela waited a few seconds, mind racing for a way to get a little more blood out of this job without losing any of her own. But Candace's abandonment had messed with her blood-spilling mojo and after an awkward silence she pushed herself up off the floor and brushed herself off. "Okay, then. What's the subject?"

King Noway put Assassin's Ass In point down and rested his hands on the pommel. "I let your little assassin party get all up in here because I have a job I need done and I need the best."

Angela stood up a little straighter and nodded. So far everything was making perfect sense.

"And now that the best just dropped out of sight from that window, I'm stuck with you."

"Hey!"

"Ah, ah. Let's be honest. The best assassin is the one that didn't get caught, am I right?"

Angela just glared.

"Anyway, a former teammate of mine in the old Rape and Pillage game, also known as Noble Life, took something from me and I need someone to get it back—"

"Ah! Stop right there." Angela held up a hand. "Can't do it."

"Oh, I think even you are capable of—"

"Nope. Not gonna' happen."

"Hold on a minute—"

"Whole lotta' nope. You just said took 'something.' Unless that something is a life that needs to be ended I'm not your girl."

"Did you not see the line of asses on the wall?" The king gestured to them again, incredulous.

"Yep, saw them. Can't help you."

"Yours is going to be up there unless you hear me out!"

"Listen, you want *something*, so what you need is a *thief*. I'm an *ass-ass-in*." Angela said it slowly to let it sink in. "I belong to the *Ass-ass-ins' Guild*, which is in the business of killing people, and only killing people. I can't go stealing stuff or the *Thieves' Guild* is going to hire someone from the *Assassins' Guild* to kill *me* for crossing *guild lines*. Got it?"

The king closed his mouth and stroked his chin dramatically. "Ah yes, and since you are obviously not the best assassin—"

Angela bristled.

"—you would have to worry about actually getting killed … eventually. Whereas, if you don't hear me out you will most certainly be killed *right now*. That is a tough decision …"

Angela glared.

"So, as I was saying, I need you to steal back the Magufin from Prince Gavashat who has hidden it—"

"What's the Magufin?"

"What is wrong with you?! Can't you let a single sentence be completed without interrupting?!"

"I just like to know what I'm getting into."

"Fine." The king regained his composure and continued. "The Magufin is the MAGical Universal Fairy Immobilizing Nutsack, which is such a mouthful. We just shortened it to MAGUFIN."

"Wait, nutsack?"

"Yeah, a sack for carrying nuts. You know, hazelnuts, walnuts, acorns, you name it. Really pretty useful on its own, but if you drop this particular sack over a fairy and cinch it up the little F'er can't get out no matter what it does."

"Why do you need a sack for fairies?"

"Um, er, you know, entertainment and such …"

Angela raised an eyebrow and wrinkled her nose, some pretty sick images running through her head.

"Oh, alright. You're an assassin so you'll probably be into this stuff." The king ripped a sheet off a birdcage dangling near his bed, revealing a bruised and battered wood sprite in garish fighting leathers who spit out two teeth and glared at her.

"What the …" Angela started.

"I Sprite Fight. I know, I know, it's illegal! But I can't get enough of seeing the little people beat the glitter out of each other. What can I say? I love it."

"But you said this sack catches fairies?"

"Fairies, sprites, it doesn't matter. The thing will hold whatever you can fit in it. Sacks aren't really into the details, you know. They're just sacks. *Anyway*, the first rule of Sprite Club is 'Don't talk about Sprite Club,' so let's get back to the job. As I was saying, *yet again*, Prince Gavashat hid the Magufin inside an orphanage in the Principality of Innocence."

Angela suddenly perked up. "So, I might have to hack through some innocent orphans to get it?" The blood of the innocent had a special feel when it ran down your skin. Kind of silky and extra warm.

"Yes, yes. You will probably have to eviscerate quite a few."

Angela swallowed down her building interest. "Go on. I'm listening."

"So, I need you to hack your way in there, get the Magufin, and then get back out, without anyone knowing where you are going with it. This is absolutely critical! Nobody can know that I have it. This sport is cutthroat in more than one way, as your presence here shows. Anyway, to help insure this you will need to plant this at the scene of your crime." King Noway held up a hair pin emblazoned with the crest of his chief rival, King L'Oreal, also known as King Finehair.

Angela shook her head again. "Can't do it. Slander Guild would be up in arms. Plus, how does that make any sense? Is King Finehair himself supposed to have stolen the thing and dropped one of his hair pins on the way out? I mean, really? Who's going to believe that?"

"You obviously don't understand fake news. Anyway, not my problem. You do this or you die. What's it going to be?"

Angela shook her head and threw up her hands. "Fine, I guess I'll do it. Can I have Ralph back?"

The king looked confused. "Who's Ralph?"

Angela pointed at the dagger that lay near the king's feet. "My dagger."

"Your dagger's name is Ralph?"

"Of course."

"Ah …"

"Can I have it?"

"Sure …"

Angela scooped Ralph from the floor and sheathed him, uncleaned. She slid Throat Slitter home, too, then put her hands on her hips. "Can I go now?"

"Of course. And remember, no one can know I have it."

Angela nodded. "Yeah, yeah. Plant hair pin, yada, yada." She took the hair pin and descended the empty steps.

* * *

Angela stalked the back alleys imagining the "oh-shit-I've-been-stabbed" face the people she passed would make if she slid a knife into their kidney. She couldn't go back to the Assassin's Guild after being captured without incurring a few rounds of torture to ensure she wasn't compromised. Plus, she was pretty sure she'd kill her no-account, backstabbing, probably pre-menstruating, ex-BAFE Candace on sight if she saw her there. So instead she mumbled to herself as she walked.

"I know for a fact that if I'm not a thief and I steal something, the Thieves' Guild is going to hire me dead. And I don't want to be dead. You can't kill people when you're dead. Unless you're a wight, but then you're stuck in one place forever. And I'm not sure they can feel blood spraying all over their face and down their shirt when they kill. So that's a no-go. And I don't think I'd even know I was killing someone if I was a zombie, and technically I'd be undead which might not be enough for the Thieves' Guild. They're kind of pedantic. Vampire would be good … but then I'd be undead again and …

"Wait a minute!" Angela stopped dead in her tracks. "I don't have to die, I just have to join the Thieves' Guild!"

Most people joined only one guild, except for those gotta'-have-it-all, can't-make-up-my-damn-mind fighter/mage/thief pricks, but they never got anywhere anyway so most people just ignored them. The important thing was that there was no law that said you couldn't belong to more than one guild. But that still left the Slander Guild.

"Screw 'em. I'll just claim the story that I planted the hair pin was fake news and therefore I'm the one being slandered. It'll be tied up in the Law Guild forever and eventually everyone will just forget about it."

Her mind made up, she turned left and headed for the Thieves' Guild main meeting place, the Fish Out Of Water.

* * *

A fake bag of coins jingled on the handle as Angela opened the front door of the Fish Out Of Water and stepped in. All heads turned, eyes roving over her body looking for sacks of gold, jewelry, anything with her Sovereign Security Number on it. The thief usual. Finding nothing but a pitch black—but somehow still blood-stained—cloak and a tightly drawn hood, they turned back to their ales. The minstrel in the corner resumed strumming on his lute.

"And Quick Finger slid Barbary's coins from her pocket, but Barbary jammed her dagger into his eye socket …"

Angela resisted the urge to fling herself into the shadows and start stabbing and instead walked up to a table in the middle of the room and sat down next to the lone thief sitting at it. He was tall and thin and wore ratty clothes and had an eyepatch. Of course.

"Hey, I got a big job lined up and I want to join the Thieves' Guild."

The thief looked up at her with his one good eye. "You can't just join the Thieves' Guild, missy—"

"Yeah, yeah, I know. You gotta' apprentice and do little odd jobs until you have enough thieving credits built up to join the Thieves' Guild West, and then hope you get a Guild contract that pays the minimum and work your way up from there until you're in the big game. But this job is *big*. Capital 'B', capital 'I', capital 'G', *big*. Like notorious. From the top. I just need someone to take me on as an apprentice and then we'll both blow right past all that crap in one go and be thick as thieves." Angela stopped and looked around the bar, nodding her head confidently.

No one said anything. Some heads shook. She detected a smirk from a far, dark corner.

Angela slammed her hand on the table impatiently. "Okay, hold up, people. I'm the real deal. Hell, in the time it took you to just stare at me I could have gutted this guy and then choked him out with his own small intestine."

No reaction.

"I'm serious. I can show you—does anyone have a puppy?"

Heads jerked back in shock. People gasped.

"It doesn't have to be a very big one," she clarified.

A scandalized thief hugged her drooling Were-Pomeranian closer to her, covering his ears. Another thief dropped his stew spoon and covered his mouth to hold back vomit.

"Now just a minute!" the barkeep yelled. "We don't want any of you sick, moral-less assassins in here! This is a fine, upstanding establishment of pilferers, pinchers, grab-baggers, pocket-cleaners, and chest-ticklers— the lock-picking kind, not the feather-carrying ones. You go back to your blood-spilling kin and leave the good, thieving people in here alone!"

Angela frowned, not understanding the hubbub. "What, are you guys fresh out of puppies? The Assassins' Guild bar always has a bunch in the back—"

"Get out!" The barkeep pointed to the door with a single meaty finger. Angela glanced around the room, finding nothing but outraged eyes glaring back at her.

"Fine, I'll just steal it myself and make you all look like chumps." She shoved herself back from the table and strode towards the door, yearning for someone to jump her from behind so she could slit him open and prove her gut-choking skills. Nobody did.

"Bunch of pansies."

She yanked open the door and stepped out.

* * *

Her initial plan blown, Angela crouched in the alley closest to the front door of the Fish, blowing on her hands to take off the chill of approaching dawn. She raised a single eyebrow at the noise beside her.

"Er, excuse me."

"Spit it out, shortstuff, I've been listening to you sneak over here forever. What are you wearing, Bardish tap shoes?"

A small man stepped out from behind a bin of rotting fish and dipped his head politely. "Pardon me, miss, I thought I was moving silently, like a summer breeze."

"Well keep on breezing, clatter-trap, I'm busy."

"Busy breaking guild lines?"

Angela turned her head slowly, looking at the man for the first time. He was short, a little over four feet at most, wearing a basic linsey-woolsey cloak with a plain-pommeled dagger strapped round his waist. His round face reminded her of a meat pie, with mashed potato cheeks and a dumpling for a nose.

"Man, I must really be hungry."

"What?" the man replied, confused.

"Nothing."

"Oh. Well, my name is Thaddeus Podruck, though my friends call me

Thad—"

"Yadda, yadda—what do you want Potluck?"

"It's Podruck, miss, I was named after a famous squire—"

"It's Potluck to me. Done deal. Now get on with it."

Potluck shut his mouth, frowning for a second, then shook off his annoyance. "I overheard your predicament in the Fish Out Of Water and wanted to offer my services as a mentor, I have recently attained guild status after years of dedicated—"

"Fine, you'll do. Let's go." Angela stood and strode into the street, hailing the first horse-drawn cart she saw.

"Ah, don't you want to know my thieving history?" Potluck shouted as he scrambled after her.

A cart stopped and silvers exchanged hands. "No. Get in the cart, Potluck, you're holding up the show."

* * *

Two days and endless cut-short conversations later, Angela and Potluck jumped down onto the hard-packed dirt on the side of the road near a cherub-encrusted sign that read "Welcome to the Principality of Innocence."

"Wow, they really take their name literally," Potluck remarked.

Angela replied with her new catch phrase, "Shut up, Potluck," and peered into the woods. After some head-bobbing she pushed back a branch to reveal a narrow path. Potluck followed her, too short to bother dodging the branch.

"So, this job …" Potluck began as he labored to keep up.

Angela did not interrupt him. Somewhat surprised, Potluck continued.

"We just have to sneak in and steal something, right?"

"Pfft," Angela snorted. "If we're unlucky."

"Wait, sneaking in undetected, grabbing what you need, and sneaking out are the hallmarks of a thieving job well done."

"Boring."

"But that's what you are supposed to do! As your mentor, I—"

Angela whirled around, whipping Ralph out and pointing it a quarter inch from Potluck's eye. Potluck cried out and staggered backwards, falling on his butt. "Dear me! What was that for?"

"Look, halfing—"

"I'm not a halfing."

"—I, wait, what?"

"I'm not a halfing. I'm just short."

"Really?"

"Yeah, my mom was short, my dad was short, pretty much my whole family is on the short—"

"Nevermind," Angela waved her dagger, "doesn't matter. Potluck, I know we have to steal stuff and all that, and I'm fine doing it because if I don't I'll get stabbed in the ass and end up on some guy's wall—"

"Wha—?" Potluck started.

"—but I'm not going to skulk around someplace keeping to the shadows and evading people if I don't get to plunge a blade into some pulsating arteries before it's all over. I mean, what a waste of time! If you're going to go through all the trouble you at least need to get the money spurt at the end."

"Ah ..."

"So when we get in there you just keep out of the way. If you get lost, follow the blood splatters. All blood splatters lead to me, got it?"

"But, I don't—"

"What? It's simple. When I stab people I like to feel a lot of blood—hot, gushing—all over me. Preferably on my face and down my shirt. But a lot of it still gets on the floor, the walls, sometimes on the ceiling, so you just have to find those splatter spots and/or the trail of bodies and they'll lead to me. If you see a bunch of corpses and aren't sure which way to go, just start feeling them: the warmer they are the closer you are to me—"

"But I don't like killing!" Potluck shouted, face stricken.

Angela stopped. Her brow furrowed. "Wha—what did you just say?"

"I. Don't. Like. Killing."

Angela's mind churned. A cog ground forward then slipped a belt. The whole thing spun out without gaining any traction. "What?"

Potluck clasped his hands in front of his chest. "Please, I can't stand the sight of blood. We have to do this without killing anybody!"

"Okay, you're speaking Common, but I can't understand you. Let's just leave it at this: stay out of my way and try not to slip in the gore." Angela whirled around and strode down the path. Ten minutes of whimpering and pleading later she stopped and squinted into the light at the edge of the woods. "Wow. That is some orphanage."

Rising above hectares of fine hops and grape vines, the main tower of Saint Innocence's Loving School for Unloved Children gleamed in the afternoon sun. Impeccably white, its plaster inlaid with golden vines hugging smiling cherubs, Angela had to squint just to look at it.

"Are you crying?" Potluck asked.

Angela turned to him, tears running down her cheeks. "No. It's just too bright. I never cry, actually. Except that one time, when my daggers were stuck in someone's face and I had to chop off another guy's head with his own broadsword and both his arteries gushed blood all over me in a Crimson Shower …" Angela's eyes misted up for real at the memory. "I did cry for that. Tears of joy. Pure joy …"

Potluck gagged a bit and turned away.

Angela, not noticing, shook herself from her reverie and plunged through the underbrush. A few minutes of stealthy crab-walking through hops rows brought them to the edge of the idyllic grounds surrounding the orphanage. Angela scanned the cascading flower gardens, bubbling fountains, and hand-crafted café tables for any sign of guards or sentry gargoyles.

"Oh, hello!"

Angela whipped around, daggers swinging out and back in a classic corncob-holder-your-skull move. Liquid splashed all over her and she opened her mouth in ecstatic surprise, until she got a whiff of it.

"Ack! What the hells!" She looked down at her dripping wet clothes and then up at the towering forms of Potluck and a smiling, rosy-cheeked boy holding a water pitcher.

"Wow, that was neat!" the boy boomed.

Angela yanked her daggers from where they had buried themselves in the toe of the boy's sandal and whirled on Potluck. "What did you do to me, Potluck?! And why does it stink so bad?"

Potluck frowned and looked at the empty vial in his hand. "I threw a potion of shrinking on you, I think. Oh, wait, this is Stinkin' Shrinkin'. Somebody must have pranked me back at the guild."

Angela shook with rage and pent up almost-had-a-kill energy. She needed blood all over her, *bad*. Then she had a vision. "Wait, if I slit your throat now, your blood will spurt all over me like a tidal wave! I could swim in it!" She started climbing Potluck's leg in a mad frenzy.

"Wait, wait, wait! Hold on!" Potluck shook his leg violently, hopping around, but Angela would not come off.

"Oh, my gods, this is going to feel so good!" Bloody red fire filled Angela's eyes as she dodged Potluck's frantically brushing hands. She gained purchase on his chest with a fistful of linsey-woolsey and leapt, Throat Slitter swinging in a beautiful arc that would open Potluck's neck from ear to ear.

"Innocencias Ninety-percent-us!" Potluck cried.

Angela's muscles suddenly froze, Throat Slitter slicing a single piece of stubble under Potluck's left ear. Then Angela fell like a collectible assassin figurine to the ground.

"Ow," she said from the corner of her mouth.

Potluck fanned himself with his hand and braced himself against a nearby café chair, breathing hard.

"Water, sir?" the boy asked.

Potluck nodded and accepted the cup the boy pulled from under his tunic thankfully. He drank deeply once the pouring was done.

Angela's muscles slowly relaxed. She stood up—all five inches of her. "Okay, Potluck, what the hell was that?"

Potluck smiled at the boy and answered her. "Compliance Command. Now you can't kill anyone who is more than 90% innocent. Don't worry, that's not a lot of people."

Angela tapped her dagger on her leg, putting two and two together and coming up with three. Then she frowned and made it to four. "Wait, no thief is ninety-percent innocent, so I should have been able to kill you just now. Spill it, Potluck. Who are you?"

Potluck patted the boy on the head. "My name is the same—"

"Who cares!"

Potluck ignored her and forged ahead. "But I'm from the Guild Guild, not the Thieves' Guild."

Angela threw up her hands and shook her head. "Oh, great. An even more useless guild than the Thieves' Guild, if that is even possible. You guys don't even do anything except check documentation for Interkingdom Standards Organization compliance. I mean, how boring!"

"Actually, we have broad powers over almost all the guilds, including yours—or at least the one you are *supposed* to belong to."

Angela glared. "Are you going to put me back to my regular size?"

"Ah ..."

Angela smirked. "Obviously you are over 90% innocent so you don't have anything to worry about."

"Yeah, but the rest of the populace ..."

"Can die! I just need to get this Magufin and be done with this stupid job!"

"The Magufin! We have it in our basement. It's really cool! Seigfried caught a heckle-gnome in it and it couldn't get out. Then he let it out and it started yelling at all the brothers, which was funny, and it made Jaden pee himself, then it ran away. So, the brothers took the Magufin from us, very gently and kindly, of course, and locked it up. Do you want to see it?"

Angela and Potluck both turned to the boy as he spoke. Angela's eyes narrowed in mistrust and Potluck's widened in surprise.

"Why, yes, young man. We would very much like to see it," Potluck said.

"What are you talking about?! We can't trust this kid! He's way too innocent to be real. Probably got a whole Cacofiend stuffed up his ass."

Potluck shook his head. "I think we can trust him—"

"One way to find out!" Angela leaped with both daggers at the kid's tender neck. She froze a hairsbreadth from his delicate skin and fell to the ground, rigid.

"Fine. We can trust him," she managed from the corner of her mouth.

Potluck nodded and pulled another vial from under his shirt, dripping a few drops on Angela. She waited to regrow. Nothing happened.

"What gives, Potluck?"

"Oh, that was some ginger deodorizer. Here's the Unshrinker."

Splash!

Angela sputtered and shook her head. "Ah, freakin' a' Potluck, that got in my mouth!"

"Sorry."

"Ack. It tastes like fairy piss."

"How do you know—"

"Shut up, Potluck!"

"Wow, that was neat!" the boy beamed. Then he hefted his water pitcher and said, "Follow me!"

* * *

The chamber the orphan led them to was just as ornate as the rest of the place, filled with gold leaf and vibrant frescos showing happy orphans playing in a parentless wonderland.

"Man, the Gilding Guild must love this place," Potluck remarked.

Angela didn't hear him; her eyes were locked on the back of the person tip-toeing out the door opposite them.

"Hey, you! Stop right there!"

The figure whirled, a hair clip spinning from his lustrous hair and clattering onto the floor.

"King Finehair?!" Angela gasped. Normally she would have already leapt and opened an artery or two, but the king's hair had stunned her. It swung back and forth around the king's head as if alive, shining, full-bodied, without a single split end despite its wondrous length. When the king finally succeeded in shaking it from in front of his eyes, it streamed back on a phantom breeze, vivacious and free, offsetting his partially opened mouth and flared, inviting eyes perfectly.

"Holy fairy tits, that is some fine hair." For a moment nothing in the world mattered except for the continued sight of that magnificent, unsurpassed, man-mane. Potluck sighed beside her, pants bulging. Water dribbled out of the orphan's forgotten pitcher.

"Assassins, attack!" King Finehair bellowed.

Angela's mind instantly shifted into Cut and Cover mode as black clad figures leapt out from behind every pillar and decorative pot in the room.

"Guilds preserve us!" Potluck shouted in terror.

The orphan boy dropped his pitcher and ran from the room shouting, "Peace out, people! You are on your own!"

Angela just flared her eyes and leapt, slicing the first assassin from navel to sternum with barely contained glee, noting, blandly, that it was Stacey "Cut Your Facey" Lambert.

"Get that sack, Potluck!" Angela shouted as she sunk Ralph deep into Melissa "Murder Mom" Kirkpatrick's sternum.

Potluck scrambled from the room, dodging blood gushes and leaping assassins, focusing on the immaculate ends of beautiful hair as they slipped around a corner in the hall.

Angela's world shrunk to flashing blades and bloody sprays, her body wracked with waves of ecstasy from every warm, wet hit of the red stuff on her skin. She began slipping in the pools of blood on the floor, eyes flaring wide in sheer pleasure with each lost footing, blades digging deeper as the killing orgy reached its climax. And just when she thought she couldn't contain herself any longer, that her body would give out in sheer spent exhaustion, her blades were stopped simultaneously with a single metallic ring. She looked past them, chest heaving, heart pounding, into the eyes of her ex-BAFE Candace.

"Oh, my gods, Angela. I knew you liked killing and all, but this is pretty sick."

"Candace!" Angela gasped. "You betraying little bi—"

"Hold on, Angie! I didn't betray anyone. That guy had us, hands down. There was nothing I could do."

"You could have thrown your dagger!"

"And what, have him whack it down with his magic sword while his guards shoved pikes through my head?"

"He was probably bluffing!"

"Nah ah, I saw him block Ralph and that sword of his is totally legit. Danced like a Bardish circus monkey in his hand, all on its own."

"Hmpf. You could have done something."

"I did. I escaped to kill another day. I just didn't think I'd be killing you."

"Pshaaa!" Angela shook her head. "As if you could kill me."

Candace's eyes flared. "Oh, don't even go there. I could totally kill you."

"No. No way. I'd slit you open like a plum pie, *Candy*."

Candace shook her head. "You know what your problem is Angela? You're fey."

"What?" Angela jerked her head back in shock.

"Yep, you are totally fey, and you don't even know it."

"I am not gay! I totally love big nobleman cock!"

"Yeah, severed and in your hand."

"That was one time!"

"Anyway, I said *fey*, and that's not the point, Angela! You get off on spilling the blood of mortals. You might as well join MORKANON and work on that first step. You know, 'Hi, my name's Angela and I have a MORtal Killing problem.' Admission is the first stage of healing, *honey*."

"The only thing I'm going to admit to is to stabbing you in your hoo-ha!" Angela shoved herself back to get some room and then lunged forward. Candace sidestepped and brought Rat Bastard up for a deep gut-spilling slash, but Angela blocked it with Ralph.

"I've got it!" Potluck yelled, puffing back into the room on his short legs.

"Later! Busy!" Angela yelled.

Candace swung her leg over in a neat round kick that tagged Angela on the temple, sending her sprawling onto the blood-smeared floor. Angela rolled, blocked Candace's leaping death plunge with her crossed daggers, and kneed Candace where the Willow-O-Wisps don't shine. Candace grimaced, her arms weakening. Angela shoved her off and brought Ralph down in a wide, friend-pinning arc.

Splash!

Ralph's point pinged off of fine marble.

Angela drew back in surprise, Ralph rising high again for another strike, but Potluck dropped the Magufin over the miniaturized body of Candace and drew the top tightly closed.

"There! All done."

Angela glared, shaking with missed-kill energy. "Stop stealing kills from me, damn it! She was mine!"

Potluck gestured around the room, "Looks like you've had enough—"

Potluck finally realized what he was standing in. He fell on his knees and started retching. After the first wave, he noticed he was retching onto the steaming guts of a disemboweled corpse and retched some more. When his stomach lining had finally come out, he fell to his side and muttered, "Isn't killing a room full of assassins enough for you?"

"No." Angela looked around at the massacre. Blood dripped from the ceiling, filled urns, rolled down walls, and oozed across the floor. It was impressive. "Well, maybe."

"Good. Can we go now?"

Angela sighed. There was no one else to kill. "Fine."

* * *

"Are you sure this is a good idea?" Potluck asked for the fifth time. He and Angela crouched in the shadows of the alley near Handoff Square, waiting for King Noway to show up to collect the magical nutsack that Candace still struggled inside of.

"You said I was all clear, right?" Angela whispered back.

"Yes, amazingly there is not a single infraction I can write you up on, since I technically stole the Magufin, King Finehair planted his own hairpin, and the assassins you killed were all contracted to kill you, so you were just defending yourself. Still, I feel as if this entire affair shouldn't somehow warrant an entire new category of noncompliance, like Willful Trading of Function or something."

"Yeah, about that 'you stole the Magufin' part—how did you get it from King Finehair?"

"Oh, that was easy, as a member of the Guild Guild I have broad powers over—"

"Stuff it, Pot o'Luck. Finehair was personally stealing that thing from an orphanage in a rival kingdom; he wasn't going to give it up over some fancy Guild mumbo-jumbo."

"Um, well, yes, he was rather reluctant …"

"Potluck …"

"Okay, I pulled his hair!"

"You touched it!"

"Yes, and it was fabulous! Like a fistful of Angora rabbit mixed with unicorn down. I almost soiled myself it felt so good."

"What did he do?"

"He shrieked, like really loud. Took me to my knees actually. But I rallied and yanked hard and he just dropped the sack and grabbed his hair, wailing. I think I broke a few strands." Potluck grimaced at the thought, eyes flaring with regret.

"Oh, my gods, Potluck. You are a heartless bastard."

"There was no other way!"

"Um …" Angela pointed to the dagger at his waist.

"Oh, that's a pen." Potluck pulled it out and held it by the blade, scribbling in the air. "You know, for filling out noncompliance forms and stuff. It's got ink in the hilt so it, like, never runs out. It's pretty awesome." Potluck beamed with pride, fawning over the dagger-pen.

Angela opened and closed her mouth a few times, then just shook her head slowly. Movement from the square caught her eye.

"Here he comes! You ready?" she called.

Potluck sheathed his pen and squatted, wriggling Magufin in hand. "Yes. So it's splash, dump, swish, right?"

"You got it."

King Noway poked his head into the square in the most conspicuous manner Angela had ever seen. Slowly he tiptoed to the center, using Assassin's Ass In like a shiny, double-edge cane. "Helloooo? … Miss Assassin?…"

Angela shook her head and squeezed her eyes shut.

"Gods, that guy is an ass," Potluck said beside her.

Angela grunted agreement, stood up, and walked straight into the square, Potluck right beside her.

King Noway brightened at the sight of the sack in Potluck's hand.

"You got it! Honestly, I was thinking you'd just get killed and that would be that. But you pulled through for me, with a little help it appears. Amazing."

"Where are your guards?"

"Oh, I had them all killed because they overheard my plan. Loose lips and all, you know."

Begrudging respect welled up in Angela, but she swallowed it down and held out her hand. "Here's your hairpin."

"What? I told you to plant that!"

"Didn't need to."

"What do you mean, you didn't need to? I told you it was crucial—"

"Listen, it's taken care of. It would take too long to explain. Now do you want the sack or not?"

King Noway glared, but the sight of the sack squashed any lingering doubts. "Yes, of course. Give it to me."

"As you wish." Angela whipped out her daggers, Assassin's Ass In leapt from the ground to defend the king, and Potluck's last shrinking potion splashed in the night.

Clatter!

Assassin's Ass In fell to the ground, King Noway's hand now too small to hold it. Potluck upended the Magufin, dumping a raging, five-inch Candace onto the ground, and slammed the sack over the dripping wet, shrunken king. Angela spun and deflected Candace's miniaturized Rat Bastard before it plunged into her shin.

"Potluck!"

"Innocencias Zero-percent-us!" Potluck shouted.

Candace froze mid-spin and toppled onto her side, stricken in a sweet, fully articulated action shot. Angela looked down at her and nodded grudgingly. "I guess you are a pretty good assassin, Candy Ass."

"Bite me, Angie," Candace said from the corner of her mouth.

Angela turned to Potluck. "I thought you were going to one-percent-us?"

"I, uh, didn't want to risk it …"

"Fair enough. Okay, Candace, we got a *little* proposition for you …"

* * *

Angela leaned her head back as Potluck lifted the steaming pitcher as high as he could in the cozy confines of their ring-side box seats. Beside them, the sprite from King Noway's cage sipped honeydew from a walnut mug with a little umbrella in it and raised a bruised, but healing, fist in the air as the next combatants entered the ring.

"And now for the main event of the evening!" The ring herald bellowed through a rolled-up hazelnut leaf, spinning so everyone could hear. "Candace 'Candy Ass' Butrello, the Candy Assassin, versus the regally dethroned, about to get owned, former king of this kingdom, Reginald Noway the Fiiiiiiiiiifffffffttttthhhhhhhh."

The crowd erupted into cheers, the loudest coming from the fairies and sprites in the caged-off competitors' area.

Potluck struggled to hold the pitcher up. "You know, if you had actually changed you would have stopped this entire inhumane affair."

"Hey, I let Candace have this kill, didn't I? Pixie steps, Potluck, pixie steps. Now shut up and start pouring."

Potluck tipped the pitcher and poured the steaming red liquid all over Angela's face and down her shirt, gagging into his armpit as he did.

"Come on, Potluck, it's just cows' blood."

Potluck continued to retch.

"Hey, get more down the shirt. Down the shirt!"

In the ring, a gnome rang a bell, the crowd roared, and a five-inch-tall Candace leapt in for the final, sweet, sweet kill.

Those Who Look Back
Amelia Sirina

The celebration began with murder.

It was such a fine, bright day the way days before a heavy rain can be. The sun was too high, the air tangible in the summer's haze, lying unwelcome over Adzeo's skin and clothes. His whole body itched—with sweat, with a shiver running up and down his marrow as he followed the orderly lines of servants and guards to the palace's grand entrance. The King and his wife were already there, greeting the court and the peasants who pressed from the back rows.

Queen Amanoori stepped into the sea of plum blossoms that servants had mindfully spilled from baskets onto the festive square. No tile was free of this pink-tinted snow, and the court trampled them, bruising the tender blooms without care.

Amanoori stilled as though listening to a whisper only she could hear.

"My blessed wife?" The king offered her a hand to descend the steps together and start the parade amidst the flowers. She didn't take his hand— she lurched as though to run, and the king had to catch her wrist and hold tight to not make a scene in front of all the court. Then Amanoori plunged a wooden knife into his throat.

Everyone's eyes were on the king, falling. Except for Adzeo. He'd watched the queen's shadow all this time, standing in the first rows of servants behind her. He saw when her shadow shifted, even anticipated it.

Then the blood sprinkled the petals in a fan pattern, and Adzeo did nothing to prevent this. It was all his fault.

Poor Amanoori.

Adzeo couldn't bear the betrayed look in her eyes when she turned to him, couldn't bear the silence that drowned the great square in seconds, spreading outwards from the spot where the queen stood. He ran.

Through the colonnade into the palace and the arched galleries—away, away from people. His face felt as though it was melting under his fingers as he tried to hold it together. The back of his head hummed and throbbed.

He'd done something wrong with the mask he had given her. He had failed her. He'd failed the king. He'd failed Master Toyou and the Guild.

What a coward. He should have stayed behind and taken it, whatever would come.

Too bad the mask he'd received right after being born—the one covering the back of Adzeo's head, sunken deeply into his skin, into the essence of who he was—was the mask of Hirisa. The Survivor. Never before had Adzeo thought it was also destined to make him a coward.

His eyes blurred. The mask he'd *chosen* to wear today—the temporary one—was hot like coals on his face. Blind with pain, Adzeo crashed into a festive column alive with flower ribbons and fell to his knees.

No. Don't remove the mask, he begged himself, thoughts thrashing in his head. *Prove it's who you are.*

The agony was unbearable. His fingers clutched his face, dug deeper than the skin by the temples to find that faint outline of the mask's edge. He was a survivor, above all. This, he couldn't deny to himself.

The mask of Zunzitsu Jun, The Loyal Servant, slid off his face, and the pain lifted in an instant. Adzeo's cheeks still stung with the tears that followed. He'd wanted to prove himself. He'd wanted for everyone to see how faithful, how true to his king he was.

But he was no Zunzitsu Jun. The mask clacked on the floor, wood against wood, and its eyeless sockets looked back at Adzeo in disgust.

Soldiers and guards were storming through the halls and down the stairs. A stampede, a chase, a hunt. Hirisa at the center of Adzeo's mind charged him to rise and run, freeze quiet in the niches, wait for the guards to pass— then run as fast as he could bear.

* * *

"My son's a Survivor. Rejoice," Adzeo's mother used to tell him when he'd been young and silly, crying in the dust in the backyard most days after school. She cited the Mask master who'd looked at newborn Adzeo and said *this*: "You're a Survivor, Adzeo. Everything bad will pass. You will stay."

A mask given after birth was meant to protect its wielder from evil spirits. A second face, put on the back of the head, with the hidden, watchful eyes. It defined the person who wore it. They became one. Most people—*normal* people—wore the masks of Angun, the Lucky; or Kyin, the Clever; or coveted Rinei, the Popular. There were plenty of others, but each was meant to inspire a life to greatness, to always seek fulfilment, to strive to be better.

Hirisa, the Survivor was the absolute baseline of existence—so much it was even insulting. No one could get better at surviving. One either did it, or one died.

Adzeo always felt that some great injustice was dealt to him by the fate or by the folly of the Mask master. But at least that decided his life's ultimate goal. He chose to become a Mask master himself and maybe save some other poor child from the same foul mistake in the future. No one should suffer as he had.

His current master, Toyou, didn't carve or give out the sacred masks that defined newborns, though. She made the other ones. The masks that people paid ridiculous amounts of gold for, then put on their faces to hide who they truly were.

Oh, Adzeo turned out to have a gift for those.

"The most important thing to consider is the clash between the masks we wear."

She had such a kind, wrinkled face, like creased oil-paper. The inner face of Kua, the Kind One, hid at the back of her head. Her eyes had that spark in them, a laugh, only hidden. As if in a joke, she put masks on her face to show Adzeo the result. He didn't know how to react, to be frank. None of the other masters played around with the craft.

"Can't you even chuckle? You're a bore, Adzeo," she told him.

"Yes, Toyou." Masters know best. Good pupils can only agree.

She scoffed and brushed her hand along the wall where hundreds of masks hung from the pegs, as though searching for the one that would make Adzeo finally crack a smile at her.

Carved from wood and stone and paper and silk, masks lined the rows—faces likened to foxes, sneering, and bears, snarling, and humans with eyes rolling mad and spittle frothing the open mouths. There were also the demure, reserved masks of pretty youths made of porcelain, glazed with varnishes of all the colors. And, lastly, those eerie ones which looked exactly like human faces. Exactly. Adzeo's gaze rarely lingered on those.

"Gak, the Evil one," Toyou said and barely touched her face with the mask's inner lining, then flinched, a hiss of pain on her lips. "This one does not agree well with the mask at my core."

"What would happen if you put it on?" Adzeo didn't lift his eyes off the rosewood plank from which he carved a mask of Miri, Pretty Face, inch by inch.

Toyou laughed and threw Gak onto the table. It wasn't valuable, really—no one cared to buy it. "Ah, my boy. I surely would die."

"Die?" Adzeo drew back. His fingers with the knife were too unsteady to continue now. Hirisa chanted its old mantra in Adzeo's heart: *not me, not me, not me*. He put the knife away, far from himself, then splayed his hands on the table, forcing their tremor to subside. "Is there a mask *I* can die from?"

"Oh no. I doubt that." She went to pat his shoulders and steady his slumped back with her warm touch. "There're not many with masks as strict as mine. Most people, given an unsuitable mask, would simply go mad." At this she gave him a "so what?" smile and an old-lady-sweet shrug.

Adzeo couldn't go back to his task for a long time after that. And as though to wipe away his fears and the crushing weight of responsibility for the profession he chose, Toyou told him, "That's why we, Masters, need to know—and imagine—all the consequences within the masks we make. It's not easy, not at all, my boy. But you'll learn."

He had. It hadn't been enough.

* * *

Now the king's murder was on his hands and most people didn't even realize it. They must still think the fault was entirely Amanoori's.

At night, he ventured out of the royal forest's farther reaches and ran down into the tunnels. Only the moonlight came through the grates overhead, so when he crossed beneath the palace's walls and was ready to get back into the city, he groped blindly for the secret door's lever.

He had to keep himself together. His breath flushed so loud in his ears, he couldn't hear if there was anyone on the other side of the door. Guards, hunters, king's spies? He had to know for sure—not for the fear of his life, but only to know if *she'd* sold him out. As she should have.

The door slid aside, and there was no one.

Sweet Amanoori, she hadn't told them. She'd kept him safe even after what his mistake had cost her. It almost made him feel better—then, so much worse.

The city tasted of smoke. The muggy rain pressed it down into the streets and the lights were extinguished to mourn the King as was proper. At the street corner by his house, Adzeo finally stopped clinging to the shadows under the eaves. He had to do this on his own terms. He wasn't going to go down like a coward.

In his tiny rooms, the shadows stirred with the motion of the curtains by the open windows. The furniture inside was scarce, but Adzeo had never needed any. He needed only walls. He needed only pegs on them, in rows and lines, and the jeering, feral, amicable, savage, and grotesquely sad faces hanging from them.

Adzeo closed his eyes and reached for the mask in the center of the display with his unsteady hand. Yungu, the Brave One, lay painfully familiar under his fingers. It licked his face with warmth, then dissipated into his skin and hid beneath it. Like before, barely weeks ago—with her.

He was not a coward. He would go back to stand under her gaze and give himself to the fury of her guards. In a moment. Or another.

His fingers went clammy, twined together in a prayer he couldn't remember.

"*Coward.*"

The voice rustled through the door Adzeo had haphazardly left open. Then another voice came from beyond the window, on the roof of the next house. "What a coward, Adzeo."

"Such a coward they'll name the next Kiogisa mask after you," the first person repeated, silking through the gap in the door, three shadows of his fellow apprentices following him.

Adzeo withdrew until his back hit the wall. The wooden masks on it clacked softly.

The guildmates of his year, four? five of them? They came uninvited, but maybe at the perfect time.

Hassuna, Kyoda, Umenasyo, among others. Those he thought his friends. He could not focus on anything else but the masks they chose to wear tonight. All now wore the empty-white, grim masks of Genzhi, the Executioner, beneath their faces.

"I … I am going to the palace, to give myself up … right now." Adzeo's voice broke on the first word, but Yungu made him carry the sentence on. Yungu would make him go through with all of this—a perfect choice for one in his situation.

"Yungu won't help a Hirisa like you and you know it," Kyoda said, solemn. "The Guild decided you might need help with this."

"We take care of our own," Hassuna added, her voice almost gentle.

The meaning behind those words hit Adzeo like a slap. Yungu told him to stay, Hirisa whipped his mind to run. In between the two, he was heaving with strain, slowly pulling away along the wall.

The Executioners mirrored his step, drawing together in a half-circle around him.

"Stay, Adzeo. It will be quick and you won't feel a thing," Hassuna told him with a sweet, sweet promise in her whisper. Adzeo wanted to listen and agree and yield to this kind voice—but then, he also knew what mask Hassuna had at the back of her head. He knew, but he always preferred to forget.

Gaksin, the Cunning One. The liar.

Had it not been for Yungu, Adzeo wouldn't dare fight. He would plead and beg on his knees, or try to wriggle like a worm out of the knives' gleaming tongues. But Yungu mixed with Hirisa was a dangerous combination indeed.

He swung between Kyoda and Hassuna, grabbed their armed hands and twisted. From his shove, Kyoda flew into the others and Adzeo slipped past the lazy blades. He had no time to steal any other masks off the wall. With Yungu on his face and Hirisa at his heart, he ran out the door. He bounced off the narrow walls and climbed the stairs—up, up to the top of the building.

The deadend. He ripped through the paper screen of the nearest window and jumped onto the tiled slope. There, under the blind moon, he stopped.

His itching nerves rang as though struck and his pulse pumped.

They were following him, he heard, and still his feet wouldn't move. He knew why. Quickly, he dug his fingers through the skin of his jawline, catching the edge of Yungu and lifting it, through ache, off his face.

"You sure about that?" Hassuna called from the window behind. Beneath the surface of her skin the wild grimace of Shoza, the Hunter, now loomed.

Adzeo didn't need to reply. His legs, fleeting-fast in the opposite direction, were all his answer.

* * *

He knew all the true masks on them. Cunning, Forceful, Clever, Gifted, and the worst of all—Lucky. Umenasyo now covered his face with Shoza as well, and that combination meant bad luck for Adzeo.

Fortune and lovers and clients and the favor of the Guild masters flowed to Umenasyo as easy as gravity. Of the five Hunters on Adzeo's trail, he would be the one to catch his prey first. There was no doubt about that. He rarely failed in anything.

Except that one time, a strange, strange day two weeks ago. The day when the new Queen arrived at the Maple Leaf palace and the guild received its biggest client yet.

She had such a miserable mask at the back of her head—of Kenduan, the Forbidden One. Only three people in the entire written history had ever received such a mask: a man who became a hermit, a woman who spent her whole life in an asylum, and now the clear-eyed Amanoori—the princess promised to a King.

The mask of Kenduan warped her existence. It made having friends, loving relatives, or a husband in need of an heir such a torment, a never-ending struggle. The Tanaya guild-masters had toiled for months to relieve her. The Sacred Capital guild had taken its turn next, without success.

Most couldn't even try. Amanoori was so terrified of pain, having been tested and probed and given new masks to try on for years. And every single new mask hurt her. Every single one came in opposition to Kenduan. *Not Forbidden*, people called her. *Forsaken*.

"The woman is insane from the years of pain," Umenasyo had told everyone as he exited her quarters—all the masters and some of the brightest apprentices gathered in the antechambers, jittery with anticipation. "She can't be helped."

"Did she even let you near her?" Kyoda asked him, grim. The most talented apprentice, Kyoda was the first to enter the Queen's rooms. She'd rejected him instantly.

Umenasyo was shaking his head, a cruel smile of disbelief on his lips. "Not to touch, not to lay a glance on her, not even to say a greeting. She broke down and that was it."

The silence was never so complete as after these words.

Adzeo went next, alongside master Toyou. There, inside the splendid rooms, adorned and latticed and gilded and sprinkled with flower petals of all the sweet trees, he choked on the words he was meant to say in proper greeting. He stuttered and froze at the threshold. As soon as Amanoori met his eye for a blinking second, Adzeo dashed in the opposite direction. His only true talent.

He didn't hear what the other apprentices asked him as he rushed through the antechamber, knocking into Kyoda, almost stumbling down. He only stopped several galleries away, clutching his chest and laboring through every breath. He had never been so terrified in his life. Seeing the Kenduan mask's faint outline at the core of another human person was like a strike of lightning up Adzeo's spine.

Bent down and trembling was how master Toyou found him.

"You all right, my boy?" Always attentive, she pulled him into a hug, and he didn't even resist. Much.

"I suppose that's the extent of my service to the Queen," he said, too ashamed to lend voice to his words. Toyou had to lean to hear him. Adzeo shook his head and added, "I hope you apologized to her on my behalf, Toyou."

"Apologize yourself. She wants to see you. Again." Toyou answered his horrified stare with a smile. From the fold of her batwing robe, she took out a mask wrapped in black silk. Even from the vague shape under the fabric, Adzeo recognized Yungu, the Brave.

"Me?"

Toyou peeled the wrapper silk off the mask, corner by corner and, holding it gently like the precious thing it was, offered it to Adzeo. "Yes, you. Of all the brash apprentices and masters, some of whom are vastly better than you'll ever be—if I may be so humble to say this—she chose you. She says you're the only one whose presence doesn't hurt."

He let her place Yungu on his face and breathed calmer as soon as the mask molded with his skin.

The glares. The "how can it be you? Such a loser?"-scowls and the narrowing of eyes that greeted him as he went back to the Queen's gilded halls. Every apprentice and master kept quiet while he passed them. Except for Umenasyo.

"Is this a joke …?" he said in a low voice, but still loudly enough that Adzeo heard.

Before going into the rooms, Adzeo turned, too bold not to answer. Under Yungu's influence he even grinned. "Yes. Laugh."

Oh, Umenasyo hated being cheated out of his luck.

* * *

Roof tiles slid and slipped from under his feet and shattered on the flagstone street. Adzeo jumped the buildings and hung from the edges of the walls and skidded his feet to climb the fences to hide behind them. He wasn't good at fighting or diplomacy. Even in childhood, he could never win a fight or talk anyone out of it. But he could run, and through the years this skill only reached new heights.

Finally, a day—a night—to make use of it.

A window sill, a rafter cross, a rain-gutter filled with mud. Jump, reach out, roll over.

The count of the Hunters and Chasers went down to one pretty quickly. The first to abandon the chase couldn't make the jump between the buildings, the second slipped on a loose tile. The others? Adzeo only heard Umenasyo's footfalls after him, and those were the ones that mattered.

He didn't have time for speaking, nor patience to run the whole city up and down to lose Umenasyo. He had to get to Amanoori soon, whatever the cost, had to speak to her and wash away the guilt and shame and horror of her deed. She did not deserve to be blamed for this and be hauled away into some asylum, kept there forever.

If only Umenasyo would break a leg or twist an ankle, just this one time. Just once.

Not possible. With Shoza, the Hunter's mask on his face, he was destined to succeed. No one could deny him that.

So Adzeo slid down into the quiet yard welled by the dark buildings around it. A moment before Umenasyo's footsteps thundered on the buttress from which Adzeo had jumped, Adzeo pulled the Yungu mask on. He retreated into the shadows of the maple trees, slow and careful. Waiting. The night was dark; he could manage this.

Umenasyo dawdled up above. Only his paced breathing broke the silence in the yard. Then he hopped down onto the gravel, knife ready in his hand.

He chose the exact direction in which Adzeo had hidden.

"Lucky Hunter," Adzeo said and sprang on him, aiming for the knife. He missed, and Umenasyo swerved around to keep away. Adzeo staggered upright, sneering. "You caught me, Shoza. What now?"

Umenasyo held the blade steady, his hand jerking as though to stab the air, as though readying for the actual hit.

"Hunters don't kill," Adzeo reminded him. Then he stepped aside, ducked under the branches that rained petals on him. His eyes didn't stray from Umenasyo's. He could see the doubt, the waver behind them. "Hunters catch, Umenasyo. You have to change back to the Executioner to succeed in *this*."

Umenasyo spat and turned the knife's handle in his grip to strike easier. "I can act without a mask guiding me." With this, he reached for his cheekbones, swept his fingers around and peeled Shoza off. He threw it on the gravel. "You?"

Adzeo rammed himself into Umenasyo's chest. They clutched each other, and Umenasyo whipped his hand in a slicing strike. Adzeo dodged.

The knife struck, again and again, and not once could it hit. Umenasyo growled, spittle flying from his mouth, and Adzeo echoed the pain, the anger, the frustration as they rolled amidst the flowerbeds. Adzeo's hands on Umenasyo's throat slipped, his punches missed and hit the ground. For one split second, Umenasyo curled his fingers around the Yungu mask on Adzeo's face. But he didn't rip it off. His hand fell away without trying.

"Damn it!" Umenasyo roared and kicked Adzeo off himself. He grimaced, holding his injured rib, while Adzeo got on all fours. Both of them were out of energy or hope to win this encounter. "A Survivor fighting a Lucky One is a joke, for heaven's sake. It's not me you need to fight."

"Surrender my life? Never."

Umenasyo stared, eyes slowly calming from their anguish. "No. Are you insane? No."

"I know how it goes." Adzeo sat back on his heels, glowering at the tree shadows sprawled in a lace pattern on the ground. "I know one of you has to kill me for bringing dishonor to the Guild."

Umenasyo muttered a curse. "It doesn't mean I can do it, you ungrateful swine. I, or anyone else. We chase you and we hunt, but none actually wants to succeed tonight. Do you not know us at all?"

They sat in silence for a while, trading looks that didn't linger for more than a second. Finally, Adzeo asked, "Then what? What are you doing with this knife, chasing after me for half the city?"

Umenasyo groaned again and flung his knife away. "I don't know. I am Angun. Everyone expects me—*me*—to chase you down. Everyone expects *me* to be the one who kills you. Do you know the pressure of being the Lucky One, all the time?" In the darkness, his eyes reflected the moonlight. "Do they care what I want to do and what I don't? They just think since I can't fail, I should be the one to do *everything*. Well, guess what …" He laughed bleakly and flashed a rude gesture to the moon.

"Umenasyo …"

He went on, ignoring Adzeo's feeble attempt to reach out to his hand. "Sometimes that's who you need to fight. Not others, or any of the people put against you in life, but the stupid mask at the back of your head."

Adzeo slowly rose to his feet.

"I am. I'm trying. Right now, I am going to Amanoori, to plead guilty."

This time Umenasyo's laughter was full of genuine joy, or folly. It started soft and rippling, ended with a sigh. "That's rubbish, Adzeo."

But Adzeo didn't need to listen to this. He went around to get the knife, matter-of-factly, without hurry.

Umenasyo continued, "We all know it. You can't—you won't—go through with it. Don't lie to yourself. You can't defeat the Hirisa on your own and give up your life, even for someone else. However much you want to. It is better to let others deal with that before it drives you crazy." At last, he returned Adzeo's stare, and held. "I hope you understand this."

It was too late to try to respond. Umenasyo flinched at the last possible moment, and Adzeo nearly missed. The knife sunk into Umenasyo's thigh.

He screamed.

God, how he screamed, high and breaking.

"You bastard! I will tear you apart myself, you—" Umenasyo flung palmfuls of gravel after Adzeo as he scuttled away, up the rafter beams to the roof.

Umenasyo would be fine, Adzeo knew. No major arteries were hurt. He was fortunate like that.

Most importantly, he didn't have to chase down Adzeo now—precisely as he wished.

"I was lucky to be your friend," Adzeo called from the roof, but heard only the inane curses in return. The best goodbye a friend can give.

He descended to the street level of the city to run towards the palace, all the while trying to avoid gloomy strangers and inebriated drunks who had their share of free alcohol tonight, in mourning. And, as the distance between him and Amanoori wasted away, so did his resolve.

Hirisa numbed his limbs and dread and chill spread under his skin. His traitorous heart fluttered faster, and he had to pause to catch a breath after every bout. Each of his steps was leaden the closer he got to the Maple Leaf groves. Until he stopped completely.

Yungu snarled in a feral grin under his skin—demanding, ordering Adzeo to go on. But his body locked down, unable to so much as stir.

Please ... Adzeo begged himself, the paralysis that clutched him, all in vain.

Umenasyo was right. It wasn't the chasers and hunters and guards he needed to defeat tonight. It was Hirisa. Himself.

He had to defeat his own survival instinct, honed to perfection through the years. Yungu wasn't nearly enough help against it. Adzeo had to find another mask to put on.

He had no idea if one like that existed.

* * *

Hirisa and Yungu worked together so well that first time, in Amanoori's quarters, under her gaze. Adzeo was stiff and aching in every bone and every taut muscle, but he didn't run away. And she stood so close, too.

He showed her masks and wrote down her answers and her history with the previous tries. He avoided her eyes as much as he could while all she did was watch—and watch, dark lashes still, her gaze coming to life through a film of tears that hadn't dried yet.

"Adzeo … is it?" she asked when he'd exhausted the long list of masks the other masters and apprentices had given him to try to help the poor woman. Amanoori wasn't interested in masks. Maybe, just one. "What mask is on the back of your head, Adzeo?"

"Hirisa, my queen."

"Ah. The Survivor. I wore it once. It nearly killed me." She kept quiet for a long time, withdrawing back to the curtained part of the room. Adzeo could see only her vague outline beyond the fluttering silks. It was easier when the two of them were so far apart, so he didn't have the urge to buck when she turned to him again. "Is that why you ran? It told you that I am a danger to you?"

Probably nobody would call her beautiful from simply seeing her face, as Adzeo had now the courage to. But Kenduan had such a visible emanation, a corrosive warping force around her, that it made her more than a mere human woman. Her misery drew people to her like magnetism. The pain followed.

Behind the curtains, she never let her teary eyes wander off Adzeo. "Do you want to run away now?"

He didn't lie. "Yes, my queen. I wish to be anywhere else but here. That is probably the only reason my presence doesn't hurt you like the others'."

"I thought so. It never happened, before." She smiled, a faint ghost of joy. "It's funny. And cruel. Because it now hurts you instead of me."

"Serving you is my honor." Adzeo bowed. "I will help you find the mask that will fit you, even if that *kills* me, my queen." Saying these words was agonizing—Hirisa squirmed all through Adzeo's body, down to the marrow of his bones—but Adzeo meant them. From all of the mask makers Amanoori had encountered, of course he had to be the one who understood her suffering perfectly. Maybe this was his call—to help this poor woman fight the vile mask at her core even if he couldn't do the same for himself. Maybe dying for this cause was even worth it. When he rose again, Amanoori slipped through the curtains, a step closer. Had any woman ever smiled at him before, like she did?

His heart squeezed and he wasn't sure if it was because of Hirisa's fear, or because of how she looked at him—as though he was the only person in the world worth looking at.

"You want to give up your life to find a mask for me? I hope you'll never find it, then," she said.

Of course, he lied when he told her he hoped differently.

Two weeks went by like this—in pain and hidden hopes.

They rushed, each day bearing doom, full of worry and betrayals of the heart. How could he have been so careless? How could he have deafened his ears to Hirisa's frenzied screams in the background? How did he let her get so close and start thawing in laughter and giggles and tender looks in his presence, filling his thoughts, day and night, with her voice?

There were masks lying between them, and all of them had failed. But Amanoori didn't need them, really. She was happy just with this—talking and sharing comfort in silence. That seemed more than enough.

Sometimes she looked long at him and he basked in that gaze. Sometimes her slick black hair brushed against his cheek as he bent down to carve new masks shaped to fit her profile perfectly. She looked from beyond his shoulder, and then, for a tiny fraction of time, they shared the same breath before she would get self-conscious and withdraw.

"This one is so beautiful." She picked up Riani from the velvet cushions on the floor. It was a lovely mask made to endear those who laid eyes on it. Adzeo had brought it among the other similar ones today, because tomorrow the Flower Parade would start, and the Queen had to join her regal husband for the celebration. She could do it, she said, but it was a torment to endure, and so she was already miserable, waiting.

Adzeo's fingers trembled when he took Riani and offered its silk-lined side to Amanoori. She didn't even need to try; her features distorted in agony. "I … can't," she said. "What is its name?"

"Lover." Adzeo pulled it away to put back into its case, cradling it like a treasure in his hands.

"Lover?" Amanoori smiled, as though in a joke she wanted to share. "Take Yungu off," she asked and took Riani, held it up—for him.

"My queen … I—"

"I want to see it on you."

"Isn't it forbidden?"

She wrinkled her nose up in a grimace. "Is that a distasteful joke, Adzeo? I would have never believed you could be so insensitive."

"My Queen …" Adzeo said, mortified, but she was already laughing at him. God, how he loved her laugh. His own lips couldn't help but ease into a smile, too.

"Come on. *Lover*," she said, suddenly serious. She stood too close now. She was drinking in his breath as she waited, Riani in her hand just inches below Adzeo's chin.

He shouldn't have agreed. But he did. He would agree to anything she asked.

In Riani, the world seemed different in a flash.

It now seemed entirely possible to grin back at her, even though his body wrung in helpless pain as she leaned in to give him a kiss on the lips. An agony far greater struck him: knowing that she was married to another man and would never be able to leave him, the King of Kings, the ruler of the Great River kingdoms, for someone as *nobody* as Adzeo. And with that last thought, dark, bitter jealousy sparked in Adzeo's heart.

So he said, "My queen, I have an idea on what mask to give you for the Flower Parade."

He gave her a second Kenduan—to put on her face.

"It can counteract the Kenduan at your core," he said, his Lover's words tinted with lie and covered in denial. "You can put it on tomorrow, before the Parade."

She trusted him.

* * *

Another Kenduan had suited her well; she hadn't even felt any pain. She was used to such a mask. Only at the plum-petaled square, when the king had taken Amanoori's hand, one she hadn't allowed him to seize …

It all had come crashing down.

The night began to pale, and the city slowly came to life as the bakers and the milkmen woke up, first of many, lighting the windows with dim glows through the dark. Adzeo couldn't go to the Palace, but that didn't mean there was nowhere for him to go. At the cross of the Potters' Street and the Eucalyptus Alley, he stopped, tired, dirty, Yungu sitting serene on his face. Master Toyou's shop was at the end of the street and Adzeo eyed it with no true hope left inside him.

Maybe Toyou knew what mask could counteract a Hirisa completely, but he didn't want to ask her either. She was loyal to the Guild. She would also have to exact justice upon him, if he came near. Putting such a weight on someone's shoulders, such guilt, such choice—was beyond cruel.

He knew that. Yet he went anyway.

All the shop's lanterns shone through the entrance curtains and Adzeo went in unannounced.

Master Toyou didn't look up from the ledger books stacked on the table. She drummed her fingers over the table's surface and said, after a heavy sigh, "Of course you came. Poor boy, you had no choice."

Adzeo didn't let that get to him. How much resignation, how much disappointment was in those words. He braced himself against the shame. "Once, you told me there's hardly a mask in the world that would silence the Hirisa. I need to question that 'hardly.'"

"Nothing can defeat the will to live, my boy. Nothing," Toyou said, and finally looked up—not at Adzeo, but to the side of him.

In the shadowed corner, a motion stirred the air. Hassuna, hidden safely beyond the shelves of crude prototype masks, slipped out and smiled at him. Her freckled face was nothing shy of amiable now. She wore the mask of Yasa, the Friend, beneath her skin.

"Hello there, we were waiting for you for so long."

She had a knife in her hand that she rested casually on Adzeo's shoulder. Adzeo tried to ignore that, but Hirisa overtook his mind again. He shuddered. His legs carried him out of the shop, as though on their own, aching to sprint.

"Hey, stop. Come back!" Hassuna laughed, arms raised. She dropped her knife to the ground, flouncing, then rolled her eyes. "Don't be like this. We can talk, all of us like friends. After all, what you came here for—it's in everyone's interest now, isn't it?"

Adzeo noted every motion of her hands, every tiny shift in her eyes and change of conduct. She was as relaxed as usual when she moved out of the entrance and swept the curtains away for him to come back. Rigidly, he went.

"Did you count on me coming here from the start?"

"Yeah. I'm not an idiot, to chase after you through the whole city, am I?" Hassuna snapped the curtains closed behind him and stuck her thumb towards Toyou. "We had quite a talk while waiting. Many interesting things—"

"Enough, Hassuna." Only now could Adzeo see his Master's face in full. She had chosen an exquisite mask to wear tonight. Giyeu, the Necessity. It hurt to look at her directly and Adzeo averted his gaze. "Adzeo, look at me."

He couldn't bear, but she took his hand in both of hers, and stroked them with her dry warm fingers. "It is not your fault, my boy. Don't even think of it like that."

"I brought shame to the Guild and now—"

"The laws that govern the masks state so, yes. We—our profession—are fiddling with dangerous forces. But we aren't exempt from the spirits that inhabit these masks. We can fall prey to them just as easily." Adzeo welcomed her hand over his cheek, and Toyou said again, "I don't blame you, not at all."

"Will you help me do what I must?" he whispered, through budding tears.

Without another word, she put a mask in Adzeo's hands. He turned it around, the golden surface marked with ink stars and hearts. A single beautifully-rendered tear stained the mask's cheek, above the mouth curved in a savage smile. Adzeo didn't know what to say.

"The Fool?" he breathed, beyond any attempt at actual laughter. "Abau, the Fool, can defeat Hirisa?"

"Nothing else comes even close." Toyou withdrew. Her back was too round, her step heavy, and she had to put her hand on the wall to hold herself upright. "Please go, Adzeo. This is the only thing I can do for you. The only thing my heart can endure."

"Will it kill me, or—"

"Madness," Toyou replied.

Adzeo nodded, not to her but just—to accept this. His grip trembled as he leaned his head to strip Yungu off his face. Too shaky, he couldn't even hold Yungu in his hands and it dropped to the floor.

"Hey." Hassuna was there, beside him. She took Abau from him and gave it an appreciative smile. "What an ugly mug." She snorted. "Still better than what you got."

Adzeo trembled, holding still against his instincts.

"Hassuna, could you … help me …"

She punched him lightly in the shoulder.

"That's what friends are for," she said, eyes crinkling. She pressed Abau to his face, gently but with quiet, unwavering resolve. The mask seeped into his skin and, as soon as it did, Adzeo stopped shaking. Fear washed off him like grime under the rain.

Adzeo waited.

The Fool came to life inside him—itchy to move, desperate to dance in the blades or to rival an open flame, and Adzeo's face dissolved into a rictus of a smile.

Hassuna watched him closely. "Better?"

"Yeah. That feels more like it," he said. Within, Hirisa had finally stopped murmuring into his ears and it was such a blessed, divine silence. Empty and echoing. Only a wicked laugh rang back and forth through his mind now. Or maybe it was out loud, in Adzeo's own voice—it was hard to tell. "Amanoori, my love. Here I come."

He swung around and made towards the threshold, as weightless and easy in his step as he had never been. But he didn't reach the exit.

At first, he didn't understand what had happened, what the red wedge of metal coming out of his chest from behind meant. He watched it, transfixed, and even touched the hot liquid flooding the wound that it opened with his chilly fingers.

"What's this, I wonder?" he asked, not sure to whom.

Hassuna caught him in her arms and eased him onto the floor. It was so eerie to see her remove the mask of the Friend and let her own beautiful face shine through, in all its glory. "It's you, defeating the Hirisa, silly," she said, such a proud look on her face.

"Is it?" Adzeo said. Joy fluttered in his numbing limbs, in the chant of his heart, slower with each strike.

Hassuna beamed at him, leaning close and wrenching her knife out of his back. "Oh, I swear to you."

* * *

He didn't come.

Amanoori spent days waiting, in her rooms, hidden from all the people who came to ask her—questions upon questions. She couldn't answer any. She didn't know what, or why. As usual, even their presence carried pain, and she only waited to be left alone, or to be killed for what she had done.

But neither happened.

Instead, one foggy morning, Amanoori woke up, weary and lost, to find a person in her room. It was a young woman. She stood above Amanoori's bed, having passed beyond the silk curtains and the paper screens made into a maze for Amanoori to hide behind, as close as any intruder had ever come before. Amanoori should have felt the woman's presence. She should have been in pain, so near to her.

The woman was tall and lean and she was smiling, her cheeks dimpled amidst the freckles. Amanoori had never met her, yet there was something so familiar and recognizable in her. So endearing.

Amanoori gulped a breath, eyes not straying from the woman's face. "Did you come to … execute me for the—"

"No, my Queen. Never." She shook her head, still smiling. "You've been cleared of any accusations. Your people and your servants know you're not to blame for what has happened. The one who was, is punished enough."

Adzeo. Amanoori steadied her voice as well as she could. "Is he …" she began, but the woman brought a finger to her own lips.

"Our Guild has succeeded in creating a mask for you, my Queen. I carved it personally. It's not for you to wear, but for anyone who wants to come in contact with you. See? I'm wearing it now. It works. You will never be in pain again." She was so proud, almost little-girl-excited to share this, and Amanoori wanted to be nice to her.

It was *him* she wanted, not other people, but that was not something she could tell anyone.

"A new mask? That is … great. What is it called?"

"Oh." The woman rocked on the balls of her feet. "It's called Adzeo, my Queen."

Amanoori froze. "Excuse me?"

"The name just suits it very well. This—" the woman tapped a finger to her cheek "—is a prototype, but we can maybe make five or six more, with the material we have."

"What … material?"

"Let's say—a very special one." The woman spoke in a secretive whisper, then giggled. "So these masks will last you a lifetime. A lifetime of friends and family and lovers you can share them with."

It took a long time for Amanoori to reply.

She wanted to hate the woman in front of her, wanted to despise or even feel a tiny bit of mistrust towards her. But how could she be angry with that dear, familiar face looming underneath? She couldn't.

She was happy to just be near it.

"It's perfect," Amanoori told her.

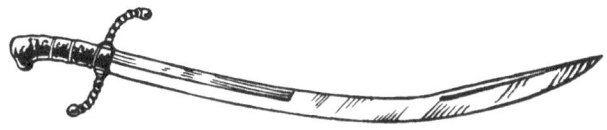

About the Authors

JAMES ENGE lives in northwest Ohio with his wife and two crime-fighting, emotionally fragile dogs. He teaches Latin, Greek and classical civilization at a medium-sized public university. His stories have appeared in *Black Gate*, in the Stabby-Award-winning anthology *Blackguards*, in *Tales from the Magician's Skull*, and elsewhere. His first novel, *Blood of Ambrose* (Pyr, 2009) was nominated for the World Fantasy Award in 2010; and the French translation was nominated for the Prix Imaginales in 2011. You can reach him through Facebook (as james.enge) or on Twitter (@jamesenge) or, if all else fails, via his website, jamesenge.com.

ANITA ENSAL has always been intrigued by possibilities inherent in myths and legends. She likes to find both the fantastical element in the mundane and the ordinary component within the incredible. She writes in all areas of speculative fiction and has stories in several fine anthologies including Love and Rockets and Boondocks Fantasy from DAW Books, as well as a novella, A Cup of Joe, out now. She will be re-releasing her The Neighborhood series in late 2018. You can reach Anita (aka Gini Koch) at her website, Fantastical Fiction (http://www.ginikoch.com/aebookstore.htm).

DAVID FARLAND is an award-winning, bestselling author with over 50 novels in print. He has won the Philip K. Dick Memorial Special Award for his science fiction novel *On My Way to Paradise* and over seven awards for his fantasy novel *Nightingale*. He is best known for his *New York Times* bestselling series *The Runelords*. Farland has written for major franchises such as *Star Wars* and *The Mummy*. He has worked in Hollywood greenlighting movies and doctoring scripts. He has been a movie producer, and he has even lived in China working as a screenwriter for a major fantasy film franchise.

Nebula Award winner **ESTHER FRIESNER** is the author of over 40 novels and more than 200 short stories. She is also the creator/editor of the Chicks in Chainmail series (Baen Books). The sixth, Chicks and Balances, appeared in July 2015. Deception's Pawn, latest in her popular Princesses of Myth YA series (Random House), was published in April 2015. Esther is married, a mother of two, grandmother of two, harbors cats, and lives in Connecticut. There is no truth to the rumor that her family motto is "Oooooh, SHINY!"

LAWRENCE HARDING is the literary alter-ego of a PhD medievalist from Cambridge, England. After filling his life with medieval literature and folklore on the one hand and fantasy fiction on the other, it was inevitable that he would combine the two. This is one of the results of that (un)holy union. In between penning stories and marking essays, Lawrence also reviews at: exploringotherwheres.wordpress.co and can be found lurking on Twitter at @lhardingwrites.

D.B. JACKSON (http://www.DBJackson-Author.com) is the award-winning author of twenty novels and as many short stories. He is best known for the Thieftaker Chronicles, a series set in pre-Revolutionary Boston that combines urban fantasy, mystery, and historical fiction. As David B. Coe (http://www.DavidBCoe.com), he writes epic fantasy, urban fantasy, media tie-ins, and just about anything else. He is currently working on a new fantasy trilogy for Angry Robot and a tie-in project with the History Channel. David has a Ph.D. in U.S. history. His books have been translated into a dozen languages.

HOWARD ANDREW JONES lives beside the Sea of Monsters with a wicked and beautiful sorceress. His newest novel, *For the Killing of Kings*, will be released from St. Martin's in the fall of 2018. He's the writer of a critically acclaimed Arabian Fantasy series, four Pathfinder novels, and a slew of short stories. He's the editor of the print magazine *Tales From the Magician's Skull*, among other things, and lurks at www.howardandrewjones.com, where he blogs about writing craft, gaming, fantasy and adventure fiction, and assorted nerdery.

VIOLETTE MALAN is the author of the Dhulyn and Parno sword-and-sorcery series (now available in omnibus editions) and *The Mirror Lands* series of primary world fantasies. As VM Escalada, she's the author of the Faraman Prophecy series. Book One, *Halls of Law,* is available now, and Book Two, *Gift of Griffins*, will be out next year. She's on Facebook, she's on Twitter, and website-wise check either www.violettemalan.com or www.vmescalada.com. She strongly urges you to remember that no one expects the Spanish Inquisition.

ASHLEY McCONNELL's first novel was a finalist for the Bram Stoker Award. Since 1990, she has sold horror, fantasy, and numerous media tie-in novels, as well as a handful of short stories and assorted articles. ("A" and "the" featured prominently among them.) She is responsible for the erratic publication of the Bloodstained Bookshelf, a list of forthcoming traditionally-published mysteries at http://mirlacca.com/Bookshelf.html, and for the vet bills of one horse and far too many cats.

R.K. NICKEL works as a screenwriter in Los Angeles. His first feature film, *Bear with Us*, is available on Amazon Prime, and "Stellar People," a sci-fi comedy series he wrote for Adaptive Studios, will be coming out sometime in 2018. He dove into his prose journey in 2017, and since then has made 6 sales and attended both the Odyssey Writing Workshop and the Launch Pad Astronomy Workshop. When he's not writing, he's probably playing an escape room or some Magic the Gathering. Or drinking coffee. Mmm…coffee. For more, check out @russnickel on Twitter or www.rknickel.com.

JASON PALMATIER is co-creator/co-writer of the epic comic fantasy series *Plague* published by AAM-Markosia (available on Comixology) and a contributor to the indie comic *Lords of the Cosmos* by Ugli Studios. His short stories *Heart of the Empire* and *Zorlar the Terrible* appeared in the anthologies *Clockwork Universe: Steampunk vs Aliens* and *All Hail Our Robot*

Conquerors! published by Zombies Needs Brains, LLC. He has completed his first novel, *War Mind*, a near future military thriller, and is currently working on a second book titled *Xenoslammer*, a parody/rage-piece about the travesty that is the Aliens movie franchise.

JENNA RHODES is a pen name for a prolific author with over 55 books published to date, with several more on the horizon, as well as short fiction. "Rainbow Dark" is her second appearance with Zombies Need Brains. Look for "The Windlost" in the wondrous SUBMERGED anthology. Check out www.rhondiann.com for more background on what she's working on under this and other names, in the fields of fantasy, science fiction, mystery, thriller, and romance.

AMELIA SIRINA is a Buryat-Russian speculative fiction writer. She studied Classics in Moscow State University, she falls in love with any new myths or fairytales easily and loves learning new languages. In her free time she travels. She currently doesn't have a website, but she's working on it.

LEAH WEBBER has been telling stories since she was three years old; the more fantastical, the better. After touring the world in the military for almost a decade, she's finally back where she started in the wilds of Portland, Oregon with her two dogs, a feral computer, and assorted overflowing bookshelves. Find out more at www.leahwebber.com/.

About the Editors

S.C. BUTLER is a writer living in New Hampshire with his wife and son. He is the author of the Stoneways trilogy: <u>Reiffen's Choice</u>, <u>Queen Ferris</u>, and <u>The Magicians' Daughter</u>, published by Tor Books; and a contributor of short stories to several anthologies and magazines. He made his editorial debut with the anthology <u>Submerged</u>.

* * *

JOSHUA PALMATIER is a fantasy author with a PhD in mathematics. He currently teaches at SUNY Oneonta in upstate New York, while writing in his "spare" time, editing anthologies, and running the anthology-producing small press Zombies Need Brains LLC. His most recent fantasy novel, *Reaping the Aurora,* concludes the fantasy series begun in *Shattering the Ley* and *Threading the Needle*, although you can also find his "Throne of Amenkor" series and the "Well of Sorrows" series still on the shelves. He is currently hard at work writing his next novel and designing the kickstarter for the next Zombies Need Brains anthology project. You can find out more at www.joshuapalmatier.com or at the small press' site www.zombiesneed-brains.com. Or follow him on Twitter as @bentateauthor or @ZNBLLC.

Acknowledgments

This anthology would not have been possible without the tremendous support of those who pledged during the Kickstarter. Everyone who contributed not only helped create this anthology, they also helped solidify the foundation of the small press Zombies Need Brains LLC, which I hope will be bringing SF&F themed anthologies to the reading public for years to come . . . as well as perhaps some select novels by leading authors, eventually. I want to thank each and every one of them for helping to bring this small dream into reality. Thank you, my zombie horde.

The Zombie Horde: Glennis LeBlanc, Kiya Nicoll, Jenny Barber, Ash Marten, Simon Dick, Y. K. Lee, Katherine Malloy, Stephanie Cranford, Chris Matosky, David Perkins, Maureen Brooks, Kevin Wallace, Jonathan Briggs, Laura and Bill Pearson, Sheryl R. Hayes, Kim Lloyd, Tanya Gough, Matt K., Millie Calistri-Yeh, Caitlin Jane Hughes, Harvey Brinda, Julie Haddy, Carolyn Petersen, Konstanze Tants, Nellie B, Bryan Wetterow, Austin, Teresa Carrigan, Aurora N., Michael Fedrowitz, Darrell Z. Grizzle, Debbie Fligor, Mark Carter, Rebecca Sims, Sarah Cornell, David Zurek, Duncan & Andrea Rittschof, The Bowers, Paul McNamee, Pam Blome, Arej Howlett, Troy Chrisman, Larisa LaBrant, Mollie Bowers, Andrew Wilson, Patrick Thomas, melme, Noah Bast, Joseph Hoopman, Stephen Kissinger, Christine Swendseid, Mary Alice Wuerz, Chad Bowden, John Appel, M Harold Page, Lyndsey Flatt, Jesse Klein, Chris Huning, Lorri-Lynne Brown, Mary Soon Lee, Kevin Winter, Ronnie J Darling, John O'Neill, Lily Connors, Casey Sharpe, Kitty Likes, Wolf SilverOak, Elektra, Nicholas Adams, Benjamin C. Kinney, Cherie Livingston, Jaq Greenspon, Howard J. Bampton, David VonAllmen, Kristine Kearney, Erik T Johnson, Andrew Hatchell, Regis M. Donovan, Stephanie Lucas, Brian Quirt, Paul Musselman, Wendy Cornwall, Jaime O. Mayer, Gina Freed, Vy Anh Tran, Elizabeth Kite, Claire Sims, Debbie Matsuura, K Kisner, April Broughton, R. Hamilton, Vincent Darlage, ANDREW AHN, Carol J. Guess, Cathy Green, Stephen Ballentine, Céline Malgen, Penny Ramirez, Julie Pitzel, Jake, Chrissie, Grace & Savannah, jjmcgaffey, Gabe Krabbe, Bregmann Roche, Patrick Osbaldeston, Lori & Maurice Forrester, Pat Gribben, Robert Claney, Patti Short, Shades of Vengeance, Patricia Bray, Leah Webber, Jen Woods, Rolf Laun, Tibicina, Martin Greening, Judith Bienvenu, Ty Wilda, Sasha, C. Lennox, Brendan Lonehawk, Tom B., Michele Fry, Helen French, Auston Habershaw, FrodoNL, Simba Pipsqueak, Vespry Family, Nancy Edwards, Melissa Tabon, Andy Arminio, K Crowell, Lawrence M. Schoen, Colette Reap, Michael Skolnik, Amy Goldman, Chris 'Warcabbit' Hare, Jo Carol Jones, Eduard Lukhmanov, M.J. Fiori, R.J.H., Eddy Black, Connor Bliss, Yaron Davidson, Annika Samuelsson, Sarah Cottell, Jerrie the filkferengi, Rick Galli, Jakub Narębski, Tanya K., Todd V. Ehrenfels, Liz Wyatt, Uncle Batman, David Eggerschwiler, Tibs, Orla Carey, Jessica Reid, Paul Bustamante, Henry Schubert, Melissa Shumake, William Hughes, Donovan DiPasquale, Gary Phillips, Jay Lofstead, Nathan Turner, Becky Allyn Johnson, Evan Ladouceur, Colleen R., L.C., Jenni Peper, Curtis Frye, Kayliealien, Richard James Errington, Kristi Chadwick, Rick Dwyer, Katchoo, Queen of the Nowells, Revek, Leila Qışın, Heidi Berthiaume, David J. Fortier, Gavran, Sarah Hester, Joanne Burrows, Elise Power, Tasha Turner, Scott Raun, Miranda Floyd, Jörg Tremmel, David A. Holden, Angie Hogencamp, Vicki Greer, AM Scott, SometimesKate, Mike Hampton, Lisa Kruse, Nick W, David Drew, Sidney Whitaker, James Conason, Nancy M. Tice, Sally Qwill Janin, Paula Morehouse, Elaine Tindill-Rohr, Christine Ethier, Kai Delmas, Todd Stephens, Mark Newman, Phillip Spencer, Deanna Harrison, Susan Carlson, Sharon Goza, Marty Poling Tool, Yankton Robins, Linda Pierce, Victoria L. Sullian, Niall Gordon, Peter T, 'Jonesy' Oberholtzer, Michael Abbott, Jonathan Collins, R Tharp, Dave Hermann, Paul y cod asyn Jarman, Hoose Family, Andrija Popovic, Keith Nelson, Paula & Michael Whitehouse, Tory Shade, Brenda Moon, Tina & Byron Connell, Deborah Crook, Moonpuppy61, Nathaniel Pohl, Ian Chung, Beth LaClair, L. E. Doggett, Kerry aka Trouble, Brad L. Kicklighter, Kristine Smith, Michelle L., Elyse M Grasso, Roy Sachleben, Jason Palmatier, Ajay O., Cyn Armistead, Brenda Carre, Alli Martin, Catherine Gross-Colten, Rebecca M, Gary Ehrlich, Mark Hirschman, Anthony R. Cardno, Mark Kiraly, Ed Ellis, David Rowe, Clare Deming, Kat S., VeAnna Poulsen, Sharon Wood, Chuck Wilson, C. L. Werner, Morgan S. Brilliant, Andy Miller, Anders M. Ytterdahl, Heidegger and Mocha, A. Walter Abrao, Max Kaehn, Barbara Becc, Chloe Turner, Jen1701D, Andrew Taylor, Mervi Mustonen, Kimberly M. Lowe, Amanda Nixon, 2-Gun Bill, T. England, Heather Kelly, Darryl M. Wood, Belkis Marcillo, Meredith B, Mark Slauter, Arin Komins, Svend Andersen, Jomelson Co, rissatoo, Misty Massey, Anne Burner, Keith Jones, Jenn Whitworth, Doc Concrescence, Anders Kronquist, Keith West, Future Potentate of the Solar System, Stephanie Cheshire, Ian Harvey, Erin Penn, Beth Lobdell, Khinasidog, Erin Kowalski, Helen Cameron, Kendra Leigh Speedling, Mary-Michelle Moore, Micci Trolio, Amanda Weinstein, Catherine Sharp, K. Gavenman, RKBookman, H. Rasmussen, S Baur, Eagle Archambeault, Keith E. Hartman, Tom Connair, Ivan Donati, Brian Hugenbruch, Paul D Smith, CGJulian, Jeffry Rinkel, Mark F Goldfield, Chuck Hickson, Michelle Palmer, Alexander Smith, Bill Harting, Sean Collins, Paul Alex Gray, Jason Tongier, Pierre, Lark Cunningham, Brenda Cooper, Fen Eatough, Alysia Murphy, Ilene Tsuruoka, Sheryl Ehrlich, Tina Good, Shel Kennon, Judith Mortimore, Breagha, Fred and Mimi Bailey, Robby Thrasher, Rachel Sasseen, Thea Cooke, Peter Bernstorff, Dino Hicks, Margaret S. McGraw, Lace, Erin Himrod, Steven Mentzel, Samuel Lubell, Linda Bruno, Amanda Stein, Julie Holderman, D-Rock, Adam Thompson, Timothy Nakayama, Antonio Carlos Porto, Melinda Seckington, Nirven, Kristin Evenson Hirst, Mick Gall, Missy Katano, Ken Finlayson, Camden, Steven Torres-Roman, Jennifer Della'Zanna, Gretchen Persbacker, Crystal Sarakas, Michele Hall, K. Hodghead, Marla Anderson, Jennifer Berk, Christina Roberts, Steven Halter, R. Hunter, Ken Woychesko, Firestar, Cindy Cripps-Prawak, David Roffey, Coleman bland, Drammar English, Cheryl Losinger, Peter Hansen, Bryan Easton, Deirdre M. Murphy, Zion Russell, Danielle Hinesly, Dana, Jonathan S. Chance, Nick Martell, K. R. Smith, SwordFire, Jennie Goloboy, Chantelle Wilson, Jenni Hamilton, S. E. Altmann, Lara Ortiz de Montellano, Donna Gaudet, Thea Maia, Jamie Ibson, Wendy Kitchens, Sarah FW, Axisor and Mike, John B. McCarthy, Andrew Barton, Gordon Rios, Kerri Regan, M. E. Gibbs, Kelly Melnyk, Greg Vose, Joe Borrelli, The Mystic Bob, Chris Brant, R Kirkpatrick, Marzie Kaifer

www.ingramcontent.com/pod-product-compliance
Lightning Source LLC
Chambersburg PA
CBHW020056030726
47498CB00006B/1807

* 9 7 8 1 9 4 0 7 0 9 2 0 8 *